The Gilded Chain

A Tale of The King's Blades

DAVE DUNCAN

An Imprint of HarperCollinsPublishers

EOS
An Imprint of HarperCollins*Publishers*
10 East 53rd Street
New York, New York 10022-5299

Copyright © 1998 by Dave Duncan
Cover art by Hal Just
Excerpt from *Signal to Noise* copyright © 1998 by Eric S. Nylund
Excerpt from *The Death of the Necromancer* copyright © 1998 by Martha Wells
Excerpt from *Scent of Magic* copyright © 1998 by Andre Norton
Excerpt from *The Gilded Chain* copyright © 1998 by Dave Duncan
Excerpt from *Krondor the Betrayal* copyright © 1998 by Raymond E. Feist
Excerpt from *Mission Child* copyright © 1998 by Maureen F. McHugh
Excerpt from *Avalanche Soldier* copyright © 1999 by Susan R. Matthews
Library of Congress Catalog Card Number: 98-18691
ISBN: 0-380-79126-9
www.eosbooks.com

First Avon Eos paperback printing: September 1999
First Avon Eos hardcover printing: November 1998

Eos Trademark Reg. U.S. Pat. Off. and in Other Countries, Marca Registrada, Hecho en U.S.A.
HarperCollins® is a trademark of HarperCollins Publishers Inc.

Printed in the U.S.A.

15 14 13 12 11 10 9 8

*This book is dedicated with
all my love to my grandson
Brendan Andrew Press
in the hope that one day he
will find pleasure in it*

• Contents •

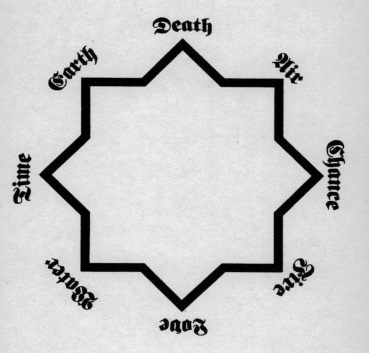

· Prologue ·

Grand Master looked even older than the Squire, but he had a hard trimness that age had not softened, as if he would still be deadly with that sword he wore. There was a ferocity in his gaze that the boy had never seen before in any man's; so he forced himself not to flinch when those terrible gray eyes turned on him, meeting the stare as impassively as he could, determined not to show any sign of the tumult in his belly. While the two men discussed him, he stood in silence, clutching his cap in both hands. He had never seen the Squire be so most-wondrous polite to anyone before, fawning at Grand Master the way the goose wife did to him.

The boy had expected the famous Ironhall to look like a castle, but it was just a cluster of buildings all alone on barren Starkmoor, black stone walls and black slate roofs. The inside was even bleaker: bare walls, plank floor, wooden ceiling; a cold wind sighing in one unglazed, barred window and out another. Two big chairs, a table, a shelf of books, a grate so clean that it was hard to believe any fire had ever burned there—no prison cell could be grimmer. If this was Grand Master's room, how did the boys live?

"Vicious!" the Squire said. "Intractable. Don't suppose even you can make a man out of such trash." He had been telling everything—the boy's entire life from his shameful birth out of wedlock fourteen years ago to last week's attempt to run away and the subsequent whipping, with not one prank or misdeed overlooked. That was no way to sell a horse. After that catalogue of wickedness

1

there could be no chance at all of his being accepted. He was going to be sent home to Dimpleshire most-wondrous fast.

Grand Master drained his wine and replaced the goblet on the table. "You will withdraw, please, while I speak with the lad."

The boy watched uneasily as the Squire rose, bowed low, and departed. What was the use of prolonging the matter? Why not throw them both out and be done with it? The iron-studded door thudded shut.

He was not invited to take the vacant chair. He met the gaze of the terrible gray eyes and steeled himself not to twitch, fidget, or even swallow. After several long minutes, Grand Master said, "Why did you steal the pony?"

"It's mine. My mom gave it to me before she . . . long time ago."

The old man smiled grimly. "If it was only this high, couldn't you have walked faster on your own two feet?"

The boy shrugged. "They'd always caught me on foot. Thought it might confuse the dogs."

"Worth a try," Grand Master admitted. He reached his left hand into his doublet and brought out a bag. It clinked. Now what? "You don't get to keep this money—I take it back. Put your cap on the table."

The boy obeyed suspiciously.

"Go back to where you were standing. Catch!"

The boy caught the coin. Most-wondrous!

"Can you throw it into your cap? Good. Ready?" Another coin.

The boy caught it and tossed it beside the first. The next throw went wider. Then higher, so he had to jump— and there was another coming already and he was throwing and catching at the same time. Soon he was going in four directions at once, grabbing and throwing with both hands.

The barrage stopped. He had put every one in the cap.

"That was impressive. *Very* impressive!"

"Thank you, my lord." It wasn't bad. Kids' stuff, though.

"Call me Grand Master. Your grandfather was certainly correct when he said you were agile. But he did tell me one untruth, didn't he, although he uttered no deliberate falsehoods? What is the real story?"

The boy resisted a need to lick his lips. Would he rather be thought wicked or stupid? The old man must be using some sort of conjurement to detect lies, so stupid it would have to be.

"The girl, Grand Master. That one was not me."

The old man nodded. "I guessed that from your reaction. The rest don't matter—only signs of a spirit caged. Violence against women is otherwise. Yet you took the punishment without protest? Why?"

Because I am stupid! "He's a serf's son. They'd have hanged him. She was only scared, not real hurt."

"And suppose the next time he does rape someone? Won't that be your fault?"

"I don't think he's truly evil, Grand—"

"Answer my question."

The boy thought for a moment. "Yes."

"Do you regret your decision now?"

"No, Grand Master."

"Why not?"

"Because I don't think he's truly evil, Grand Master."

"You have confidence in your own judgment. Good. Well, the choice is yours—not mine, not your grandfather's. Yours. If you wish to stay, I accept you. If you do not, then I shall tell your grandfather that I refused you. I warn you that you will be embarking on a whole new life, a life of complete obedience. It will be made a hard life, deliberately, for we have no use for the soft. For the first few weeks you will not even possess a name; you will be only the Brat, the lowest of the low. You will be free to leave at any time—and many do—but what happens to you then will be no concern of ours. You will walk out of the gate with nothing and never return.

"On the other hand, if you survive your training, you will have achieved a position of some honor in society.

You will very likely live at court, one of a very select brotherhood, the finest swordsmen in the known world. Again, you will be embarking on a life of complete obedience. You will serve your King or whomever else he decrees. You will have no say in the matter. Indeed, this decision you take now is in a sense the last decision you will ever make of your own free will.''

And the first one, too. The boy had not expected to be offered a choice.

Grand Master said, "Have you any questions?"

"Who picks my new name?"

"You do, usually from the list of former Blades, although other names are sometimes accepted."

That was fairer than he had expected. If he left, he would never know whether he could have been man enough. Being the Brat in Ironhall could not be much worse than being a bastard son in a family with very little money and no social importance. The alternative was to be apprenticed to some craftsman or merchant, a nobody evermore. He would not be the Brat for long. "I wish to stay, Grand Master."

"Don't be too hasty. There are many things you do not know. Ask more questions or just think about it. You can have five minutes."

"No, Grand Master. I wish to stay."

"To make such a decision lightly can be taken as a sign of folly."

"I have confidence in my own judgment, Grand Master."

The dread eyes narrowed. "If you were already a candidate, that remark would be treated as insolence."

The only safe answer to that was, "I understand, Grand Master."

The old man nodded. "Very well. You are accepted. Brat, go and tell the man waiting outside that he may go now."

HARVEST

I

"Treason," Kromman whispered. He repeated the word, mouthing it as if he found the taste pleasing: "Treason! Your treachery is uncovered at last. Evidence has been laid before the King." He smiled and licked his wizened lips.

Human wood-louse!

Roland considered drawing his sword and sliding it into Kromman until the blade would go no farther, then taking it out again—by another route, for variety. That would be an act of public service he should have performed a lifetime ago, but it would create a serious scandal. Word would flash across all Eurania that the King of Chivial's private secretary had been murdered by his lord chancellor, sending courtiers of a dozen capitals into fits of hysterical giggles. Lord Roland must behave himself. It was a pleasing fantasy, though.

Meanwhile, the winter night was falling. He still had work piled up like snowdrifts, a dozen petitioners waiting to see him, and no time to waste on this black-robed human fungus.

Patience! "As you well know, Master Secretary, such rumors go around every couple of years—rumors about me, about you, about many of the King's ministers." Ambrose probably started most of the stories himself, but if his chancellor said so to Kromman, Kromman would tattle back to him. "His Majesty has more sense than to listen to slander. Now, have you brought some business for me?"

"No, Lord Chancellor. No more business for you." Kromman was not hiding his enjoyment; he was up to something. Even in his youth, as a Dark Chamber inquisitor, he had been repugnant—spying and snooping, prying and plotting, maligning anyone he could not destroy. Now, with age-yellowed eyes and hair trailing like cobwebs from under his black biretta, he had all the appeal of a corpse washed up on a beach. Some days he looked even worse. Even the King, who had few scruples, referred to him in private as rat poison. What secret joy was he savoring now?

Roland stood up. He had always been taller and trimmer than this grubby ink slinger, and the years had not changed that. "I won't send for the Watch. I'll throw you out myself. I have no time for games."

"Nor I. The games are over at last." Kromman slithered a letter onto the desk with all the glee of a small boy waiting for his mother to open a gift he has wrapped for her. Definitely up to something!

Over by the door, Quarrel looked up from his book with a puzzled expression. No voices had been raised yet, but his Blade instincts were detecting trouble.

Roland's face had given away nothing for thirty years and would not start doing so now. Impassively he took up the packet, noting that it was addressed personally to Earl Roland of Waterby, Companion of the White Star, Knight of the Loyal and Ancient Order of the King's Blades, et cetera, and closed with the privy seal, yet it bore no mention of his high office. That odd combination warned him what he was going to find even before he lifted the wax with a deft twist of his knife and crackled the parchment open. The ornately lettered message was terse to the point of brutality:

> *is therefore commanded to divest . . . will absent himself from business of our Privy Council . . . will hold himself available to answer certain grave matters. . . .*

Dismissal!
His first reaction was sweet relief that he could now

throw down all his worries and go home to Ivywalls and the wife whom he had never been allowed time enough to love as she deserved. His second thought was that Kromman, here designated his successor, was an unthinkable choice, totally incapable of handling the work.

He looked up blandly, while his mind raced through this deadly jungle that had suddenly sprung up around him. He should not be surprised, of course. Ambrose IV tired of ministers just as he tired of mistresses or favorite courtiers. The King grew weary and sought new beginnings. He would hope to shed some of his current unpopularity by blaming his own mistakes on the man who had faithfully carried out his policies. Loyalty was better to receive than to give.

With the silent grace of an archer drawing a longbow, Quarrel rose to his feet. For most of the last two days, the poor kid had been slouched on the couch by the door, leafing through a book of romantic verse, bored out of his mind. He would have registered that the latest visitor was unarmed when he entered and then lost interest in him. Now he had sensed something amiss.

"Your treason is uncovered!" Kromman said again, gloating.

Roland shrugged. "No treason. Whatever forgeries you have concocted, Master Kromman, they will not withstand proper examination."

"We shall see."

They stared at each other for a moment, lifelong foes harnessed too long together in service to the same master. Roland could never consider himself guilty of treason under any reasonable definition of the word; but treason was a slippery concept, a mire he had seen trap many others—Bluefield, Centham, Montpurse. Especially Montpurse. He had organized Montpurse's destruction himself. To be dragged down by the odious Kromman would be excessive irony, though. That would hurt more than the headsman's ax.

Again he found himself contemplating murder and this

time he was not altogether joking with himself; this might be his last chance to slay the vermin. Alas, the revenge he should have taken years ago would now be seen as an admission of guilt, so he would die also and leave Kromman as posthumous winner of their long feud. Better to stay alive and fight, face down the deceit and hope to win, however unlikely that might be—Kromman was very sure of himself.

Meanwhile, the dusty files on the desk and the garrulous petitioners in the waiting room could equally be forgotten. Lord Roland could walk away from them all with a clear conscience and head home a day earlier than he had planned. Tomorrow would be soon enough to start worrying about treason and a trial and the almost inevitable death sentence.

"Long live the King," he said calmly. He walked around the desk, lifting the weighty chain from his shoulders. "This is not gold, by the way, only gilt. Chancery knows that, so don't try accusing me of embezzlement."

With a leer of triumph, Kromman bent his head to receive the chain. It rattled around his feet like a golden snake as Roland released it.

"Put it around your neck yourself, Master Kromman, or have the King do it. The writ does not require me to bestow it."

"Oh, we shall teach you humbler ways soon!"

"I doubt it." Then Roland recalled the wording of the warrant and the authority it granted to his successor. "Or are you contemplating immediate action against my person?"

The new chancellor's amber-toothed smile was answer in itself. "Indeed, I shall now have the pleasure of completing a task I was prevented from completing many years ago." Meaning he had a squad of men-at-arms waiting in the anteroom to escort the prisoner to a dungeon in the Bastion, probably in chains. What sweet triumph that would be for him!

But he was still unaware that there was a third person

present. He had come scurrying in with his mincing, pigeon-toed walk and gone right by the witness beside the door, too impatient to notice his victim's guardian. As quiet as mist, Quarrel had crossed the room to stand at the inquisitor's back—tall and supple and deadly as a spanned crossbow. He could be Lord Roland's twin brother, born forty years too late.

For the first time Roland looked directly at him. "Have you met Master Kromman, the King's secretary?"

"I have not had that honor, my lord."

Kromman twisted around with a gasp.

"It is no honor. He plans to have me arrested. What say you to that?"

Quarrel smiled at this sudden improvement to his day. "I say not so, my lord." One hand rested on his sword. He could draw faster than a whip crack.

"I thought you might. This is Sir Quarrel, Chancellor. I deeply regret that I shall be unable to accept your gracious invitation voluntarily. I hope you brought adequate forces?"

Kromman's jaw hung open. Quarrel's hose and doublet had been outrageously expensive, his jerkin and plumed hat even more so, but they could be matched on a score of young dandies around the court. It was not his athlete's grace or his darkly sinister good looks that proclaimed him unmistakably as a Blade, nor yet his sword, for his hand concealed the distinctive pommel. Perhaps it was his bearing. There could be no doubt that even if he were one against an army, he would litter the floor with bodies before he let anyone lay a hand on his ward.

Kromman had a problem he had not anticipated.

"Where did you get *him*?" he squeaked.

"On Starkmoor, of course." Roland should have guessed that something unexpected would happen right after he went back to Ironhall. Every visit he had ever made to that gloomy keep had marked a turning point in his life.

2

As Durendal raised his wineglass to his lips, loud booing broke out at the far end of the hall, which could only mean that the Brat had come in. An immediate cheer announced that he had been tripped up already. The kid scrambled to his feet in a shower of crusts and chop bones, and was promptly tripped again. He had a long way to go, because he was not past the sopranos' table yet and must still run the gauntlet of the beansprouts, the beardless, and the fuzzies before he reached the seniors. Undoubtedly Grand Master had sent him to summon Prime and Second to a binding, and it was his misfortune that they happened to be at dinner.

It was a rough game, but some of the games were even worse; and everyone started out as the Brat. Durendal had endured that ordeal longer than most, beginning right after the supremely joyous moment when he had been able to tell his grandfather to go back to Dimpleshire and stay there. Spirits! Had that been five years ago? It was hard to believe that he was Second now and the Brat was heading for him. Most-wondrous!

He glanced at the high table to confirm that Grand Master's throne remained unoccupied. Master of Horse and Master of Rapiers caught his eye and smiled knowingly. Nothing but a binding would be keeping the old man away on Ironhall's most important night of the year, the Feast of Durendal, the legendary founder whose name Second himself had assumed in a mad act of defiance. Tonight the seniors were allowed wine. Soon the Litany of Heroes would be read out and speeches made. For Grand Master to be absent required something epic afoot. Possibly the King himself had arrived.

Durendal had been Second for less than a week. He had not expected to make the leap to Prime just yet. He glanced at Harvest beside him, but Harvest was arguing so intently with Everman that he had not even noticed the disturbance.

Five years, and soon it would be over—possibly as soon as tomorrow night, if the King wanted more than one Blade. Manhood in place of adolescence; farewell to Ironhall. Feeling his mind strangely concentrated by this sudden nostalgia—and possibly also by the wine, he realized—he scanned the great hall, as if to fix it more tightly in his memory.

Servants hastened back and forth from the kitchens, striving unsuccessfully to keep platters heaped against the onslaught of voracious young appetites. Candlelight flickered on scores of fresh faces at the long tables and reflected on the famous sky of swords overhead—a hundred chains slung from wall to wall, with a sword dangling from almost every link, more than five thousand blades. Visitors and newcomers notoriously lost their appetites when offered their first meal in the hall, especially when it was accompanied by vivid descriptions of what would happen if just one of those ancient chains should break. Residents soon learned to ignore the threat. The oldest of those swords had been up there for centuries and would probably remain there for a long time yet. The oldest of them all hung alone in a place of honor on the wall behind Grand Master's throne, and that was Nightfall, the sword of the first Durendal, which had been found so inexplicably broken after his death.

Soup sprayed over the Brat as he passed the bean-sprouts' table.

There were seventy-three candidates in Ironhall at the moment. Second was responsible for keeping them all in line, so he had that number branded on his heart. There ought to be a hundred or so, but there was a new King on the throne. In his first year Ambrose had replaced more than a score of his father's aging Blades. He had slowed the pace a little since then, but lately he had been gifting Blades to his favorites. The candidates considered that Ambrose IV was being profligate with his precious swordsmen, although they were hardly unbiased observers. How many did he want tonight? Harvest was Prime, and candidates invariably left Ironhall in the same order they had entered.

The Brat arrived at last, panting and well spattered with gravy and fragments of salad. He stared in dismay at Harvest's back, hesitant to interrupt the awesomely exalted Prime while he was talking; but all the seniors except Durendal were still arguing at the tops of their voices, blissfully unaware of the drama. The hall hushed as the audience realized what was happening and waited in amused suspense. The distant sopranos had climbed up on their benches to watch.

Young Byless was in full throat. "And I say that we're the most deadly collection of swordsmen in all Eurania!" He apparently meant the seniors, including himself. This was certainly the first time in his life he had ever tasted wine, and it showed. "We'd be a match for a whole regiment of the King of Isilond's Household Sabreurs. We ought to send them a challenge."

"Shinbones!" said Harvest. "We'd be massacred!"

Byless turned an unsteady gaze on him. "What if we were? We'd have created a legend."

"Besides," said Felix, "I think they're a lot more deadly." He gestured over his shoulder at the tables behind him.

He was making better sense. That was where the masters and other knights sat, those Blades who had played out their game and retired to teach another generation. There were bald heads and liver spots and missing teeth there. Some were truly ancient, but not one of them was fat, senile, or even stooped; and by and large they were all still functional. Blades might rust, but they did not rot.

Among them were some unfamiliar faces, visitors enjoying the nostalgia of a Durendal Night. Knights who had completed their stint in the Royal Guard might be anything from doorkeepers for rich merchants to senior ministers of the Crown. The only one Durendal recognized there tonight was Grand Wizard, head of the Royal College of Conjurers. They were all having as much trouble as the juniors in suppressing their laughter.

Red-faced, Byless drained his glass and went on the offensive with a loud burp. "*Urk!* Them? They're *old!* There isn't one of them under thirty."

Durendal decided it was time to stop his friends making fools of themselves. He scowled at the Brat, who was a smartish nipper and had been Brat long enough to know that the current Second was no danger to him.

"Miserable lowlife!" he shouted. "Bottom-feeding, snot-nosed, festering slug, you dare to creep in here and mar the merriment of your betters?"

The Brat shot him a wary glance. Harvest looked around, gaped in horror for a moment, and then made a fast recovery. "Scum! Bed-wetting troglodyte!" He swung a blow at the Brat's head, but it was well signaled and failed to make contact.

The Brat sprawled realistically to the floor and groveled appropriately. When he had been Brat, Durendal had found groveling the hardest duty required of him. He had learned, of course—oh yes, he had learned! The hall whooped in approval. They had all been there once, every one of them, down on the floor, butt of all Ironhall.

"Honored and glorious Prime!" the kid squeaked. "Most noble, most illustrious Second, Grand Master sent me to summon you!"

"Liar!" Harvest boomed, tipping his wineglass over the lad. "Get out of here, you human pestilence. Go and tell Grand Master to eat horse dung."

The Brat sprang to his feet and fled, running the gauntlet of flying food and extended feet again. The knights joined in the laughter as if they had not witnessed such scenes a thousand times before.

Tumult died away to an excited murmur.

"That was good," Durendal said. "'*Bed-wetting troglodyte*' was good!"

Prime tried to hide his apprehension and failed miserably. "You suppose there might be something in what he said?"

"It's your blood, brother," Durendal declared confidently.

It would not be his blood, not tonight. Only Prime was going to be bound, or Grand Master would have summoned more than two. They rose together, bowed to high table together, and headed side by side to the door. An ominous hush settled over the hall.

Most-wondrous!

* 3 *

Durendal closed the heavy door silently and went to stand beside Prime, carefully not looking at the other chair.

"You sent for us, Grand Master?" Harvest's voice warbled slightly, although he was rigid as a pike, staring straight at the bookshelves.

"I did, Prime. His Majesty has need of a Blade. Are you ready to serve?"

Candles flickered. Durendal had not been in this chamber since the day he caught the coins, five years ago, yet he could see no change. The grate had never been touched by flame, the same stuffing was still trying to escape from the chairs, and even the wine on the table was the same deep red. Of course Grand Master's eyebrows were thicker and whiter, his neck more scraggly, but Durendal had watched those changes coming day by day. He himself had changed far more. He was as tall now as Grand Master.

He remembered how, that epic first day, he had gone to report to this same Harvest and seen his face light up with ecstasy. Three months later, Durendal himself had reacted the same way when his own replacement had appeared. Three months of hell—and yet those three months had been nothing compared to what had followed right after, when the ex-Brat had insisted on taking the sacred name of Durendal. Master of Archives had warned him what would happen if he defied a tradition hallowed by three hundred years' observance. Well, they hadn't broken him. He had survived, struggled to be worthy of the great name, won the grudging respect of the masters and his peers. And he was worthy—the best of them all. By tomorrow night he would be Prime and Byless Second. Byless wouldn't be able to handle the juniors.

Not Durendal's problem.

What was his problem was Harvest's appalling silence. He must have been expecting the question, because he had been Second when Pendering was called. What choice did he have? Did any man ever refuse? Presumably he still had the choice all candidates had, the dismal election of walking out of the gate forever; but to contemplate surrender after so many years of effort—it was unthinkable, surely?

The only sound in the room was a faint crackling as Grand Master crumpled a sheet of parchment in his massive fist. The wax of the royal signet broke off in fragments. After five years of learning to read Grand Master's moods, Durendal knew that now they were proclaiming *hurricane*! Enforced absence from the feast might explain some storminess, but not so much.

Harvest spoke at last, almost inaudibly. "I am ready, Grand Master."

Soon Durendal would be saying those words. And who would be sitting in the second chair?

Who was there now? He had not looked. The edge of his eye hinted it was seeing a youngish man, too young to be the King himself.

"My lord," Grand Master said, "I have the honor to present Prime Candidate Harvest, who will serve you as your Blade."

As the two young men turned to him, the anonymous noble drawled, "The other one looks much more impressive. Do I have a choice?"

"You do not!" barked Grand Master, color pouring into his craggy face. "The King himself takes whoever is Prime."

"Oh, so sorry! Didn't mean to twist your dewlaps, Grand Master." He smiled vacuously. He was a weedy, soft-faced man in his early twenties, a courtier to the core, resplendent in crimson and vermilion silks trimmed with fur and gold chain. If the white cloak was truly ermine, it must be worth a fortune. His fairish beard came to a needle point and his mustache was a work of art. A fop. Who?

"Prime, this is the Marquis of Nutting, your future ward."

"Ward?" The Marquis sniggered. "You make me sound like a debutante, Grand Master. *Ward* indeed!"

Harvest bowed, his face ashen as he contemplated a lifetime guarding . . . whom? Not the King himself, not his heir, not a prince of the blood, not an ambassador traveling in exotic lands, not an important landowner out on the marches, not a senior minister, nor even—at worst—the head of one of the great conjuring orders. Here was no ward worth dying for, just a court dandy, a parasite. Trash.

Seniors spent more time studying politics than anything else except fencing. Wasn't the Marquis of Nutting the brother of the Countess Mornicade, the King's latest mistress? If so, then six months ago he had been the Honorable Tab Nillway, a younger son of a penniless baronet, and his only claim to importance was that he had been expelled from the same womb as one of the greatest beauties of the age. No report reaching Ironhall had ever hinted that he might have talent or ability.

"I am deeply honored to be assigned to your lordship," Harvest said hoarsely, but the spirits did not strike him dead for perjury.

Grand Master's displeasure was now explained. One of his precious charges was being thrown away to no purpose. Nutting was not important enough to have enemies, even at court. No man of honor would lower his standards enough to call out an upstart pimp—certainly not one who had a Blade prepared to die for him. But Grand Master had no choice. The King's will was paramount.

"We shall hold the binding tomorrow midnight, Prime," the old man snapped. "Make the arrangements, Second."

"Yes, Grand Master."

"Tomorrow?" protested the Marquis querulously. "There's a ball at court tomorrow. Can't we just run through the rigmarole quickly now and be done with it?"

Grand Master's face was already dangerously inflamed, and that remark made the veins swell even more. "Not unless you wish to kill a man, my lord. You have to learn your part in the ritual. Both you and Prime must be purified by ritual and fasting."

Nutting curled his lip. "Fasting? How barbaric!"

"Binding is a major conjuration. You will be in some danger yourself."

If the plan was to frighten the court parasite into withdrawing, it failed miserably. He merely muttered, "Oh, I'm sure you exaggerate."

Grand Master gave the two candidates a curt nod of dismissal. They bowed in unison and left.

· 4 ·

ﬡarvest clattered quickly down the stairs and strode off along a corridor that led to nowhere except the library. Durendal, with his longer legs, had no trouble keeping up with him. If the man wanted to be alone, he could say so; but if he needed support, then who else should offer it but Second?

The glow of a lamp appeared ahead as someone approached the corner. Harvest muttered an oath and moved into a window embrasure. Leaning on the stone sill, he thrust his face against the bars, as if trying to fill his lungs with fresh air.

"You go back to the hall, Second. Take—" His voice cracked. "Sit in my chair. So they'll know."

Durendal thumped a hand on his shoulder. "You forget that I have to fast also. Look on the bright side, warrior!" You can always cut your throat, which is what I would do. "You might have been gifted to some tinpot princeling in the Northern Isles. As it is, you'll live at court, romancing all the beautiful maidens. What a sinecure— wenching, dancing, hunting, and not a worry!"

"An ornament?"

"A long, quiet life is better than a short—"

"No, it isn't. Never! Five years I've slaved here, and I'm being wasted. Utterly wasted!"

This was so obviously true that Durendal found himself at a loss. He turned hopefully to the lamp approaching and saw that it was being carried by Sir Aragon, who was even older than Grand Master. He contributed nothing to Ironhall these days except a glorious reputation, for he had

20

been Blade to the great Shoulrack who had pacified Nythia for Ambrose III. He was reputed to have been the general's brains as well as his personal sword and shield.

"Leave me," Harvest howled to the sky. "For spirits' sake, Second, leave me, go away, and let me weep like a crazy woman. Like that dissolute, useless namby who is going to own my soul."

Durendal stepped back. Aragon came shuffling closer with his lamp in one hand, a cane in the other, and a thick book under his arm. He was frail, but he had not lost his wits. He took in the situation at a glance.

"Bad news, lad?"

When Harvest did not answer, Durendal said, "Prime is a little shocked, sir. He has been assigned to the Marquis of Nutting."

"Who, by the eight, is he?"

"The brother of the King's current mistress."

The old man pulled a hideous face, all wrinkles and yellow stumps of teeth. "I trust you are not implying that a private Blade is in some way inferior to a member of the Royal Guard, Candidate?"

Huddled in his cloak of misery, Harvest mumbled, "No, sir."

"It is a rare honor. There are a hundred Blades in the Royal Guard all going mad with boredom, but a private Blade has his work cut out for him, a lifetime of devotion and service. I congratulate you, my boy." Propping his cane against the wall, he held out a gnarled claw that would never again draw the sword hanging at his side.

"Congratulate?" Harvest shouted, swinging around but ignoring the proffered hand. Two red lines framing his face showed where he had been leaning on the bars. "Nutting is a nothing, a bag of dung! What need has he for a Blade?"

"The King must think he has need, Candidate! Do you presume to overrule your King? Do you know things that he doesn't?"

Nice try, Durendal thought, but it wouldn't console him, were he in poor Harvest's half-boots.

Prime shuddered and made an effort to control himself, although he was obviously close to tears now. "The King knows what he is doing! Grand Master's told him I'm not good enough for the Royal Guard, so he's palming me off on a worthless buffoon, a panderer. He isn't even a genuine noble."

Aragon's shock seemed genuine enough. "You are raving, Prime, and you know it! Neither Grand Master nor anyone else ever passes judgment on the candidates like that. Anyone who fails to measure up is thrown out long before he becomes a senior—you know that, too. I am well aware that you can't fence like Durendal here. Who can? That does not mean that all the rest of us are useless! The reason the King always takes the first in line is because even a below-average Blade is fields ahead of any other swordsman anywhere. It doesn't matter how you rank in Ironhall, you're first-class by the world's standards. Now stop making a fool of yourself." The rheumy eyes glanced briefly at Durendal. "If Grand Master were to hear of this exhibition, he might indeed change the assignment—but he would do it by striking you off the roll completely!"

Then Durendal would have to take his place, but he was more concerned for his friend than he was for himself—or hoped he was. Harvest's trouble was that he wasn't quite ripe. He did not have his emotions under adult control yet. He needed to do some more growing up.

He had twenty-four hours to do it.

Durendal said, "You're an Ironhall Blade, the deadliest human weapon ever devised—loyal, fearless, and incorruptible. How long since anyone died in a binding, Sir Aragon?"

"Before my time. Sixty years ago, at least."

"There you are. You're not afraid, are you?"

Harvest flinched. "Curse you, no! I'm not a coward!"

"It's beginning to look like it."

"No!"

"Well, that's all right, then." Durendal laid a friendly

but powerful arm around Prime's shoulders and propelled him bodily along the corridor.

Aragon stared after them wistfully.

· 5 ·

The secret, sacred heart of Ironhall was the Forge, a vast and echoing crypt watered by its own spring. The eight hearths around the walls—each with its own bellows, anvil, and stone trough—were where the magnificent cat's-eye swords were made; but the focus of power was the coffinlike slab of iron in the center, for there the human Blades were tempered. Puberty alone would have transformed the boys into men, but few of them would have become the superb swordsmen who graduated. The King's Blades were all stamped with the same die—lean, well-muscled athletes. When Harvest had stopped growing too soon, conjuration had coaxed his body into another effort. When Durendal had been in danger of growing too big, then he in turn had lain on the anvil while Master of Rituals invoked the appropriate spirits to come to his aid. The final drama, the binding of a Blade to his ward, must inevitably be consummated among the fires of the Forge.

On the day of a binding, the echoing cavern was relinquished to the participants, who were required to meditate there, starting before dawn. By the end of a very long day, Durendal was still not sure he had succeeded, because meditating wasn't something he'd ever tried before; but if boredom was the measure of success, he had done splendidly. Harvest sat and chewed his fingernails to the elbow, while the Marquis paced, fretted, and whined about hunger. Once Master Armorer came in and asked Harvest what he wanted to name his sword. Harvest muttered, "Haven't decided." The man shrugged and went away.

At sunset Master of Rituals appeared and ordered the three of them to strip and bathe in four of the eight troughs, in a particular order. After poking a finger in the icy spring water, the Marquis squawked and refused so vehemently that a pathetic smile briefly warmed Harvest's pale face. Alas, offered alternatives of calling off the binding or being forcibly stripped and dunked by four smiths, Nutting decided to cooperate; but he must have set a record for the shortest bathing on record.

Close to midnight, the knights and the rest of the candidates filed in to begin the ritual.

Bright flames frolicked in the hearths, but the shadows of six score men and boys made the crypt dark and creepy. As the chanting soared amid strange acoustics and the metallic beat of hammers, Durendal sensed the spirits gathering. Some spirituality always lingered there, for any forge sustained all four of the manifest elements—earth from the ore, fire from the hearths, air from the bellows, water from the quenching troughs. Of the virtual elements, the swords attracted spirits of death and chance, while time and love were essential ingredients of loyalty. Binding was a very potent and complex conjuration.

His fast had left him vaguely light-headed, yet he was buoyed up by the surging powers. Hard to believe after so long that his life in Ironhall was almost over. Soon he, also, would be bound and stride out into the world behind his ward, whoever that might be. He could not possibly draw a shorter straw than poor Harvest had.

The procedure was very familiar. He had first played a role in a binding on his third day in Ironhall, because one part of the ritual was assigned to the Brat. As the spirits of chance had caused him to remain the Brat so long, he had assisted no less than eight Blades at their bindings, which might be a record, although a petty one to be proud of.

Now he had emerged from the chorus to play a major role once again, gathered with the other participants inside the octogram. The locations were obligatory: Prime stood at death point, directly across from his future ward at love and flanked by Second at earth and Byless, the next most senior candidate, at air. Chance point was always given to the Brat. The three who performed most of the conjuration took the remaining points—Master of Rituals as Invoker at fire, Master of Archives as Dispenser at water, and Grand Master as Arbiter at time.

Dispenser chanted the banishment of death, casting grain across the octogram, grain being a symbol of life. Banishing all death spirits when there was a sword present was an impossibility, of course; and the element of chance was fickle by definition. When he had completed that second revocation, Invoker began summoning spirits of the required elements. The onlookers joined in the triumphant dedication song of the Order, a paean to brotherhood and service that made the Forge throb like a great heart. Although the chamber was stiflingly hot, Durendal felt the hair rise on the back of his neck.

Grand Master went forward to scatter a handful of gold coins on the anvil. He peered at their distribution and seemed satisfied that they hinted at no bizarre improbabilities afoot. As he gathered them up again, he nodded to the Brat, who strutted forward to play his small role. So fast was the King calling for Blades now that this Brat had done it three times already. He was still a long way behind Durendal's record, if it was a record. Piping out the dedication in his reedy soprano, the boy laid the cat's-eye sword on the anvil. Harvest had never touched or even seen that sword before, but the skilled armorers of Ironhall had wrought it to be a perfect fit for his hand, his arm, and his favored style.

Everything was going as it should, yet Durendal was worried by the two principals. Neither seemed quite right, somehow. Most Primes approached their binding with a glow of excitement and fulfillment, but Harvest looked miserable and unsure. The Marquis's air of contemptuous bored amusement might be an acceptable affectation at court but was no way to approach a dangerous elementary ritual. He still seemed to expect some meaningless fakery.

Master of Rituals nodded to Byless, who stepped over to remove Prime's shirt for him. Only a week ago, Durendal had done that for Pendering. If Harvest was a borderline Blade, young Byless needed at least a year's training yet. Surely Grand Master must soon advise the King that the supply of ready candidates was running out? And in that case, if they wanted to keep at least one in reserve for emergencies, how long might Durendal have to wait for his own call?

Prime turned. Durendal went to him, smiling cheerfully and trying to ignore the pale lips and eyes stretched too wide. Oh, let that only be an illusion of the firelight! He put a thumb on Harvest's hairless chest to locate the base of the sternum, although all the bones were clearly visible. He made a mark with a piece of charcoal directly over the heart. He went back to his place at earth point.

Harvest stepped forward and took up the sword, barely sparing it a glance. He jumped up on the anvil and raised the blade in salute as he swore the oath—to defend Nutting against all foes, to serve him until death, to give his own life for his ward's if need be. Words that should have rung through the Forge like glorious trumpet notes came out as a mumble. Durendal disliked what he saw on Grand Master's face.

Prime sprang down and knelt before the Marquis to offer the sword—which Nutting accepted with an air of bored indifference—and then backed away and sat on the anvil. The Marquis followed to aim the point of the sword at the smudge of charcoal. This was the culmination of the ritual, but even now he seemed to be expecting some sort of trickery. Durendal and Byless closed in to assist. Harvest took several deep breaths, raised his arms. Durendal took a firm grip on one and Byless on the other, together holding him steady for the thrust. The Marquis hesitated, glancing around at Grand Master as if suddenly realizing that what he had been told must happen was not some elaborate joke or fake.

"Do it, man! Don't torture him!" Grand Master snarled.

The Marquis shrugged and spoke his three words of ritual: "Serve or die!" He poked the sword into Harvest's chest.

No matter how good the conjuration, that must hurt. All Blades admitted that the binding had hurt, although briefly. In this case, the prospective ward did not strike very forcefully, for the point failed to emerge from Harvest's back, and yet the spurt of blood was much heavier than usual. With a faint moan, Harvest let his head droop. He did not wrench back at the friends supporting him, which was what Pendering had done the previous week. Instead he pulled forward, causing them to stagger off balance. He pulled harder and harder, as if he was trying to double over. What was the fool playing at? Had he fainted? Durendal and Byless resisted, took the strain, then stared at each other in horror as the awful truth dawned. Three knights ran forward to help them lower the body to the floor. Nutting screamed shrilly and dropped the sword.

The conjuration had failed.

Now it was Second's turn to try.

· 6 ·

The candidates were warned early in their training that binding could kill, and there were even records of Second dying as well. The conjurers blamed such failures on mistakes in the ritual, but Durendal had witnessed a hundred bindings now and was certain he would have noticed any deviation from standard procedure. He assumed the problem had been lack of will. Harvest had been reluctant to serve, Nutting skeptical and indifferent. Harvest had distrusted his own ability, while Nutting had wanted a Blade as a plume in his hat to flaunt around the court, not as a vital defender. Two unenthusiastic principals had combined to create disaster.

Durendal's first concern was to look at the wound. The charcoal mark he had made had been blotted out by the blood, but the hole in poor Harvest was exactly where it should be, so the error had not been his.

Then, while knights and seniors milled around, removing the body and making ready for the next attempt, he headed for the Marquis, who was down on his knees near the door, miserably retching between frantic protestations that he could not possibly go through all that again. Grand Master and Master of Rituals stood over him, blocking any further effort to flee, lecturing him before he had even recovered his wits.

"With so many spirits assembled, we have raised the potential to levels where discharge of the elemental forces—"

That sort of talk wouldn't work on a pseudo-aristocratic pimp.

"Excuse me." Durendal elbowed the two knights aside in a way he would not have believed possible even five minutes ago. Detecting the preliminary intake of breath that would become a roar from Grand Master, he said, "This is my problem!" He hoisted the Marquis to his feet by his padded jerkin, spun him around, and steadied him before he toppled over.

Nutting rolled his eyes in horror when he saw who was manhandling him. Even in the ruddy light of the Forge, his cheeks were green. "No! Not you, too! I can't, you hear? I can't. The sight of blood nauseates me." His boots scrabbled on the rock, but he did not go anywhere with Durendal holding him.

"You prefer to die?"

"*Argk!* W-what do you mean?"

"You killed one of our brothers. You expect to walk out of here alive?"

The aristocratic vapidity made a croaking noise. Master of Rituals opened his mouth to protest, and Durendal aimed a cow kick at his shin.

"You only *thought* you needed a Blade yesterday, my lord. You most certainly need one tonight. Without a Blade you can't possibly leave Ironhall alive. Do you want me or not?"

"Leave him, Prime—we'll let the juniors have some sport with him." Grand Master had caught on. Master of Rituals, who had not, looked as if he were about to have a seizure.

"Please?" whimpered the Marquis. "I need protection! I'm no good with a sword."

"Come then, my lord." Durendal hustled him through the crowd of sullen watchers to a trough where water trickled endlessly from the rocky wall. "Rinse your mouth, drink, compose yourself." He gestured at the onlookers—the dismayed and the enraged—waving for them to leave. He ducked Nutting's head, pulled it up, and wiped the splutters away with his sleeve. By that time the others had moved more or less out of earshot. He put his nose very close to Nutting's.

"Now listen, my lord! Listen well. The King wants you to have a Blade and now I am Prime. My name is Durendal, in case you've forgotten, a name revered for more than three hundred years. I chose it so I would have to live up to it and I did. I am the best to come through Ironhall in a generation. If you want me, I am yours."

The Marquis nodded vigorously.

"I would rather see you die to avenge poor Harvest," Durendal said truthfully, "but I won't feel like that after I'm bound. I can get you out alive if I have to fight our way out, and probably not even Grand Master could say as much." He wondered if he was flying too high now, but Nutting seemed to be believing every word of this rubbish.

"What went wrong?" he moaned.

"Mostly Harvest wasn't quite ready. I am." Was this human chicken even capable of playing his part in the ritual? He was shaking like a broom out a window. "And you did not strike hard enough."

"What?"

"You didn't strike as if you meant it, my lord. Next time—when you put the sword in my heart—remember you are fighting to save your own life. Ram it all the way through, you hear? That's how the King does it. Push till the point comes out of my back."

Nutting moaned and began to retch again.

· 7 ·

Somehow love point seemed inappropriate for the still-sniveling Marquis, but he was back there. Now Durendal stood opposite, at death. He was flanked by Byless and Gotherton. He wondered if they would be strong enough to restrain him when his reflexes took over, and if a man could cut himself to shreds from the inside out. The singing was over. The Brat had trilled the dedication, whey-faced and staring at Prime with owlish eyes, as he laid another sword on the anvil.

Master of Rituals had invoked the spirits, and either he had summoned far more than before or else Durendal was just more attuned to them. He sensed the haunted chamber quivering with power. Spirituality fizzed in his blood. Strange lights dancing over the stonework made every shadow numinous. His hand itched to take up the superb weapon gleaming on the anvil.

The Marquis had shrunk till he looked like a shivering,

cowed child compared to the awesome Grand Master. Could a real man serve such a craven nothing all his life without going crazy? Could Durendal endure to be only an ornament, as poor Harvest had put it? Yes, by the spirits! This was what he had aimed for, worked for, struggled for—to be one of the King's Blades. If his ward was useless in himself, then he would still have the finest protector in all Chivial. Perhaps a man might make something out of that worthless human rag if he tried hard enough, or perhaps the King had some secret, dangerous mission in mind for him. With real luck, there would be a war, when a young noble would be expected to raise a regiment and his Blade could go into battle at his side.

The invocation ended. At last it was his move, his moment, his triumph—five years he had worked for this! He turned to summon Gotherton forward, felt Gotherton's fingers shake as he unbuttoned the shirt. He winked and almost laughed aloud at the disbelief he saw flood over the boyish face. In that oppressive heat, it was a relief to shed the garment, to flex his shoulders, and spin around. He winked at Byless also when he came, and this time was rewarded with a stare of open admiration. Why were they all so worried? Things only went wrong once every hundred years or so. He was not poor Harvest! He was the second Durendal, come into his destiny. He felt the thumb press on his chest, the cool touch of charcoal.

Now for that sword! *His* sword. Oh, bliss! It floated in his hand. Blue starlight gleamed and danced along the blade and a bar of gold fire burned in the cat's eye cabochon on the pommel. He wanted to whirl it, caress it with a strop until it would cut falling gossamer, hold it in sunlight and admire the damask—but those luxuries must wait. He sprang up onto the anvil.

"My lord Marquis of Nutting!" The echoes rumbled and rolled—wonderful! "Upon my soul, I, Durendal, candidate in the Loyal and Ancient Order of the King's Blades, do irrevocably swear in the presence of these my brethren that I will evermore defend you against all foes, setting my own life as nothing to shield you from peril, reserving only my fealty to our lord the King. To bind me to this oath, I bid you plunge this my sword into my heart that I may die if I swear falsely or, being true, may live by the power of the spirits here assembled to serve you until in time I die again.''

Then down to the floor and down on one knee.

Sallow and trembling, the Marquis accepted the sword, seeming ready to drop it at any moment. Durendal rose and stepped back until he felt the anvil against his calves. He sat.

Grand Master pulled the Marquis forward. He needed both hands to raise the sword this time. It wavered, flashing firelight, and the point made uncertain circles around the target—idiot! It would do no good if it missed Durendal's heart, no good at all. He waited until the terrified noble looked up enough to meet his eyes. Then he smiled encouragingly and raised his arms. Byless and Gotherton pulled them back, bracing them against their waists. He must try not to thrash too hard when the shock came. He waited. He could hear Nutting's teeth chatter.

"Do it now!" he said. He was about to add, "Do it right!" but the Marquis shrieked, "Serve or die!" and thrust the sword. Either he remembered Durendal's instructions or he lost his footing, for he stumbled forward and the steel razored instantly through muscle, ribs, heart, lung, more ribs, and out into the space beyond. The guard thudded against Durendal's chest.

It did hurt. He had expected pain at the wound, but his whole body exploded with it. Through that furnace of agony he became aware of two terrified eyes staring into his. He wanted to say, "You must take it out again quickly, my lord," but speaking with a sword through his chest proved difficult.

Grand Master hauled Nutting back bodily. Fortunately he remembered to take the sword with him.

Durendal looked down to watch the wound heal. The trickle of blood was astonishingly small, but then it always was—a heart could not pump when it had a nail through it. He felt the healing, a tickling sensation right through to his back, and also a huge surge of power and excitement and pride. Byless and Gotherton had released him. The Forge thundered with cheers, which seemed like an unnecessary commotion, although he'd always cheered for others in the past. A binding was routine, nothing to it.

He was a Blade, a companion in the Order. People would address him as Sir Durendal, although that was only a courtesy title.

"You didn't need us!" Gotherton gasped. "You barely twitched!"

They could be thanked later, and the Brat, the armorers, and all the others. First things first. He rose and went to recover his sword before the glazed-looking Marquis dropped her. Now he could inspect her properly. She was a hand-and-a-half sword with a straight blade, about a yard long, the longest he could wear at his belt without tripping. She was single-edged for two-thirds of her length, double-edged near the point. He admired the grace of the fluted quillons, the delicate sweep of the knuckle guard, the finger ring for when he wanted to use her as a rapier, the fire of the cat's-eye pommel that gave her her balance, which of course was perfect, neither too far forward for thrusting nor so far back that he would not be able to slash. The armorers had created a perfect all-around weapon for a swordsman of unusual versatility. Had they laid her among a hundred others, he would have picked her out as his. He admired his own heart's blood on her, then slipped her through the loop on his belt. He would name her Harvest—a good name for a sword, a tribute to a friend who'd been treated badly by chance.

Byless was fussing, trying to help him into his shirt, Grand Master was congratulating him, while he was still trying to think of all the people he must thank before . . .

Suddenly his attention was caught by the Marquis, that green-faced, shivering pimp in the background. How strange! It was as if that pseudo-aristocratic ninny was the only illuminated thing in the room, with everyone and everything else in darkness. Nobody, nothing else mattered. The turd was still a turd, unfortunately—the binding had not changed that—but now he was obviously an important turd. He must be looked after and kept safe.

Most-wondrous!

Sir Durendal walked over to his ward and nodded respectfully. "At your service now, my lord," he said. "When do we ride?"

· 8 ·

The Marquis did not ride, he traveled by coach—but that came later, in the morning. First there was the customary small-hours dinner in the hall, when the new Blade and his ward sat with the knights, when juniors went quietly to sleep with their heads among the dishes, when men made foolish speeches. Harvest's death should have cooled the merriment this time, but it did not seem to.

"We were all so sorry for him," Master of Archives explained. "Two weeks is average. I only had to endure a couple of days of it myself. But here, this poor little fellow—" The hall guffawed in unison. "—this unfortunate mite had been the Brat for three whole months! And he really wasn't good at it. He couldn't grovel. He cringed badly. His whining was just appalling. But, finally, at long last, something crawled in the door, something that Grand Master could in reasonably good conscience accept. No, I don't mean Candidate Byless; he came later. So the Brat was allowed back into the human race. He came to see me to choose a name. 'No,' I said, 'you can't have that one. It's special.' And he said, 'But you said . . .' "

And so on. If it kept the children happy, *Sir* Durendal could smile tolerantly. It had been the sopranos who had hung that name on him and he had turned the tables on them by keeping it.

Master of Rapiers was next to rise up on his hind legs. ". . . not true that he could beat me on his second day in Ironhall. Absolute nonsense! It was the *third* day."

More howls of mirth. It had been two years, and three before Durendal had been able to do it consistently. He sipped his wine—and almost choked.

"What in the name of the evils is this piss?" he whispered.

Master of Sabers chuckled as if he had been waiting for that. "It's an excellent vintage." Other faces were smiling.

"It tastes like—"

"Yes, but only because you're on duty, Blade. One glass is your limit now."

Durendal glanced at his ward, who was pouring the stuff down his throat like a dairymaid washing out a churn. He looked at the amused Grand Master on his throne and then at all the other grins.

"When am I off duty?"

"Probably about forty years from now," said Master of Horse.

The Marquis's coach bore his arms in cobalt enamel and gold: *azure, two squirrels adorsed or.* It had padded leather seating, was drawn by eight matched grays, and represented a splendid example of the benefits to be gained by being brother of a woman the King wanted in bed— Olinda Nillway, now Countess Mornicade, the greatest beauty of the age. Gossips whispered that she had enhanced her natural charms with conjuration, but they could not explain how she might have smuggled an enchantment into court without the sniffers detecting it. Not only a great beauty, she was also a shrewd negotiator, who had won titles and estates for all her relatives. A couple of her uncles served the King as minor officials. Her brother was controller of naval provisions and made weevils seem wholesome.

Two hours after leaving Ironhall, Durendal had not raised his opinion of his ward at all. The man wrapped in ermine was a small-minded, vainglorious nonentity. His gossip was pointless, his humor spiteful, and his general conversation utterly lacking in tact. "Can't you grow a beard yet?"

"Never tried." But he'd been shaving every day since he ate at the beansprouts' table. His chin grew stubble like marble-cutters' grit.

"Try. That's an order. His Majesty sets the standard for the court, and at the moment it is mustache and full beard."

Yesterday, while wondering what to meditate upon, Durendal had decided to let his beard grow in. Now, clearly, he would have to keep shaving it off.

"Is your hair naturally wavy, or do you curl it?"

Spirits preserve me! *Curl* it?

"I asked you a question, boy."

"I heard it."

Nutting fell silent, looking puzzled. He could not remain silent long. Soon he laughingly mentioned that a Blade had been his sister's idea. "She persuaded the King to make out the warrant and gave it to me at my birthday banquet last week—such a lovely surprise!"

Up until then Durendal had hardly spoken, being intent on viewing the world he had not seen since he was fourteen, but at that news he felt a sort of high-pitched twang, like a string snapping on a lute.

"My lord, I am not your servant. I am the King's. He has decreed that I shall serve him by defending you to the death, so that is what I shall do. How I do it is entirely up to me. I don't need to pander to your whims. I am a Blade, not a gift from a harlot to a pimp."

Nutting's jaw dropped. "You can't speak to me like that!" he screeched.

"Yes, I can. I won't do it in public unless you provoke me."

"I will have you flogged!"

Durendal chuckled. "Try. I'll bet you I drop six of them before they lay a hand on me." Three for certain and why not six?

"I'll report you to . . . to . . ."

"Yes?"

"To the King!"

"He can bring me to heel, I admit. But I shall be with you when you tattle, because from now on I am always going to be with you. I advise you not to have too many other witnesses."

The rest of the journey was more peaceful.

Still the coach continued to bounce and rattle through fields and pasture, with no sign of Grandon. Just as Durendal realized it was not going to the capital at all, a bend in the road revealed gates ahead and a high stone wall that stretched almost out of sight. Over it showed glimpses of fine trees, gable roofs, innumerable tall chimney pots. A Blade should be a saturnine, silent, menacing sort of person, but there would be time enough for that later. Not today.

"This's the palace?"

"Oldmart Palace." The Marquis shrugged. "It's better than most. Newer, for one thing."

"The King's in residence?" Flames and steel! He was babbling like a child. Why else would they be going there?

His lordship curled his shapely mustache in a sneer—he had been complaining again of the grand ball he had missed last night. "Today he's hosting a reception for the Isilond ambassador. It will be a very august affair."

A man could relax, then. He would not be invited to . . . but where the Marquis went, his Blade went. Mustn't ask. Didn't have to.

"Of course," said the turd, "correct protocol requires a new Blade arriving at court to be presented to His Majesty as soon as possible. I imagine even the Lord Herald will not object if I change first. Can't do much about you, though. It is regrettable that you have nothing decent to wear.''

Durendal glanced down at the smart new hose, doublet, and jerkin Ironhall had provided for his departure, much as a merchant might package an expensive purchase leaving his premises. ''These are the finest garments I've ever worn, my lord.''

''Bah! Rags! Disgusting. Those slashed sleeves went out two years ago. As my Blade, you will have to be suitably arrayed, but we can't help that today.''

''If I may presume, my lord . . . you could take me into town, dress me, and present me tomorrow.''

''No! It must be today.''

Obviously the Marquis could not wait to flaunt his new symbol of greatness before the court. Durendal sank back on the bench in silence.

An hour or so later, he followed his ward down marble steps and out into the palace grounds. Ironhall had taught him the basic skills he would need for court—protocol, deportment, etiquette, and even how to tread a reasonable minuet or gavotte. This was all real, so why did he feel like a child playing make-believe? He surveyed acres of lawns and flower beds and little ornamental lakes, all divided by waist-high hedges and paved paths, with striped marquees and bright flags in the distance. Orchestras played under the trees. It was grandiose and fairy-tale, but it was *real*. The weight at his side was Harvest, a real sword, his own personal sword.

His eyes picked out other Blades right away, the distinctive blue and silver livery with a royal lion emblem over the heart, the uniform of the Royal Guard, which he would give all his teeth to belong to and now never would. Soon he was close enough to recognize some of those who had been ahead of him in the school and others who had accompanied the King on his visits there. Two of the former noticed him and beamed a welcome from a distance. They must know the man he was warding. Would he have to live with their pity all his life?

There were also men-at-arms holding pikes, wearing helmets and breastplates, probably secular, although he must never assume that a possible opponent was not spiritually enhanced. There seemed to be more servants than courtiers. The women in white, wearing high white conical hats trimmed with muslin—those must be the White Sisters, the sniffers.

Nutting plunged straight ahead through the throng of silks and satins, jewels and ermine, ruffs and gold. He smiled and waved and cried out greetings to those he deemed worthy of his notice. Heads turned, which was the whole idea. Had he no shame, no sense of rightness? Had he never heard of subtlety? The better Durendal came to know him, the worse he seemed.

As the Marquis led his Blade through a gap in the final hedge, entering onto the lawn where the royal party stood, he brushed past two men-at-arms, undoubtedly without seeing them. Even Durendal assumed they were ceremonial, for they were chatting earnestly with a sniffer, but suddenly she shouted, "You—stop!" and there was an emergency.

The men-at-arms began to level their pikes to challenge, but Durendal had already thrust the Marquis aside, drawn Harvest, and was just about to spit the first man through the eye when the woman screamed.

"No! Stop! Stop! It's all right!"

He managed to halt the sword about an inch from its target and retain his balance too. Which was good.

The sniffer waved both hands at the guards, who had not finished reacting to her original shout. "I made a mistake."

Fortunately there was no one else close enough to have noticed. Even more fortunately, the woman had retracted her challenge extremely quickly. Now came reaction, analysis, reproach—he had erred. He had been *too* quick.

There had been no threat to Nutting, only to him, but he had almost slain two of the King's men-at-arms on the King's lawn.

"My lady, your mistake was nearly fatal!" He slid Harvest back into her scabbard, noting with unworthy pleasure that his potential opponents had both turned almost as white as the stupid woman's antique clothing.

She was about thirty, old enough not to make such dangerous errors. Her face was pleasantly plump, the scarlet blush of embarrassment intriguing. The towering hennin made her seem much taller than she actually was.

The Marquis had begun to splutter predictably. "What is the meaning of this outrage?" He kept trying to dodge around Durendal, and Durendal kept moving in front of him.

"My lord, I apologize!" she said. "Your Blade is very recently bound, my lord?"

"What of it? Confound it, boy, get out of my way!"

"The smell of the Forge on him is very strong, my lord."

The Marquis flustered like a mad duck. "That's no excuse! Don't you know who I am? You dare accuse *me* of practicing conjuration, and against His Majesty at that? You almost provoked a major scandal, sister!"

"I was merely doing my duty, my lord, and what I almost provoked was a lot worse than scandal."

Good for her! She was not going to take any nonsense from the turd, even if she had made unpleasant allegations about Durendal. She nodded stiffly to him. "My apologies to you also, sir knight."

He bowed. "Mine to you for startling you, sister."

"I shall complain to Mother Superior!" Nutting snapped. "Now come along, Blade, and let us have no more embarrassing scenes."

He strode off huffily. Durendal risked a wink at the sniffer and followed his ward.

He had seen the King often at Ironhall, although to the King he would have been just one of dozens of faces. He would not have known the Queen from any other well-dressed lady in the land. He took note of her features, realizing that they were singularly nondescript and someday he might meet her by chance in a hallway. Godeleva was a slender woman, but she might not have seemed so frail and colorless had she not been standing next her vibrant, domineering husband. In eight years of marriage, she had not yet brought a baby to term, which might explain her air of worry and sorrow.

But the King . . . Ambrose IV was thirty-four and had reigned for two years already. He was taller than any other man around him, monolithic in his sumptuous attire of fur and brocade and jewels, blazing brighter than the rose-bushes behind him. His hair was tawny, the cropped fringe of beard closer to red. He broke off what he was saying to frown at the Marquis's brash intrusion.

Nutting could bow gracefully, give him that. But he did not wait to be acknowledged.

"My liege, I have the great honor of presenting the Blade Your Majesty so generously assigned to me. Sir Durendal has—"

"Sir Who?" The royal bellow could be heard all the way to the hollyhocks. Every head turned.

The Marquis blinked. "Durendal, sire."

Ambrose IV stared at the young man kneeling before him. "Stand up!"

Durendal rose.

"Well!" The famous amber eyes raked him up and down. "Durendal, hmm? A descendant?"

"No, Your Majesty. Just an admirer."

"We all are. Welcome to court, Sir Durendal."

"Thank you, sire."

"Very impressive! I don't believe," the King said loudly, "that I intended to be *quite* so generous."

Amid the thunderstorm of laughter, the Marquis turned redder than the geraniums. A royal jest like that one would linger around the court for days, like a bad smell.

· 9 ·

The Marquis, surprisingly, had a marquise he had not thought to mention. She was even younger than Durendal—although not younger than he was feeling by then, which was about seven. She was another gift from the King, having been a ward in chancery, but her husband seemed genuinely fond of her. She was very pretty, impeccably well mannered, incapable of rational thought. Her family tree was as tangled as a briar patch and blighted by inbreeding; and her only serious interest was clothing.

In the Marquis's absence, his establishment had been moved to a vast new suite in the main wing of the palace. He preened at this additional evidence of royal favor, ignoring his wife's complaints that the servants were laughing at her for not having enough gowns to fill all the closet space. She told her husband's Blade to stand there. And there. And there. Look at the window. Perfect. When company called, would he please lean against the mantel with his left profile to the door. She assumed she was giving an order, so he did not need to answer the question.

He thought he could detect invisible hands at work on his behalf, though, because the new quarters had obviously been designed with security in mind, having but a single entrance and windows accessible only to bats. Any midnight intruder must pass through the outer rooms, where he would be. The servants were billeted elsewhere. There were ropes available in case of fire. What else need he worry about?

Two things. The first was that no assassin in the world had the slightest interest in harming Tab Nillway, Marquis of Nutting. The second was that Durendal knew that and could no more stop himself behaving like a real Blade with a real ward than a sheepdog could resist herding sheep.

Fortunately on this, his first night on the job, his ward announced that he was incredibly exhausted by the hardships of his visit to Ironhall and was going to bed early. The Marquise went with him; valet and maid departed. Durendal locked and barred the door, checked every cranny for concealed murderers, and then settled into a comfortable chair in the outermost salon. There he chewed over his problem while he stropped Harvest into the sharpest sword in the known world.

As he had not been warned of all the side effects of a binding conjuration, he must be expected to work them out for himself. He already knew he could not drink more than one glass of wine. Now, after two nights without sleep, he felt as fresh as a new-laid egg. Bizarre! Blades were normally assigned in pairs or larger groups, and he should have realized that sooner. He was all alone, but he already knew that he could not bear to let the unspeakable Marquis out of his sight. How were the two of them going to stand each other for the next thirty or forty years? How was he ever going to take exercise, make friends, and even enjoy a little romance?

He must have advice. The logical source was the Royal Guard, but how could he consult them? Even now, when his ward was as safe as he could ever be, Durendal could not walk out and leave him, not if that door had a hundred locks on it. During the day, he would be in constant attendance.

He was going to go crazy.

An hour later, when the tap came, he had guessed the answer. Even so, he had Harvest in his hand as he opened the door a crack on the chain and peeked out. There were two of them, and one of them was Hoare, who had left Ironhall only two months ago. The other was Montpurse himself.

"You're late," he said brashly and let them in.

They were both typical Blades—lean, chiseled men who studied the world intently and moved like cats—but Hoare had not yet lost his distinctive juvenile nonchalance, an insouciance that gave him a permanent air of knowing some secret joke. He was about a month into an ill-advised beard, much fairer than his hair. Montpurse was clean shaven, with hair like flax and eyes the blue of buttermilk. His babyish complexion made him seem ten years younger than his companion, but he must be in his middle twenties now. Was it an advantage to be always underestimated? Did it amuse the King to have a permanent adolescent in charge of his Guard?

"Brother Durendal, Leader," Hoare said, cuing Durendal to call him "brother" and Montpurse "Leader." Hands were clasped.

"I'd never have forgotten that name," Montpurse said. "You must have been after my time."

"Yes, Leader." Not quite, but Durendal would not say so.

Then the mist-blue eyes lit up. "No! You were the Brat! You gave me my sword!"

"And you came and thanked me afterward. You have no idea what that meant to me!"

"Yes, I do," Montpurse said firmly. "Now, you must have questions."

Durendal remembered his manners and bade his visitors be seated. He apologized for not having refreshments handy.

Montpurse settled onto a chair like a falling leaf. "You can get anything you want by pulling that bell rope. Don't bother now, though."

"First question, then. How do I guard a man twenty-four hours a day?"

For a moment the Commander reflected Hoare's secret smile. "You can't. You'll find that the urgency wears off in a couple of weeks. As you learn the ropes you gain confidence. You stay out of the bathroom, is how we describe it. In the Guard, of course, we take turns; and whenever your ward is in the palace we can spell you off also.'' He cut off Durendal's thanks. "No, we do it for any single. We regard it as part of our job. There are far too many of us just to guard the King, and it would be no advantage to him to have crazy Blades running around.''

Durendal had guessed right, which was satisfying. "Do I ever sleep?''

This time the smile was broader. "You may doze in a chair for an hour or so, but you'll waken every time a spider sneezes. One gets used to it. Take up a hobby—study law, finance, or foreign tongues. Helps to pass the time. Even Blades age, you know. You can't be a crack swordsman forever.''

Durendal thanked him again. There was something exhilarating in this frank, brotherly talk with two men he had admired for so long. Hoare had been part hero, part friend, permanently ahead of him although Durendal had been the better fencer for years. All the candidates worshiped Montpurse in absentia for his legendary swordsmanship and meteoric rise in the King's service.

"Is there any reason I don't know why the Marquis needs a Blade?''

Awkward pause.

"Not that I am aware of,'' Montpurse admitted reluctantly. "The King will refuse the Countess nothing. But don't feel slighted. Look on the sunny side—your assignment will stretch you to the limit. We guard the King, but there's a hundred of us. Most of the time we're bored silly.''

That was Sir Aragon's Rationalization to Comfort Unfortunate Colleagues.

Hoare leered. "Tell him about women!''

"You tell him, you lecherous young beast.''

"I hope one of you will,'' Durendal said frankly. They knew how innocent he was. They'd been there.

"Oh, they're overrated. They always drift off to sleep.''

Montpurse rolled his eyes in disbelief. "You wear them

out, you mean. That's part of the legend, Durendal, one of the best parts.''

"I'll find you a good tutor," Hoare said thoughtfully. "Let's see . . . Blondie? Ayne? Rose? Ah, yes . . . married to a royal courier, so she gets lonely and won't chatter or start dreaming of permanent arrangements . . . bonny, bouncy, eager . . .''

"He knows a hundred like that," his commander said scornfully. "I won't let him play tricks on you."

Durendal gulped and said, "That's kind of you."

"Now, how about leaving our philandering friend here to guard your gate and coming for a stroll with me?"

Every muscle tensed in alarm. "Not tonight, if you don't mind. I'd love to, but it just feels a little soon, if you understand?" He could see that they had expected that response and were trying not to laugh at him. But he couldn't! No matter what they thought of him, he just couldn't.

"I give you my oath, Blade to brother," Hoare said, keeping his face as solemn as it could ever be, "that I will guard your ward until you return."

"It's very kind of you, but . . .''

Montpurse chuckled and stood up. "The King wants you.''

"What?''

"You heard. The King wants to speak with you. Coming?''

That made a difference! He was a King's Blade. "Yes, of course. Um, I'd better shave first."

"You'll only nick yourself," Montpurse said. "Come! We don't keep him waiting."

There could be no more argument. Although Durendal heard the bolts and chains closing behind him, he still felt unsettled as he headed off along the corridor with Montpurse.

"Like ants walking all over you, isn't it?" the Commander said. "But it does wear off, I promise you. Or you get used to it."

They clattered down a long flight of marble stairs. The palace had fallen silent; the corridors were dim as the candles burned low.

"I'm a King's Blade bound to a subject. How does divided loyalty work?"

"Your binding is to the Marquis. He's first, the King second. If they ever come into conflict, you will have a serious problem."

That seemed like a good cue for a very tricky question, and the middle of a huge, deserted hallway a good place to ask it. "Why would the King give a valuable property like a Blade to a man who has no enemies?"

"I thought I told you that."

"Tell me again."

"Are you questioning the royal prerogative?" Montpurse opened an inconspicuous door to reveal narrow fieldstone stairs leading downward.

"I would not want to think my sovereign was a fool, Leader."

The Commander closed the door behind them and then caught his companion's arm in a steely grip. "What do you mean by that?" The pale eyes were ice-blue now.

Durendal realized that he was being held under a lamp, where his face was clearly visible. How had he managed to stumble into quicksand so soon? "If the King had doubts about a man's loyalty—perhaps not now, but his loyalty in future—well, conspiracy would be very difficult with a Blade around, wouldn't it? And he would make a good touchstone. If he suddenly goes insane, investigate."

Hard stare. "Oh, come, Brother Durendal! You don't suspect your little marquis of treasonous ambitions?"

"No, not at all. But His Majesty couldn't plant Blades only on the doubtful, could he? He would have to spread some dummies around too."

A longer stare. Faint sounds of male laughter came drifting up from the cellar. "I do hope you won't spread such crazy notions around, brother."

Spirits! That meant *yes*! "No, Leader. I won't mention them again."

Without seeming to move a muscle, Montpurse shed about ten years and was a boy again. "Good. Now, one thing more. If His Majesty should choose to try a little fencing with you—about three times in four, understand?"

"No."

"Any less than that and he gets suspicious. Any more and he may be a little resentful. It is foolish to upset the mighty, brother." He led the way downstairs.

Puzzled, Durendal followed.

· 10 ·

The cellar was rank with odors of ale and sweat, plus the eye-watering stench of whale oil from lamps hanging low overhead. There were no chairs or tables, only a row of barrels and a basket containing drinking horns. Of the thirty men standing around laughing and chattering, at least twenty-five were Blades in the blue-and-silver livery of the Guard. The rest were almost certainly Blades of other loyalties or just out of uniform—all but one, the largest man present, who was the center of attention. Judging by the relaxed din, Blades off duty had no problem drinking their fill and this was their private haunt.

The King completed a story that sent his listeners into peals of mirth. What a king! After only two years on the throne, already he had reformed the tax system, ended the Isilond War, and gone a long way to master the great landowners who had so defied his father. Yet here he was, one of the greatest monarchs in all Eurania, roistering with his Blades as if he were one of them, making them laugh and—much more important—bellowing with laughter himself when they responded. This was the man Durendal had been created to serve, not that wretched Marquis of Nothing now snoring away upstairs.

Ambrose swung around to stare over heads at the newcomers. Although his face was flushed at the moment and sequined with sweat, the gold eyes were clear and steady. Durendal offered a three-quarter bow that he judged appropriate to a first personal audience set in an informal atmosphere.

"I have heard some impressive tales, Sir Durendal," the King boomed.

"Your Majesty is most gracious."

"Only when I want to be!" He glanced at his companions to trigger another laugh. Then he frowned. "What happened to Harvest?"

The room stilled instantly. It also seemed to grow much colder, in spite of the stuffiness.

"I am not qualified to judge, sire." That was not good enough. The King knew that. "But, if you are asking for my opinion, I believe he was not ready. He lacked confidence in himself."

The royal brows frowned. "Come over here."

He led Durendal to a dark corner. Backs turned and the rest of the room became very noisy again. Nothing was less visible than a monarch incognito, but the King's personality at close quarters was an experience akin to being trapped in a cave by a bear. It was a long time since Durendal had needed to look up to anyone.

"It was unfortunate."

"Yes, sire." Oh, yes, yes, yes! But a man should mourn a lost friend for the friend's sake, not for what that death had cost him personally.

"Who's next? Give me your assessment of the next six."

That would be tattling. Officially even Grand Master did not pass such information on to the King, although no one believed that. Conflicting loyalties howled in Durendal's mind—loyalty to Ironhall, to the men who had trained him, to his friends there. But the Order was the King's, and a companion's fealty was to the sovereign.

"My liege. Candidate Byless is Prime now, excellent all-round material, but he's only seventeen—"

"He lied about his age?"

Byless told tales about a sheriff after him and Grand Master rescuing him from a hangman's noose, but no one believed them. "I expect so, sire. He needs at least another year—better two." Three would be better yet, but who would dare say so to this impatient King? "Candidate Gotherton is very sound, probably better at thinking than he can ever be at fencing, but not at all below standard. Candidate Everman is a year older than me. He's superb. Candidate—"

"Tell me about Everman." The King listened intently as Durendal raved about Everman. Then he said, "Is he as good as you?"

Trapped! A man should fall on his sword.

"Not yet."

"Will he ever be?"

"Close, I'd say."

The King smiled, showing he was aware of the feelings he had provoked. "Good answers, Blade! The ancients taught us: Know thyself! I admire a man who can assess his own worth. I also appreciate honesty. It is a quality rulers treasure above all others—except loyalty, of course, and I can buy that. Grand Master agrees that Everman is exceptional, but he still ranks him well below you."

Durendal's mouth opened and closed a few times. He could feel himself blushing like a child. He had never dreamed that the King followed the progress of the school so closely. "Your Majesty is very kind."

The King pouted. "No I'm not, I'm ruthless. I have to be. Just now I have an urgent need for a first-rate Blade. I wanted you."

Blood and steel! Harvest's death had thrown Durendal

away on the turd, and the King's reaction at hearing his name today had not meant what he thought it did.

"Byless and Gotherton—can they endure binding? Would they snuff out like Harvest?"

Durendal held two friends' lives in his hands and wanted to scream. He took time to think about his answer. Mouth dry, he said cautiously, "Sire, they're good men. I think they'll do it."

The King smiled. His breath reeked of ale and garlic. "Well spoken. Repeat this conversation to no one, ever. Now, I've heard so much about your ability with a sword . . . I'm not without merit myself, you know."

This night was going straight down and accelerating. Oh, to be back on Starkmoor! Even to be the Brat again would be better than this.

"Your Majesty's prowess is legendary, but I am supposed to be an expert. I hope you will not humiliate me in public, sire."

"Well, let's see about that! Fair match, now—honesty, remember? No pandering to my feelings. Sir Larson! Where are the foils? Rapiers, I think. The rapier is my weapon. Even I would hesitate to try this brawny lad with a broadsword. What do you think?"

A Blade Durendal did not know had already produced foils and masks, apparently from nowhere. "I am sure Your Majesty would massacre him with a broadsword."

The King guffawed. "Be a shame to end his career so soon, yes?"

Willing hands helped Durendal out of his jerkin, doublet, and shirt as the audience cleared back to the walls. Obviously this reeking cellar had a long history of Blades, ale, and fencing. Fair match? Did the King always order what he really wanted? How could he possibly hope to make a showing against a Blade? Montpurse's baby face was shooting more warnings.

Aha! The new boy was being hazed, of course, and the King was in on the joke. Perhaps hazing was a tradition for all greenies, but the bright new star who could thrash all the fencing masters at Ironhall would be an irresistible target. The famous expert was going to flounder against a mere amateur and would never hear the end of it.

No, he wasn't! If His Majesty had ordered a fair match, then a fair match he must have. A man could never go wrong obeying his king. Surely very few monarchs would shed their dignity so willingly just to play childish games with a band of guards. But it was with this kind of understanding that a great man inspired unquestioning loyalty among his followers.

Stripped to the waist, the contestants raised foils in salute. Durendal scuffed his feet in the sawdust to test the footing.

"On guard!" cried Ambrose IV, King of Chivial and Nostrimia, Prince of Nythia, Lord of the Three Seas, Fount of Justice, and so on, who was large and sweaty, with too much fat under his skin and a pelt of tawny hair outside it. The most famous face in the kingdom was hidden behind the chain mesh of a mask.

Right foot forward, left arm up, the King advanced and lunged like a three-legged cow. Deciding to play along for a moment or two, Durendal parried, riposted well wide of the mark, parried again, and almost struck the King by accident on the next lunge. The man was slower than a watched pot. He was trying to use the Ironhall style and he didn't know Lily from Swan. Parry at Willow, riposte to Rainbow. It was a ballet of tortoises. Enough.

"A touch!"

"Ha!" said His Majesty in a tone that sounded convincingly like displeasure. "It was indeed. Well, good luck is a valuable attribute in a Blade. Let us see how you fare on the next pass, Sir Durendal."

Durendal went to Swan again.

"Have at you!" cried the monarch.

Eagle, Butterfly— "Another touch . . . sire."

The King growled realistically, but he must be grinning hugely behind the mask. Montpurse made frantic gestures in the background. If the victim had not seen through this jape, he would be getting very worried about now.

"Again, sire?"

"Again!"

Better spin this one out, just for good manners. Egg-beater. Stickleback. *Oh flames!* Cockroach. He hadn't really meant to do that quite so soon. The King uttered another growl and swished his foil up and down a few times as if he were truly surprised and angry at the way the match was going. He was a marvelous actor. They all were. Peering through his mask, Durendal could not see one surreptitious smile in the room.

Three–nothing so far. Three times out of four, Montpurse had said, so the next pass would show them that their pigeon had smelled the cuckoo. . . .

"By the spirits of fire, my liege, the lad is on form!" shouted a voice somewhere.

The note of desperation in that voice was so amazingly realistic that it froze Durendal's sweat. *Fire and death!* Had he misunderstood? Did the King really think he could fence worth a pot of spit? Surely men like Montpurse would not prostitute their honor by indulging his crazy fancies?

This *had* to be a joke!

Didn't it?

Suddenly his new apprehension switched to anger. If this was a prank, then it was in stinking bad taste. If it wasn't, then he had already shown the King up as a deluded buffoon, which was probably high treason, and Montpurse as a bootlicker, which meant that all the generous aid promised to the newcomer would fail to appear.

"Now, by death!" Snarling, the monarch charged his foe, and Durendal poked him on the belly. Four out of four.

"Again!" roared the King, and the button of Durendal's foil flicked him again in exactly the same place.

The royal chest was turning red, as if all the hair might start smoking soon. "By the dark, I'll not quit till I have laid steel on this whelp! On guard again, sirrah!'' That was a threat. This was no friendly test of swordsmanship, it was rank intimidation.

''It is spirituality, Your Majesty!'' shouted one of the onlookers. ''He is too fresh from the Forge for any man to beat him.''

Ambrose ignored that ingenious invention. He took eight hits before he admitted defeat and hauled off his mask. Inflamed and incandescently furious, he glared around the room as if searching for the least trace of a smile. The King was a stumblebum swordsman, and the Royal Guard were a gang of sycophants.

Durendal saluted and removed his own mask. ''Permission to withdraw, Your—''

''No! Put that on again, boy! Montpurse, let us see how you can fare against this superman.''

Sending Durendal a look that should have melted his bones, the Commander began to strip. Of course there could only be one ending to the coming match—he would have to lose almost as dramatically as his King had lost. Anything else would be a public admission that he was a liar and a toady.

The new Blade could win at fencing, but he had lost a lot of powerful friends on his first night at court.

· 11 ·

The next day it was the Marquis's turn again. He called in the tailors. His wife assisted the discussion with the air of a child given a new doll to dress. Durendal stood patiently while they draped swatches over him, trying to match his hair and eyes. When bidden, he went off and returned in various absurd apparels. And when the final decision on cut and color had been made, he said, "No."

"What do you mean no?" Nutting snapped.

"I will not wear that, my lord."

"You are under oath to serve me!"

"Yes, my lord. I have also been enchanted to serve you. But you do not buy a bulldog and harness it to a plow. You set it on bulls. My purpose is not to look pretty but to defend you, and I cannot fight in those garments."

"Bah! You will never be required to fight. You know that."

"Yes, my lord. Sadly, I do know that. But the conjurement does not, and it will not let me swaddle myself in a gabardine mattress cover."

"Insolence!" snapped the Marquise. "Don't let him talk back to you like that, dearest."

"I will follow you naked, my lord, before I wear that tabard." Seeing that defiance was going to be stalemate, Durendal added, "May I presume to advise?"

"What?" Nutting growled.

"Something more like the livery of the Royal Guard. It is serviceable and appealing."

The turd considered the suggestion, tugging his little beard. "You know, that idea has merit! My colors are blue and gold. Dearest, why don't we specify exactly the same design but with gold instead of silver?"

The Marquise clapped her hands. "Why, he will look beautiful in that, my dear!"

Fire and death! Durendal had been talking about the cut, not the heraldry. The Royal Guard would have a hundred apoplectic fits.

Montpurse was furious enough already, as Hoare reported that evening—but Durendal knew that from the tongue-lashing he had received the previous night, after the King's departure. He thought he would carry the scars to his grave.

But the Commander was not a vindictive man, Hoare

said. His offer of help still stood, which was why Hoare
had appeared at the Nutting suite after midnight in the
company of a beautiful child named Kitty. He departed
quite soon, but she remained.

Durendal discovered that she was not a child, and she
was beautiful in ways and places he had hitherto only
imagined.

Later in that first memorable week, things began to improve. Even the black glares that greeted the appearance
of the Marquis's Blade in his new livery came to a sudden
end. The Guard's acceptance of the upstart was promoted
by the King himself.

It happened at the Birthday Reception. Blades at official
functions, like the frescoes on the ceilings, were invariably
present and universally ignored. Thus Durendal stood by
the wall on the far side of the hall and watched as the
Nuttings waited in line to pay their respects to the monarch. The other Blades present, both royal and private, had
gathered in small clumps; but he was alone and likely to
remain so.

The Queen was not there. Rumor whispered that she
was with child again. The Countess was in evidence, but
she could not stand at the King's side on such an occasion.
He was attended on the dais only by Commander Montpurse, Lord Chancellor Bluefield, the forbidding Grand Inquisitor, and an imposing matron in white robes and
hennin, who must surely be Mother Superior of the Companionship of White Sisters.

There were other sniffers present, of course. About the
end of the first dull hour, Durendal observed the Sister
who had accosted him on his first day at court, standing
by herself not far from him. He eased unobtrusively in her
direction; but before he reached her, she looked around,
frowning. He strolled the rest of the way quite openly and
bowed to her, bidding her good morrow.

Her response was barely civil. "What do you want?"

She eyed the golden squirrel over his heart with distaste, which meant they had at least one thing in common.

"I came for reassurance that I no longer reek of the Forge quite so strongly, Sister."

"We resent being referred to as sniffers, young man. Your question is both vulgar and insulting."

It was she who had begun the talk of sniffing by accusing him of having a bad smell.

"I beg pardon, then. I give offense through ignorance, being but a new-forged Blade, fresh from the coals. How does one detect a conjurement?"

"The sensation is indescribable. At the moment I feel as if I am required to sing a very difficult song and you are standing beside me humming another one loudly in the wrong key. Does that make matters clearer?"

Somewhat. He tried one more smile, probably a rather desperate one. "And what will you do if you detect the handiwork of an evil conjurer, Sister?"

"Call on the King's Blades, of course." She tossed her head so sharply that no secular power should have been able to keep her tall hat from falling off, but it didn't. She stalked away.

A quick glance around the hall told him that Blades and White Sisters nowhere stood together, so he had learned something new by offending someone else. He went back to watching his ward's progress, a process duller than breeding oak trees.

When, at long last, it was the turn of the Marquise to curtsey and the Marquis to kiss the royal hand, he prepared to move with a sense of relief, although he knew that he was merely about to exchange this ordeal for another, even longer one in the banquet hall. Then the King looked up. The bright amber eyes scanned the room and fixed on Durendal as if they were measuring him for a coffin—one that came up to his shoulders might be adequate.

The King beckoned.

Blood and steel! Was this the end? Exile to some hyperborean desert? Durendal hastened across miles of oak floor, conscious that heralds and pages were heading to block him and stopping as they intercepted gestures telling them there had been a change of plan. He arrived at the dais unchallenged and contorted himself in a full court bow.

"I have a question, Sir Durendal!"

The Nuttings turned back to see what was going on.

"My liege?"

The King pouted dangerously. "After our little fencing match the other evening . . . did you by any chance have a *further* exchange with Commander Montpurse?"

Flames and death!

If Montpurse had a weakness, it was that his babyish complexion could color very easily, and now it colored very much. The King ought to be able to feel the heat of it on the back of his neck.

"Yes, sire," Durendal said. "We did try a few more passes."

For about an hour, with both rapiers and sabers, with and without shields or parrying daggers.

"And who won that time?"

"He did, Your Majesty." Not by very much, though.

"Indeed? Isn't that very peculiar, considering that you had given him such a drubbing earlier? He fared no better against you than I did."

"Um, well, these things can happen, sire."

"Can they?" The King turned to look at the Commander. Then back at Durendal. Very slowly, the royal beard twisted around a grin. Abruptly Ambrose IV burst into enormous bellows of laughter, startling the whole court. He slapped his great thighs in mirth; tears ran down his cheeks. He thumped Montpurse's shoulder, and Montpurse blistered Durendal with another of his bone-melting glares.

Still unable to find words, the King waved dismissal. Durendal bowed lower than an Alkozzi and beat a hasty departure, more or less dragging the startled Marquis with him. And then, of course, he had to explain, which meant

admitting that he had delegated his responsibility, shamed
the King, antagonized the Guard, and launched a scandal,
for now the story must come out. The Marquise became
almost hysterical and insisted that her husband dismiss his
errant servant. She refused to believe that he could not
be dismissed.

The worst part of being a Blade, Durendal decided, was
that he could not simply disappear down a rabbit hole
when necessary. Perhaps other Blades, lacking his genius
for causing trouble, never felt the need.

The reception ended at last and the court sat down to
eat the King's health at a twelve-course banquet. Blades
stood around the walls again, but this time Durendal
attached himself to a group of them. They were civil to
him, no more. They made little jokes about men who wore
gold uniforms, although they were careful not to make
them about squirrels or upstart pimps who invented such
uniforms, because that sort of talk might trigger Durendal's still-tender binding. They came and went, visiting a
buffet in the next room. Since none of them offered to
spell him and he was determined not to ask for relief, he
did not expect to eat at all.

Montpurse drifted into the group, acknowledging the
problem Blade with a curt nod.

About two minutes after that, a diminutive page appeared in front of Durendal, bowed, handed him a box of
polished rosewood bearing the royal arms, and departed.

"You have your lunch delivered?" Montpurse stepped
closer to see. The others gathered around.

"I don't know anything about this!"

"Then you'll have to open it, won't you?"

Anything but that! But he had no choice. He opened it.
On the red velvet lining lay a sword breaker of antique
Jindalian design—a dagger with deep notches along one
side. Its hilt and quillons were inlaid with gold, malachite,
and what appeared to be real lapis lazuli. At a guess, it
was worth a duke's castle and change. The card bore a
brief message:

For him who broke the King's sword,

                                        A.

"Flames and death!" Durendal slammed the lid before anyone could steal the contents. He hugged the treasure to his chest in both arms and stared at his companions with a sense of panic.

Montpurse's pale eyes were twinkling. "Been robbing the crown jewels, have you?"

"No! No, no! I don't understand. What do I do?"

"You wear it, you flaming idiot. If the King is watching, as I expect he is, then you bow now."

He was, his grin visible right across the hall. Durendal bowed.

"Right. Then—here, let me help." Montpurse hung the marvel on Durendal's belt over his right thigh and said, "Oh, that's very nice! I'm jealous. What do you think, lads?"

· 12 ·

A few days after that, an excited Byless turned up at court, bound to Lord Chancellor Bluefield, who already had two Blades. Then Gotherton was reported to be in Grandon, assigned to Grand Wizard of the Royal College of Conjurers, who had three and ought to have less need of them than anyone in the kingdom.

Although the Guard had numerous well-informed but ill-defined sources, there were some secrets it could not penetrate. When word came that Candidate Everman had been bound to a certain Jaque Polydin, gentleman, no amount of prying could discover anything at all about him, except that Blade and ward together had vanished off the face of the earth the following day. Even Montpurse claimed to have been kept in ignorance. Men whispered longingly about high adventure and secret agents traveling in foreign lands.

Durendal wanted to scream with frustration and wring his ward's neck. His self-control prevented the first and his binding the second.

It became official: The Queen was with child. The King showered wealth on every elementary order that could provide her with appropriate charms, amulets, and enchantments.

Over the next couple of months, Durendal adapted to his strange double life in court. By day he was bored to insanity, following the Marquis from party to ball to reception to salon to dinner, and almost to bed. All suggestions that his lordship should take up riding or hawking or fencing or anything at all interesting fell on deaf ears. Besides, such pastimes would all incur a slight element of danger, and thus the binding conjurement impeded Durendal's efforts to promote them. He tended to stutter and develop a headache.

Boredom was not the worst of it, though. Nutting's official duties for the navy occupied about ten minutes a week, when he signed the documents that his staff prepared and brought to him. Unofficially he ran a thriving business of his own. Much of it was dealt with through clandestine correspondence—letters he burned as soon as he had read them—but some of it required face-to-face negotiations. During those meetings with various savory or unsavory persons, he would order his Blade to stand at the far end of the room, so he could not eavesdrop. The details did not matter. Durendal was soon able to work out that his lordship was taking kickbacks on contracts, accepting bribes to overlook defects in the supplies delivered for the unfortunate sailors, and selling access to the King himself by passing petitions on to his sister. It was all nauseating, but there was nothing Durendal could do about it. He could never endanger his ward in any way at all.

By night he flew free. One of the Guard would relieve him as the palace went to sleep, so he could join the others in their revels. Two horns of ale was his limit, but one satisfied him. His body absolutely demanded exercise, so he fenced. When there was moonlight he went riding in mad chases over the fields or joined bacchanalian swimming parties in the river. He indulged in quick romances, having no trouble finding willing partners.

He learned how to beat Montpurse with sabers, if not with a rapier.

He wore the royal sword breaker everywhere except in bed.

The King never indulged in fencing now, and for that the Guard was duly grateful to Durendal.

He saw the King frequently. Even if they just passed in a hallway, when the King had acknowledged the Marquis, he would always greet his Blade by name. It would be very easy to fall victim to that famous charm—and what it would be to be bound to such a man!

Alas, fickle chance had decreed otherwise. However great his swordsmanship, he knew he was stuck with the job of guarding the obnoxious Marquis for the rest of his days. Never would he serve the king he revered, never ride to war at his side or save his life in lethal ambush, never battle monsters, unmask traitors, rise to high office, travel on secret missions in far dominions—never be anything at all except a useless ornament around the court.

Even the greatest of swordsmen can be a lousy prophet.

Nutting

II

"**V**ery well!" Kromman spluttered. "You may leave. You will remain at your residence until you are summoned." He was scarlet with fury.

"Let go your sword, Sir Quarrel," Roland said, edging between the two men.

But Quarrel was a very newly bound Blade, and the new chancellor very obviously a danger to his ward. For a moment it seemed as if that order would not be enough. Then the white-faced boy made an effort and released the hilt he was holding.

"As you wish, my lord." He glared hatred at Kromman.

With a silent sigh of relief, Roland headed for the door. Quarrel arrived there before he did and opened it to peer out, as a well-trained bodyguard should.

Roland whispered, "Mask!" It was an old Ironhall warning, a reminder that in real contests a man's face was not hidden from his opponent's view.

"My lord." The boy's mouth smiled as he swung the door wide. The angry glitter in his eyes remained, but none of the watchers would be close enough to notice that. Few of them would even be astute enough to realize that the new Blade's face might not be as uncommunicative as his ward's notoriously was. It was the principle that mattered, for serenity would deceive no one tonight. The King's Secretary had arrived posthaste from court and gone into the Chancellor's office; if Lord Roland then emerged without the chain of office he had worn for twenty years, was the conclusion so hard to draw?

Half a dozen men-at-arms were standing in a bored and

puzzled huddle. Obviously Kromman had not told them what he had expected them to do, for they sprang to attention at the sight of the former chancellor and made no effort to block his departure. Six? Even Quarrel might have had trouble with six—but of course Roland would have been there to help him. He was gratified that Kromman had thought six might be necessary to arrest a man of his years.

The first ordeal would be just to stroll across this wide antechamber, crowded with men and women waiting to see him, some of whom had been there for days. Now none of them had reason to see him and most would prefer not to be seen anywhere near him, lest his fall from favor prove to be infectious, as it so often did.

He watched the news flash through the room ahead of him—the startled gasps, the exchanged glances, the calculating looks. Who was smiling, who frowning? It did not matter! He had no friends now, only enemies.

"They say," Quarrel remarked, "that the Earl of Aldane is already clear favorite to win the King's Cup this year."

Ah, the disgraced minister still had one friend! Even royal disfavor could not alienate a Blade from his ward. "Too early to tell, my lad! Don't lay any bets yet. Is he another of the Steepness school?"

"I believe so. Steepnessians are fast, I understand."

"Lightning with diarrhea." The onlookers were watching, listening, but now none came crowding forward to clutch Lord Roland's sleeve.

"What do they use—air and fire?"

"Plus a hefty dose of time, I imagine. That's what's dangerous. The subjects rarely live to see forty. The present duke, his father, was one of theirs, although he is still hale, last I heard. I fought against him once, when he was the earl." The great lout had never forgiven him for that day.

"Oh, I have heard tell of that bout, my lord! It is one of the legends of Ironhall." Quarrel babbled more appropriate nonsense, his youthful face displaying pure innocence. He was doing splendidly, and his ward must tell him so as soon as they were alone. They would first go around by his personal quarters and collect a few keepsakes. After that, the gauntlet would continue down the great staircase . . . on and on, until he could clamber into the coach, leave Greymere Palace forever, head home to Ivy-walls. There he would await the King's pleasure. The King's displeasure would be a more apt description.

What was he going to do about his Blade, though? The ex-chancellor's troubles suddenly seemed very minor as he contemplated Quarrel's. He had brought disaster upon the boy only three days after his binding. If the King tried to arrest him, Quarrel would resist to the death. No matter how hopeless the defiance, he would have no choice.

A Blade whose ward was accused of plotting against the King—Lord Roland knew that dilemma from personal experience.

· 2 ·

Sunlight shone on the brilliant array of watchers massed in the stands like flowers in boxes. The wind snapped bright-colored pennants and flapped the brilliant awnings; it ruffled striped marquees. The court was assembled in a great display of tabards and blaring trumpets, heraldic banners and fair ladies in sumptuous gowns.

Clank, clank went the armor as Durendal plodded over the muddy grass. The broadsword in his hands already weighed as much as an anvil and would soon feel like an overweight horse. He could swing it convincingly if he did not have to keep up the effort for long. In a few minutes, a much larger man than he was going to start smashing at him with an even larger sword, and the two of them would chop away brutally until one of them went down. Encounters in full armor involved very little skill, only strength and endurance—and quite often serious injury. He was not looking forward to the contest, but he had only himself to blame for this predicament. He had made a mistake that morning and must now pay the price.

Curse Ambrose and his stupid broadswords!

Although the King no longer fenced, he had not lost his interest in fencing. Each year he sponsored a great tournament modeled after the jousting of olden days before advances in conjuration made armored knights an absurdity and trial by combat unnecessary. Each year he donated a gold cup worth a hundred crowns, enough to attract contestants from all over Chivial. The first King's Cup had been won by Montpurse and the second by Durendal himself, so he was now defending his title. He had reached the semifinals without trouble. This morning Montpurse had lost to Chefney, another Blade, so tomorrow the finals would pit Chefney against either Durendal or Aldane, that mountain of metal now thumping forward to meet him.

The Duke of Gaylea was a smallish man but rich enough to have had his son's growth enhanced. He must have paid well, because at sixteen his little boy now stood a full head taller than any Blade and was muscled like a bull. He looked more fearsome stripped than he did in plate armor. Ironically, this young giant had developed ambitions to be a fencer, which was absurd for one of his size; but wealth could always find a way. The Steepness school specialized in quick results for aristocrats unwilling to waste years in secular learning; it substituted spiritual speed for skill. As a fencer, the Earl of Aldane was technically crude and unbelievably fast for his size—for any size.

Durendal had lost to him that morning at rapiers, which he should not have done. He had then won at sabers; and perhaps that success counted as a second mistake, for under the King's elaborate rules it forced a deciding match with two-handed broadswords. Few contests had gone so far, and the crowd was buzzing with anticipation. At broadswords, when strength was vital and skill unimportant, Aldane had an almost insuperable advantage.

Right foot forward, left foot forward, right foot forward . . . every move was a conscious effort. Armor was ridiculous stuff. The padding stank as if someone had lived in it day and night since the Fatherland Wars. It was already growing unpleasantly hot. His right knee squeaked. When he lowered his visor, he would peer out at the world through a slit, which turned fighting into a mindless brawl with no art whatsoever. Unlike the rapier and saber matches, this bout would be decided by a single round, when one contestant could not or would not fight longer. Contrary to popular belief, it was possible for a man who fell down in plate armor to get up again without help, but not if someone else was beating on him with a six-foot sword.

One of the red-and-gold umpires gestured for Durendal to come no closer. He stopped and clanked around to face the royal box, noticing at once that the Queen was there now. She was reported to be expecting another child, although Princess Malinda was still a few days short of her second birthday. The Countess was rarely seen at court anymore. Gossip had it that she would soon be banished completely.

A trumpet stilled the crowd, sounding unpleasantly muffled inside Durendal's padded helmet. The umpires bowed to the King. The contestants raised their swords in salute, which seemed no small concession, considering what they weighed. He turned himself to face his opponent, seeing again the kid's confident smirk from inside the cave of steel encasing his head. The bigger they are the harder they fall.

The harder they hit, too. Durendal's shoulder still throbbed from this morning's saber bout, where a padded plastron had not completely absorbed the Earl's vicious blow. The broadswords were blunt, but his armor would crumple like parchment when Muscle Brat started beating on it. Because a Blade could not guard his ward if he were injured, Durendal's spiritual binding might compel him to escape the dilemma by losing the match. He must gamble everything on a very quick win.

This was not a fair fight.

"My lords, prepare!" cried the senior umpire. Aldane raised a gauntlet the size of a bucket and closed his visor.

Durendal did nothing.

"Prepare, my lord!"

"I'll fight like this. It's hot in here." Fighting with an open visor was rank insanity, but it was also a bluff. Aldane would be sorely puzzled, wondering what exotic technique his Ironhall opponent knew that he did not.

The umpire hesitated, glanced at his colleagues and even across at the King's box, and then shrugged.

"May the spirits preserve the better man. Do battle!"

The umpires scuttled out of the way. The contestants lumbered forward over the grass. Durendal aimed his sword like a lance and tipped himself forward into a near run. Aldane copied him at once, for if they collided he would contribute twice Durendal's weight and knock him down like a skittle. Soon he was sprinting in full armor, an awesome display of strength. He raised his blade, aiming at that temptingly open visor.

Of course, he could not see very well. He must have been sorely puzzled when his opponent disappeared.

Durendal dropped to hands and knees in front of him. That act alone was reckless, for armor was no place to try gymnastics and he might injure himself before taking a single blow. As a tactic, it was insane. If he failed to trip the Earl, he would be at his mercy. If both of them were knocked prone, he would have gained no advantage. Its only merit was that no one had ever done that before.

Aldane pitched headlong over him, striking the ground like a falling smithy. Fortunately his weight neither toppled Durendal nor came down on top of him—it just tried to push the Earl into his own helmet. The bout was reduced to a question of which man could regain his feet first and start hammering the other into scrap metal. As Aldane was at least momentarily stunned, Durendal had no difficulty in clanking himself erect and setting a foot on the kid's back. He put the point of his sword at a suitable gap in the armor.

"Yield, miscreant!" he declaimed.

The umpires went into a hurried consultation. The crowd's jeering was a constant roar, like a mountain torrent.

Aldane began screaming, "Foul!" and tried to rise. Durendal poked him in the kidneys with a dull edge—a fairly dull edge. After that the noble earl just lay and beat mailed fists on the turf, still yelling muffled protests.

The umpires waved a flag to declare a victory. The crowd became even noisier.

· 3 ·

The contestants clattered side by side toward the royal box with their helmets tucked under their arms. Aldane was demonstrating a virtuoso command of indecent language.

"Did they teach you those words at Steepness?" Durendal inquired sweetly.

The kid glared down at him with the beginnings of two lush black eyes. His nose had not stopped bleeding yet, and his purse would bleed even harder to pay for all the expensive healing he would need. "Did they teach you to cheat at Ironhall?"

"Look, you've got another twenty years ahead of you. Making the semifinals at your age is a wonderful feat."

"Losing the match doesn't matter, you oaf! It's the flaming money!"

Not being a gambling man, Durendal had forgotten that side of the tournament. "What odds?"

"I was taking thirty to one at lunchtime," the Earl admitted.

It was very hard to sound sincere. "That's a shame."

"There are hundreds of losers out there. You'll be lucky to leave the palace alive, you blackguard peasant!"

Not so funny.

The King was not amused either. When the contestants came to halt in front of the royal box, he leaned back in his chair of state and glared at Durendal. At the King's side, the diminutive Duke of Gaylea was an alarming gray color. How much had he wagered on his baby boy? Indeed, most of the nobles present seemed to have bet on the favorite, but Blades in the background were grinning like pike.

The Marquis was there, being guarded by Hoare. He was smiling, which was something he did only in public now. He had been seated three rows behind the King, almost in among the baronets, and likely would not have been admitted at all had his Blade not been fighting, because the entire Mornicade family was seriously out of favor at the moment. He had been dismissed from his naval office; his uncles and cousins had all lost their sinecures and privileges.

"You disapprove of broadswords?" the King inquired menacingly of Durendal.

Tricky! "I do prefer rapiers, Your Majesty."

"My liege!" Aldane bleated. "I protest the decision!"

The royal glare was turned on him. "We did not address you."

The Earl made unpleasant noises, as if gargling blood.

The King looked back at Durendal. "And what is it you prefer about rapiers?"

"Um. I suppose it is the greater element of skill, sire."

"I see. Well, we saw no evidence that brawn triumphed over brains in this instance." The amber eyes had begun to twinkle.

"Your Majesty flatters me."

"You won a duel without striking a blow! You have created another legend. It seems to be a habit of yours. Congratulations."

Relieved, Durendal managed a small bow without falling over.

"And as for you, my lord, I applaud your remarkable showing in our tournament. You and your honored father will dine with us tonight, of course."

Aldane stepped forward to the barricade. The King rose and hung a ribboned semifinalist's star around the giant's neck, even he having to stand on tiptoe to do so. Everyone else was upright also, of course, applauding politely.

The Marquis had not been invited to dine. When the royal party had left, he came down to the barricade and beamed at his Blade, undoubtedly for Hoare's benefit. He had grown plump in the two and a half years Durendal had known him. He was seldom sober.

"Well done, my man! How soon can you get out of that bear trap?"

Displaying his habitual cryptic smile, Hoare said, "I will be happy to attend his lordship until you are ready, Sir Durendal."

"About ten minutes, my lord."

"Hurry, then. I have business to attend to. Meet me at the coach yard."

As Durendal trudged off to the marquee, the crowd began booing again.

• 4 •

Nutting was waiting beside his carriage with the footmen and driver already in place. What business could be so urgent? His only occupation these days was supervising the decoration and furnishing of the grandiose mansion he had built, and his wife invariably overruled his decisions. He drank excessively and wandered the halls at night.

Durendal nodded his thanks to Hoare, who rolled his eyes sympathetically, bowed to the Marquis, and strode off. Nutting scrambled aboard. The carriage began to move as Durendal followed him in.

"That was very well done!"

"Thank you, my lord. I should not have lost to him this morning, though."

"Yes, but you will be pleased to hear that I had faith in you. It has been a most lucrative afternoon for me."

It might prove less profitable if an angry crowd was waiting outside the palace gates. As it happened, the few spectators there confined themselves to booing. The Marquis did not seem to notice, and the carriage rumbled unmolested into the cramped and dirty streets of Grandon.

After several minutes of idyllic silence, he said, "Unfortunately, the odds will be less favorable on tomorrow's match. You are the favorite, at four or five to one."

"I do not deserve so much. Sir Chefney is a brilliant fencer."

"Um, yes." The Marquis chewed his lip for a moment. "I hate to mention a subject as sordid as money, Sir Durendal . . ."

The title was meaningless, but he had never used it

before. Durendal felt a sharp stab of worry. What was coming? He had absolutely no money of his own. He was given his board and his clothes but never wages. He sponged his recreations off the Royal Guard—horses and ale. The only purpose for which he would have liked to have some cash was to give presents to women, but pride forbade him to ask for it. They had to be satisfied with the legend, which fortunately they always seemed to be.

"My lord?"

The coach rattled over cobbles, making slow progress through the crowded streets. It seemed to be heading for a very seamy part of the city.

"Nutting House has cost considerably more than I anticipated, you see."

"If I win the cup tomorrow, then of course it belongs to your lordship, as my patron." As he had taken last year's, the skinflint.

"Yes, but . . ." The Marquis's eyes wandered shiftily, not meeting his Blade's. "I'm afraid a hundred crowns is a drop in the gutter. My winnings today are in the thousands and I have staked them all on the finals."

Death and flames! "Am I to infer, my lord, that you are *counting* on winning tomorrow? I am by no means certain that I can beat Sir Chefney. He trounced Commander Montpurse very convincingly."

"I was pleased to see— What I am suggesting, Sir Durendal, is that you should lay a bet of your own."

"I have nothing to wager, my lord."

Nutting pointed at the sword breaker on his thigh.

"No!" Seeing his ward flinch in alarm, he drew a deep breath. "I mean, I cannot in honor hazard losing a gift from the sovereign, my lord! He would most certainly notice its absence."

"Bah! He will never know. You don't wear it to fence. You need only part with it until the match is over. I have a friend willing to advance six thousand crowns against it."

"It's worth ten times that!"

"Only as an outright sale, boy. This is a merely a short-term loan."

"And if I fail to win the match, what then?"

The Marquis sniffed plaintively. "Your task is to defend me, yes?"

"Of course. But only—"

"Does debtors' prison rank as a specified peril? If I cannot raise certain amounts within days, Sir Durendal, then that is where I will be. I presume you must accompany me."

"You poxed pig's bastard." Durendal did not raise his voice—shouting was unnecessary when stating facts. "You mean your harlot sister can't wring any more money out of the King?"

Nutting's eyes glittered for a moment, then his air of dejection returned. "As you say. And no one will pay my debts, so we shall rot in jail for the rest of our lives. Men die quickly in Drain Street, Blade. Will you defend me against the coughing sickness?"

"By the eight, I am a healthier man than you are! When you die, I can walk free—free of you and free of the worst duty ever laid upon an honorable swordsman."

"As you please. We have arrived. Is that your final decision?"

The carriage had stopped in an alley, gloomy and stinking and so narrow that men could barely have squeezed by. As if the visitors had been expected, a door opened in the wall alongside, revealing a fat, bald man, who smiled to show black and broken teeth.

Durendal discovered that he was trembling violently. Never had the binding been so at odds with his personal inclinations. He wanted to strangle this human toad beside him and stamp his corpse into mud.

"The King gave it to me!"

"And you shall have it back."

"Don't you trust me?" His voice cracked. "Do you fear I won't try my best? I swear, my lord, that I will fight tomorrow as if your life depended on it. I don't need talk of debtors' prison to keep me honest!''

''But it is true. My life is at stake—indirectly, I admit, but very surely. I merely ask to borrow that thing on your belt for a day. Is that so much to ask of a man bound to defend me against all foes? Decide. Shall I signal the coachman to proceed?''

It was true that life expectancy in debtors' prison was a matter of weeks. The binding might ignore a danger so indirect, but Durendal had sworn an oath. Sick at heart, he detached the sword breaker from his belt and handed it over.

Smiling, the Marquis passed it down to the man waiting in the doorway, receiving a roll of vellum in return. He scanned it quickly, nodded his assent, and rapped on the window to the driver. The carriage clattered into motion. Not a word had been said.

How had the turd arranged all this without his Blade knowing? Of course Durendal had spent much time fencing in the last few days, leaving his ward in the care of the Guard. There had been more letters coming and going than usual, so he should have suspected something evil was afoot. What difference would it have made? He could not oppose his ward in anything that mattered.

''You realize,'' he said, his mouth dry, ''that if I lose and the King asks me what happened to the breaker, I shall tell him the truth?''

The Marquis of Nutting smiled slyly. ''You *will* lose, dear boy, and he won't notice, because it will not be missing. We are betting on Sir Chefney, not on you. I can get odds of five to one and he will win. You must lose to get your sword breaker back.''

The autumn evening was fading into night when the Marquis arrived back at Nutting House, but he at once proceeded to inspect the gardens, complaining loudly to his Blade that the army of workmen had left without achieving anything during the day. Indoors, it was the same story. All those painters, artists, carpenters, and plasterers had obviously been idling since dawn, wasting his money.

My money, Durendal thought. The King's money.

The Marquise had been dispatched a few days previously to visit her parents, so the half-completed house was empty except for the fifty-two servants. Nutting screamed for his valets, demanding a shave and fresh clothes—bathing was a danger he seldom risked. While the lackeys tended his noble carcass, Durendal prowled restlessly around the grandiose dressing room.

There was something wrong, something that should be obvious but remained maddeningly out of sight. Foul as the turd's explanations had been, the whole truth must be even worse. He had, in retrospect, dismissed his wife very brusquely; she had not wanted to visit her family, but he had insisted. That was a reasonable precaution if he expected to be arrested, so it could not be the missing clue. A man facing financial ruin ought to be trimming his construction costs and household expenses, surely? Well, perhaps not. Courtiers were notoriously lax in paying tradesmen and domestics, and any hint of economy might spook his creditors. The turd probably did not know what economy was, anyway. He could no longer swindle money out of the navy or sell his sister's influence with the King. Fixing fencing matches might be a lucrative sideline, but he was up to something more. What was coming next? He was demanding full evening wear, as if planning to go to a ball or banquet. Nobody invited him to those anymore.

What else was he up to? Why was he not more morose? *That* was what was wrong! Ever since he came home, he had been smirking. Six thousand crowns at odds of five to one meant, um, thirty thousand. Was that enough to save him from ruin? Or was there some other foulness in the wind?

The Marquis ordered dinner and ate in satisfied silence with his Blade sulking at the other side of the table. Then, instead of calling for his coach, he demanded a cloak and boots. Apparently he was going out for a walk—in the dark? This was utterly unprecedented, completely out of character.

Durendal spoke for the first time since he gave up the sword breaker. "Where are we going, my lord?"

His ward smiled mysteriously. "Wait and see."

There was moonlight, but for a gentleman to walk the ill-reputed streets of Grandon by night was a rashness that set his Blade's binding jangling like bells. It was his clear duty to prevent such folly, even by force if necessary. Against that, Durendal was so exhilarated by the thought that his skills might possibly be required at last that he suppressed his wiser instincts. Thus he found himself escorting the devious Marquis through noisome, sinister alleys without even a lantern between them. He quivered with joy like a racehorse at the gate, praying for someone to leap out of the shadows at them. Fortunately or unfortunately, no one did. Once or twice he thought he detected footsteps some distance behind them and cursed himself for a nervous ninny.

The Marquis obviously heard nothing. He knew where he was going, although he seemed to have learned the route by rote, for he muttered to himself at every corner.

Then he began counting doors, but when he found the one he wanted, it was clearly defined by an octogram sign that glowed with enchanted light. A conjuring order that hid itself in a slum must specialize in very murky conjurations, and supplicants who came in the middle of the night must have very murky needs. Two footmen in imposing livery admitted the callers and led them to a salon whose decor of jarring reds and purples, salacious paintings, and contorted erotic sculptures revealed exactly what sort of enchantment was available. Soft music played in the distance and the air was fetid with hot, musky odors. Shamefully, Durendal felt his flesh responding to the sensual mood.

Other conspirators had already arrived. The elderly man was easily recognizable as the Earl of Eastness, former governor of Nostrimia and the elder of Nutting's notorious uncles. The woman was veiled, but her identity could be in no doubt.

She sprang up in alarm. "You fool! Why did you bring him here?" Even her voice was unforgettable. The pale hand she pointed at Durendal was long-fingered and graceful.

The Marquis laughed and strolled across to her. He lifted her veil back and kissed her cheek. "I can't shake him off. He sticks like a birthmark. Besides, he is an ideal accomplice. He wouldn't betray me under torture. Would you, Sir Durendal?"

Durendal ignored the mockery and tried to ignore the loveliest face in the kingdom as well. "What foulness are you plotting, my lord? You must remember that I am a servant of the King."

"But I come first! And I stand or fall with my accomplices here, so you can betray none of us." Smirk, smirk, smirk!

Anyone else who provoked Durendal like this would be dead already, although he had never drawn his sword in anger and had believed he never would. "I cannot betray you, so I must stop you. It is obvious that you are planning to use conjuration against His Majesty, and that is a capital offense.'' His logic was leading him to an unbearable conclusion.

Nutting glanced briefly at his sister and his self-confidence wavered. "Indeed? Just how do you propose to stop me?"

Durendal, too, looked at the Countess. She shrank back, anger turning to fear.

He said, "You are plotting to restore the whore to royal favor. I cannot harm you, Tab Nillway, but she is not so favored." Could he really slay a woman in cold blood? Yes, if his ward's safety demanded it. Perhaps mutilation would suffice, but that might be even harder to do and would be less certain. Disfigurement could be cured. Death could not.

The Countess gasped and made a dive for the door. She stopped with Harvest's razor edge before her face like a rail. Eastness roared an oath and reached for his sword.

"Don't be a fool, Uncle!" Nutting snapped. "He'll filet you before any of us can move an inch. You are too late already, lad. You cannot possibly hope to kill a countess and not have the crime discovered. The inquisitors will question us, perhaps even put one of us to the Question— you, most like, as you are not of the nobility. Our intentions will be revealed, and intentions are enough in cases of treason. There is nothing you can do."

A carillon of conflicting emotions clamored in Durendal's mind. His voice came out hoarse and shaky. "It is still a better chance than letting you attempt an impossible crime."

"A very possible crime. Put up your sword and I shall explain."

"No. Say what you must and be quick."

The Countess backed away from the sword, and he let her go. Whatever was coming, he knew that he had lost.

The Marquis, also, seemed to have realized that, for his oily smoothness flowed back. "A candle, only a candle. Quite harmless. It will be attuned to my sister's body. When it burns and the King inhales the fumes, his desire for her will return, stronger than ever. He will reinstate her at court; my fortunes will be restored also. I was not lying about debtors' prison, Sir Durendal. The King will take no harm.''

Durendal shuddered. ''Others may be affected also.''

''What matter? Hundreds have lusted for her in their time. Only one counts.''

''You cannot hope to bring such a conjurement within reach of the King.''

''No? You underestimate me. The Queen has retired to Bondhill for her confinement. Ambrose already has the place so stiff with enchantments that no sniffer can go near it. He visits her there regularly. We have made arrangements.''

It sounded all too horribly plausible, just the sort of slimy trick the turd would think up. And, no, there was nothing Durendal could do to stop him. Treason! Where was honor now? Where were the bright hopes of his youth? Where . . .

''A dramatic scene,'' said a new voice. In the doorway stood a woman dressed all in scarlet. Only an ageless pale face was visible within the wimple that enclosed her head, and the irises of her eyes were red, also. Rich robes of the same shade cascaded from her shoulders to the rug. Her bearing left no doubt that she was in charge of the elementary and the order that ran it.

The Marquis bowed. ''It had its moments, my lady, but I think my young friend has seen reason.''

The Prioress turned her nightmare gaze on Durendal. ''Do you think we are unaware of the dangers? Would we undertake this venture lightly? If you misbehave, young man, then none of you will leave these precincts alive. We have ways of disposing of evidence.''

He hesitated even then, wondering if he could slay that foul creature as well. The need to keep his ward from harm restrained him, for obviously an order that dealt in such evils would have strong defenses. The Marquis knew he had won, smirking already. The Countess was recovering her anger. The old uncle had shrunk back into unwilling despair.

Durendal sheathed his sword. Truly, he had no choice. He must carry on as normally as he could, being a perfect accomplice, trustworthy to death itself. Tomorrow he would even throw the final bout of the King's Cup in a demonstration of his shame and failure. His binding would not let him kill himself.

He watched in sick self-hate as the Marquis paid over the money that had come from the sword breaker, the King's gift. The prioress scanned the scroll with satisfaction and then led the way into a chapel that was itself an octogram, a tall chamber of white marble with sixteen walls defining eight points. Each of these alcoves was in some way—mostly very obviously and crudely—dedicated to an element. One was empty, representing air, with a ewer of water opposite, a sword to portray chance, and so on. Fire's brazier provided the only light in the big chamber. Durendal considered much of the symbolism questionable or just in bad taste, like the skull for death or the huge gold heart for love. It set his teeth to scraping, but perhaps it impressed the sort of customers such a place attracted. Although he could sense the presence of spirits strongly, here they did not give him the comforting feeling of support that he had experienced at Ironhall. Here they unsettled him and felt wrong.

The four supplicants were joined by three more conjurers in scarlet gowns—two men and another woman. All eight were then placed in position by the prioress. Durendal was ordered to stand before the black pedestal from which the skull grinned down, so he was at death—which felt very appropriate in his present mood. It was the standard octogram, so he had air on his left and earth on his right. Nutting was at chance, his uncle at time, and the Countess, of course, was love, opposite Durendal.

When the conjurer chanting the role of Dispenser began banishing unwanted elements, Nutting, his uncle, and Durendal were required to turn their backs. That was their only participation in the ritual, but Durendal could make out enough of the chanting to guess roughly what was going on behind him. Standing in the place of death he should be less involved in the proceedings than any of the others, and yet—to his utter disgust—the erotic spirits roused him to panting, sweating, trembling lust. The only consolation he was able to wring from the night's events was that he was not forced to watch the obscenities being performed upon the naked body of the most beautiful woman in Chivial.

· 6 ·

It was near dawn when the Marquis returned to Nutting House and demanded his valet be wakened to put him to bed. Durendal just paced—up and down stairs, through completed rooms and rooms still being plastered, along corridors, past piles of furniture in dustcovers. Even for a Blade, it was no way to prepare for an honest fencing match but perhaps a good way to prepare for a match he must throw. It might be the start of madness. He looked back with contempt on the idealism of his youth, the time before Harvest's death had sealed his fate. He marveled at how far he had fallen from those dreams, how fast he had become a cheat and a traitor.

He could still hope for the conspiracy to be uncovered, yet he could do nothing to expose it. He would cheer with the best of them when the headsman raised the Marquis's head for the crowds to see, even if his own neck was to be next on the block. He hoped it would be. A ward's death was always a shattering bereavement for his Blade;

when the ward died by violence, the Blade rarely survived. Beheading definitely classed as violence.

A clatter of hooves at sunrise roused him from his brooding. He sprinted downstairs and slithered to a halt at the front door just ahead of the porter, a former sailor named Piewasher, who had regaled him during many a long night with improbable tales of travel, foreign ports, foreign women, and children of various shades. Before either of them could say a word, a stave thundered against the panel and a voice demanded that it open in the King's name.

Piewasher gasped with dismay, then stared blankly at Durendal who was laughing.

So! The fox had been tracked to its lair already. The jig was up. Now it had happened, he had no doubts about what he must do. He spun Piewasher around. "Go and tell the Marquis! Quickly!"

Sailors did not question orders. The old man scurried off across the hallway at the best speed he could muster.

The Marquis's only hope of escape was the servants' stair at the back. The chance that any exit from the house had been left unguarded was very slim, but Durendal's duty now was to give his ward the longest possible start. He could die with his sword in his hand.

He waited for the second demand, then snapped open the spy hole cover. He saw a gaunt and bloodless face framed by lank, mousy locks and topped by a black biretta. That and the black robes were the uniform of His Majesty's Office of General Inquiry. Behind the inquisitor stood at least a dozen men-at-arms of the Watch.

"His lordship is not at home."

"That is a lie."

The prospect of action had lifted the burden and set all Durendal's muscles tingling. "I did not mean it literally. It's a social fiction. You can't possibly believe that I would be so foolish as to try to lie to an inquisitor, can you? No, I was merely presenting the customary excuse the gentry use whenever they do not wish—"

"You are trying to delay us." The young man had a harsh, unpleasant voice.

"I am attempting to further your education. Now, it is possible that his lordship might consent to receive visitors if he were—"

The inquisitor gestured without taking his glassy stare off Durendal. The nearest man-at-arms slammed the butt of his pike against the door and bellowed again, "Open in the King's name!"

Even a marquis did not rate more than three warnings. Durendal shut the peephole and marched across the hallway, detouring past the fireplace to pick up the poker. He mourned the absence of his sword breaker in what would be his first and final real blood-on-the-floor fight, but the poker might deflect those heavy pikes better. It was a pity, too, that when her ladyship insisted on a main staircase of pink granite, her grandiose taste had required it to be of such width that it required at least three men to hold it adequately. Why hadn't she thought of that? The defenses could be improved, though. On high pedestals at either side loomed pretentious creamy marble statues of mythical figures. The Marquise had been very excited when these two eyesores were delivered a week ago, but she would not grudge them in a good cause.

The lock on the front door clicked open. The chain rattled loose of its own accord. Bolts slid. Inquisitors had ways of entering anywhere.

The statues required a surprising effort, but they toppled, one after the other, setting echoes rolling and spraying fragments of stone across the tiled floor. That would make the footing a little trickier for the opposition, while Durendal could stand on the steps. Moreover, the noise would bring fifty or so servants running, which might delay the invaders a little.

The inquisitor led in the Watch. His black robes should have made him an ominous figure, but he had a comical in-toed strut like a rooster crossing a farmyard. He hesitated when he reached the scattered debris. His men came to a halt behind him.

His fishy gaze fixed itself on Durendal. "You are under arrest."

Durendal smiled. "Talk is cheap."

Sounds of voices and running feet overhead meant that the back stairs would be full of servants, at least for a few moments. If the Marquis had reacted fast enough he might be down in the kitchens now, or even the cellar, which had an exit to the alley.

"Your cause is hopeless."

"Of course."

The glassy eyes did not change expression. "We know everything you have been up to: how you pawned your sword breaker, how you went to Werten House—"

"Was that its name?" Durendal itched with eagerness for the action to start, but delay was the game. He admired his opponent's unwinking sharklike stare, wishing he could keep his face impassive like that. "I needs must defend my ward, you know."

"You have already betrayed him. It was you our sniffer was following."

Ouch! He must not let himself be rattled, although he was trained in swords, not words. "Then my obligation is all the greater."

Startled faces were appearing at doors and balustrades as the servants flocked to witness this confrontation.

"Sergeant, arrest that man."

The sergeant looked at the inquisitor in disbelief. "He's a Blade! Can't you enchant him, like you did that door?"

"No. Try to take him alive."

The men-at-arms exchanged worried glances. None of them moved.

"I won't be taking prisoners," Durendal said, feeling sorry for them. They were only doing their duty, like him; and he would certainly fell some of them before they overpowered him. "Inquisitor, I regret this. I hope you catch them all and chop off their heads, but I will do everything I can to stop you."

"You are being illogical. Why throw away your life on a hopeless cause?"

"You can't understand, pettifogger. The only cause a Blade knows is the defense of his ward. What he's up to doesn't matter—I will die here and write my name in the Litany of Heroes. My sword will hang in the place of honor at Ironhall forever."

"You fool, Kromman!" Montpurse shouted. With Chefney at his side, he came striding around the Watch to accost the inquisitor. "How dare you start before we got here?"

Durendal had not seen them come in the door; and his heart dropped solidly into his boots, for he had absolutely no chance against those two together. But at least now it would be quick and he would not be butchering secular men-at-arms. Harvest leaped from her scabbard in a flash and hiss of beautiful steel. He laughed joyously. "Come on, then! Let's get it over with. Both of you!"

No one paid any attention to him.

"Normal rules for dealing with Blades do not apply in this instance," said the inquisitor's hoarse voice. He dragged a scroll from somewhere inside his robes. "The warrant names this one as a conspirator, not just as witness. Our readings register him as a danger to His Majesty."

"You can take your reading and stuff it down your throat. The King will pardon him."

"He is not pardoned yet. He goes to the Bastion with the others."

"Come on!" Durendal shouted from the stair. "What are you waiting for? Are you scared?" The talk of pardons was terrifying. Far better to die quickly doing his duty than languish as a failure, an emotional wreck, an outcast unable to hold up his head among men. If the Marquis wasn't safely out of the house by now, he never would be. Time to die.

He was ignored. The others continued to discuss him like a troublesome damp patch in the plaster.

"Don't be a fool, Kromman!" That was Chefney. "You can't lock up a ward and then expect to treat his Blade like any other prisoner. He'll go mad."

Montpurse spared Durendal an appraising glance. "He's gone already."

The inquisitor shrugged blandly. "We can put madmen to the Question, Commander. They often seem saner afterward. And we shall see how he behaves now we have his ward under restraint. Stand aside, up there! Let them through."

Durendal heard muttering and whispers above and behind him, up among the servants at the top of the stair, but he was too close to Chefney and Montpurse to take his eyes off them. He backed up a couple of steps. It was probably a trick. It must be a trick. The alternative was that all the time he had been thinking he was distracting the inquisitor, the inquisitor had been distracting him. *No! No!*

"You idiot, Kromman!" Montpurse said. "Oh, you flaming moron!"

Durendal backed up another step, still not daring to turn his head.

"Look up, Sir Blade!" the inquisitor shouted. "Your cause is hopeless. Throw down your sword."

"Death and fire!" said Montpurse. "Hoare, bring the net! Quickly!"

Durendal risked a quick glance above and behind him. The goggling servants had been cleared away from the top of the stair. Now the Marquis was stumbling down between two men-at-arms, barefoot and pathetic, his red woollen nightcap askew, his creamy silk nightshirt torn and spattered with blood, although apparently only from a nosebleed. A length of chain connected his ankles, his hands were tied behind his back, and the left-hand guard held a sword under his chin. There were six more men-at-arms in the squad, but they were all coming behind the prisoner. That was foolish of them.

Durendal went up the pink granite staircase much faster than he would normally have dared go down it. He cut the left-hand guard's throat before the man could even pull his sword away from the Marquis's chin. The man on the other side tried to draw and died. Durendal pushed his ward aside so that he could get at the three on the next step. He promptly hamstrung two of them, but either his shove or the falling bodies caused the bound prisoner to lose his balance. The superhuman reflexes of his Blade might have saved him even then, had not Montpurse and Hoare at that moment enveloped Durendal in the net. With a thin shriek of terror, the Marquis tripped on his ankle chains and fell headlong. He rolled all the way down his pink granite staircase and arrived at the inquisitor's feet with a broken neck.

Durendal screamed. He went on screaming.

The Guard bundled him in enough stout hemp to rig a galleon. He still held his sword, of course, and they did not try to remove it, knowing what that would mean to a Blade, but they slid Hoare's scabbard over it so he would not cut either himself or the mesh in his struggles.

Chefney took his feet and Montpurse his shoulders. They carried him out like a roll of carpet and loaded him into the coach. They took the west road, to Starkmoor. He still screamed.

· 7 ·

Being both ward and suzerain, the King could release his own Blades from their binding just by dubbing them knights in the Order—that was how the conjuration worked. For private Blades, with their divided loyalty, the only way out was a reversion ritual, which rarely succeeded. When the ward was already dead, and possibly by the Blade's own hand, there was no ready answer at all.

The group that assembled in the Forge that night included no candidates. The innocent slept in their dormitories, unaware that a Blade who was already one of their heroes had been returned in a seriously damaged condition. A couple of the smiths had been recruited to help with the dirty work, but many of the masters and other knights refused to attend. Knowing the odds against a reversion succeeding, they were unwilling to endure the ordeal of watching this one.

After a whole day of screaming, Durendal had at last fallen silent, unable to force another sound through his battered throat. He lay on the floor in his rope cocoon, unresponsive to all queries or entreaties, although some gibbering corner of his mind registered the horrible things happening. He was knotted with cramps; he had fouled himself. He cared for nothing except the fact that his ward had died by violence and he had done that terrible thing himself.

"I don't suppose we can do it without untying him?" Grand Master mumbled. He walked with a cane now and was seriously deaf. He was well over eighty.

Master of Rituals ran fingers through hair that resembled

91

a field of seeding dandelions. "No. We need his sword first." He had brought a bundle of scrolls from the library, but he knew the ritual by heart. He had always been aware that one day he might need it and the need would be urgent. "He must be chained. That is essential. Even if he were in his right mind, he would have to be chained."

Montpurse said, "How could he be in his right mind? Let's get started."

"Wait a moment," suggested Master of Archives. "Can we get his sword out first? I don't like the idea of him loose with his sword."

"That's a good idea."

"Let's try that. . . ."

No, they discovered, they could not free the hilt from Durendal's grip while he and the sword were all wrapped up together. There was a delay while Master of Arms went off to the armory and returned with some steel gauntlets and a couple of shields. Then Montpurse cut the knots. As the ropes fell away, Durendal began to draw Harvest free of the scabbard. Chefney and Master of Horse managed to grasp the blade with the gauntlets before the madman could wield it. Four men pried his fingers off the hilt. The shields were not needed. It took eight men to hold him down while the smiths fettered his wrists and ankles; then Montpurse and Hoare cut away his clothes and dunked him bodily in one of the troughs, then toweled him dry. He was trying to scream again.

The ritual was long and complex, for all the elements that had been invoked in the binding must be invoked again. Through it all, Durendal lay chained on the anvil, mostly in silence now, although he cried out when his sword was plunged into the coals. Two masters worked the bellows.

Prolonged roasting on charcoal will ruin a blade, making the iron brittle.

At the end of the invocation and revocation, when the sword had been quenched, the participants sang the dedication song, for that was what the texts demanded, although it seemed incongruous to include part of a ritual in its own reversal. Then Master Armorer, a bull of a man, took the sword Harvest and swung her, bringing her down with all his might across the subject's heart. As he saw the blow coming, Durendal screamed one last time.

The blade shattered, the body did not. The ritual had apparently succeeded.

"Can't even see a mark on his skin," Grand Master said cheerfully, leaning forward on his cane to peer. "Sir Durendal?"

"He's unconscious!" Montpurse said. "Wouldn't you be? Let's get those flaming chains off the poor beggar and put him to bed."

· 8 ·

When the need for a privy became unendurable, Durendal opened his eyes to admit that he was conscious. Montpurse closed his book instantly; he had been lounging on the window seat for the last three hours or longer, apparently reading. Perhaps he had been faking, too.

"How do you feel, brother?"

Whisper: "Sore throat."

"I'm surprised you have any throat left."

The room was large and well furnished, finely paneled. The bed alone would have stabled two oxen, the draperies were of rich velvet—faded in places, originally good stuff. The scenery beyond the window resembled the useless, rocky hills of Starkmoor, but there was no chamber like this in Ironhall.

"Where?"

The Commander rose, his smile becoming visible as he

moved away from the light. "Back home in the Hall. This is the royal suite. The kiddies never get to see it. Is this what's on your mind?" He reached under the bed and produced the necessary receptacle.

The ensuing procedure took all of Durendal's strength—Montpurse had to help him stand up and steady him. He flopped back on the bed again like a landed fish. Montpurse offered a water flask so he could drink.

"Roast venison? Pease pudding? Chicken broth?"

Durendal closed his eyes in silence. It was almost three years since he'd had a good sleep.

The battle of the Royal Guard versus Sir Durendal went on for three nights and three days. They never left him alone—Montpurse, Hoare, Chefney, and others, taking turns. They brought trays of steaming dishes. They lectured. They bullied. They pleaded. Hoare even wept. They sent in Grand Master and other knights. They showed him the royal pardon, and his sword breaker, and eventually even Harvest reforged to prove to him that she was as good as new again, and now she had her name engraved on the blade in these neat little letters near the top, see? Nothing worked.

He would not speak. He would not eat. He drank water and passed it and slept. That was all. His face grew ever thinner under its stubble.

As another night was falling, the door flew open and the King marched in. He barked, "Out!" and Montpurse departed like a hare. The King slammed the door behind him, shaking the building to its roots.

His Majesty strode to the bedside, put his hands on his hips, and said, "Well?" He seemed to fill the room.

Durendal whispered, "No."

The King swelled like a bullfrog, filling the room with his amber glare. "I don't accept that word from any man. So Tab Nillway is dead? He would have died anyway on the block. Perverting a Blade is a capital offense in itself. Utter trash!"

His Blade had killed him. Nothing else mattered, or ever would.

The royal glowering darkened. "Why should you care now what happened to that traitor? You're free of your binding now."

He did not feel free.

"Well?" Ambrose boomed. "Where's your loyalty to me, mm?"

"Long live the King," Durendal whispered.

"You think that pus-face Nutting defeated you? No, you defeated him! He thought I gave him a Blade because he was important, but I was marking him as dangerous. Mold like him creeps under the furniture and rots things unseen, but he couldn't be unseen when he had you at his heels. You blazed. The whole court noticed you wherever you went. And I always remembered that I had marked Master Tab Nillway as dangerous."

That was a lie. Durendal had been assigned to the Marquis because a sniffer could follow a Blade in the dark. He had been a double traitor, betraying both ward and sovereign.

The King waited for a response that never came. Seeing that loudness wouldn't work, he tried louder, like a rising thunderstorm. He kicked the table beside the bed. He threw a scroll on the covers. "There's your pardon. I'll make you a knight in the Order, and you can put all that fencing skill of yours to work teaching, here in Ironhall. Well, what do you say?"

To live out the rest of his days in these barren hills? To be a permanent horrible example of a failed Blade, pointed out to all those youngsters, and helping to trap them as he had been trapped? It was unthinkable. "No."

"Thought not." There was a dangerous glint of satisfaction in the King's cunning stare. "Well, I didn't ride all day on an empty stomach just to pander to a self-pitying namby-pamby. You're interfering with the business of the kingdom. You're an almighty nuisance, but I'm going to try another binding on you."

"What? Will that work?"

"Probably not. The conjurers say it will kill you. I'm going to find out." A royal bellow rattled the casement. "His Majesty has need of a Blade. Are you ready to serve?"

Durendal shook his head.

The royal yellow eyes flashed dangerously. "You refuse our command?"

Making a great effort, Durendal said, "Binding is evil. It steals a man's soul."

"Steals it? It gives him one, you mean. If your past had had any future in this world, boy, you would never have been brought to Ironhall. A Blade has pride, status, and above all a sense of purpose. He matters. His life matters. His death may matter even more. And you certainly don't look as if you've got any future at the moment. Serve or die!" The King raised a clenched fist. "But I won't be a laughingstock, even for you. Can you stand on your own feet? Will you say the words?"

To climb up on the anvil or lift a sword in his present state would be an impossible effort. "No."

"Very well. I take back the pardon." The King did, crumpling it into a pocket. "Now you have a choice. You can either be put to the Question, stand trial, and then have your head chopped off, or you can get a sword through your heart tonight. Which is it to be?"

Since he couldn't just will himself to death, the quicker way was the more appealing choice. Besides, it would make fat Ambrose do his own filthy executions.

"All right. I'll say the words."

"Then get out of that putrefying bed and bow to your sovereign lord."

"I haven't any clothes on."

"I won't scream. Up!"

Durendal forced himself upright. The covers were made of lead, but he heaved them aside and put his feet on the floor. He stood, swayed, straightened.

"Go on, man! We are waiting!"

Durendal began to bow and collapsed.

"I didn't say grovel, I said bow!" The King took him under the arms and hoisted him to his feet like a doll, big as he was. For a long moment they stared at each other.

Then the King pushed, and he fell back on the bed like a dirty shirt.

"Get dressed. We'll start as soon as you're ready. Cold baths come first." The door slammed behind the monarch. The building trembled again.

· 9 ·

"For the last time," the King roared, rousing long-sleeping echoes, "I am not going to meditate. Not five minutes, not one minute. I have meditated all day on a horse to get here. The candidate has meditated in bed for even longer. I am hungry. Begin now!"

Eight hearths flickered in the deep stillness of the hold. More than a hundred men and boys held their breath in the spirit-sanctified gloom.

Master of Rituals cringed. "My liege!"

Candidate? Yes, Durendal was a candidate again. He was as weak as a newborn babe again. Even standing without swaying was an effort, and there were all those shocked young eyes staring at him. *Young!* It wasn't even three years since he had been one of those apple-cheeked kids, but they had not looked so innocent then, surely? Could those be *seniors*? When he'd agreed to go through with this, he had forgotten there would be an audience. He was the celebrated, the famous, the renowned Sir Durendal, who'd taken the King's Cup away from Montpurse last year and just a few days ago had won a broadsword duel without striking a blow. He must look like a geriatric paralytic to these adolescents, ruining all their dreams. Every one of them was going to have to go through the ordeal in the next few months or years, and seeing their King strike the famous Durendal dead in front of their eyes would give all these kiddies nightmares.

There was Montpurse, shining like a gold figurine in the firelight, going to be Second for him in the ritual. Poor old Grand Master, failing fast—soon another sword would hang in the hall. But Harvest was going there even sooner, because Sir Durendal was going to die tonight, and good riddance to all of them and the whole stinking world.

Master of Archives was Dispenser, just as he had been the last time. He hadn't shut out death for poor Harvest. There was the other Harvest, the remade sword, and a badly undernourished Brat stumbling his way through the dedication.

He felt the spirits rally and his skin pucker. Weak, weak! Why did he have to be so weak? Three days without food shouldn't make his knees shake like this. He staggered in to join hands with the others around the anvil. The singing soared erratically, half the Forge trying to stay in one key and the other half trying to follow the King as he bellowed out the words in several. But the song still worked. Tears blurred the firelight. He wondered if the others noticed.

He didn't really want to die. It was just that life wasn't worth living anymore.

He made it back to his place and Hoare arrived to remove his shirt. Why was he leering like that? Was he looking forward to Durendal's death? Oh, perhaps he was trying to appear cheerful. Then came Montpurse's thumb on his chest . . . and a frown on Montpurse's face as he realized how far off-target the scar was. It felt as if he put the mark where it ought to be, one rib lower.

Back to the center for the sword. Why had they made Harvest so heavy this time? And the anvil seemed a foot higher than he remembered. He climbed onto it, straightened up, and swayed. The King put a foot forward, then stopped.

Deep breath. "My Sovereign Lord, King Ambrose IV, upon my soul and without reservation, I, Durendal, companion of the Loyal and Ancient . . . defend you, your heirs and successors, against all foes . . . bid you plunge this my sword into my heart that I may die. . . ." Last time he had shouted. Now he had no cause to shout, but he did not mumble, either.

He very nearly fell headlong getting down off the anvil, and he did twist his ankle. He limped over to the King and disposed of the sword. It was a great relief to be able to sit down. This was it, then. Time to die. All over.

The King put the point to the charcoal.

They stared hard at each other.

Will you live?

Will you kill me?

Hoare and Montpurse were waiting to take his arms.

Why live? Was being a Blade purpose enough?

Well, perhaps it was better than nothing. Show the fat toad! Show them all. On sudden impulse—just as he'd once trounced the King at fencing, and just as he'd dropped in front of Aldane's charge—he put his hands on his thighs and lifted his chin. "Do it now!"

"Serve or die!" The King was fast, but then he'd done this fifty times or more. The guard was almost touching Durendal's chest before the awful explosion of pain came; then it was all over, the sword was out again, and he felt that rush of life and healing.

Marveling, he rose. Sweat cold on his skin . . . crazy, hysterical cheering . . . the King returning his sword and clapping a hand on his shoulder . . . Life! He had a life to live.

Beaming as proudly as if he'd been on the other side of the gruesome ordeal, the King shouted over the tumult, "Ready to ride, Sir Durendal?"

Slipping the bloody sword through the loop on his belt,

Durendal gave fat Ambrose his own treatment—the steady stare first. "Against whom, Your Majesty?"

The King's fist clenched, but he did show a trace of doubt. "Against all foes, of course!"

Then the smile. "Of course, my liege."

Everman

III

At last the great door and the snowy steps beyond—Lord Roland was about to leave Greymere for the last time, venturing out into a very unpleasant-looking winter's night. Never would his own fireside seem more welcome.

The King came and went from palace to palace: Nocare, Greymere, Wetshore, Oldmart, and others. Court was where the King was, but government was where the paper was; and the clerks and counters, lawyers and lackeys, labored year-round in the capital, Grandon. Even now, when the King had shut himself up in Falconsrest for Long Night, the pens still scratched busily in Greymere chancellery. Carriages were held ready day and night for the convenience of senior officials.

The weathered, square-faced head porter had borne the grandiose title of Gentleman Usher for longer than anyone could remember, perhaps even himself. Roland had bid him many thousands of good morrows and good evens. Now the old man looked ready to melt like the slush on the cobbles. All he could say was, "I got my orders, my lord." There was a coach and four in clear sight sheltering under the arch, awaiting his hail, but he had his orders. He probably had hopes of a small pension from the King if he continued to behave himself for the next couple of years—and did not die of misery in the next few minutes. He had his orders.

Lord Roland had never owned a coach of his own, unless one counted the one his wife used. He had rarely in his life carried money. He did not even have a horse of his own at the palace just now, but he needed to proceed home with as much dignity as possible, and a two-hour walk through the streets and out into the countryside in his chancellor's robes would not be dignified. Kromman wanted to hurt, but then Kromman had been nursing his hatred for a generation.

Quarrel's eager young face seemed dangerously inflamed under the rushlights. He was practically quivering. Roland gestured him forward and took a step back.

"Gentleman Usher," he said from behind his guardian's shoulder, "this is very embarrassing for me. My Blade, Sir Quarrel, has not been with me long enough to learn how things are done in the palace. Thus, when I sent him on ahead to order a carriage, he did not understand that the ensuing problem was not of your devising. I am sure he would not really have hurt you, but—"

Quarrel's sword hissed from its scabbard.

Gentleman Usher lost his look of despair. "Ah, noble Sir Blade! Pray be not hard on a poor old man or deprive his fourteen grandchildren of their beloved grandfather!"

"Verily!" Quarrel said. "Dost thou not summon yonder carriage full speedily and direct it to a place congruous to my ward's desires, then I shall expeditiously slit thee into elementary eighths."

"Forsooth? Hold it under my chin, lad—it'll look better. Coach! Coach!"

As Roland climbed into the carriage, he could hear Gentleman Usher directing the driver, still at sword point. When the horses began to move, Quarrel swung nimbly aboard and closed the door. The team pulled out of the palace gates, clattering into the night-filled streets.

Farewell, Greymere!

"Thank you, Sir Quarrel. That was a very nice piece of highwaymanship. And I congratulate you on your verbal feinting earlier."

"My pleasure, my lord." He did not laugh, but his smile was audible.

What was Roland going to do about this boy, trapped in a fatal allegiance? Binding only worked one way, but a man's instincts and standards insisted that loyalty must be a two-edged sword. Long ago, he had survived a reversal conjuration unscathed, but he knew of only one other who had. He would drag Quarrel with him in his downfall, and that was unjust.

As he would drag down many others, no doubt. What, for that matter, of his wife? His shameful dismissal would upset her if he were upset, but she would be very glad to have him to herself at last. She had never cared for court life, all glitter and sham. How long would they have together before Kromman sent the inquisitors?

What sort of a fool would expect gratitude from a monarch?

The clattering and jingling of the coach was overridden by a voice from the darkness opposite. "May I ask a question, my lord?"

"You are trying to stop me brooding, I presume?"

A chuckle. "Of course. But I do want to know the answer."

"Ask then. Ask questions anytime. The old can still be useful as sources of information."

"Will you tell me about the time you saved the King's life?"

Oh, that! They always wanted to know about that.

"I wish I could. You really ought to ask the King. He saw it all, and he was the only one who did. Absolutely as cool as an icicle." He heard himself sigh. Those had been the days! "It happened back in 355—in Nythia, of course. Outside the walls of Waterby, about the third week of the siege, I think. It was a foggy morning. And there was a great deal of smoke and dust about, too."

And noise, of course—deafening thunderclaps as Destroyer General and his men tried to bring down the walls, and the defenders retaliated with conjurations of their own. The King would never listen to reason. He wandered the camp in full view, ignoring arrows and flying rocks and explosions of elemental power, driving his Blades insane with the risks he took. They crowded around him like swarming bees until he cursed at them to give him room to breathe. Yet somehow, that morning, for just the critical few moments, there was only one. . . .

Roland remembered he was supposed to be telling Quarrel this story, not reliving it. He pulled himself back from that misty morning, from golden youth and high adventure, back to Grandon's bleak winter, the swaying carriage, shame, and dismissal. Old age. This was 388 already. Where had the years gone?

"I just chanced to be walking with the King and no other Blades close. I don't know why. It must have been conjuration, I suppose."

"I thought our bindings were spirit-proof?"

"So did we. If the rebels had that much control, you'd have thought they would have blasted the King directly. The conjurers at the College never could explain it, although they speculated that my double binding might have made me more resistant than the others; or it may have been fickle chance. We were going through marsh and low scrub, so we tended to spread out, avoiding puddles and so on. The others had wandered farther off than they realized. The King and I were discussing horses, ambling along like blind turtles.

"As to what actually happened—I don't know, I really don't know. Four armed men jumped out of the bushes." Not men, just boys. "The next thing I recall is being a little short of breath, blood on my sword, four bodies on the ground. Then Commander Montpurse arrived at a scream. You never heard such language! His Majesty laughed at him, calm as milk."

Yes, those had been the great days—days of youth and love and war, the days when he had been a simple Blade in the Royal Guard, wanting nothing more in the world, when life had been pleasure from dawn till dawn.

• 2 •

"**Y**ou missed an interesting display of swordsmanship, Commander!" The King was enjoying his Guards' collective dismay. "Another Durendal legend, I fancy."

"Take it, my liege!" Montpurse was on his knees in the mud, offering up his sword. "Take it. Cut off my useless head if you want, because I certainly—"

"Stand up, man! Keep your sword. You won't escape that easily. Well, perhaps I need to borrow it for a minute."

A nearby copse exploded with an earth-shattering roar, hurling branches and rocks everywhere. The King ignored it, although some of the debris went dancing past his feet. The river plain was pockmarked with craters, most of them now full of water. The honey-colored walls of Waterby were in worse shape, with half the towers in ruins; but archers on the battlements had been sending arrows this far. Not accurately, fortunately. Another thudded into the turf close to Chefney, who jumped.

Bewildered, Durendal was examining Harvest. That was fresh blood on her and those were dead men on the ground, but the last few minutes had vanished in a confused blur of leaping and slashing and parrying. Four?

"What was your family name, Sir Durendal?"

"Family . . . Roland, sire." He had not spoken the word in a dozen years. He almost had to think to remember it. Of course a King could ask questions that others must not, but what on earth was Ambrose after now?

The King frowned. "The Rolands of Mayshire?"

"Who? Oh, no, sire. Dimpleshire, very minor gentry. My grandfather held lands in tenancy-in-chief from the

Priory of Goodham.'' Why ask? And why was Montpurse pressing a hand on his shoulder so heavily?

Then realization—the Commander was signaling him to kneel. Mystified, he dropped to one knee and then to two as full understanding came. Oh, no! He felt the mud cold through his hose.

Oh, yes! The blade came down on his shoulder. Then on the other.

''Arise, Baron Roland of Waterby.''

He arose. Montpurse grabbed his hand and pumped it, hugging him with the other arm. The rest of the Blades started a cheer and gathered around to thump him on the back.

''My liege! I—I thank you, Your Majesty. But I do not deserve—''

''Deserve?'' Hoare bellowed. ''Four dead men and you don't deserve? The rest of us ought to be hung, drawn, and quartered—every day for a month.''

One of the towers of Waterby dissolved in a ball of stones and dust that floated leisurely to the ground. Everyone looked quickly to the battery where the conjurers of the Royal Office of Demolition were at work, to see if they had all survived, because sometimes they blew themselves out of the octogram as well as the shot. Then came the sounds—first the distant cheering of the army, second the roll of thunder over the plain.

Durendal turned back to face the King's smug smile. ''But, Your Majesty . . . I trust that this does not mean . . . that I don't have to . . .'' How could a peer belong to the Royal Guard? Unthinkable!

Chuckling, the King returned Montpurse's sword to him. ''Not unless you wish. We grant you leave to retain your present style at your own pleasure.''

That was honor indeed! He could retire at will and be a lord. Not that he ever would, of course. A noble must live nobly, which required vast amounts of money.

Another explosion showered mud and pebbles. They all ducked, and one or two swore at being struck.

"They are finding the range, sire!" Montpurse said angrily.

"True. Well, let us proceed to the battery and hear how Destroyer General views his progress." The King set off at a leisurely stroll, anxious not to appear to be retreating. With much relief his Blades accompanied him.

Hoare edged close to Durendal to whisper, "My lord, may I kiss your backside?"

"No. You aren't worthy."

"I know that. I was just hoping."

Baron Roland of Waterby. Meaningless, really. He could never afford to use the title, even if he would ever want to.

That evening, as the new peer was whetting Harvest to remove a few recent nicks, a herald came to the tent and presented him with an official notice from Chancery. The honor and lands of Peckmoss in Dimpleshire had been estranged from the royal demesne and granted in freehold to Baron Roland of Waterby; said lands would be henceforth administered to the avail, benefit, and profit of the said baron, pending his further instructions.

He was rich. It didn't matter.

He was more worried about getting the bloodstains off his jerkin.

· 3 ·

Those were the great days. In the four years between his second and third visits to Ironhall, he was never far from the King. Of the hundred or so Blades in the Royal Guard, five or six were especially favored; and Sir Durendal was one of them, companion at both work and play.

Ambrose was a ferocious horseman still, in spite of his ever-increasing size, and rode in mad hunts. He hawked and followed hounds. He danced and attended masques. He went on progresses through town and country, while the crowds roared their loyalty. Seldom, if ever, had Chivial loved a monarch as much as this one. He repaired highways and built bridges, fostered trade, wenched notoriously, and kept the nobility under control. He had managed to conclude a treaty with Baelmark, ending a war that had dragged on for fourteen years, so now the coasts no longer lived in dread of Baelish raiders. Almost the only complaints ever heard in Parliament concerned the lack of a male heir, so when the King divorced Queen Godeleva and married the Lady Sian, the country rejoiced and his popularity soared even higher. From any viewpoint, he loomed larger than life. The fickle spirits of chance were his handmaids in those days, and Durendal was there to share in the glory.

When the King did not need him, he never lacked for recreation. There was Rose, soon after he joined the Guard, but Rose's father disapproved and married her off to a man of better breeding.

There was Isolde. They spoke seriously of marriage until the rebellion in Nythia called him away. He had thought they had an understanding, but on his return he found her betrothed to another.

That summer of the Nythian Rebellion was perhaps the finest time of all—living with the army, fighting a war. Apart from the vague few minutes when he earned his barony, he experienced little real battle, for the days of kings in armor leading charges had long gone. Only very hard talking by Montpurse kept Ambrose out of several skirmishes, though; and even Montpurse could not stop him on the day Kirkwain fell. Then the King rode through the breach directly behind the vanguard with his Blades around him. Four were killed, a dozen wounded, but they gave more than they took. Harvest alone avenged the four, and the legend of the second Durendal crept a little closer to the legend of the first.

Then there was Kate.

He had seen her around the palace many times, but never close. He took a long time to find the resolution to address her, for he feared rejection—not from most women, for he knew his abilities, but from her—because he still remembered the last time he had presumed to approach a White Sister. One evening, while he was considering whom to invite to a masque, he saw her on the terrace, admiring the swans. Her robe and tall hat were the same snowy white as they, and the blossoms overhead matched as well. . . . A little rejection would not kill him.

He walked closer and closer and closer, and she did not sniff inquiringly and turn around to glare. She just watched the swans. He saw that she was smaller than he had realized; the tall hennin was deceptive. Size did not matter when everything else was perfection. When he judged the distance to be about right—interest, but not threat—he rested his forearms on the stone balustrade, to bring his eyes nearer to the level of hers.

"Ugly brutes!" he said.

She turned her head with a frown. "I think they're beautiful."

"You're not standing where I am."

He had always been puzzled by the fact that he could never predict a person's laugh until he heard it. The largest men might titter and the smallest women guffaw. She had a wonderful laugh, like birdsong.

"You are flattering me already, Sir Durendal!"

"You know my name?" He pretended surprise, although everyone knew his name.

"You have quite a reputation." She had a lovely smile, too, and eyes of cornflower blue. He presumed her hair would be the same gold as her eyebrows, but it was hidden by her veils and hat.

"What sort of reputation?"

"I don't think we should both indulge in flattery. It might be dangerous."

"I spurn such danger." He proved it by moving closer.

"That's part of the reputation."

This was definitely promising, but before his hopes soared any higher he must discover if his binding made him repugnant to her. "I have been told that White Sisters can detect Blades at a considerable distance."

"Thirty paces or so. Less in a crowd."

"Upwind or downwind?"

She laughed again. "Any wind. I could detect you behind a wall, too, or in the dark. Your binding is a powerful enchantment."

"Detect how? You really sniff?"

She smiled. "That's an old superstition. Not by smell nor sight nor touch nor sound, and yet by all of those. Explain color to a blind person."

"I asked you first. What does a Blade look like, otherwise than other men?"

She considered, head tilted cutely. "More intense. A Blade in a group seems more solid, more important, I suppose. Detecting conjurements is my duty, after all, and my skill. A dagger in a box of kitchen knives."

"This is very interesting. And hearing? You can tell by my voice?"

"Even when you are silent. All the time. Like the highest note on a trumpet, very high, very clear. . . . That sounds unpleasant, but it isn't. Sort of rousing."

"Rousing?"

"In a military sense," she said hastily. "And as for smell, you know that dry sort of odor from very hot iron?"

"The smell of the Forge, I expect." He laid a hand on hers. "And how do I feel?"

She stiffened. He feared he had moved too soon, but she did not snatch her hand away. She turned it over, so that they were palm to palm.

"Strong."

"So a Blade is not too horrible to be with?"

"One could get used to it."

"Would you begin by accompanying me to the masque tomorrow?"

She looked up in astonishment. "Oh, I should love to! You mean it?"

They parted an hour later, when he had to go on duty. He had forgotten to ask her name. He knew it by the end of the masque the next night, and he also knew that this was a fish he wanted to land. He must play his line very carefully.

Kate had other ideas. On the afternoon following the masque, as they strolled hand in hand under the spring blossoms, she said, "This dramatic sword-through-the-heart ritual, does it leave a scar?"

"Two—one front and one back. I have four."

"I should like to see those."

Earth and fire!

He led her to his quarters—a small room, poorly lit and cramped by an oversize bed. He locked the door, for the Blades had informal ways among themselves, but she did not protest. She turned to peer at the lithographs on the wall, while he went over to stand in the light under the window. As he removed his doublet, then his shirt, he could feel his heart pounding as it had not pounded for a woman in years. Then she turned. He held out his arms; she came to them.

She ignored his scars completely.

He knew very soon that she had no experience of love-making. He did, though. He was skilled and, in this case, extremely careful. And extremely successful.

Later, as they lay entwined, he said many things, but one of them was, "You astonish me. We have only known each other for two days."

She snuggled even deeper into his embrace. "I have loved you for months. For weeks I have been putting myself in your path and you never seemed to notice me."

"I did notice you. I was always frightened that you

would think . . . that you might find a Blade unpleasant
at close quarters.''

''Very pleasant.''

''Trumpets and hot iron, daggers . . . what am I now?''

''Mm?'' She stroked the hairs on his chest. ''Like being
in bed with a sword.''

''A naked Blade, you mean?''

''Exactly.''

''Months, you say? Then I have a lot of catching up
to do.''

She sighed and stretched her body against his. ''Begin
now.''

· 4 ·

He was on duty in the antechamber the following day
with Parsewood and Scrimpnel, surreptitiously rolling dice
on a cushion so they made no noise, while pointedly ignoring disapproving stares from the officials who waited endlessly in the big brocade chairs and understood perfectly
that the Blades would not misbehave like that if there was
anyone of real importance present. Dusk was falling, pages
were lighting the lamps, the Chamberlain fussed with papers at his desk. From time to time a secretary would
shuffle in and out again.

The antechamber was boredom incarnate. Eaves-
dropping on what went on in the King's presence could
sometimes be interesting. At least one Blade was normally
present when the King granted audience, but at that moment he was receiving Grand Inquisitor, and not even
Blades overheard her reports.

The outer door opened a handbreadth to admit a pint-sized page, who scurried over to Sir Durendal and handed him a note, thus prompting sarcastic whispers about billets-doux from his insubordinate subordinates.

Must see you. Very urgent. K.

It had better be urgent! Cataclysmic!

Ignoring all the curious and disapproving stares, he went over to the door and peered out. She was right there, with the two men-at-arms scowling at her. Montpurse would have him racked for this, but his anger melted as he saw her pallor. She would never weep, but something was very wrong.

"Quick!"

"I've been reassigned!" she whispered. "First thing in the morning."

"No!" Then quieter, "To Oakendown?"

"No. To Brimiarde. It's a new posting."

"How long?"

"Probably forever."

To lose her so soon? It was unbearable. "Will you marry me?"

"What?"

"They won't transfer you if you're married. Marry me."

"But, but . . . but we can't! There isn't time. It takes days, weeks. . . . I need permission from—"

Parsewood coughed. Durendal glanced around and saw the door to the council chamber already opening.

"No, it doesn't. I'll ask the King to declare us man and wife. Then it'll be done. You agree?"

She gasped, took one breath. . . . "Oh yes!"

"I adore you!" He closed the door and moved away from it, aware of amused grins from Scrimpnel and Parsewood and wondering what the men-at-arms thought.

Grand Inquisitor backed out of the council chamber, making a final curtsey with one hand on the doorknob and the other clutching files. Her age was a state secret, for a black gable headdress concealed her hair and her pale moon face bore no wrinkles. She turned and began to cross the anteroom in the shuffling, flat-footed walk of the grossly fat, black robes whispering around her ankles. Her fishy gaze swam from face to face as she went, noting exactly who was present and who sat next to whom. No one would look her in the eye except the Blades, who stared back coldly—a point of honor, to prove they had nothing to hide.

The Chamberlain gathered up more papers and hastened in to learn His Majesty's pleasure. Durendal headed for the desk.

Words whirled in his head: *Your Majesty, I crave a boon.* Utterly ridiculous! *Sire, may I humbly beg a favor?* Better. The King would certainly consent. Married by royal prerogative!—it would amuse him. He loved to flaunt his power, especially if the demonstration did not cost the Exchequer anything. Durendal was, after all, one of his favorites. Montpurse should have been advised beforehand, but would understand. Married! To Kate! No doubts, no hesitation. What a woman! But first, of course, he must get by the Chamberlain. "I seek a brief audience with His Majesty concerning personal business." Personal business might take months! He certainly must not try to bring it up when it was his turn to stand guard in the council chamber itself. That would call down royal thunderbolts, even on him.

The Chamberlain emerged, but he hung onto the handle and peered shortsightedly around the anteroom. "Ah, Sir Durendal! Thought you were here. Just the man. His Majesty wants you."

Even for a Blade who prided himself on his fast reflexes, this afternoon was moving a little too quickly. He straightened his doublet and his shoulders, then walked into the inner sanctum.

The council chamber was a square room, poorly lit by mullioned windows at the far side and made gloomy by paneling of black walnut and a dozen dark leather chairs set around the walls. One of them was piled with an untidy heap of red dispatch boxes and a snowdrift of spilled documents. The two high fireplaces were white marble, but neither was lit.

The chairs were sometimes offered to foreign ambassadors. Everyone else—ministers, officials, petitioners; high and low, male or female—remained standing because the King did. Hoare, the Guard humorist, maintained that if the King sat down, you tried to remember when you had last updated your will, but if he began to pace it was too late to worry. He was an erratic worker, driving his ministers to desperation by refusing to look at a single paper for weeks, then working them for days and nights until they were half dead of exhaustion. He could snatch the substantive points out of a long-winded report like a sparrow hawk taking sparrows. His memory for detail was legendary, his temper even more so, his tenacity infinite. He made the policies. His ministers found ways to carry them out. Or were carried out themselves, Hoare said.

The lamps had not been lit. He was brooding by the window, peering out at the sunset and darkening the room like a hay wagon. Durendal walked to the center of the room, bowed to that massive royal back, and then waited. Never before had he been more than a single pace from the door.

The King swung around and grunted as if surprised. He pointed vaguely at a group of chairs. "Sit. I need to think."

Fire and death and more fire! Durendal obeyed, although his scalp prickled. He could not recall anyone sitting when the King stood. Invalids, no one else, not ever.

The King put his hands behind his back and began to shuttle—door, window, door. "I made a mistake once. Now I'm going to make another."

Silence was the only possible comment.

Window, door . . . "I suppose I'm just pigheaded. Hardest part of being a King—being any sort of leader—is knowing when to quit. You've wounded the quarry, you've tracked it all day, and now night is coming. Do you give up and go home? Lose all that effort? Or do you push on, knowing you'll have to spend the night in the woods and may gain nothing? Hmm? How do you decide?''

He seemed to be speaking to himself, but he suddenly stopped and peered at his uneasy Blade.

"Hmm? Well? Which?''

"I've never known Your Majesty to give up when there was any hope at all.''

Grunt. "Pigheaded, you mean. You're probably right. If I send you, can you go?''

"Huh? I mean—''

The King snarled impatiently. "You will be gone some time. Can you stand it, or must I release you first?''

Release? Durendal shivered. Blades notoriously resisted being released from their bindings, although most of them were very relieved to be free of them afterward. Unexpectedly faced with that dread prospect, he felt a surge of panic. Of course, he would then be able to snatch up his barony, marry Kate, do all sorts of things with his life. . . . No, unthinkable!

The alternative, though, seemed to be to be absent from his ward for an extended period, and that might be torture unendurable. But at least it would be temporary, and the other permanent. He wiped sweat out of his eyes. "I think I can trust Commander Montpurse to take care of you, my liege.''

The King beamed. "Good man! Remember Everman?''

It took a moment. It had been six years. "Candidate Everman? Three behind me at Ironhall.''

"That one. The one who got the job I wanted you for.''

No reply was required except a faster heartbeat.

"He's still alive,'' the King said. "We have an agent in Samarinda. Sends reports in every few years. This time he reports that there's a Chivian— You don't know any of this, do you?'' He peered suspiciously at Durendal.

Fortunately, it was possible to answer as truthfully as if he were being put to the Question. "Nothing at all, sire.

There were rumors that he had been bound to a mysterious gentleman whom no one had ever heard of and they both disappeared. Nothing more.''

''Master Jaque Polydin, merchant, adventurer, perhaps a trickster.'' The King cleared his throat uneasily. ''It's a long story. Grand Inquisitor will provide you with the details. There were reports that the knights of Samarinda owned the philosopher's stone—the gadget that turns lead into gold and lets you live forever. If you ever breathe a word of this around court, my boy, I will have you shortened by a head!''

''I understand, sire.'' The King had been younger then, and every man was entitled to a few youthful follies. He'd been older than Durendal was now, though.

''Grand Inquisitor will explain. I assumed they were both dead, but apparently Everman is still alive, fighting as some sort of gladiator. Of course, the news is two years old, so he may be dead now. But I won't have it, you hear? I won't have one of my Blades turned into a performing bear! Go and get him back.''

''Yes, sire.'' Durendal rose to his feet, but he felt as if he were falling.

What else could a man say when the bottom dropped out of his world? It was the challenge of a lifetime. Where was Samarinda, that news took two years to arrive? Not even in Eurania. Oh, Kate! He could not refuse an order from his liege. He could protest and explain, but something as strong as the binding prevented that—pride. What a fool Kate had been to fall in love with a Blade!

The King studied him for a moment and then smiled grimly. ''Or at least find out what happened. Create another legend! I don't want to lose you, but I can't think of any other man to choose. Only you. See Grand Inquisitor in the morning. She'll assign one of her own men to accompany you. And Privy Purse will provide all the money you need. May the spirits favor your cause.''

Dismissal—so easily may a prince send a retainer to his death.

How? When? Where? Who else? Take what? All those matters were being left to his discretion. It was Ambrose's way. Mind racing, Durendal said, "One question, sire?"

"Ask Grand Inquisitor."

"Your orders, sire? Am I to bring him back whether he wants to come or not? And further . . . what about the philosophers' stone?"

The King opened his mouth and seemed to think better of what he had been about to say. "Use your own judgment. I can't make decisions at the other side of the world. That's why I picked you. It's your enterprise; do what's best. Oh, yes, before you go . . ." He stalked over to the paper-littered chair and began to rummage in a flurry of vellum and parchment.

Kate, Kate, Kate . . .

Other side of the world?

He could resign! He had a barony in his pocket, and the King had given him the right to claim it at any time. No, his binding would not let him exercise that right, as the King had known all along. And to mention Kate now would seem like cowardice and weaseling out.

"Ha!" The King had found what he wanted down on the floor. He heaved himself upright again. "I keep meaning to amend the Ironhall charter. Allowing boys of fourteen to choose their own names is utter . . . *Ahem!* Nothing personal, you understand. Nothing wrong with your name, and you have amply lived up to it. You may be *the* Durendal by the time you're finished."

"Your Majesty is gracious."

"Sometimes. When I have my foot in my mouth, I am. But what about Sir Snake, for example? Now we have Candidate Bullwhip. Young idiots! The current Prime is Candidate Wolfbiter."

Durendal had planned to be Bloodhand if they wouldn't let him be Durendal. "I believe there are precedents for all those names, sire."

"Yes, or Grand Master wouldn't have allowed them. Anyway, Grand Master says this Wolfbiter is the best thing they've produced since you. I've been saving him for something special. Now he's turned twenty-one and he's tearing the walls down.''

Hardly surprising! "I look forward to meeting him."

"Well, you will. Here." The King thrust out a parchment sheet bearing the personal signet. "He's yours."

· 5 ·

Durendal bowed and closed the door. For a moment he just stood there, staring at the oak panel in front of his nose, sick with the thought of what he had done. *Oh, Kate, Kate, Kate!* He had given the king the best six years of his life and owed him nothing more. By any sane standard he should have demanded his release then and there and carried his beloved off to whatever that estate of his was called to happily ever after. The knowledge that his binding had overruled his own desires and judgment was no consolation at all.

But what was done was done. He turned and beckoned the nearest page. He bent to whisper into a none-too-clean ear. "Go and find two Blades. I want them, the first two you see. Say please if one of them is Commander Montpurse, otherwise don't."

The lad bowed and hurried off, impressed with his sudden ability to give orders to Blades. The Chamberlain bustled away into the King's presence. Durendal sat down at his desk, ignoring all the curious and disapproving faces. He selected a blank sheet of parchment and wrote out his will, leaving everything to Kate. Most Blades would have nothing to bequeath, but he owned a manor he had never seen. He had no idea what it was worth.

Then he took another sheet.

Grand Master:

*You are hereby authorized and requested to pre-
pare Prime for binding on the night of the fifteenth
instant.*
*Done by my hand and in the King's name this
fourteenth day of Thirdmoon, in the three hundred
and fifty-seventh year of the House of Ranulf.*

Durendal, companion.

He folded the papers, held wax in the candle flame,
sealed them with his ring. He wandered over to rejoin
Scrimpnel and Parsewood, enjoying their baffled stares and
hoping his own face was not too scrutable.

"Whose throw?"

"Yours, obviously," Scrimpnel said. There were two
groups in the Guard now, and he was one of the young
ones, those who had not been in on the Nythia campaign.
Good man with a rapier, though. "May spirits of chance
favor you wherever you're bound."

"Writing out your will?" asked Parsewood, who was
newer yet, but a powerful saber fighter and clearly another
good guesser. "You won't tell us a thing, you big bastard,
will you?"

Before Durendal could frame a reply with enough
scathe, the door swung open to admit the most recent
Blade of them all, although even he had several months'
experience now—a reminder of just how long the King
had kept the respected Wolfbiter dangling. Despite His
Majesty's disapproval, Sir Snake's name was apt, he being
about as long and as slender as a Blade ever was. He
affected a thin mustache, a supercilious manner with a
nose to match, and he sat a horse like the shine of its
hide. He would do very well.

Durendal sprang up and intercepted him before he could

join the group. He passed him the letter. "Deliver this to Grand Master, no one else."

The kid raised his eyebrows. "The Moor? Tonight?"

"Yesterday. And keep your mouth shut, totally. Report to Leader when you return."

"But tonight is the—" Snake took another look at the deputy commander's face. "At once, sir."

As he went out, Chefney came in. Excellent! His luck was holding.

"Take over from me here, please, brother?"

Chefney nodded, curious but not questioning. Durendal followed Snake out, almost colliding with the returning page. Kate was no longer in the hall, but that was to be expected.

He tracked down Montpurse as he left the fencing gym. A distinctly frosty stare suggested the Commander already knew there was something afoot and he had not been informed. He still looked no more than fifteen.

"I've been detached for special duties," Durendal said. "May be gone some time. Will you hold this for me— it's my will—and see my things are put in a safe place? The cups are worth a fair bit."

The Commander's face went bleak. "Talk to Chancery. That's their job, and Blades can't always keep promises. Friend . . . I'm going to miss you."

"These things happen. He's the boss."

"Yes." Montpurse's ice-pale eyes were asking how bad it was.

"I'd like you to wear my sword breaker for me, though."

"I'll see it's kept safe." He was not going to wear it, obviously, any more than his deputy would say where he was going. "Is this good-bye?"

"I'll leave tomorrow." Durendal told him about Snake and the changes that would be needed in the duty roster. Then there was nothing more to say and nothing left to do except go and find Kate.

· 6 ·

He headed first for the White Sisters' quarters. Crossing the western courtyard, he saw her coming toward him. They both began to run, shocking several elderly sniffers and a few grandly dressed courtiers. Before they even met he watched the hope die in her eyes and wondered if his face was as readable to everyone or if women were more perceptive than men.

They embraced in an impact that should have knocked her hat flying but didn't. Eventually they broke loose and began to walk, holding hands still. Passersby coughed disapprovingly.

"It didn't work," she said. Statement, no question.

"I had no chance to ask. He called me in and gave me a posting, too."

Her eyes scanned his face for clues. "Dangerous. And long. If it were short you'd be making plans."

He would not lie to her. He never lied to women or had reason to lie to men. "And yours?"

"Just a dull guild of merchants in Brimiarde, worried in case some conjurer tries to steal their money." She shivered. "Their halls will all be stinking with conjurements. Never mind. Is it true that Blades never sleep?"

"Almost never."

She forced a smile. "Then we have the whole night ahead of us."

They talked. They made love. They did both all over again. Moonlight crept down the wall, across the bed, and up the other side, dragging inevitable morning behind it.

124

"I will wait for you," she said many times.

His heart ached. He had always believed that was only a manner of speaking, but there was a real pain in his chest.

"No, dearest, you must not. A Blade is not meant to be loved, because the King will always come first in his heart. I could have told him about you. Then he might have withdrawn his orders or delayed them. He's not a cruel man by nature. I just couldn't. Much as I adore you, I had to obey. Find a better man and forget me."

"Will you come back? Do you expect to come back?"

"I hope to come back, but not for years."

"I will wait for you, no matter how long."

Once, after a long kiss, he said, "You have told me how Blades sound and feel and seem, but how do they taste?"

"Like strong wine."

"'Tis passing strange! So do White Sisters."

"I will wait for you."

"You mustn't, but if I do come back and you are still free, then I shall sit on your doorstep till I die or you agree to marry me."

Although he had revealed nothing about his task, he did let slip a remark about inquisitors—a breach of security, perhaps, but his mind was on other matters. It was one of those times when women like to talk and men don't but will humor them in a good cause.

"Horrible people!" she said. "All time and earth and death. No love or air at all."

He was sitting up cross-legged, admiring her body in the moonlight, exploring its contours with his fingers, not really listening. "You can tell what elements were used in a conjuration?"

"Usually. You do have scars! I hadn't noticed them before. Let me see your back."

"No, I'm busy. What elements do you sense in a Blade?"

"Love, mostly." She sat up also. "I want to see your back."

"No. Lie down and submit. Love, you say? I'm a killer, and you think I was made by spirits of love?"

She kissed him in passing, climbing around and over him. "Love isn't only man and woman. It is many other things—motherhood, man and master, brother and sister, men in bands, simple friendship. Turn around; your back's in shadow. There they are. They're closer together at the back. Love can be dying for someone, even. Understand?"

"Love can be this, too!" He pulled her back into her proper place. She had already found his ticklish spots. The wrestling became heated.

"Now you see why Blades are such great lovers," she said. "Because they're bound by mmmph—"

Her lips were too precious to waste on speech.

It was dawn.

"I will wait for you."

"I will be true to you."

"Just come back safe and I will never ask if—mmmph!"

· 7 ·

"We have met before, Sir Durendal."

"So we have. I was not at my best that day."

Durendal knew the sallow face, the bloodless lips, the lank hair, because they were part of his Nutting nightmares. He would not have known the name, Ivyn Kromman.

Grand Inquisitor's gloomy office was a room oppressed

by too many papers, folders, bookshelves, tomes, and unhappy implications. Even the dust and cobwebs seemed to whisper of broken lives and buried secrets. Mother Spider herself had her back to the window, a huge and hunched blackness against the light. Durendal had been placed across the desk from her, better lit. Kromman sat at the end so that he, too, could watch the Blade's face. Making other people uneasy must be an inquisitors' instinct, like dogs' barking.

"Have you reservations about having Inquisitor Kromman as your colleague, Sir Durendal?" Grand Inquisitor's fish eyes neither blinked nor moved. Her fat white hands lay like dead things on the desk.

"I welcome his help in my mission."

"You do understand that he has been working on the case for a long time and that your experience of foreign travel is considerably less than his?"

"I have the King's word for it that I am to be the leader."

She ignored that. "How much do you know of the matter?"

"Assume I know nothing at all and begin at the beginning."

"Why do you not answer questions directly?"

Perhaps he was managing to give her a rash—he hoped so. "Why do you never blink?"

"Is that question relevant?"

"Yes. If Inquisitor Kromman stares at everybody as he likes to stare at me, then he will attract suspicion."

She smiled without making a wrinkle. "I assure you that Ivyn can evade attention most expertly and has done so many times on His Majesty's service. Does staring make you uncomfortable?"

"No. It just annoys me as a demonstration of bad manners. I have nothing to hide."

"Do you feel happy at being chosen to undertake such an exotic quest?"

"Any man would be honored to be so trusted."

She smiled again, but only with her mouth. "You see? You do have something to hide. By 'any man' you mean 'all men' and thus you are lying, because you have some reservation you do not wish to admit. A romance, perhaps? Ah!"

He reminded himself sternly that she was just guessing. She had a conjured ability to smell a spoken lie, but if he remained silent she was forced back on purely secular skills like face watching—at least that was what the Blades believed. It was also why criminals were put to the Question. Nevertheless, she had nettled him.

"Must we fence all day, or can we start shedding blood?"

"As you wish. Six years ago now, Master Polydin came to His Majesty with a wild tale of faraway lands. He told of the city called Samarinda in Altain, wherever that is, at the back of nowhere—ancient and isolated, a place of strange legends. Yet he swore that he had been there and that the strangest of these legends was true. The city is ruled by a military order, the Knights of the Golden Sword. He thought that there were twelve of these knights. They possess the secret of the philosophers' stone and so they live forever."

"Wild indeed! A sword of gold would be useless, of course, soft as wax. Unless it was enchanted, I suppose. What proof did he offer?"

"Only what he had seen. He may have been deceived, but he believed that he was telling the truth. I can testify to that—he was convinced in his own mind. He told us what he had witnessed. Each morning at dawn, the order will accept a challenge from any man of quality. One of the knights comes out to the courtyard of their castle, and the two of them fight with real swords. Almost always, the knight slays the challenger."

Durendal was both skeptical and intrigued. Of course the King would have chosen to send a Blade to investigate such a story. His first choice had been Durendal himself, the candidate reputed to be the finest fencer Ironhall had produced in memory.

Grand Inquisitor smiled, reading his interest in his face or just guessing it. "A champion who succeeds in wounding the knight—a rare event, apparently—is rewarded with as much gold as he can carry to the gate. In so poor a land, there are aspirants aplenty. Men wait months for the chance to win their fortunes with a single stroke. And some do, that is the surprising thing. The house does not win every time, so it never lacks for players. It charges no entry fee and pays out in real gold. Where does the gold come from, if not the philosophers' stone?"

It might be always the same gold, "won" by accomplices and smuggled back into the castle by night.

"You mentioned wounded? The knight is never slain?"

"Apparently not, although Master Polydin swore that he had seen one run through. A wounded knight reappears the next morning, healed and ready to fight again. They are reputed to be immortal. Old men swear that the current knights are the same ones they saw in their youth, still as young and virile as they were then."

Durendal tried to consider the problem and decided that considering the problem would be a waste of time. The King and others must have investigated thoroughly and been convinced. He wasn't, though. There would be a trick somewhere. "Our conjurers could not manage any of that."

"Exactly. His Majesty resolved to send an expedition to the city in an effort to buy or steal the secret."

"Buy? From men who own the philosophers' stone? What could you offer them in return?"

Grand Inquisitor shrugged her heavy shoulders. "Knowledge. The King authorized Master Polydin to steal the secret if he could. He provided him with many arcane conjurations to offer in trade if he could not. If both approaches failed, and if he believed there was anything to be gained, Sir Everman had royal permission to accept the challenge.''

Everman had been a daredevil. He would not have been able to resist.

''And now? The King said he has an agent in Samarinda.''

''Hardly an agent. A collaborator at best. A local merchant who had befriended Master Polydin in the past and had dealings with him. He wrote a letter, which reached us a few months ago, claiming that Sir Everman has himself joined the order, the first new member admitted in centuries. He lives in the castle. Every twelve days or so, he answers the challenge.''

Gladiator, the King had said. But when Durendal had asked if Everman was to be brought back even if he did not want to return, the King had evaded the question. An immortal swordsman, the ultimate Blade.

''Those are the bones of the matter,'' said Grand Inquisitor. ''Ivyn knows the details and can provide them to you at leisure. You will have much time together for conversation.''

Durendal glanced at that flesh-crawling inquisitor and thought of several million people he would rather have as companions on a long journey. Almost anybody except Mother Spider herself, in fact. ''I need a lesson in geography.''

''Ivyn has studied the route and spoken to merchants with connections in the east. In brief, the day after tomorrow you will sail from Brimiarde to Isilond, landing at Furret, and thence proceed overland to the Seventh Sea by whatever route seems advisable. The shortest route is across Fitain, but they have a civil war raging at the moment. Your way then takes you across or around the sea to Thyrdonia and up the Yvusarr River until you find a caravan traveling the Jade Road. A few deserts and mountain ranges later, you should arrive at Samarinda, probably on the back of a camel.''

He had been wondering if he should recruit more helpers, and the answer was obviously no. More people would merely find more opportunities for trouble. "Money?"

"His Majesty has been more than generous. Ivyn has been provided with ample funds in drafts drawn on reputable banking houses. You will have to convert most of them to gold before you enter Thyrdonia, of course."

Ah! Someone was feinting. He turned to consider Kromman's waxen features. "These drafts? Do they specify you by name?"

"Most do. Some are bearer instruments."

"The King put me in charge of this mission—am I speaking the truth?"

The well-remembered croaky voice said, "Of course, Sir Durendal."

"And are you prepared to accept my orders until we return to Chivial?"

After a barely perceptible pause, Kromman repeated, "Of course, Sir Durendal."

"I want those drafts redrawn. I do not mind your keeping some minor amounts in your name in case we become separated or I meet with misfortune, but the bulk of the funds will be under my control and I will carry them." Whoever had the money would have the power.

The inquisitor looked to Mother Spider.

"Your request is much less reasonable than you realize," she said. "Ivyn must leave in a few hours, and the clerks of Privy Purse are overworked as it is. To burden them further for a purely symbolic personal advantage seems very petty."

"I will accept no other terms. Attend to it please, Inquisitor."

Kromman nodded impassively. "As you wish, Sir Durendal."

"I must be at Ironhall tonight. I can meet you tomorrow in Brimiarde. Where?" He had never been there. He had seen the sea only once.

"The Brown Fox in Seagate is adequate, Sir Durendal. I shall take a room in the name of Chalice, posing as a successful merchant who has hired two mercenary soldiers down on their luck for service in a private militia. You and your Blade should be dressed in suitable style—patched and threadbare. Please remember that cat's-eye swords are well known in this country and keep the hilts under your cloaks. Make quite certain that you bear nothing that can be identified—no papers, letters, lockets, signets, nothing. The same goes for your horses' tack, but you may lodge the horses themselves at the inn and I will have them attended to. You are listed in the ship's log under the name of Sergeant-at-arms White, accompanied by Man-at-arms Ayrton, so you may as well use those names at the Brown Fox. The names on your passport for Isilond may be different, of course.''

Barely controlling his temper, Durendal said, "I can see why we may have to behave like criminals in Samarinda, but when did Chivial become so dangerous that a gentleman cannot use his own name?''

Kromman revealed a brief flicker of amusement, undoubtedly deliberate. "A swordsman should understand the importance of practice, Sir Durendal. His Majesty's Office of General Inquiry is not merely responsible for the internal security of the realm, it also watches the King's enemies in foreign lands. I have been smuggled in and out of other countries so often that all these habits are second nature to me. You and your Blade have much to learn if we are to survive our journey.''

"I accept the rebuke, Inquisitor. Thank you for correcting me. By the way, can you use a sword?''

"Not by your standards, Sir Durendal.''

"He is an expert by any others','' Grand Inquisitor said dryly. "He has slain several men. Did you think I would choose an incompetent?''

Two inquisitors were certainly cutting one stupid swordsman to shreds. Keeping his anger as far from his face as possible, he said, "Chalice, White, Ayrton, at the Brown Fox. Is there anything else I need worry about?''

Grand Inquisitor produced her closest approximation yet

to a genuine smile. It was an unpleasant sight. "What about languages?"

He had not given a thought to languages. "I suppose we must hire local guides." He saw at once that he had again displayed total incompetence for the task the King had set him.

She shook her head, and there was a disapproving set to her mouth now. "At His Majesty's insistence, we have arranged for you to receive a spiritual enhancement known as the gift of tongues. With that you will be able to pick up any foreign language within hours. After a day's exposure you will speak it like a native."

He had never heard of that conjuration—an intriguing insight into the Dark Chamber. "Inquisitor Kromman is already so enchanted, I presume? A specialty of your office, ma'am?"

"We employ it," she admitted. "The conjuration itself belongs to the Silk Merchants' Guild. They charge a fortune for its use, I may add."

Had the guild's sudden new wealth enabled it to hire the services of some sniffers, including Sister Kate? She would be in Brimiarde when he arrived there. The Everman Affair spread its tentacles ever wider.

Kromman said, "Tomorrow night, in Brimiarde."

"And my Blade will be enchanted as well, of course."

Grand Inquisitor pursed her lips. "I am afraid not. The budget will not run to two fortunes, Sir Durendal."

Here was a place to stand and fight. "I am afraid I must insist. Tomorrow night he will be freshly bound. It will be virtually impossible for him to leave my side. More important, the gift of tongues will make him much more useful." He tried to look as if he were prepared to take his case to the King. He knew his pride would not let him go running for help, yet he was certain that the King would agree with him if he did.

Perhaps that certainty was what Mother Spider smelled, for she scowled and said, "Very well. Anything else?"

Kromman and Durendal glanced at each other and shook their heads simultaneously.

"Until tomorrow then, Master Chalice." Durendal rose and bowed. "A most interesting meeting, ma'am. My thanks for all your help."

She acknowledged the courtesy with a queenly nod. "I suggest you visit some convenient elementary and spend a little of the King's money on a good-fortune conjuration. You will need it."

♦ 8 ♦

He rode up to the royal door at Ironhall with his hat pulled down to hide his face, for it would be unfair to reveal the identity of Prime's ward until Prime himself was told. The last few miles he had ridden by the light of the full moon, chivied by a bitter moorland wind. He had cut it fine, for the ritual must begin at midnight and with a man's life at stake he would not dare dispense completely with meditation, as the King sometimes did. His day-long fast had left him shaky and depressed.

The door opened before he had even dismounted. Wallop had been a servant there since long before his time, perhaps since before he was born. If Wallop recognized the cloaked visitor, he did not say so. He mumbled, "You are expected, my lord," and led the horse away.

Durendal went in and began to climb a dark and narrow spiral stair. This was his third visit to Ironhall, and might well be his last, but he could see that no Blade could ever wholly escape its clutches. Would Harvest ever hang in the hall, or would she rust away in some distant jungle?

The door at the top opened into Grand Master's private

study, with lamplight and a crackling fire, comfortable chairs and shelves of books, and heavy drapes drawn over the casements to keep out the drafts. Grand Master was standing in front of the hearth, toasting himself. Old Sir Silver had died in the winter, honored and sincerely mourned. His replacement was Sir Vicious, who had been Master of Rituals in Durendal's day and was one of the best. He had grown a little shorter and somewhat wider, but his hair was still a field of seeding dandelions and his cheerful face glowed red from the fire.

"You?" The astonishment was almost comical. "I expected the King. My! How very . . . unexpected."

Tossing his cloak over a chair, Durendal headed for that seductive hearth. "I thought you would guess. That's all right, isn't it—one Blade binding another?"

"It's been done. Not in this century, I suspect. No, I never dreamed. Can you tell me why?"

" 'Fraid not." He squatted beside the knight's knees to warm his hands. The respect with which the old man was treating him was a little unnerving, for his memories of Ironhall were memories of his boyhood. He had not realized how the years had flown.

"Well! We must break the good news to Prime right away!" Grand Master seemed almost as excited as if he were about to be bound again himself. Without waiting for consent, he went to the door and spoke to someone outside. In a moment he came back to the hearth. "I'd offer you wine if you weren't fasting."

"I understand. Tell me about Wolfbiter."

"Oh, the best. Absolutely first class. Not quite Durendal, but he'll be giving you a run for the King's Cup in another couple of years." Grand Master chuckled. "It's time somebody else got a chance at it anyway."

"Tell me about the man, though."

"Solid steel. Mind you, the last six months have been hard on him—can't recall any Prime having to wait that long. Make allowances for that."

Blast fat Ambrose for being so unthinking! Durendal

rose and leaned an elbow on the mantel. Watching for a reaction, he said, "Is the boy going to be resentful that he's not being bound to the King?"

"Resentful? Resentful?" Grand Master chortled. "Well, no, I don't think I expect resentment. You realize that this is your night you've picked?"

"My night?"

"We have a hard time explaining that Durendal Night isn't named after you. No, I don't think Wolfbiter will be resentful. Delirious, perhaps. Hysterical joy is a possibility, I suppose. Being torn limb from limb by all the other—"

Horror! "You're joking!"

"Not much. You are the Blade of Blades to them. Win the cup every year, saved the King's life, bound twice, deputy commander of the Guard, the Aldane bout—they think the sun won't rise if you don't pee in the morning. We postponed the Durendal Night dinner until after the binding. That thunder you can hear is all those young bellies growling." Grand Master rubbed his hands. "And now we discover that the guest of honor will be the second Durendal himself with his new Blade at his side! No, I don't think Prime will have any complaints."

Death and fire! How could a man live up to such expectations? He was not worthy of absolute loyalty. He had been feeling unhappy about becoming a ward ever since the King ordered it; this news made him feel much worse. He was going to lead his Blade on a useless trek halfway around the world, with very few prospects for a safe return.

"Bring your cloak," Grand Master said, producing one of his own. "We'll await them in the flea room."

Durendal followed, stooping along a low-roofed corridor and down a short flight of stairs. This was the oldest part of the keep, an ants' nest of passages. It smelled of rot. "Why do you play these tricks?"

Grand Master stepped aside for him to enter the little room he remembered so well, where he had caught coins, where he had first met the Marquis. Candles already flickered on the table and mantel, but the air was icy and unused.

"Dunno. Because it's always been done, I suppose. Because the tricks were played on us, so we play them on others. You sit there. Maybe it is childish," he conceded.

He settled in one chair, Durendal in the other, where he would not be readily visible. Yes, Grand Master's glee as he prepared to spring the great surprise was juvenile. What happened to a Blade when he retired to these forsaken moors to forge more Blades? From the shimmer and glitter of court to—what? Bleak nothing and a house full of children. Were the knights and masters perhaps all a little crazy? It was not a welcome thought, but it might be one to ponder when he succeeded Montpurse as . . . but he was going to Samarinda, wasn't he? He would never succeed Montpurse.

"You had a fire last summer, I heard."

The older man nodded. "Lightning. Happens every hundred years or so. It was one of those freak late storms, middle of the night. We were lucky all the boys got out safely. That was only thanks to—"

Knuckles rapped on ancient boards.

Grand Master winked. "Enter."

How many times had this scene been played out? Five thousand swords in the hall . . . For a moment the door blocked Durendal's view. When it closed, two boys stood at attention between him and the other chair.

"You sent for us, Grand Master?"

Wolfbiter was unusually short for a Blade, and slight of build—a rapier man. From that angle he certainly did not look twenty-one. His hair was black. Second was very different, fair, big-boned, and meaty. They represented the two end limits of the Blade type.

"I did, Prime. His Majesty has need of a Blade. Are you ready to serve?"

"More than ready, Grand Master."

No hesitation there!

Grand Master smirked and gestured. "Then pray greet your assigned ward."

Wolfbiter spun around and completed the turn without stopping, a complete circle until he was looking at Grand Master again, and snapped, "Is this some kind of a joke?"

Second was staring at the visitor with his mouth hanging open. It was less than four years since Durendal's second binding. These lads would have been juniors then, so they knew his face, but Wolfbiter's reaction had been incredibly fast—so fast that it could not have been faked, even. If he had been forewarned he would have faked better than that.

Grand Master spluttered, totally taken aback. "Joke? What do you mean by insulting—"

"To bind a Blade to Sir Durendal would be setting a lamb to guard a wolf! I do not understand." The bantam cock was furious! Was this the resentment Durendal had feared?

It was time for him to intervene. He rose. "No joke. Grand Master does not describe you as a lamb, nor even a ram. But my own first experience with binding had terrible consequences for me, and I have no wish to put you to the same ordeal. If you would prefer to wait for another ward, Prime, then this episode can be quietly forgotten, as if it never happened."

The kid had blushed scarlet. "No, no, no! I meant no disrespect, Sir Durendal! Quite the reverse. To be bound to you is an unbelievable honor, that's all—one I could not have dreamed of." He bowed with a fencer's grace.

Durendal offered a hand. "The honor and the burden are mine. I shall strive to be worthy of the loyalty you pledge."

Wolfbiter's grip was powerful. His dark eyes gleamed bright and clear in the candlelight, and undoubtedly those quick wits were now trying to calculate why a Blade should need a Blade. His gaze kept darting toward Durendal's right hip. Either he wanted to see the famous sword breaker, or he had glimpsed its absence under the cloak but could not be sure.

Yes, this one would do.

Then . . . "By fire! You were the Brat! You gave me my sword!"

Intense satisfaction flashed back at him. "Yes, sir. And you came and thanked me afterward. You can't imagine what that meant to me!"

"Yes, I can." Montpurse and himself. Déjà vu!

"Second?"

"Candidate Bullwhip, Sir Durendal," Grand Master said.

"My pleasure. I have heard much good of you also."

It was Bullwhip's turn to blush, but he also stammered incoherently. His grip was positively crushing—a broadsword man. Wolfbiter would be the better man for the job.

Grand Master rose. "I expect you will all wish to start the preliminary stages of the ritual as soon as possible so we can start on the banquet."

Wolfbiter looked inquiringly at Durendal, who said, "The sopranos won't starve if we keep them waiting a few more minutes. If we may stop by the gym, I'd be interested in trying a couple of passes with Prime."

"In this light?" Grand Master protested.

"If the candidate has no objections."

"None at all, sir. My honor." Dark eyes gleamed in triumph. "We shall be leaving before dawn, then, sir?"

Quick!

Word must have flashed through Ironhall like a bolt of lightning. By the time the contestants had removed their doublets—retaining their shirts against the cold—the entire school had assembled around the walls of the gym, most of them holding candles or lanterns. Durendal could hear his own name being whispered everywhere. He stipulated rapiers to let his future Blade show his best weapon. The lighting was certainly tricky, as all the myriad flames danced on the foils like a mist of stars.

Wolfbiter was sunlight on water. He flashed from position to position, making even tricky transitions gracefully:

Swan, Violet, Steeple. . . . He was aggressive as a bee
swarm but never predictable. The foils clashed and clattered, feet tapped like a patter of raindrops. Durendal let
him lead, holding him off but finding himself stretched
almost to his limits. Deciding not to let the lad get too
cocky, he switched to attack, seeking a touch. But Wolfbiter was never there. Incredible speed! Ah!

"A touch, sir!" He was ready to go again, barely
even puffing.

Durendal saluted and tossed his foil to a waiting junior.
"No. I daren't risk my reputation. I know only three men
other than myself who might beat you, Candidate, and I'm
not sure of any of them. I do not flatter."

He felt ill. Who was he to own this superb young man
body and soul for the rest of his life?

· 9 ·

By the time the familiar ritual rose to its climax, Durendal had lost most of his doubts. Perhaps the singing was
spinning its old seductive spell around him again, the love
of men in bands that Kate had mentioned. He could ratio-
nalize that Wolfbiter had chosen this life, just as he had.
If a man must serve his King indirectly, that was still
service. Of course it was a shame that his first duty was
to risk his skin in a distant land to no real purpose, but
the King must be the judge of such matters. Kings' whims
were not as other men's. There might be more to the
foolish tale than Grand Inquisitor knew or had admitted.

It was strange to watch the candidate jump up on the
anvil and address him in the words of the oath. It was
even stranger to stare at that ominous smudge of charcoal

below the dark fuzz on his chest and take up a sword to try and kill him. The sword was a surprise, too. It had a slight back curve and its point of balance was far forward, so Wolfbiter was a slasher, not a point man after all. If he was so good with rapiers, how must he be with his preferred sabers?

Now he must find the lad's heart. Wolfbiter was seated on the anvil, pale but determined as he stared up at death, but exactly as Kate had described a Blade—strong, intense, a dagger in a box. Bullwhip and another stood ready to grasp his arms, but suddenly Durendal guessed what was going to happen. Hero worship . . .

Prime slapped his hands down on his thighs, lifted his chin defiantly, and said, "Do it now!"—the Durendal way.

"Serve or die!" In, three feet of steel through the chest, back out again. Done! Durendal saw the contortion of agony, the instant relief. Surprise, pride . . . All so familiar! Almost no blood at all.

Wolfbiter did not smile even when the waves of cheering boomed back from the roof and his friends poured around to congratulate him. He just stood there, acknowledging the acclaim with quiet dignity, as if to say that it was no more than his due. He was obviously popular, which was a good sign in Ironhall, and his assignment to Durendal was being hailed as incredible good fortune.

Durendal knelt to give him back his sword, for that seemed a fitting tribute to courage and years of effort. The King could not do it that way, but another Blade should. With more heartrending déjà vu he watched the boy inspect the bloodstains and then hang the sword on his belt.

Wait for it!

Wolfbiter was distracted by more knights coming to compliment him. Suddenly he turned from them impatiently and glanced around, seeking his ward. When he located Durendal, his eyes widened in shock. That was it, the moment of realization, the moment when the ward became the sun and the moon, the light of the world.

Remembering the King's words to him four years ago, Durendal said, "Ready to ride, Sir Wolfbiter?"

"Yes, sir."

"I think we can eat first."

"As you wish, Sir Durendal."

Did the kid never smile?

During the raucous festivities that followed, he was shocked to discover that the Litany of Heroes now included his own exploit at Waterby. The roar that followed seemed to make the sky of swords shimmer and glitter more brightly and would not stop until he rose and took a bow. Very few Blades lived to hear their own names in the Litany.

Somewhat later he found himself on his feet giving the Durendal Night speech and mouthing all the platitudes he had suffered through five times during his own youth—honor, duty, service. Yet the hundred young faces out there did not seem to recognize banality when they heard it. Perhaps it helped to have a real hero spreading the fertilizer, or perhaps fertilizer was more welcome when one was still growing. No soprano went to sleep, no senior yawned, and Grand Master swore that was this an unprecedented compliment.

Prime Candidate Bullwhip conducted the real hero around the hall, introducing him to everyone, even the servants, even the Brat. His Blade followed two steps behind. When Sir Durendal went to the privy, Sir Wolfbiter was immediately overcome with the same need.

Dawn found the two of them miles away, riding into the rising sun. Of course Wolfbiter was as impressive with a horse as he was with a rapier—if he had any failings at all, they would have been mentioned. Even his manner was appropriate; he knew he was good, but he would let the world find that out for itself. Everyone wanted to compare him to Durendal. Had he been like this: bright, sharp, untested, dangerous? He suspected he had been a lot more cocky. He had been younger, of course.

"Ready to hear the story?"

"Yes, sir." Not a smile, though, only that intense dark stare. Why had he not died of curiosity before now?

"First, though . . . I couldn't tell you this earlier, but Grand Master submits detailed reports on all the seniors. The reason you stayed Prime all those long months is that you are so fiery good! The King has been saving you for something special."

Wolfbiter nodded as if he worked that out, but he did not comment.

"This is the special something. Remember Everman, just behind me?"

That won a faint frown. "Yes, sir."

"Did you give him his sword, too?"

"No, sir."

"He and his ward were sent on a dangerous mission to a mythical city halfway around the world, in Altain. They never returned and were assumed dead, but word arrived a few months ago that Everman at least is still alive, probably enslaved. Two days ago, the King ordered me to go and get him back. He gave me a Blade because I'm going to need one. We sail with tomorrow's tide."

The hooves drummed on the dewy trail. The riders squinted into the rising sun. Wolfbiter seemed to be thinking. He certainly did not volunteer any remarks.

"The journey there will take us at least two years, by ship, by horse, and eventually by camel. We shall cross seas and deserts and mountains. We must evade brigands and wild beasts, storms and disease, pirates and hostile tribesmen."

Still no reply.

"Well?" Durendal said, exasperated. The hawk was loosed from the hand at last; he had been assigned to aid the hero of his dreams on a fairy-tale mission to the ends of the earth. Was he pleased or scared? Couldn't he say anything at all?

His Blade's swift glance seemed to appraise him: What does he want of me? What am I doing wrong? "Sir?"

"Sonny, not one Blade in ten ever draws his sword in anger from the night he is bound till the day he is knighted and released—his whole career is one big sham. He struts and postures and does nothing of any interest except prod girls. You are going to be fighting for my life and yours about once a week for the next five years. Your chances of ever coming back alive are worse than slim. How does that future look to you?"

"Oh." Wolfbiter did not exactly smile then, but he came close. "Very satisfactory indeed, sir."

WOLFBITER

IV

1

Eight hundred days later, they rode into Samarinda, mounted on the shaggy, tough ponies of Altain, which had no great speed or beauty but could amble on forever. The Blades were posing successfully as free swords, two of the dozen nondescript guards hired to guard Sheik Akrazzanka's caravan of linen, ivory, and dyestuffs. Ironically, despite all Kromman's skilled efforts at masquerading as an itinerant scholar, the wily traders were quite convinced he was a spy, just on principle. They did not care, since most of them were spying for someone or other.

The sheer size of Altain made men feel like fleas. Ice-clad peaks lined the horizon—clear at dawn, fading under the sun, and yet revealed the next morning unchanged, as if a whole day's ride had achieved nothing. Compared to those giants, the nearby gray-brown hills seemed insignificant, but hours of riding were needed just to descend a slope or climb out of a valley. Water holes were scattered and precious, trees nonexistent, villages even rarer. From time to time Durendal would catch a glimpse of watchers in the distance but never of tents; rare tracks and droppings were the only sign of herds. In this parched emptiness, life was a constant struggle against wind and dust, the gentle, misty landscape of Chival an incredible dream. A man might vie all day with a sadistic sun searing his eyes and flesh, and at night be fending off bitter frost under crystal stars.

A line of laden camels wound up the long hillside ahead, but one lone rider came cantering back, shouting to every trader, driver, and guard he passed, "Samarinda in sight!'' Most laughed or cheered. When he reached the end of the column, he wheeled around to retrace his path; he drew alongside Durendal. He smiled, teeth very white against his deep-tanned face—Sir Wolfbiter, of course.

What would the court of Chivial think of the two of them now? Under conical, comical felt hats, their faces were as brown as dried dates. They wore the baggy trousers and shapeless smocks of the country, colored a muddy shade, and they reeked of man and horse and camel. Hair and beards blew wild in the ceaseless wind. Only the cat's-eye swords at their sides marked them for what they were—or what they had once been and might hope to be again.

''We'll make it before sundown?''

Wolfbiter nodded firmly. ''Journey's end! Praise to the spirits!''

Amused by this rare display of enthusiasm, Durendal said, ''It has been an interesting trip, has it not?''

His Blade glanced appraisingly at him. ''Moderately, sir. You promised me seas and deserts and mountains— no complaints there. Brigands, yes. Wild beasts, I think you mentioned. Not too many of those. Or pirates. But hostile tribesmen . . . yes, you delivered those.'' He did not mention the snakes, scorpions, fevers, shipwreck, avalanche, forest fire, and dysentery.

''You delivered me. I'd be rotting in an unmarked grave in Thyrdonia if you had not been with me. Or feeding fish.''

The Blade's faint smile indicated satisfaction. At least twice he had saved the life of his friend and ward with a flashing thrust—and that put him one ahead of Durendal. ''But the same goes for me, too. And we still have to find our way home again.''

''Enjoy it. The rest of our lives will seem dull after this.''

''I am enjoying it, every minute.'' He stared at the skyline, where the horses showed as dark dots. ''I'm considering killing Kromman.''

"You don't say? Why?"

"He makes my binding itch."

He was probably joking—it was never easy to tell. Wolfbiter was a peerless companion, as tough and reliable as a cat's-eye sword, uncomplaining, resourceful, and usually a voice of prudence to restrain Durendal's wilder impulses. Though he was four years younger, his blood was colder. He would kill the inquisitor without a scruple if he thought he had reason to.

"We'd never have made it here without him," Durendal said hopefully. "He will probably be as useful on our way home. Murder needs evidence, Wolf." Not necessarily, because some Blades could detect danger to their wards by pure instinct.

"He told me that they did a reading on you once, and it foretold that you were a danger to the King."

Durendal laughed with a confidence he did not quite feel. "I know that, and the King knows it. It doesn't worry him, so why should it worry you? Readings are about as reliable as old wives' weather lore."

"And I know that. What matters is whether Kromman believes it. If he does, then he's a danger to you, out here in nowhere. He may not want you ever to get home."

"I honestly think he's more of an asset than a threat, Wolf."

The Blade glanced thoughtfully at his ward. "But how much of an asset? One reason I don't trust him is because he doesn't trust us. He has brought along conjurements he hasn't told us about. I'd like to know why Inquisitor Kromman's blanket looks like mine and feels like mine and yet weighs three times as much."

Durendal had not known that, and Wolfbiter's satisfaction was irritating.

"I suppose he's just naturally secretive."

"Then why did he tell me about the reading? Why is he so unfriendly all the time?"

"Because he was taught sneering at inquisitors' school. I think he's never forgiven me for escaping his clutches once, that's all. I know he's a human slug, but sarcasm isn't a capital offense. He does have many good qualities.''

"Name one."

"Resourcefulness. And he's loyal to the King—you just admitted that yourself. Come on, friend, you can't kill a man just because you don't like him!''

After a moment Wolfbiter said, "You are an old sourpuss!''

When they crested the rise and looked down the long slope to Samarinda in the distance, it seemed disappointingly similar to other places they had visited in this last stage of their trek. Like Alzan or Koburtin, the city itself was only a slightly rougher patch of the same drab brown as the overwhelming landscape, with a striking lack of shining towers or domes of jade, but the flat valley bottom beyond it displayed the lush green of cultivation. Water made crops, crops made food, food must be stored, stores required defenses. In another hour or so, Durendal discerned walls and a central building higher than anything else: palace, castle, or monastery?

Somewhere between Altain and the court in Chivial, the legend had become distorted. The military order that Grand Inquisitor had described was known here as the Brethren of the Gold Sword. She had spoken of knights in a castle, which in the local tongue became monks in a monastery. Durendal had concluded that the distinction was of little significance; the building would be fortified and the men would rule by force or reputation, as required. Otherwise, the tale seemed to be standing up. He had expected it to retreat as he approached, like a rainbow, but it had grown stronger all along the Jade Road. Yes, agreed the traders, there was much gold in Samarinda. They had chuckled at his questions. A swordsman asking about Samarinda could have only one thing in mind, wealth. What he would find would be death.

"You are a fool to dream so," old Akrazzanka wheezed

in the talks around the campfires. "Many strong young men have I guided to Samarinda on that quest. Only two have I brought out again, either to east or to west."

"But some win?" Durendal had asked. "Some succeed?"

"A few. Not that they manage to keep their gold for long, you understand—any man foolish enough to enter that contest will succumb to the first woman or rogue he meets—but yes, a few live and depart with much fine gold. I have touched it."

All the rest of the legend might be faked, but real gold leaving the city was inexplicable. No one knew of mines or miners in the district, and everyone agreed that Samarinda gold was the purest gold in all the world, yellow butter-metal so soft you could score it with your fingernails, let alone your teeth. Taking gold to Samarinda was a byword for futility. If the answer was not the philosophers' stone, what was it?

Journey's end. The two guards would leave the caravan here, as would the spy who pretended to be a scholar. At Kromman's insistence, they had concealed their relationship. If they did not die in Samarinda, they could catch an eastbound caravan in a few days or a month or two, or when the spirits willed.

Not an end, then, a halfway point. Say a week in Samarinda to solve the Everman mystery, or a month for a return caravan, and then two more years home. Two more years until he saw Kate again.

Or the King.

Kate and the King, the King and Kate. He was still bound—many nights he woke up sweating, wondering if his ward was safe.

The true defense of Samarinda must be the monks' skills in conjuration, for the city walls stood only three spans high, which was modest for a place with a reputation for wealth. Few rooftops within the walls overtopped them except the castle, or monastery, itself, which brooded above everything like a hen within her chicks; yet Durendal had seen many fortresses in Chivial more impressive. Four stubby towers rose at the corners of the main keep, each built of the same brown stone and capped with a low-pitched roof of green copper. No faces peered from the tiny windows, no pennants flew—no, nor even birds. It was strange not to see at least crows or pigeons around an inhabited castle.

When the sun turned pink in the dust of the horizon, he slid with relief from his pony's back outside the city gate, amid an untidy clutter of shanties and paddocks— businesses not worth the high rents within the walls, constructions that could be sacrificed if enemies attacked. He handed the reins to one of the Sheik's drivers and bade him farewell; then he hefted his bundle on his shoulder and headed for Wolfbiter, who was doing much the same.

He made a conscious effort to speak in his mother tongue. "Now we can be about the King's business!"

"After we have collected our pay, you mean." Wolfbiter's eyes glinted as they did when he was playing nursemaid. "Sir!"

"You're right, I suppose. Where is the old scoundrel?"

They still carried great wealth strapped around their waists and had no need of money, but it would be imprudent to begin their activities in Samarinda by showing that they were not what they said they were. Wolfbiter was probably anxious not to give Kromman a chance to criticize—the inquisitor insisted that a careful agent never broke out of his role.

Finding the Sheik and extracting their due was a slow process. Akrazzanka was busy making arrangements for his livestock, workers, and trade goods. When he had a moment to spare for two wandering swordsmen, his memory of their agreement naturally did not coincide with theirs, so everything had to be haggled out all over again.

Thirsty, hungry, and almost weary enough to think of himself as tired, Durendal strode at last toward the gate with his bundle on his shoulder and Wolfbiter at his heels. He need never fear a knife in the back while he had his

Blade with him. As soon as they left the anonymity of the caravan, they were identified as visiting swordsmen and surrounded by a yabbering mob of men, children, and even a few women.

"The finest house in all Samarinda . . ."

"My wife's cooking . . ."

"My beautiful sister . . ."

The voices were hoarse and harsh, for every city in Altain had its own dialect; but by tomorrow they would seem as intelligible as the Chivians at court. He pushed on through the jabber, the waving hands. In a few minutes he spotted Kromman and headed toward him. Kromman turned to go into the city, following a bent old man; and the Blades in turn trailed after him at a distance. Eventually the pimps and hawkers gave up and scuttled off to find more willing prey.

Poky alleys wound between walls still giving off the day's breathless heat, although dusk was almost over. In Altain night fell faster than a headsman's ax. The overpowering smells of cooking, animals, people, and ordure seemed very close to visible. Strains of music drifted from barred windows, children wailed, mules and cattle bellowed in the distance. Old, old, old! Stairs and doorsteps were hollowed by generations of feet, cobbles were rutted, even the corners of the houses seemed rounded off; mortar had crumbled and fallen out. Alzan was old and Koburtin even older, but Samarinda was more ancient than anywhere. Along the Jade Road it was a truth ordained that when the gods built the world they began at Samarinda and worked out from there. If each of the eight elements must have a source, then Samarinda was the fount of time.

The people were olive skinned and broad faced, hiding their eyelids when they were not in use. Some of the women went veiled, not all. Most men had mustaches but either shaved their cheeks and chins or else grew very little hair on them. Yet here and there were other types, a blond man and one with near-black skin. . . . They bore swords. They must be visitors come to seek their fortunes.

Feeling a thrill of excitement, Durendal caught up with Kromman and fell into step. They had hardly spoken since leaving Koburtin. Wolfbiter remained at his post, one pace behind his ward.

The inquisitor wore the same filthy, shapeless clothes as the Blades, and even his fish-belly face had turned brown on the trek. His beard was straggly and already streaked with gray. "Congratulations!" he said in supercilious Chivian. "You made it all the way to Samarinda."

"I should not have done so without your help, of course. Do you think I am unaware of that?"

"Even you could not be so obtuse."

"Who is your friend? What is he peddling—his daughters or worse?"

"His name is Cabuk. He offers accommodation for visiting swordsmen, just like them all, but when he said his place was the best, he was lying less than any of the others were." Inquisitors were undeniably useful companions. It was a shame they could not be more pleasant people.

Murder would be going a little far, though.

The ragged old man had reached their destination, a set of staggered stone slabs protruding from a wall to form a narrow and precarious stair, well worn by use. He scampered nimbly up to a massive iron-studded door set about head height above the street; he unlocked it and disappeared inside. Wolfbiter went first—it would have taken an army to stop him. Durendal and the inquisitor followed.

The single room was furnished with a few dubious rolls of bedding, a handful of stone crocks in one corner, and a knee-high, rickety table. It was loud with flies and hot as a sweat house, although the two grilled windows were unglazed and there was an open trap-door in the awkwardly low ceiling. Immeasurable time had stripped all but a few traces of the original plaster from the walls and reduced the floorboards to a creaking mesh of gaps and splinters. Twilight showed through the roof in places, giving just enough light to see little Cabuk standing in the middle of this ruin, beaming at his visitors as if he expected them to go into raptures over such luxury.

It was much better than most of the places in which Durendal had lived during the past two years. The long journey had been less arduous than the months spent waiting for ships or caravans.

"Noble lords!" Cabuk declared. "Behold the finest lodging in all Samarinda! No one disputes that it is the most fortunate for all swordsmen; for many, many who slept here have won vast wealth in the arena." This was clearly a well-rehearsed speech. "I have it most expertly enchanted every month without fail for that purpose. Here, while you wait your turns, you have privacy and security. Here you will not be molested by rats and other vermin, as you will be in all other establishments without exception. Here is cool by day and warm at night, see? My wives are the most excellent cooks in the city and my daughters will attend most expertly to the personal needs that strong young men like yourselves must have. Their beauty is famed throughout Altain and they are absolutely free of lice or disease or defects—practically virgins and yet very skilled. I also have two charming young sons, if you seek variety, no more than this high, see? Anything whatsoever that we can do to make your stay in Samarinda more pleasurable, you have only to ask. And for this, a mere two dizorks a night, although my wives rail shrilly at me for my insane generosity."

In cash, of course. Swordsmen would be poor credit risks in Samarinda.

Directly underfoot, two of the wives or near virgins began screaming at each other. Wolfbiter dropped his bundle and went to climb the ladder, which creaked even louder than the floor did.

"He's lying through his beard about the daughters," Kromman said in Chivian. "The rest is probably not far off the truth. Apart from the money, naturally. You want one boy or both, Sir Durendal?"

That was a typically Krommanian sneer. Fidelity was a difficult concept for him to appreciate. He could not understand Durendal's celibacy, and even Wolfbiter thought it odd.

"You are the expert, Ivyn," Durendal said wearily. "Negotiate realistically, but don't make a career out of it, please. No boys for me."

Kromman said, "One obit per night, including all the food we can eat and fresh water whenever we need it."

Cabuk screamed as if impaled. "One obit? I have never accepted less than a dizork and a half, and that was in midwinter."

"I bet you've taken four obits and been glad of them."

"Never! But since there are only three of you and you seem honest and well-behaved persons, I will make an exception and take one and a half dizorks."

"Four obits," Kromman said with a satisfied tone. "Here, take it and begone."

"Wait!" Durendal cut off the next flood of protest from the landlord. "I have a whole dizork here for information—in addition to the rent, just this once. We want food and beer, but no daughters."

The old man hesitated and then nodded grudgingly. "But tomorrow we must reach a more reasonable arrangement."

Durendal dropped his bundle near the wall and sat down, leaning back against the wall. Kromman folded down where he was standing.

"Aha!" the old man said. "You want me to tell you how you go about winning all the gold you can carry. You could not have asked a better expert. But first . . ." He dropped to his knees and put his mouth to a gap in the boards. "Food!" he screamed. "At once, food! A feast for six mighty warriors! Do not bring shame upon my house by scrimping, you bitches! They are huge men and starving. And send up beer at once for these nobles. Enough for all six to drink themselves into a stupor, or I shall whip you to death's door." He sat back and crossed his legs. "Now, my lords, I shall tell you the truth of the wonders of Samarinda."

2

Wolfbiter came squeaking down the ladder and nodded to say that there were no problems on the roof—security being his responsibility, of course. They would probably sleep up there. He settled himself cross-legged, close to the door.

Cabuk rubbed his spidery hands, producing a rasping sound. "Around dawn, noble lord, you go to the courtyard of the monastery and give your name to the monkeys on the gate. There is a long waiting list, you understand." He rubbed his hands again gleefully at that thought. "About an hour after sunrise, they start calling out names. If yesterday's challenger won, then he is called again— given a chance to double his fortune, see? Else the next name in line is called. If that man does not answer, then the monkeys call the next, see? No man is ever given a second chance if he misses his first."

That was the first new information. Durendal had heard the rest many times already, even the peculiar stories of monkeys. The traders insisted that the Monastery of the Golden Sword was guarded by man-size talking monkeys.

"Wait. These monkeys? Do they write down the names?"

Cabuk cackled, sounding startled. "Monkeys cannot *write,* my lord!"

"I never heard of any that could talk, either. How long is the waiting list?"

"Usually a couple of weeks, my lord."

"I heard a couple of months."

157

"It is very rarely that long. I have not checked recently."

Kromman scratched his knee. It was understood that the inquisitor moved his left hand when he smelled a lie.

"So the monkeys remember every name in the correct order? For months?"

"These are no ordinary monkeys, my lord. They will remember a man's face for years. Where was I?" Cabuk's speech was obviously given by rote. Having been interrupted, he might have to begin at the beginning again.

"The monkey just called out my name."

"Um, yes. When a man responds, then he comes forward to challenge. The monkeys make sure that he is armed only with a sword, and he must strip to the waist to show that he is not wearing armor. He beats on the gong. The door opens and one of the brothers comes out with the golden sword and they fight. If the challenger wounds the brother, then he is taken inside and comes out carrying all the gold he can move. Anything he drops before he reaches the gate must remain. If he falls over, then he loses it all, but that is a fair penalty for greed, yes? It is very simple. I have seen it done many times."

"What happens if the brother kills him?"

The old man shrugged his tiny shoulders. "He dies, of course. But you seem a most noble and virile swordsman, my lord, and your companions also." He glanced uncertainly at Kromman who did not, although in fact he was an outstanding amateur. "I am sure you will prosper, especially if you are living under this roof of great good fortune."

The door creaked open. A woman waddled in, carrying a leather bucket with both hands and holding three drinking horns tucked under her arms, bringing an unmistakable stench of beer. The foul Altain brew was made from goats' milk and probably other things even worse, but the traders insisted it kept away the flux. It did seem to settle the stomach.

"My eldest," Cabuk said. "Is she not ample? In all

Altain there are no more generous breasts. Drop your gown, child, and display your charms to these noble lords.''

''That will not be necessary,'' Durendal said sharply. ''Leave the beer, wench. We will serve ourselves.'' He waited until she had gone. ''How else can one approach the brethren?''

''Er . . . I do not understand, my lord.''

''If I just wanted to speak with them, or one of them—can I go to the door at some other time of day without issuing a challenge?''

''But why?'' Cabuk sounded so puzzled that perhaps none of his customers had ever asked him such a question before. ''What other business could you have with them?''

''Suppose I just wanted to ask them a question.''

''I never heard of that being done, my lord. No one ever goes in or out of the monastery except as I have told you.''

Kromman's fingers did not move.

Durendal persisted. ''Who delivers their food?''

''I—I do not know, my lord!''

''How often does the challenger win? Once a month?''

''Oh, more often than that.''

Kromman rubbed his chin.

''And are these brothers truly immortal, as the legends say?''

''Indeed they must be, your honor,'' the old man said unwillingly. ''I have seen them all my life. When I was but a child, my father would sit me on the wall to watch the duels, and they were the same men then as they are now. I know them all—Herat, Sahrif, Yarkan, Tabriz, and all the others. They are no older now than they were then.''

Kromman's fingers were still.

''Thank you. The food soon.'' Durendal flipped a coin, which Cabuk snatched out of the dark with surprising agility—take him back to Ironhall, maybe?

As the door closed behind him, the inquisitor spoke in Chivian, "Mostly true."

"But not once a month?"

"No. What did the caravan guards say?"

"About once a year. Or less."

Wolfbiter snorted with disgust. "They must be fiery good fighters! And the challengers are earth stupid! Three or four hundred to one? Those odds are not worth it."

"Not to Sir Wolfbiter," Durendal said. "But if you were a strong young peasant with absolutely nothing—no herds, no lands, and could see no other way of winning a wife—they might seem reasonable."

His cautious Blade obviously disagreed. He would be a lot less likely ever to accept such a gamble than his impetuous ward would.

Kromman rose and creaked across to inspect the crocks in the corner. "Do you suppose the odds are adjusted to draw the required number of challengers?"

Durendal had not thought of that. "You mean the brothers deliberately lose once a year? Flames!" They might be even-better-than-fiery good.

"You did not ask about Sir Everman." Wolfbiter made the statement a question.

"I wanted to see if our flea-bitten friend would mention him on his own. Now I want to know why he didn't. Besides, we have the rest of our lives ahead of us. We'll take this mystery one step at a time."

"I may make a competent agent out of you yet," Kromman remarked in his unpleasant hoarse rasp.

Observing a dangerous glint in his Blade's eye, Durendal said hastily, "After we've eaten, if we don't fall ill immediately, I'll take a stroll around the town."

Wolfbiter rose and took a step to stand before the door. He drew Fang and raised her in the duelists' salute. "Over my dead body."

"Put it away; you're bluffing."

Fang went back in her scabbard. "But I'm not joking, sir. All those strong young peasants you mentioned, trapped here for months waiting their turn, running out of money . . . Do you remember where I put the manacles?''

He had a good point. Samarinda after dark would not be a haven of tranquility and a prudent man would explore it first in daylight. ''All right, nurse, tonight I'll behave myself.''

''Thank you.''

The inquisitor said, ''This is the water jug and this is the chamber pot, I think. Confirm that please, Sir Wolfbiter.''

About once a year, Kromman showed signs of a sense of humor.

· 3 ·

They left at first light, locking the door behind them in the certain knowledge that it would not keep Cabuk from rummaging through their packs while they were out. The alleyways were deserted still, but the monastery was so high that it could not be hard to find. Soon they were walking parallel to it, seeing it looming over the adjoining buildings.

''Makes no sense!'' Wolfbiter complained. ''These houses must butt up against it. Why give your enemies a three-story leg up?''

If his quick wits did not understand, then his ward's certainly would not. ''Because you defend yourself with conjuration, I expect. The fortifications are just for show.''

Then they turned a corner into a square, the first open space they had found in the city. The side to their left was the front wall of the monastery, a smooth and forbidding curtain of stone between two corner towers. The other three sides were a tightly packed jumble of the ramshackle,

chaotic houses of Samarinda, a continuous frontage broken
only by a few narrow alleys. Most of the square itself was
occupied by the fateful courtyard of the legends, defined
by a chest-high wall on three sides, directly abutting the
monastery on the fourth. The terrace between the wall and
the houses provided both access to the dwellings and a
grandstand for spectators, for the flagstones of the court
lay a man's height below street level.

"The bear pit. Once you're in you're in." Durendal
leaned on the wall and peered over. He wondered how
often some poor wretch lost his nerve down there and
was pursued around and around by an immortal conjurer
wielding a golden sword. The coping of the wall was too
smooth to offer any hope of a handhold; it had been polished by centuries of arms leaning on it.

In the chill dawn light, the courtyard stood deserted and
the monastery door was closed. The arch was large enough
to take a loaded wagon, which was clearly impractical, as
the only other way in or out of the courtyard was a barred
gate directly opposite, and it was only man-size. Steps
outside it led up to street level, while close inside it stood
a post with a single arm, like a gallows, and from that
hung a bronze disk about shield size. Cabuk had mentioned a gong.

A dozen or so men were already leaning on the wall
near the gate. Durendal set off to join them, in the belief
that they would have chosen the best place to view the
show. Before he reached the corner, a door in one of the
houses opened and the biggest man he had ever seen
emerged, bent almost double. He straightened up to tree
stature and put his hands on his hips. He looked up at the
morning and then down at Durendal. He was obviously
not a native of Altain, for his hair was the wrong color.
He was all hair: tawny beard trailing to his waist, a cinna-
mon mane hanging down his back, a black bearskin around
his loins, and man-fur everywhere else. He bore a shiny
steel battle-ax on his back. He would have curdled blood
had he not at once grinned from ear to ear.

"You're new! Do you speak Puliarsh? I am Khiva son of Zambul."

"Durendal the Bastard."

"Chalice of Zuropolis."

"Wolfbiter the Terrible."

"Welcome!" He looked doubtfully down at Wolfbiter, who did not come up to his nipples. "How terrible?"

The Blade gave him a malignantly calculated glare. "Appalling when I have to get up before dawn. Quite patient otherwise."

The colossus took a moment to work that out and decide it was a joke. He laughed, a sound like runaway barrels. "Are you going to put in your names today? Come!"

He set off with long strides. Durendal walked with him, letting the other two follow.

"We'll decide if we want to enter when we've seen a few fights."

"They're very good, all of them. But I am better."

Was he? A warrior who let his hair or beard grow long was inviting opponents to catch hold of it. "Will they let you fight with that ax?"

"Yes. The monkey said it would be all right."

"How long have you been waiting?"

Khiva pondered. "Weeks. But I'm due soon, because I don't know anyone who was here when I came, except Gartok son of Gilgit. It will be nice to have someone else who can speak Puliarsh. I have been lonely since Ysog was called."

"Have you seen any winners?"

"No. But you will, if you watch me. I have a woman waiting for me, friend Durendal! Her father said I could not have her because I had no flocks. When I go home, I shall buy up all the flocks in the village and buy her with them and everyone will be amazed. And I may take her sisters, too."

Alas, when the brains and brawn were passed out, Khiva son of Zambul had been served twice from the same pot and missed the other one altogether.

A couple of dozen aspiring swordsmen had gathered at the gate now, and more were drifting in. As soon as the newcomers introduced themselves, it became clear that many of the other contestants had the same cognitive shortcomings as Khiva son of Zambul, but a few were quite impressive. It made sense that only fools or very skilled swordsmen would venture their lives in the Golden Sword Stakes. One man in particular stood out as having a following. He was large but not ungainly, past his first youth but still lithe. His swarthy, hooked-nosed features probably came from somewhere on the shores of the Seventh Sea, and his curved sword certainly did. He gave his name as Gartok son of Gilgit.

"Ah! Then you are next?" Durendal said.

His dark eyes gleamed in a smile. "I believe so. It is impossible to be certain. There were forty-six here when I put in my name, but many become dispirited and go home. I have been here forty days. It must be soon."

Durendal wondered why he could not just ask the monkeys to tell him where he stood on the list, but the question seemed so absurd that it stuck in his throat. "And you believe you can win?"

Gartok shrugged. "If they send out Tabriz or Valmian, I have a very good chance. Against Karaj or Saveh, a reasonable one. I have not seen all the brethren in action, and a couple of them only once. If Herat comes or Everman or Tejend, then I am dead."

Aha! "I was told that Everman was a recent recruit to the brotherhood?"

Gartok shrugged again. "So they say. He has a strange style, but he is deadly. I have watched him twice. He does not toy with his victims as Karaj and Herat do. He goes straight for the heart. Stab! Like that!"

Everman had been a rapier man.

Before Durendal could ask more, a murmur of excitement drew his attention to the courtyard. The sun was over the rooftops now, already hot. One of the flagstones had lifted like a trapdoor, and the monkeys were emerging.

He left Gartok and strode along the terrace a few yards to watch this performance more directly.

The only monkey he had ever seen had been a pet chained to a beggar's wrist in Urfalin, and that had been a tiny animal. These were as tall as he was, although they walked stooped with a shambling gait; and they most certainly outweighed him. They were all female, wearing loose trousers of many-colored material—scarlet, blue, green, and gold—and each had a sword on her back, the scabbard held by shoulder straps. He counted seven of the strange beasts before a dark hairy arm pulled the trapdoor closed. Two shuffled toward the gate; the others spread out to the sides of the yard. Then they just stood, waiting.

He glanced behind him, and for once his Blade was not there. He went back to the group at the gate, receiving an angry stare from Wolfbiter, who could not have noticed him leave.

Nothing very much seemed to be happening. Gartok, the senior contestant, was holding forth to a dozen or so intent disciples, passing on his own observations of the monks' personal styles, plus wisdom collected by others— the group folklore of a unique, ever-changing gladiator society.

"Yarkan I have not seen. He is of great stature, like Sahrif, but may be known by his chest hair, which is black and in a cruciform pattern. He has been wounded either twice or three times in living memory, always on the left leg and always with a rapier. He is left-handed and often uses a broadsword. That is a very tricky combination, my friends, a broadsword coming from your right! They may well send him out against Khiva son of Zambul."

One of the listeners made a remark about Khiva son of Zambul that sent the others off into nervy laughter. Fortunately the giant was not within earshot, or else the joke had not been phrased in Puliarsh.

A newcomer went by and started down the stairs. At once everyone fell silent and crowded around the railing to listen. He was older than most, with silver in his beard, but he moved well and bore a very long single-edged sword on his back. He peered through the bars at the two waiting monkeys.

One said, "Give me your name and you will be called in turn." Her voice was deep and throaty but perfectly intelligible. Her lips and tongue were black. She had dangling breasts, although not as prominent as a woman's, and the nipples were black also.

"Ardebil son of Kepri."

"You will be called, Ardebil son of Kepri."

"May I use this sword?"

"It will be permitted."

Ardebil climbed back up the steps and was at once hailed as a welcome addition to the group. Had that been a person of grotesque appearance he had spoken with or an intelligent animal? Suppose Durendal went down and asked the monkey to deliver a message to Brother Everman—what then?

The terrace was filling up as the hour of challenge approached, so he strolled off in search of a clear space of wall to lean on. Wolfbiter joined him on one side, Kromman on the other.

"There must be forty contestants here."

"Forty-two," said Kromman. "A good agent collects exact information. And here come another three. Those six over there with the women are unarmed, probably just spectators. So is the man with the boy."

"Would it be easier to enchant a monkey into a thing that size and make it talk or to enchant a woman into looking like a monkey?"

The inquisitor sneered. "I am not a conjurer, Sir Durendal. My guess would be the latter, but conjuration is not always logical. Do you agree?"

"Yes. They seem to be intelligent, not just trained animals, although I can't be certain. The feat of memory still troubles me. Is there such a thing as a memory-enhancing conjuration?"

"Possibly. We must find out what else the brutes do."

"I think they prevent anyone else interfering in the duel." Wolfbiter was clearly having nightmares of his ward down there fighting for his life.

One of the monkeys by the gate shambled over to the gong and reached up a very long arm to rap on it with her knuckles. A metallic note reverberated through the court. She went back to the gate as her companion there bellowed out a summons.

"Jubba Ahlat!"

Heads turned this way and that along the long line of spectators.

"Jubba Ahlat!"

"Master Ahlat has apparently thought better of his rashness," Kromman said. "Prudent young fellow."

"I have never heard you speak sense before, Inquisitor," Wolfbiter retorted.

"You do not listen. One of the camel drivers told me that if a man comes back years later to try again, the monkeys will always remember him and refuse him a second chance, no matter what name he gives."

A third time Ahlat's name was called, and still there was no response. More spectators were drifting into the square. Faces had appeared at the windows of the surrounding houses.

"Gartok son of Gilgit!"

"Here!"

The Thyrdonian hauled off his tunic and then his shirt. Each was snatched from his fingers by a group of small boys who had gathered near the steps and promptly began fighting over the loot with many shrill curses. When he contributed his dagger, one of them grabbed it and ran; others pursued. Finally Gartok emptied his pockets, showering coins over the remaining scavengers, and hurried down the steps to the gate that now stood open for him.

"This is barbaric!" Kromman growled.

"My Blade and I do not disagree."

One of the monkeys clanged the gate shut and locked it. The other intercepted Gartok, pawing at him to make sure he had brought no concealed weapons. Then she stood aside and let him stride out into the sunshine, naked to the waist, flashing his scimitar as he flexed his arms for battle.

He went to the gong and struck it with the flat of his blade, crashing out an earsplitting boom that echoed back and forth.

Barbaric, yes, but there was some horribly primitive attraction in a contest to the death. Durendal could not have torn himself away for anything except immediate danger to his ward, the King.

A second boom on the gong, then a third—the challenge delivered.

The great iron-bound door of the monastery began to open, swinging slowly inward to reveal a blank wall of sunlit stone, which was to be expected in a castle, where an invader breaking down the front door would find himself confined to a passage and defenders dropping missiles on his head.

A man strode in from one side and advanced until he was in the center of the arch, then turned to face his opponent across the width of the court. Experienced spectators began whispering a name, which in a moment worked its way along to the Chivians: Herat!

Gartok had named three who could certainly kill him and two who toyed with their victims. Herat had belonged to both groups.

The monk was clean-shaven and wore his black hair cropped short. He had the hollow belly and hairless chest of a youth barely into manhood, but appearances were reputed to be deceptive in Samarinda. He emerged from the archway and paused to raise his sword in a duelist's salute while the great door silently closed behind him. His blade shone gold.

Gartok returned the salute. The two men marched toward each other. They looked more like man and boy, though.

They met in the center, Herat stopping first and raising his blade at guard to let the challenger strike first. He turned his right shoulder toward his opponent and placed his left hand on his hip, fencer style. Gartok leaped in at once with a dazzlingly fast two-handed slash. The youngster parried it easily, and the challenger jumped back. He began to circle, making feinting movements, now using a matching one-handed grip. The monk turned slowly to keep facing him.

Kromman said, "An expert commentary, if you please, Sir Durendal."

"That was a very wild stroke. Gartok told me that Herat likes to play cat and mouse. He was gambling on surprise and assuming Herat would not strike him dead if it failed."

"Could he have done?"

"I think so. Too early to be sure."

Gartok closed again, but Herat leaped back, barely parrying. And again. The fight moved swiftly across the court.

"Now who's winning?" asked the inquisitor.

"Why play ignorant?" Wolfbiter snarled. "We know how good you are with a sword."

"Herat is," Durendal said. "Did you see how neatly he avoided being pinned against the wall? Gartok's good. Nothing fancy, but fast and accurate. Herat's going to wear him out, though."

True enough. Herat let his opponent drive him three times across the full width of the court, until the older man began to tire. The third time the monk was almost backed into a wall, he changed tactics without warning and went on the offensive in a flurry of clangorous parries and ripostes. Round two had begun. Now the pace was even faster, and it was Gartok who was in full retreat. Monkeys shambled out of the way whenever the battle came near.

"Do we have to watch this?" Wolfbiter asked bitterly.

"That bad?" said the inquisitor.

"The only thing left to bet on is how long he'll be made to suffer."

Or how long flesh and blood could stand that pace,

Durendal thought. He had never seen a bout continue so long without a touch, and those were real swords, not lightweight foils. "The kid is superb. I wouldn't last a minute against him. Well, maybe two. But he'd always beat me. You agree, Wolf?"

"Loyalty forbids me to answer, sir. Look at that! Point, edge, point again. He hasn't repeated a move. He's just playing!"

The crowd was becoming noisy. Even Kromman was showing signs of excitement, drumming his fists on the wall. "This is it!" he rasped as Gartok was expertly herded into a corner.

But no. With a wild slash at the monk's head he broke out of the trap—*was allowed* to break out. And round three began, for now Herat switched to a very dirty game, pricking his opponent here and there as the fancy took him: chest, arms, face, even legs. None of the wounds seemed serious, but soon the older man was streaming blood, while still fighting desperately. He was driven methodically backward around the courtyard, as if to allow all the spectators a clear view of his humiliation. In a moment they passed below the Chivians, both fighters gasping for breath.

They did not progress much farther before pain and despair and sheer exhaustion triumphed. The challenger conceded. With a howl, he dropped his sword and spread out his arms, waiting for the *coup de grâce*. The two men stood in tableau for a moment, chests moving like bellows. Durendal was fairly sure that Herat had been slowing down near the end, so he was not without human limitations, even if he was immortal.

The boy spoke and gestured, pointing at the ground.

Gartok shook his head, and spoke a word that was audible over the whole silent square: "Never!"

Herat laughed and flicked his golden sword in the older man's face. Gartok screamed once and doubled over, but then he straightened up again, clasping his hands to his eyes, bleeding and blinded, still too proud to kneel. That was a game he could never win. Herat paced around him like a giant cat circling its prey, making random cuts, but seemingly just amusing himself, not playing to the gallery, for he never once looked at the spectators. Gartok was being flayed alive and could not see the strokes coming. He screamed and staggered; it sounded as if he was begging, but again he refused a command to kneel. Eventually Herat cut his throat and walked away, leaving him to bleed to death.

The great door swung open to receive him. Something about the way he wiped sweat from his forehead and the relaxed way he walked suggested a young athlete returning from a strenuous but enjoyable workout.

"I think we have seen all we need," Durendal said thickly. His gut was heaving.

"Why?" Wolfbiter asked. His face was pale under his deep tan.

"What?"

"Why, sir? What is the purpose of all this?"

"I wish I knew."

It was a curious question. Did barbarity need a purpose?

* 4 *

They walked in silence through alleyways already stiflingly hot under the midsummer sun, bustling with people and carts and pack animals. Durendal chose to leave the square by the far side and continued to bear left, staying as close to the monastery as he could. A couple of times he had to retrace his steps at dead ends, but he had no serious trouble in circling all the way around. He found only two places where he could stand in the street and touch the fortress. Everywhere else it was behind houses. There was no other door.

Having now given himself time to think, he led the way back to their room at the top of the precarious stairway of slabs. He saw at a glance that the packs had been emptied and carelessly stuffed back together. Cabuk had not been subtle. Knowing his guests expected him to snoop and steal, he would see no need to be devious about it.

Durendal scrambled up the ladder to the roof, which was admittedly a superior feature of Hotel Cabuk. At one time the house had possessed another story, and most of the walls were still there, even to windows blocked by the stonework of adjoining buildings. When the original roof had burned away to a few charred beams, the owners had spread clay over the floor. The result seemed likely to collapse at any moment, but the resulting patio was private and as cool as anywhere in Samarinda could be.

He kicked away enough litter to make a clearing on the shady side and sat down. The other two did the same. Finding he had a view of the monastery towers, he glared at them with sudden hatred. Why? Why murder a man every day? According to the legends, this had been going on for thousands of years. The Monastery of the Golden Sword had always been there. There was no record of its founding. Two years he had spent coming here, two years he would need to return, and it seemed as if it would all be wasted. He would go home with only failure to report.

"Anyone want to eat?" he asked eventually, and his companions shook their heads.

"Ideas, then. His Majesty told me to rescue Everman or at least find out what happened to him. We have—did have—an eyewitness who saw him fight, so he's almost certainly still alive." Was that progress? Yesterday at this time, he had not expected as much. "At worst we must linger here until he fights again and Wolf and I can identify him. But how we go about getting a message to him, I can't for the life of me . . . The castle—or monastery, whichever you want to call it—seems to have no other door. Even if it has own well for water, they still have to get food in and night soil out. Cabuk didn't know, but he wouldn't care.''

Wolfbiter was wearing his steady, calculating stare. "And women. Monks may abstain, but knights rarely do, even in theory. Those houses crammed against the walls, they bother me, they really do.''

"You noticed the monkeys are all female? Perhaps they don't always look like monkeys.'' The alternative did not bear thinking about. "You think there's a secret way in?''

"Must be. Several, through the houses. One of the merchants told me that Samarinda is a good place to buy swords. We can try to find out who sells them and where he gets them.''

"They may just leave them on the flagstones for the scavengers.''

"Yes, sir. But why not put Inquisitor Kromman to work interviewing harlots and see if any of them ever get called in by the brethren? He's good at that sort—''

"Don't you start being childish. He's bad enough. Today we explore the town and ask some guarded questions. And we ought to find that merchant who sent the letter. What was his name—Quchan?''

"Why?'' Kromman asked with a disagreeable pout.

"I'll write one and give it to him to send on the next eastbound caravan. Then at least the King may learn that we arrived.'' Assuming it ever arrived, which was probably not probable. "If we fail to return, he'll be less tempted to send anyone else.''

"But Quchan may very well be in league with the brethren. I suggest you wait a few days first.''

Durendal conceded the point with a nod, knowing that the inquisitor was much better at intrigue than he would ever be.

For a moment Kromman sat with a sour expression on his face. Then he sighed. "I wish I could show you both up as stupid musclebound louts for missing something obvious. I do think that's what you are, but I can't expose you at the moment. We must prepare an escape route in case we need to leave in a hurry. I suggest we buy five horses and saddles and stable them at one of those establishments outside the gates. If we pay a high enough daily rate, they should remain available.''

"Five?'' Wolfbiter said. "You think Polydin's still alive too?''

"Everman was only twenty-two when he came here. Few musclebound louts could be bribed with a promise of immortality at that age.'' The inquisitor sneered. "The brethren found a Blade's weak spot, that's obvious.''

He meant Everman's ward, because if they held Jaque Polydin hostage, they could force Everman to do anything. It was a horribly logical way to explain how an honorable swordsman had been turned into a cold-blooded killer.

"Well, there's our first day,'' Durendal said. "We'll see about horses, and explore the city and make inquiries. I suppose we had better eat something now before it gets any hotter. Tomorrow we'll watch another man die.''

It was small consolation that Kromman seemed to be as baffled as he and Wolfbiter were.

· 5 ·

The next day began very much like the first, with the Chivians arriving at the courtyard as the sun was rising. Durendal walked only a few yards along the wall and stopped before he reached the house from which Khiva son of Zambul had emerged the previous morning.

"I want to watch from here today.''

"Why?'' demanded the inquisitor.

"Just a whim. You go 'round and talk to the human sacrifices if you want."

Glowering suspiciously, Kromman remained. So, of course, did Wolfbiter.

The challengers were gathering by the gate, conspicuously including Khiva son of Zambul, that hairy giant standing head and shoulders above even the tallest. The sun crawled up over the buildings, spreading brightness across the flagstones. Yesterday's bloodstains were a darker black, but the whole of the courtyard was a dark color, dyed by the dried blood of centuries.

The previous day's inquiries had done nothing to solve the mystery. Neither the inquisitor nor the two Blades had managed to learn anything about the monastery's domestic arrangements. No stall keeper had admitted to delivering food or knowing who did, and the men who gathered the night soil claimed they did not collect any from the brethren. None of which meant anything if Wolfbiter's guess about concealed entrances was correct.

The expedition had purchased horses in case it must make a quick getaway. Whether a small party could travel across Altain unmolested was another problem, but if they could just reach Koburtin, they could wait there for a caravan.

The trapdoor rose, and the first monkey clambered out.

Durendal began to walk then, and his companions followed in puzzled silence. They joined the contestants, who greeted them cheerfully and asked if they were now ready to submit their names.

Suddenly he decided to tackle the monkey guardians. He had not intended to, for he would be drawing attention to himself and might even put Everman in danger, but he had learned to trust his impulses. Swordsmen who waited to analyze problems tended to die without finding answers. He headed for the steps. Wolfbiter muttered a curse and followed. Although the gate was still closed, the monsters were clearly visible through the bars. They had long tails, huge yellow fangs, an acrid animal stench, and calluses on their shoulders where the scabbard straps had worn the hair off. They were certainly not people in costumes, yet the dark eyes seemed intelligent.

"Give me your name and you will be called in turn," one of them said.

When he did not reply, she repeated the statement in another language, and then again in a tongue he did not know.

"I am not ready to do that. I wish to speak with one of the brothers."

The monkey scratched herself with big black nails.

Feeling his skin crawl, he tried again. "I have something important to tell the brethren."

Still no reaction. He glanced at Wolfbiter. "Do you think she doesn't understand or won't?"

"Won't. I'd be happier if you stood farther from the bars, sir. I don't know how fast she is."

Durendal moved back against the wall to ease the strain on his ward, although the monkey's long arm might still be able to reach him there.

"If you are going to put our names in," Wolfbiter said tensely, "give them mine first. I will not be able to remain in the gallery if you are down here fighting." He was speaking Chivian, but could monkeys have the gift of tongues also?

"I'm not going to put anybody's name in. I am not crazy, and I have a duty to report back to my ward. Don't you answer questions?"

The monkey scratched again impassively.

The answer was no. The other one turned and shambled toward the gong to begin the day's spectacle. With an angry sense of failure, Durendal trotted back up to the street and went in search of a place to watch from. He had gained nothing and might have warned the opposition that Everman's friends had arrived at last.

The summons of the gong died away.

"Khiva son of Zambul!"

"Here!" roared the giant. He ripped off his bearskin

and hurled it to the waiting scavengers, then went plunging naked down the stairs. He emerged through the gate, crouching under the stone lintel, and strode past the monkeys. He was much larger than they but not much less hairy. If his nudity was not just bluff and he truly was a berserker, then today's match might not be the pushover Durendal had been expecting.

At that moment Kromman inquired, "What odds on Khiva the Short?"

When his ward did not answer, Wolfbiter said, "A thousand to one on the golden sword. Khiva hasn't got a brain in his head."

"He has a lot of muscles in his body."

"I'd take the same odds on me against that lout—and cut him down to my size, or less."

Boom!—boom!—boom! The giant's fast blows seemed designated to tear the gong from its chains. They reverberated like thunder through the square, echoing off the monastery wall.

The great door began to open.

"He does not lack enthusiasm or courage," the inquisitor said. "Intelligence in swordsmen is a relative matter, and that ax of his is at least six feet long. His arm can't be much less. How do you close with him, Sir Wolfbiter?"

"I wear him out. I dodge his stroke and come in behind it. It must weigh— Oh, death and fire! Sir, isn't that Everman?"

Steady! Durandal forced his fists to unclench and laid his palms on the wall. Everman had been one of the best. Superb, he had told the King. Trouble was, he was short, like Wolfbiter. He looked tiny, standing there in that huge archway. This was to be a battle of the bull and the bulldog.

The two men advanced toward the center as the monastery door closed. Sunlight glinted on Everman's auburn hair. He had always been pale skinned, rarely taking a tan even in midsummer, and now his chest and arms seemed almost milk white. The closer he came to the giant, the smaller he became, like a boy facing an ogre.

Khiva had no use for duelists' courtesies. He roared out a battle cry and charged, swinging that enormous ax around his head with one hand. Hair and beard streaming behind him, he bore down on his opponent within a whistling circle of flashing steel, safe from any swordsman's reach. That was not the technique Wolfbiter had predicted.

Everman halted and watched him come, waiting in a half crouch. Which way would he jump—left or right? He would be far more nimble than Khiva, who would need five or ten paces to come to a halt and reverse direction, but even that great bone-brain must know that Everman would dodge. Khiva could lunge sideways at the last minute. If he guessed wrong, he could try again, but Everman would have no second chances. The contest would end when the challenger ran out of wind or the monk out of dodges.

They met and both men went down. Everman rolled clear and bounced to his feet at once, unharmed and unarmed. The giant slid to a halt face downward, while his ax clattered and clanged across the flagstones halfway to the monastery door. He had grown a bloody horn between his shoulder blades.

The encounter had been almost too fast for even Durendal's expert eye. Everman had simply dropped to his knees under the ax and then sprung up, thrusting his sword two-handed into Khiva's chest. The son of Zambul had done the rest, impaling himself on the blade with his own momentum. Stab! Gartok had said, right to the heart. The wonder was that Everman had not been crushed by the giant's fall, but he was upright, dancing from foot to foot, and Khiva was prone, spread-eagled, hardly twitching. The spectators were silent.

The victor took hold of the corpse by one ankle and walked around it until it flopped over on its side and he could retrieve his sword. Then he headed back toward the monastery door. He had won his bout in little more than a minute, spilling almost no blood. He had not once looked at the audience, any more than Herat had the previous day—mortals must be beneath immortals' notice. There was no cockiness in his walk, as there had been in Herat's, but there was no dejection either.

Impulse: Durendal cupped his hands to his mouth and bellowed at the top of his voice, "Starkmoor!"

Everman missed a step and then kept walking, not looking around. He passed under the arch, turned to the left, and disappeared from view. The door swung shut.

The swordsmen began to disperse in gloomy silence.

"Oh, I approve," said Kromman. "Very sharp and concise. Merciful pest control. Stamp on them quick so they don't suffer."

Durendal rounded on him. "Will you shut up, you slime-mouthed reptilian shit bucket? That man is a friend of mine, and he is in trouble!"

Kromman stared back at him with the fish-eyed gaze of an inquisitor. "Men are known by the company they keep, Sir Durendal."

"Sometimes we have no choice. Let's get out of here."

"This way, sir." Wolfbiter was wearing his warning expression, the one that made him look like a constipated trout.

"Lead," Durendal said, puzzled.

But his Blade moved only a few paces, to the middle of the terrace, and then turned. "Here, I think. Pretend we're having an argument or a discussion or something." He was facing the monastery and the other two had their backs to it.

"You are behaving very much out of character," Kromman complained. "I do not know what could provoke a Blade to start cultivating the superior habits of an inquisitor, but of course I am prepared to stand here all day if it will further your education and progress."

A group of four contestants went by. Muttering, they disappeared into an alley.

"I just keep wanting to know why," Wolfbiter said apologetically.

Kromman beamed like a toad. "You're watching to see what happens to the body!"

The Blade gave him his familiar dark appraising stare. "Yes. And at the moment the monkeys are trooping back down the— Ah! The last two have gone for it. Yes, they're carrying it to the trapdoor."

Durendal said, "Only two?" Khiva would have outweighed an ox.

"Only two, sir, and not making heavy work of it, either. Gone. You can look now."

The trapdoor had closed. The courtyard was deserted, bearing no sign of Khiva's death except his great ax, which lay abandoned in the sunshine.

"What does it mean, Wolf?"

"I think that must be how they feed the livestock."

"But—but they can't go through all this just for that, surely?"

"Look!" Kromman snapped.

A wiry adolescent had dropped over the wall on one side of the yard, and two more came down on the other. They all raced for the ax. The solitary youth reached it first and sprinted back the way he had come with the other two in close pursuit. Reaching the wall, he hurled his booty up to his waiting friends. The opposition abandoned the contest and ran back to their own helpers. Thief and would-be thieves were hauled up, over the coping. The rival gangs vanished into convenient alleys and the courtyard was truly deserted again.

"Very slick," Durendal grumbled, leading the way homeward. "They do it every day. I don't think I could have handled Khiva as neatly as Everman did, though." He would not have wanted to, that was the difference. "What you were hinting, Wolf, is that the monkeys are the masters and the brethren are the servants. A murder a day just to feed the apes on human flesh?"

Wolfbiter glanced appraisingly at him and said nothing.

They walked on in silence through the morning crowds.

"We have broken cover," the inquisitor said suddenly. "You spoke to the monkeys and then shouted to Everman. I think your idea of a letter sent through Master Quchan may now be a wise precaution. If the brethren are opposed to our meddling, they will probably have little trouble tracking us down very shortly and—"

Durendal caught his companions' arms to halt them. Cabuk's house was straight ahead. Waiting there, seated on the third block of the staircase with his feet resting on the second, was a man in the anonymous dusty garments of Altain. The face under the flapped, conical cap was Everman's, and he had already seen them.

· 6 ·

He stepped down to the road as they approached, offering a hand and a wary smile. "Durendal! I did not expect you. And . . . Wait, don't tell me. Not Chandler . . . Wolfbiter!" The smile broadened. "Sir Wolfbiter now, of course! Fire, how the years go! And?" He looked quizzically at Kromman.

"Master Ivyn Chalice, merchant." Durendal's conscience squirmed. He was lying to a brother Blade. "Our infallible guide. Let's go up."

"No, we'll talk here. How are things back in Chivial? And Ironhall?" Everman had not changed on the outside, whatever he had become inside. His face was unusually pale for Altain but the same face it had been eight years ago. The gingery eyebrows and eyelashes were the same, his eyes perhaps more cautious. Immortality must agree with him.

"The land's at peace. The King was well when we left—remarried, expecting a second child. Queen Godeleva produced a daughter and he divorced her. Grand Master finally died. Master of Archives succeeded him." Durendal felt waves of unreality wash over him as he tried to discuss such matters in this exotic alleyway—with bizarre crowds trooping by, mules and even camels, beggars chanting, conical caps with earflaps, hawkers wheeling carts and waving hot meat on sticks, alien scents, harsh voices, slanted eyes without visible lids.

Everman nodded as if none of it mattered very much. "I was afraid he'd try again. I didn't expect you, though. You were not bound to the King."

"I am now."

"You have had a long journey for nothing, brother." His red-brown eyes stared intently at Durendal. "There is no philosophers' stone. Discard the first wrong answer. There is no secret in Samarinda that you can steal for good King Ambrose."

"There are mysteries, though." Not the least of them was whatever had changed a former friend into this stranger. "There is a source of gold. And apparently there is immortality."

Everman shrugged sadly. "But nothing you can take or use. Look . . ." He reached for his sword and Fang flashed into Wolfbiter's fist.

Everman jumped and raised both hands quickly, palms out. He glanced from one Blade to the other and then smiled. "I can tell who is whose ward. I just want to show you something."

"Put your sword up, Wolf." Fortunately none of the passersby had taken alarm. "Show us what?"

Everman pointed at the stone on the pommel, keeping his hand well away from the hilt. "The cat's eye is coated with wax. The blade's covered with gold paint. I was going to draw it and show you the scratches. This is Reaper, the sword I took from the anvil in Ironhall. You want to look closer?"

"What's the significance?"

"Discard the second wrong answer. There is no enchanted sword in the monastery, in spite of its name. There are some fiery good swordsmen, but no enchanted swords."

"There's you. Why? Why did you join them?" What are you now, who were once my friend? Why kill men the way you swatted that half-witted giant this morning? What harm had he ever done you?

A passing wagon caused them to move closer together. Everman sighed and leaned an elbow on one of the slabs of the stair.

"My ward died, so discard the third wrong answer. Master Polydin died of a fever in Urfalin." He peered around at their faces. "You know what that does to a Blade. I decided to carry on, and I made it all the way here. I prowled around like you've been doing, I expect, and couldn't find out anything at all. So I put my name in. The day my turn came, Yarkan drew short straw. He brought out a broadsword and I managed to prick his knee. They took me inside. . . . There's a stack of gold bars there. I tucked one under each arm and walked out again. That night I sat in my room and stared at them and tried to decide what on earth I needed gold bars for."

Durendal could not see Kromman's left hand and suspected he was not signaling anyway or else that all this was true. "And?"

"And the next day I answered my call again—they give you a second chance, you know. If I hadn't taken it, then Yarkan would have fought again, but this time they sent out Dhurma. I won again."

"Ironhall would be proud of you."

A brief smile made Everman's face seem absurdly boyish. "Our style was new to them. They know it now— I've taught them. The third day they sent Herat."

"Third?"

He shrugged, almost seeming embarrassed. "You haven't heard that part? Three wins and you're in. I couldn't resist. I'd been sent to discover the secret, remember.''

"You were always a daredevil."

"Oh? The well is calling the puddle deep, Sir Durendal."

"We watched Herat yesterday. Vicious. You beat Herat?"

"Nobody ever beats Herat. He says I gave him the best sport he'd had in a century or two, though. When I was about to pass out from loss of blood, he dropped his guard. I was so mad I disemboweled him."

Wolfbiter whispered, "Fire and death!"

Everman chuckled. "Fire, maybe. We staggered back to the monastery together, but he was helping me more than I was helping him—holding his guts in with one hand and me up with the other. Their healing conjurements are vastly better than anything we have back in Chivial. By next morning I was good as new. I became one of them."

"And you're staying there of your own free will?"

Everman nodded. "I'm going to stay here forever." He met Durendal's stare defiantly. "Of my own free will."

A beggar boy started wailing for alms. Kromman clipped him on the ear to send him packing. He used his right hand, though, not signaling. How much of Everman's tale was true? What should Durendal ask next? Gold? Immortality? Monkeys eating human flesh?

"The King sent me to get you back. If there was a philosophers' stone, and I could find it, well and good, but my prime directive is to bring you home. He won't have one of his Blades made into a performing bear."

"Kind of him. And since I don't want to leave?" Everman had lost his smile. He was as tense as if he had his sword in his hand.

"He said I could use my own judgment."

"You always had good judgment, even if you were a worse daredevil than me. Go home and meddle no more in Samarinda."

Durendal glanced inquiringly at Kromman, but the inquisitor's fishy stare told him nothing. How much of the story was true? None of it, if Polydin was chained in the monastery cellar.

"In the King's name, Sir Everman, I command—"

"Screw fat Ambrose."

Wolfbiter hissed at this sedition. Everman laughed.

Appeal had failed, duty had failed. The renegade seemed ready to terminate the discussion. If he dodged off into the crowds, he would be gone forever. All Durendal had left to try now was force.

"There are three of us, brother, and only one of you. We could take you, I think."

Everman stared hard at him and then shook his head sadly. "Brother, you say? Oh, brother, brother! Look over there."

They all looked. Three youths were lounging against the opposite wall, watching. The middle one was Herat. He smiled.

"My brothers now," Everman said. "Go home, Sir Durendal. Go home, Sir Wolfbiter. There is nothing in Samarinda for you or for the King. Whatever secrets the monastery holds will not work in Chivial, I promise you. You will find only death here, and this is a long way from home to die." His lip curled. "And take your tame inquisitor with you. Give my regards to Ironhall. Reaper is one sword that will never hang in the hall, but you don't have to mention that."

• 7 •

*I suppose I'm just pigheaded. Hardest part of being a
King—being any sort of leader—is knowing when to quit.
You've wounded the quarry. . . .* No, Durendal thought,
the quarry had wounded him. The quarry had run him out
of town with his tail between his legs. He was going home
to report failure.

Sunlight blazed like a furnace door. The morning was
still young, yet the air was unbreathably hot and the peaks
had already vanished in purple haze. Five ponies followed
their shadows over the dusty hills—three with riders, two
spares. They could travel no faster than a caravan, so five
days' ride to Koburtin, maybe. No one spoke a word until
they crested the long rise and Samarinda disappeared from
view, then Durendal said, "What went wrong? Obviously
Wolf was right and they have secret doors, but how did
they catch us so quickly?"

After a moment, it was Kromman who answered. "An
efficient spy system. The brethren must be very interested
in strangers—who they are, where they stay. We asked
strange questions. . . . Or perhaps conjuration—who
knows? They must have some sort of sniffers to make
sure the challengers are all secular."

"Very few good swordsmen are purely secular, Inquisitor, any more than you are. Wolf and I are not, certainly.
Herat can't be. I think even Gartok had some spiritual
enhancement."

"Or we were betrayed," Wolfbiter suggested. "How
did Everman know we had an inquisitor with us?" As

186

always, his face was expressionless. Was he contemplating murder again?

"You mean me?" Kromman sneered. "What do I have to gain by treachery, Sir Blade? If you want to search my pack for gold bars, then go ahead."

"You wouldn't have told them you were an inquisitor," Durendal said. "That's out of character. How much of Everman's story was true, if any?"

Kromman twisted his straggly mustache over a pout. "I don't know. You let him talk in a busy street. We normally question people alone. If others are present, they must at least keep still. A crowded alley with people going and coming is absolutely the worst possible situation for smelling falsehood."

Was he lying? Why should Kromman lie? Durendal did not know, and yet he knew he trusted his inquisitor ally no farther than he now trusted Everman. Killing might be inevitable for a Blade or man-at-arms on duty, but killing for no purpose was unforgivable.

"Give me some opinions."

"He was lying about Polydin's death. That I am almost certain of."

"And later, when he said he was a willing member of the gang?"

"No—at least, he wasn't saying that just because the three bullyboys were watching him. He may have been holding something back."

Durendal looked at his Blade, riding on his left to cover his vulnerable side.

"No arguments, sir. I thought much the same."

"Yes. Me too. Who needs inquisitors? But if he was lying about his ward, then he needs rescuing. On the other hand, the brethren now look absolutely invincible, and any further efforts on our part will be rank suicide. But that's what we came for. But, but, but! Do we go home or ignore the threats and double back to try again? Look—shade! Let's see if we can get down there."

He turned his mount to the right and rode over to a

rocky wadi that cut the landscape like an open wound. The surefooted pony seemed to approve, for it picked its way eagerly down the stony slope and in a few minutes brought him to a patch of shadow against a beetling cliff. The rising sun would soon wipe out even that small shelter, but at the moment it was a heavenly refuge. Without dismounting, he turned to face his companions as they closed in beside him.

"We can't fight conjuration without using conjuration. You have not been open with us, Kromman. We all know that inquisitors have resources they prefer not to discuss, but now we need your help. What tricks have you got with you that you haven't told us about?"

Kromman scowled through his lank beard. "It is true that I was provided with certain devices that may prove useful—you have already benefitted from the enchanted bandages, Sir Durendal—but the Office of General Inquiry does not proclaim all its resources hugger-mugger. I am forbidden to reveal them unless and until they are needed. If you tell me what you are planning to do, I shall be happy to advise you how I may be able to assist. But don't expect very much."

"How about a golden key?"

Wolfbiter groaned in dismay. "You can't be serious!"

The inquisitor smiled thinly. "Of course he is serious."

"Break into the monastery?"

"You should cultivate your powers of observation, Sir Wolfbiter. When that trapdoor in the courtyard opened yesterday, your ward walked along the terrace until he was opposite it and then looked behind him. This morning he stayed at the east side until it opened again—at which point he started to walk, glancing at the houses he was passing. He now has two bearings on the opening, so he can find it again. A unusual display of thinking from a sword jockey, I admit, but obviously he had burglary in mind, even then."

Durendal tried not to show his annoyance. Wolfbiter was naturally impassive, the inquisitor had training or enchantment to help him conceal his emotions, but he always felt he was an open book to both of them.

"Before we left, there were rumors going around of a handy little gadget called an invisibility cloak."

The inquisitor laughed harshly. "Most of the legends about the so-called Dark Chamber are absolute swamp gas, and that definitely includes invisibility cloaks. Pure myth. But if you are intent on suicide, I shall do everything I can to help, of course."

He was about as likable as something dug out of an outhouse pit.

Wolfbiter glared at him and then equally at Durendal, who reached for his water bottle to give himself a moment to think. It was ironic that the man he disliked and distrusted was supporting him, while the one he called friend must be opposed. Wolfbiter was smarter than Durendal when it came to logic, even if he did not have the same gift of intuition. Was intuition much different from what Everman called daredeviltry?

"Sir, this is crazy talk! We'll be caught for certain. Why throw our lives away like this? What can you possibly hope to achieve?"

"There's no secular way to open the trapdoor from the outside—I'm sure of that—and I'm gambling that it won't be guarded. It must lead into the cellars."

"Dungeons? Polydin?"

"That's what I'm hoping. If we can rescue him, then their hold over Everman disappears. At worst, we may gain useful information."

"At worst we get skinned alive, like Gartok." Wolfbiter wiped an arm across his forehead, searching for arguments. "I do, I mean. One of us has to go home to Chivial, to report to the King. That's your mission, sir. You do that—start now—and I'll go into the monastery for you tonight. Wait for me at Koburtin."

"You know me better than that, Wolf."

"You have a duty to report to the King!"

"The inquisitor will. He can let us in, but then he heads

down to the city gate and at dawn he leaves, with us or without us.''

''Sir! There's no point both of us walking into the lions' den, and you know I can't let you go.''

"Everman was my friend.'' Was that Durendal's motive? Or was it just stupid pride, a pigheaded refusal to crawl home to his ward, the King, and admit defeat? He did not know. He did not care. He just knew he was going back to Samarinda to try again.

Kromman had been listening to the argument with his customary disdain. Now he said, "I certainly won't go in there myself, but I can open the trapdoor for you, unless it is itself a conjurement. I can provide you with lights. . . .'' He screamed, "Call off your dog, Durendal!''

Wolfbiter's left hand had caught hold of the inquisitor's reins and his right was drawing Fang—slowly, though, so he was not quite certain. Kromman's hand fluttered over his own hilt, but he knew that he would die before he could draw.

"Wait!'' Durendal said. "That won't stop me.''

Wolfbiter stared at him with eyes that seemed strangely empty. "It needs three of us to find the way in, doesn't it?''

"It would help, but two could do it, perhaps even one. And I'm going back there if I have to do it over your dead body, Wolf.''

For a moment Kromman's life balanced on a sword edge.

Then Wolfbiter let go the reins with a sigh. "Why did I have to be bound to a raving lunatic?''

• 8 •

The day was long, and the night even longer.

"Plan for both success and failure" was an Ironhall maxim. Failure in this case was death at best or enslavement at worst, so no contingencies need be considered. Success would consist of rescuing Master Polydin—and possibly Everman himself, although that was even more unlikely—and escape from the city when the gates opened at dawn. Two hours would be ample. More time could only help the enemy track them down, so most of the night had to be wasted. The best place for swordsmen to waste time without attracting suspicion was a brothel.

Both Kromman and Wolfbiter expressed much enthusiasm for that part of the plan, but a Blade could not be parted from his ward in such surroundings. Thus Durendal spent many hours playing a complicated board game against a series of amused young ladies, losing large amounts of money to them while trying to ignore the continuing sounds of pleasure from the bed behind him. Kate, Kate, Kate! Would he ever see her again?

As the waxing moon was setting, the expedition prepared to set out.

"Wear these rings on your left hands," Kromman explained, "with the stone out. When you need light, turn the stone inward. You can control the amount by opening or closing your fingers. They should last several hours."

The square was deserted. No lighted windows showed in either the monastery or the houses. Durendal found the door he had noted the previous day and left Wolfbiter there. With Kromman, he went around the corner and along to the one he had marked on the first morning. The inquisitor continued alone, heading for the gate.

Durendal leaned on the wall for what seemed like a very long time, quite long enough to convince him that something had gone wrong already. Then a star twinkled in the courtyard. He turned his ring over and briefly opened his hand. The resulting flash half blinded him, and a moment later another flash showed that Wolfbiter had made the same mistake—too much!

Kromman was very close to the right line, though. Another twinkle, farther to the left. This time Durendal flicked one finger and achieved the required effect. So did Wolfbiter.

Then again. This time he flashed twice to tell the inquisitor that he was correctly aligned. And two from Wolfbiter.

A long, nerve-racking wait . . . Three from Kromman to say he had located the trap.

Wolfbiter loomed out of the dark, breathing faster than usual. Without a word, the two of them headed for the steps and the gate, which the inquisitor had left ajar. They found Kromman easily enough and knelt beside him.

"It looks good," came his whisper. "Seems to be just a slab on a pivot. If there's no secular way to open it from this side, they may not have too many defenses on it. Ready?"

Whatever the "golden key" conjurement looked like, it was small enough for him to conceal inside his hand. Metal clinked on stone. The slab shivered and slowly rose, making grating noises that sounded like trumpet fanfares in the stillness. When it reached vertical, the iron ring set in its underside clanked once. An acrid stench of monkey wafted into the night.

Kromman thrust his hand down and released a faint glow, revealing a square shaft with a floor eight or nine feet down. There was no ladder, only a few iron staples set in the wall—an entrance made for oversized monkeys with prehensile feet, not for men. Durendal rolled on his belly and dropped his legs over the edge. A minute later, three burglars stood at the bottom of the shaft and the trap had been closed.

It had indeed.

A low, rectangular tunnel led off in the direction of the monastery, and the stench of monkey was eye watering.

"I'll wait here," the inquisitor said. "You may be suicidal, Sir Durendal, but I'm not."

"You're a brave and resourceful companion, and I shall tell the King so if I ever see him again. How long?"

"There are gaps at the side of the slab, so I should be able to detect dawn. I shall go as soon as I see light coming through. You want me to leave it open or closed?"

"Open. If we're that late, we shall probably be in a hurry." Durendal was removing his boots.

"As you please. If there's no pursuit, I'll wait outside the city for a couple of hours. Then I'll go on to Koburtin and take the first caravan west."

"I approve those arrangements, so you can quote me if you ever have to testify at an inquiry. Ready, Wolf?"

"I go first. Come."

They set off barefoot along the passage.

Thirty-two, thirty-three . . . He had paced it out in the road and they ought to be under the monastery by now. Thirty-five. This was truly crazy, one of those insane impulses of his. One day he would jump and find spikes. Everman was the danger. The rest of the brethren would not expect such madness, but Everman knew him and had practically warned him not to try exactly what he was trying now. Thirty-seven . . .

Wolfbiter stopped, killing his light. Durendal bumped into him and smelled his sweat.

"What?"

"Light ahead. No? I thought . . ." He flashed a gleam. "Ha! It's a reflection."

It was gold. It was a small room almost full of gold bricks—piled ten feet high at the back, in lower rectangular stacks in front—while the narrow corridor on the far side was walled with them. Durendal eyed the stone pillars in the room, lining them up with the passageway beyond. Then he climbed up the lower heaps until his head was against the roof and he could peer through the narrow gap on top. His light showed no end, but it did reveal the heads of more pillars, rows of them. He climbed down.

"This is all the space they have left," he whispered. "I think this cellar underlies the whole monastery or a large part of it. It's all full of gold. Tons and tons of gold." He tried lifting one of the bricks and decided that Everman had done very well to carry two of them across the courtyard. "Thousands of tons, maybe millions."

"Gold is no use to the dead." Wolfbiter, that practical soul, started forward again, but inconspicuous skulking had suddenly become very difficult. The smallest ray of light he could produce reflected dazzlingly from the walls. In a moment he reached another gold corridor branching off to the right. He hesitated and then went straight. Then one to the left—he stopped.

"We're going to get lost."

"Keep left. It ought to put us under the corner tower, I'd think."

It led, eventually, to a stone doorway slightly narrower than the corridor itself, and beyond that was a dark place, with no reflections. The air did not smell good. Wolfbiter paused at the entrance and directed a narrow beam through his fingers, moving a spot of brightness over rocky walls and then a cubical structure with an obvious chimney, metal tongs, a stone crucible. . . .

"A forge?"

"No. That's a furnace, though." Durendal activated his own ring and advanced into the room. "A foundry. This is where they cast the gold." He pointed to the molds. "Where do they get their ore?" And why did the place stink so badly?

He turned his hand to light up the other end of the chamber and almost cried out at the resulting blaze. The conical mountain of raw gold heaped there filled the room from side to side and reached almost to the roof. It was not what he supposed ore would look like, being a collection of odd-shaped fragments and nuggets, from lumps the size of a man's head all the way down to gravel. He picked up a log that had rolled free, marveling at its weight. Its surface was rough, and here and there black stone still adhered . . . except it wasn't a log, it was a human tibia. Blood and fire! Ribs, vertebrae, jawbones, skulls, and the gravel was toe and finger bones. The black adhesions were lumps of dried flesh. Hence the stench.

"They don't feed the livestock, do they?" Wolfbiter said aloud.

"Sh!"

"But this is what they do with the bodies. They turn the bones to gold."

The surface of the tibia sparkled as if whatever had scraped away the flesh had scored the metal heavily all over. Durendal recoiled from trying to understand that and laid his trophy down again. On impulse he helped himself to a few finger bones and slipped them in his pocket as souvenirs. There was only the one door. The bones had been tipped in through a trapdoor in the roof, like trash.

As he followed his Blade back along the gold-paneled corridor, he marveled at the obscene hoard. A great nation could not spend this much wealth in a thousand years, and yet a mere dozen or so maniacal monks waged daily slaughter to increase it. So infinite a fortune must surely be guarded by infinite defenses. When they came to the junction, he was very tempted to tell Wolfbiter to go to the right, back to the trapdoor, but Wolfbiter went left again and he followed.

Would the trapdoor even be there? He could easily call up a nightmare of wandering in this golden maze forever, imprisoned by some potent conjuration. If Herat had anything to do with it, the reality might be worse than anything he could envision.

The corridor went on and on. As he was deciding that they must soon reach the far side of the monastery, they came to a door of stout timbers, banded with iron. In darkness, Wolfbiter tried the latch.

Whisper. "It's not locked."

"Go ahead then. Slowly! And sniff."

The worst thing they could stumble into would be a stable full of sleeping monkeys. Even Herat might not be as bad as one of those brutes.

Slowly Wolfbiter pulled, easing hinges that would be longing to creak but not giving them the chance. The room beyond was pitch-black. A momentary flash . . . A pleased breath. "Ah!" . . . More light.

They had found the jail, a double line of barred doors. It did not smell of monkey. It did smell of men, but not recent men. Stale and foul. A few of the little cells still had rotting straw in them; some had old buckets and water jugs covered with dust. The jail had not been used for many, many years.

"If Polydin is anywhere, he should be here, sir."

"Probably. Not necessarily." Durendal went to the door at the far end.

His Blade reached it first and stood before it, barring the way. "Sir! We've seen enough."

He was absolutely right, of course. They had met with amazing luck and ought not to push it any further. How long had they been inside? The brethren must certainly rouse at dawn, if not before.

"I'm going on," Durendal said miserably—knowing he was making a mistake, knowing his friend must come with him and share his fate. "Remember if we have to make a run for it, the way out is straight down that corridor." But there was an unexplored branch in that corridor. They could be cut off.

Without wasting time on argument, Wolfbiter doused his light and tried the door. Perhaps a spirit of adventure was overcoming his caution at last.

· 9 ·

The next room had been designed for jailers, for it contained ancient wooden benches and racks for weapons. Now it was merely used for junk; a heap of old swords and axes, baskets and boxes, piles of rotting clothes. It stank of rats and immemorial dust.

It did have another door at the far end. Wolfbiter eased it open in darkness, but there was a faint light beyond. For the first time, they had reached a place that might be inhabited. It might even be luxurious, for there was just enough brightness to show that the walls and floor were patterned or tiled. It was a squarish hallway with two more doors at this level and a white stone staircase winding upward. The light was coming from somewhere up there—perhaps only starlight, but probably the first stirring of dawn—and with it came unexpected odors of flowers and vegetation and a very faint sound of running water. What lay outside? The monastery was swathed in city houses all around, so a best guess was that it was hollow, a shell enclosing an open atrium.

One of the doors was ajar, showing blackness. Staying ahead of his ward, Wolfbiter padded over to it in silence and peered inside.

"Stinks," he whispered. "Kitchens. Flies." Then he crouched down and risked a single ray of light, running it around the floor to check for more open doors. He was worried about windows, although they were probably not quite up to ground level yet. Finally he rose and went in. Durendal followed.

It was not a kitchen, it was the meat locker, containing

a single carcass, although there was space for more. It had been flayed and eviscerated and hung up by a metal hook through its hocks—upside down, of course, so that the fluids could drain from the gash in its throat. It buzzed with flies. Judging by its size, it had been Khiva son of Zambul.

Wolfbiter made a retching noise and put a hand over his mouth.

"Gold ore," Durendal whispered. "Those . . . bastards!" He could not think of words anywhere near adequate. He poked the corpse. It was stiff with rigor mortis, but the way it swayed told him it was not heavy enough to have gold bones. It would probably have fallen apart if it did.

· "But why skin him and gut him?" his Blade said. "Why leave him here to go bad?"

"Some meat improves with hanging." Not in this climate, surely?

"Sir, let's go now, please?"

"I want to look outside. Just a quick peek."

Wolfbiter sighed and followed him as he started up the stairs.

Durendal knew he had given up all hope of locating Jaque Polydin and was now motivated by pure curiosity to see a little more of the monastery. Dungeons and cellars were not enough. Where was he, though? His sense of direction had failed him. Somewhere at the back, he thought, well away from the court. This stairwell was probably in one of the towers.

They reached another decorated hallway. More stairs went upward. There were two closed doors at this level and an archway open to a shadowed garden, with faint shapes of trees and bushes. Frustrated, he stood on the step and peered out at the darkness, sniffing lush odors of greenery, very unexpected in Samarinda. A few lights glimmered in windows, and above the encircling walls the stars were fading as dawn approached. Even as he watched, more windows brightened. He could see nothing of the garden itself, but its presence showed that the monastery must be a much finer place to live in than it seemed from the outside—a palace, in effect. Everman's decision might not be quite as crazy as it had seemed.

"Beautiful!" Wolfbiter whispered. "Now can we go?"

"Yes, all right. Lead the—"

Hinges squeaked downstairs in the hall they had just left. Light flared. Wolfbiter spun around, drawing his sword. Grunts and shuffling footsteps, a door closing but the light remaining . . . Someone or something was coming up. Trapped!

Without a word, the two intruders dived out the archway, down two steps to a paved path. A tangle of shrubbery to the right of the door offered cover. Dropping to hands and knees, they squirmed underneath and lay prone. Wolfbiter mouthed some obscene words under his breath. Somewhere close, a steady tinkle of water did nothing to add to the comfort of the situation.

Light from the arch grew brighter, flickering like fire and illuminating elaborate colored tiles on the path. A monkey came shuffling out to stop abruptly not five feet from the cowering Chivians. She wore the usual garish trousers and held a flaming torch. There was a sword on her back. She snuffled suspiciously. Could she smell the intruders?

Durendal might not be able to jump to his feet and put Harvest through her heart fast enough to prevent her crying out, because animal reflexes were usually faster than human. He might trip over a branch and fall flat on his face. More light had appeared in a window overhead, meaning that more people or monkeys were coming down the stairs. Light brightened behind her. She stepped aside to make way.

Two more monkeys emerged, carrying Khiva's flayed corpse like a rolled rug on their shoulders, its death-stiffened arms stretched rigidly ahead of it. A fourth shuffled along behind them, bearing another torch, and all four headed down the path. Wolfbiter started to move and then sank back with a sound of grinding teeth as he saw more light streaming from the arch.

Durendal leaned close to his ear. "I think we may have to relax here for a while. Someone has called a meeting."

"Relax? Yes, sir. Wake me when it's time to go."

Next through the door was a torch-bearing monkey lighting the way for two tottering humans. They seemed to be two women, but they were so shrunken and bent that Durendal could not be sure. He could hear voices from the stairwell.

More torches had appeared in the far corner of the garden and begun moving slowly in their direction. Once or twice their flames reflected off water. The ground seemed to be lower at that end, so the tantalizing fountain nearby probably fed an ornamental stream and a series of ponds like the Queen's Garden at Oldmart. More windows were brightening, others going dark. The entire population of the monastery must be awake, and it was a reasonable guess that they were all on their way here.

Why? The focus was just below him, a platform of white stone, probably marble. He slithered forward under the branches until he had a better view. The floor itself was irregular in shape, bounded by ornamental walls and flower beds close at hand, a lawn at the far side. Khiva's corpse lay facedown in the center of an inlay of dark tiles that outlined an octogram. The two old women were sitting on the far edge, and now a monkey arrived carrying another, whom he set down gently beside them. No, it was a man, and the next three who came shuffling into the gathering were men also. They all stayed outside the octogram and well away from the stinking, buzzing load of bad meat that yesterday had been Khiva son of Zambul. Obviously someone was going to perform a conjuration.

Sunrise and sunset were very sudden affairs in Altain. The roofline and the towers' silhouettes were clearly visible now against the sky. Even the shadowy atrium had brightened to reveal a tiny secret paradise of lawns, bushes, flowers, little gazebos, ornate bridges, tall trees.

Wolfbiter's whisper in his ear: "Kromman will have gone by now. He was going to leave the trapdoor open."

"Can't be helped. Let's just hope all the monkeys are here at the moment. Who do you think the senility cases are?"

His Blade's eyes showed white all around their irises. "You tell me."

Durendal did not try. He could not convince even himself of what he suspected, let alone put it into words. But it had begun to make a horrible sort of sense. Some very potent conjurations could be performed only at certain specific times. Now it was dawn, the start of a new day. *By next morning I was good as new,* Everman had said.

There were twenty-three of those living corpses laid out around the platform now. Most of them were wrapped in some sort of sheet or robe, a few completely naked, all gray-skinned and either bald or white haired. Some mumbled aimlessly to their neighbors, others lay prone, as if near death. Three more were brought in and set down by their animal guardians, for a total of fifteen monkeys and twenty-six human beings, if that was a fair description of those repulsive bundles of stick limbs and sagging flesh. Most of the monkeys squatted down on the grass nearby. Two climbed into trees, but four went inside the octogram with the corpse and began to chant, first one, then another. Chivian conjurations were usually done by eight people, but other lands might know other rituals.

Wolfbiter squeezed his ward's shoulder. "Now!"

"Wait!"

"Go! I'll wait and see what happens if you want, but if you stay here any longer, I shall go out of my mind!" He was right, of course. The time to make a break was now, while the livestock was engrossed in watching the ceremony.

Durendal began to wriggle back, then paused. "Listen! They're revoking time!" The ritual was unlike any he had ever heard of, a complicated sequence of invocations and revocations that seemed to leap in purely random fashion back and forth across the octogram. All the manifest elements were being invoked. He could have predicted that, because life sprang from all four in combination: air, fire, earth, and water, while to make gold must require massive amounts of fire and earth. It seemed that all the virtuals were being revoked, even love. The entire faculty of the Royal College of Conjurers would tear its collective hair out for a chance to witness this ritual, but it was making his skin prickle. The climax came as the first rays of the sun flashed on the top of the towers. The chant ended on a long note of triumph.

The corpse moved.

Impossible! The man had been dead for twenty-four hours. His guts had been removed and his blood drained; his flesh was already rotten—and yet Khiva's limbs were stirring. He seemed to be trying to rise up.

Three of the shrunken mummies reeled to their feet and staggered across to him. Four or five more began to crawl forward. As they reached the body, they fell on it and fed, tearing at it like starving dogs. Some were rolled away by its spasmodic thrashing, but they scrambled back to try again. The monkeys lifted the weaker ones and carried them over to join the feast. Soon all twenty-six were ripping and sucking at their prey, the corpse buried beneath them. The monkeys stood back to watch, some of them hooting in amusement.

A naked woman struggled to her feet, clutching a lump of meat to her mouth with both hands. As she stood there and gorged, her body grew larger and straighter. Its color changed from the sickly pallor of the very old to vibrant youth. Her desiccated dugs filled in, rising to lush young breasts. Her hair darkened and thickened. She dropped the last fragments of her feed and screamed with laughter, showing bloody teeth.

"Durendal!" Wolfbiter said in a barely audible scream. "If we don't go now, we'll never get away!"

True. Durendal rose to his knees, still unable to tear his eyes from the bestial scene. Now men were emerging from

the melee—strong young men, where moments before
there had been only feeble geriatrics. He recognized one
who had stood beside Herat in the alley the previous day,
thick muscled and hairy chested now, yet not much more
than a boy. He laughed and lunged with bloody hands for
the woman. She jumped clear and pretended to run. He
followed. They came up the path, and she let him catch
her when they reached the arch. They embraced, bloody
mouth to bloody mouth, hands smearing reddish stains on
each other's bodies in urgent passion. They were blocking
the fugitives' escape. Wolfbiter whimpered.

Sounds of laughter came from the octogram. The rest
of the pack was opening out, youths and maidens sitting
up, strong and comely, some of them still chewing on a
bone here, an arm there. Gold glinted from those bones;
the scratches Durendal had seen on the relics in the
foundry had been made by teeth. More women jogged off
with men in pursuit. Couples flopped to the grass to en-
twine and wrestle in the exuberance of newly regained
youth.

The two by the arch disappeared inside.

"Now!" said Wolfbiter.

"Yes."

They wriggled out from under the shrubbery until they
reached the path.

"Ready?"

"Yes!"

"Now!"

They jumped to their feet and dived for the arch. Howls
and roars from monkey throats told them they had been
seen. The passionate lovers had progressed only to the
hallway and lay writhing on the tiled floor—Wolfbiter
went around them, Durendal jumped over. Together they
went plunging down the stairs.

They stumbled across the junk-infested guardroom, the light from their rings barely visible in the brightness of daylight. Wolfbiter opened the door, stood aside for Durendal to pass, then closed it behind them as Durendal ran the length of the jail and threw open the next. Its hinges squeaked shrilly. He raced off along the gold-walled corridor, hearing his Blade shut that door also. He thought they could probably outrun the monkeys, although not necessarily outfight them. Thirteen young swordsmen were loose, too, and would know shortcuts. Swordplay, if it came, would not be a matter of honorable, man-to-man duels this time.

Then something roared or screamed ahead of him, the distorted sound echoing bizarrely along the corridor. Apparently he was going to have to fight his way to the trapdoor. He drew Harvest without breaking stride. Wolfbiter's feet were slapping on the stone at his back. Then the jail door squealed and light blazed up behind them. Monkeys hooted.

He passed the turnoff to the foundry. He had almost reached the other branch when he saw a body in his path. No, it was a monkey playing tricks, scrabbling on the ground. It uttered the same discordant howl he had heard a moment earlier, apparently writhing in pain. There was blood on it, blood on the rock floor, even on the gold walls. That could hardly be a trick. Surely only Kromman could be responsible for that, so the inquisitor had not gone at first light.

"Look out for this!" he shouted, and hurdled over it.

Just beyond it was a puddle of blood and some bloody footprints leading toward the trapdoor.

"With you!" Wolfbiter responded.

Then they were out of the gold-filled cellar, running along the tunnel.

"Kromman! We're coming!" Durendal almost blundered into the wall at the end.

The trapdoor was closed.

He spun around, but Wolfbiter had turned already and was waiting for the attack with Fang at the ready. Wild hoots and bellows indicated that the pursuit had found the casualty.

"Put your boots on!" Durendal hurled Wolfbiter's footwear to him, and put on his own. They were going to need those. He scrambled up the metal brackets. Balancing precariously, he freed both hands for the slab and strained. He could not budge it. *Fire and death!* He had seen a monkey open and close it with one arm.

Holding the top bracket with both hands, he turned around to put his back to the wall and then took hold of the metal ring dangling from the flap itself. The corridor was full of gibbering apes, flashing swords, flaming torches. Wolfbiter's left-hand ring blazed, and that would be a small advantage, shining in his opponents' eyes.

Meanwhile, Durendal had to get them both out of there and do so soon, or they would find Herat and his friends waiting for them above. He put his shoulders against the slab and brought his feet up as high as he could. If he slipped, he was going to fall headfirst to the floor. He heaved with all the power he could summon from legs and back. He heard joints creak. The slab quivered reluctantly.

Metal rang as the leading monkey swung at Wolfbiter. Then rang again. Fencing in a narrow corridor would be a skill all its own. A triumphant shout from the Blade and a simultaneous animal howl proclaimed first blood.

The flap tilted and blinding daylight poured in around the edges. Durendal straightened with a convulsive heave. Clang, clang, clang . . . another yell of triumph, more animal howls. Now the angle was worse but the weight was less. The slab tilted past the vertical and settled there, erect, leaving him stretched at full length over the shaft. He scrambled out and spread himself prone on the flagstones, reaching down.

Wolfbiter came backing along the corridor into the light, clanging sword against sword. Only one monkey could get at him at a time, but a single careless stroke into a wall would ruin a parry and leave him open.

"Can you keep fighting while I lift you?"

"I'll have to!" He raised his left arm.

Durendal grabbed his Blade's wrist and levered himself up with his other hand. Fire! This was impossible. It had bloody well better be possible. Gritting teeth, he hauled, taking Wolfbiter's weight to let him climb backward up the staples while still parrying thrusts from the gibbering monkey below. Gasping, Durendal forced himself up to one knee, then both knees. Below him, swords rang, the monkey shrieking furiously as her prey worked his way up the wall, step by step, defending his legs from her strokes. Durendal got one foot on the ground and prepared to snatch Wolfbiter out bodily in one tremendous heave. Just as he tried it, Herat kicked the trap shut.

· 11 ·

Wolfbiter screamed once, although that was probably only air being expelled from his collapsing chest cavity. He must have died even before the scream emerged, when his heart was crushed.

A few early-bird challengers were watching over the wall, doubtless very puzzled by this break in routine. Half a dozen monks stood before the open door of the monastery, but they were making no move to come closer. Why bother when Herat was there already? He had a rag tied around his loins and a golden sword in his hand. His smile displayed lips and teeth still streaked with blood. Durendal drew Harvest in his right hand and his dagger in the left and leaped at him.

Herat fell back a couple of paces before the fury of the Chivian's attack—but then he continued to retreat. His smile vanished. The swords rang like the Forge at Ironhall when all eight smiths were hammering at once. He was superb, incredible. Every parry was a hairsbreadth escape from death, every riposte a mad gamble. Durendal had never met a swordsman to match him, but Durendal had a friend to avenge and very little life to lose. First blood would decide the match, for the slightest nick must throw off a man's timing and concentration just enough to leave him open to the next lunge. Lily, Eggbeater, Rainbow . . . He stayed with Ironhall style, parrying often with the dagger that was his only advantage. In provoking this contest, Herat had forgotten it would not be fought by the brethren's rules. He had overlooked the possibility of the dagger. He began by countering Ironhall with Ironhall, but soon switched to other styles, trying everything he knew to slow Durendal's murderous onslaught. Wrist, fingers, arm, feet—his control was perfection. He never repeated a stroke, and yet nothing he tried could overcome the dagger handicap. Parry, riposte, parry . . . He was retreating steadily. Perhaps his watching friends believed he was playing the same game he had played with Gartok, but this time he had no choice. Every move he made was parried by the dagger, leaving him open to Harvest's deadly tongue licking toward knees or groin or eyes.

They were almost to the gate already. Butterfly, Cockroach . . . Ah!

Harvest bit into Herat's shoulder. He cried out, and then a bloody gash opened on his ribs. Durendal had the upper hand now. He persisted, trying for a kill and still managing only flesh wounds. Face, neck, chest—he was shredding Herat as Herat had shredded Gartok; but it was not play, for every stroke was attempted murder. How could a man suffer so and still keep up that superb defense?

Then Herat backed into the wall. He recoiled with a desperate thrust, which was parried by the dagger. Harvest opened his throat, his sword clanged on the flagstones, he sprawled after it in oceans of blood. But the brethren had ways of healing, and his death must be certain. Durendal chopped off his head, taking three blows to do it.

Gasping for air, he glanced around. The men at the door had at last begun to run forward. He sprinted for the gate, only a few yards away, wondering vaguely why the swordsmen leaning on the wall were cheering.

The gate was locked—more treachery.

"Here!" yelled a voice and muscular arms stretched down to him.

He grabbed a wrist with his left hand and raised his sword arm so another man could take it. They hauled him up bodily, face to the stones. Then more hands seized his shirt, his belt, and he went flopping over the wall.

He said, "Thanks!" and was on his feet, sheathing his sword as he ran.

One shout would do it: Ten gold bars for that man!

If it came, he did not hear it. He dived into an alley and kept on running.

· 12 ·

As he pounded along the alleyways of Samarinda, dodging the first early-morning pedestrians, he was convinced that he would find the brethren already in possession of the city gate. They would have sent men to close the exit; that must be why they had not made more determined efforts to stop him. To his astonishment, no one challenged. Puffing hard in the already hot morning, he trotted out under the arch to the cramped shanty market and smelly paddocks beyond. Even when he rode away over the bare hills, he would still not be safe, of course. If the monks chose to follow on racing camels, they would ride him down in no time. The bare hills hid dangers of their own, but just to be outside the accursed walls was a huge relief.

The traders and farmers had not yet spread their awnings, and Durendal needed a few moments to locate the paddock where he and Kromman and Wolfbiter had boarded their five shaggy ponies. He identified it eventually by its owner, a bloated man with a villainous pock-marked face. His name was Ushan, and Kromman had vouched for his honesty—his relative honesty. He had been there near dusk yesterday, and he was there now. Dung stains on his clothes suggested that he slept there, which would be the only way to keep his charges from being removed by others who seemed less villainous. The next question was whether the five ponies wearing red cords around their necks were still the same healthy specimens they had been when they arrived, or whether they had aged ten years in the night. Their owners had scratched signs on each front right hoof, also, but Durendal had no time to waste arguing about such details.

He fumbled in his pocket and produced his receipt for three of them. Ushan peered oddly at this sweaty, blood-spattered, out-of-breath stranger, but without a word he swayed off into the herd and returned leading two ponies. They certainly looked familiar. Others came drifting along behind, as horses would.

"Two will do for now," Durendal said. "My friends may be along later for theirs, and I do not need my third one today. I will only require one saddle. I expect to be back before evening and will pay you then for another night.'' He must try not to arouse any more suspicion.

Again Ushan looked at him oddly. He did not say anything until Durendal was mounted, with the second pony tethered behind.

Then he spat in the dust. "For three obits, I will tell you which way your friend went."

Durendal reached in his pocket and found a gold dizork. He held it up. "Tell me everything."

The obese man shrugged. "He had been running, like you. He bought another horse, although like you he had no baggage. He went that way." He pointed west. "Fast. But he cannot have gone far yet."

Durendal threw him the coin, which he bit before making it vanish in the dirty folds of his gown. "You have just inherited two more horses, friend. And the saddles. In return, have I your silence?"

Ushan's nod of agreement was worthless, of course.

Durendal mounted and rode off to the west. He felt suddenly very happy—not because he had escaped from the city with his life, which he did not value especially highly at the moment, but because he bore an obligation for vengeance and now he knew where his quarry was. He had expected to have to wait at Koburtin until Kromman arrived. Now he could hope to catch him before being himself caught by the pursuing monks.

Three men had killed Wolfbiter and he was one of them. He had pushed his luck too far, not realizing that his luck might not shelter others. Perhaps every man learned from experience the limits of his own luck. Wolfbiter had known his and had repeatedly begged his ward to leave the monastery. Durendal had refused until it was too late. He had cut it absurdly fine, surviving only because his luck had held. So he was one of the three murderers. The only recompense he could make was to punish the others; Herat had already paid. That left one more to die.

Kromman would not expect to be followed, so he would not be taking precautions. He might well be invincible when he did, for he had resources he had refused to reveal. In a crowded city, or even a forest, he would vanish without difficulty, but here on the rolling wastes of Altain his inquisitor tricks might fail him. He could not have much of a head start.

After about half an hour, Durendal saw him in the far distance, leading his spare mount. For almost another half hour, the inquisitor rode blithely on, unaware that death was creeping ever closer at his back. When he did look behind him, Durendal was close enough to detect the move; thus he was not taken unaware when Kromman's spare horse stopped to graze and Kromman himself disappeared, mount and all.

Durendal changed horses then, so he could make a spurt in the direction he had last seen his quarry, and he abandoned his spare. Rumors of invisibility cloaks had begun to circulate about the time he'd left Ironhall, but little was known about them. He must hope that they could not mask both a man and a horse, or at least not completely. Again his luck held. Soon he detected a faint blur ahead somewhat to the right of his line of travel. He angled that way. At times he seemed to be racing alone over the dry hills. At others he could see a shadow or a riderless animal. Often he could detect dust. Another hour went by in relentless pursuit. He was parched and exhausted and his horse was in worse shape, but Kromman's was flagging badly. Every time he changed course, Durendal could cut a corner.

At last, as he was descending into a small hollow, he saw the inquisitor appear ahead of him, discarding his invisibility and slowing to a walk. When he reached the bottom, he reined in and dismounted to examine his horse's hooves, bending over each and taking his time. Durendal made sure that Harvest was loose in her sheath, not gummed there by Herat's dried blood. When he drew close enough for the sounds of his pony's shoes on the stones to be audible, the inquisitor looked up with sudden alarm.

"Sir Durendal! You startled me." If fish could smile . . . "I had given you up for lost. Wonderful! What has happened to your Blade?"

At thirty feet away, Durendal slid down to the ground and looped his reins around a dead thorn bush, which would suffice as a tether if his horse believed in it strongly enough. He walked closer to Kromman, keeping his right side to his opponent, wondering what tricks were to come.

"Exactly what you wanted to happen to him."

"I don't think I quite follow." Kromman was caked with dust. He rubbed his forehead with his arm.

Twenty feet.

"You shut the trapdoor. You locked the gate."

"Oh no! I certainly did not! That was not our agreement. If you found the trapdoor shut, the monkeys must have closed it. I expect they went and checked the gate after that. Flames! but that sun is bad, isn't it?"

"You killed Wolfbiter and you are a dead man."

Either fear or anger glinted in the fishy eyes. "That is not true! I don't know what's come over you, Sir Durendal. I shall certainly include this episode in my report."

"You will not be making a report. Now throw your sword over there—still in its scabbard. And your knife, too."

"I shall do no such thing!"

Ten feet.

Again the inquisitor raised an arm to his face. How could there be sweat on him in this virulent dry heat? The dust would soak it up if there were. Durendal started to turn his head away, but only a fraction of a second before a flash brighter than the sun seared his eyes. The two horses screamed in terror; a tumult of hoofbeats shook the world.

Blind and half mad with pain, Durendal whipped out Harvest. He could see nothing, but he knew Kromman's fighting style and his distance. He had three paces to come. One, two, three—parry! The blades clanged. If Kromman had used his customary lunge to the heart, his sword was right there, so parry! again and then riposte! He swung Harvest around like a scythe and felt her strike flesh. Kromman's shriek was accompanied by what sounded like a sword falling on the rocky ground, but he was capable of any deception. Making Harvest dance random patterns in front of him, Durendal backed away. He heard no footsteps following, and a moment later he detected a groan of pain some way off. He paused then.

Lurid green fires swayed before him; tears streamed down his cheeks. That last-minute aversion of his head had saved his sight from worse damage, for a vague grayness to his left marked reality returning. Slowly the green mists cleared until he could make out blurred shapes of thorns and rocks, and eventually he located Kromman, curled up on the gravelly ground with his sword behind him.

Durendal approached quietly, cautiously. If that black puddle was blood—for some reason he was not seeing colors—then he had seriously injured his opponent or even killed him. He hooked Kromman's sword away with Harvest, then picked it up and tossed it safely out of reach.

"Tell me why."

The inquisitor whimpered.

"Why did you leave Wolfbiter and me there to die when the hue and cry started? You followed us in. You probably saw everything we saw and more, but you had an invisibility cloak. And when you left, you deliberately locked us in to die."

Slowly Kromman turned his head. Durendal's sight had cleared enough now for him to see that he had opened the inquisitor's belly from side to side. He was lying there holding his guts in place with both hands, and no doubt suffering excruciatingly. Oh, what a shame!

"No."

Durendal's knuckles ached around the hilt of his sword as he fought to restrain his hatred. "Flames, man! You are about to die. Do you want to die with lies on your lips? You wounded the monkey—I heard it cry out, and the blood on the floor was still wet. You left footprints. You turn your toes in, you scum. Tell me why.''

The inquisitor's face blanched under its tan and dust. ''I'm sorry! Yes, I was, I mean I must have been, just ahead, or at least not far ahead of you. I panicked. That's all. I'm not a trained fighter like you, remember. I lost my head. I'm just a glorified clerk who wasn't cut out for—''

''You're a glorified slug. But that isn't the worst of it. The worst of it is that you lied about the invisibility cloak. Even if you only have one of them, there was no need for three of us to risk our lives. So what's your explanation of that, Master Kromman?''

''I'm hurt! I—I need help!''

''Well, you're not going to get it. For the murder of Sir Wolfbiter, I condemn you to death. Die, but take your time. Take all the time you want. And give my regards to your brothers the vultures.''

Durendal sheathed his sword and walked away.

· 13 ·

Three men had murdered Wolfbiter and all three must die for it. That seemed very probable and very just as he trudged back up the endless dirt slope with the sun only a foot or two above his head—or feeling like that. His eyes ached and watered so hard that he could still barely see, and the tears were all he had to drink. Kromman must have known his fancy trick with the light would spook the horses, so either he had been desperate enough to take the gamble or he had arranged some way of calling his own back to him. Perhaps that was what he had been doing when he worked on its hooves. Durendal would have to survive on his own two feet. If he lasted long enough in the heat to make his way back to the city, assuming he could find it, then he would very likely be caught by the Brethren, and that would mean Durendal for breakfast with an apple in his mouth.

He made his way to the highest elevation he could find and paused there, rubbing his eyes. He assumed they would heal in time, if he had time, but at the moment a fog of tears hid Samarinda, although he knew it must be to the east. He could tell south from his shadow. There was no sign of his horses or Kromman's, and if there were he would never be able to catch one. He would run himself to exhaustion in the attempt.

Someone was coming. At first he could not make out who or what, but probably more than one and so obviously heading in his direction that he must have been seen already. He set off across the vast landscape to meet them. It might be the Brethren intent on vengeance, and in that case he had no chance of escape. It might be Everman, having had a change of heart. It could never be Wolfbiter. No matter how marvelous the monks' healing conjurements were, they could not have repaired that much damage.

Eventually he came to an outcrop of dusky rock that, while it offered no shade, would at least be a place to sit down, so he sat down. By then he knew that the others were two camels, with only one rider.

They came up the long slope under the enormous sky until the rider was close enough to identify as Everman. He had removed his cap to show his auburn hair. He made his camels crouch on the dusty grass. Dismounting stiffly, he walked over to Durendal, handed him a water bottle, and chose a suitable rock to sit on.

Durendal drank greedily, then the two men stared at each other for a long moment.

"Repentance? Coming home?"

Everman shook his head. "I would die at dawn. I really

don't want to, anyway, but I couldn't if I did. I wasn't lying to you."

"You lied about your ward." So Kromman had said—but had Kromman been telling the truth?

Apparently he had, because Everman shrugged. "Only when I said he died of sickness. He was killed in a skirmish just this side of Koburtin. I failed my ward." He looked up defiantly.

"That's why you challenged? To die?"

"I suppose so. Before you judge my new brotherhood, brother, consider the ethics of the old." Dust had collected in the fine lines on his forehead. His hair had lost its sheen and was thinning at the front; thickening neck and jaw. . . . He saw that Durendal had noticed. "Not quite the man I was, am I?" He smiled sadly, making grooves from nose to mouth. He had not had those yesterday.

"That fast?"

Nod. "A lifetime every day. By sunset I'll be middle-aged. By midnight I'm old." He smiled ruefully. "From then until dawn it gets really bad."

"So you lied about staying of your own free will? They trapped you!"

Everman leaned his arms on his knees. He toyed with his cap, then glanced warily at Durendal. "How much did you see?"

"More than enough—animals, scavengers. Starving rats."

"You don't know what it's like. Not trapped . . . Well, partly, I suppose. They do have wonderful healings, and they kept me alive in spite of all the blood I had lost, and Herat alive, also. The next morning, the monkeys brought me a mouthful of meat. I didn't know what it was, but it worked like fire. I screamed for more, and they brought more. The next day I knew what it was, but I couldn't do without it."

"It has to be eaten right after the conjuration, I presume?"

"Within minutes. It won't keep." Everman went back

to tormenting his headgear. "Rejuvenation! You can't imagine what it's like."

"You pay for it. You just told me you'll be old by midnight."

"That isn't as bad as the real thing, though. It can't be! To have to go through that—wind going first, then speed, strength . . . senses waning, pains, decay . . . to go through all that knowing that it's permanent, that it's forever, that there isn't going to be any remission. . . . No, that must be much, much worse. Life must be one long torture. You have that to look forward to." He shrugged again. "No one survives it. Except us. We start afresh every morning."

"At a price."

"They're all volunteers! Every one of them! They know the risks. They all have a chance. In drought years, or after a big war, the waiting list grows to hundreds. All volunteers."

No, there was no repentance. An honorable swordsman had sold his soul for immortality. He could not even see the evil.

"Are they really all volunteers? What happens on the days when the challenger wins?"

"Ah!" Everman sighed and replaced his cap on his head. "Yes. Well, on those days we engage in active recruitment—but we take one of them, one of the strangers. He just didn't expect to go so soon, that's all."

"And he dies in an alley with a knife in his back instead of a sword in his hand?"

"Let's not argue, old friend." Everman shook his head sadly and put his hat on. "We're not going to agree. I did warn you that the secret wouldn't work in Chivial."

"What do you want, then?" Durendal peered around at the horizon with sudden suspicion, wondering if he was being encircled.

"Thought you might need a little help. Looks like I was right, too. What happened to your horses? What's wrong with your eyes?"

"Had a disagreement with my tame inquisitor. I won on points."

Everman shrugged. "You shouldn't consort with such lowlife. I also came to say I'm sorry about Wolfbiter. He was top drawer, wasn't he?"

"They don't come any higher."

" 'All Blades are born to die.' That's what they told us at Ironhall, but they didn't know about me. Wolfbiter's what I came about. I brought you his sword to take back."

Flames! Durendal wasn't sure if the pain was anger or sorrow, but whatever it was, it made speaking difficult. He nodded.

Everman waited a moment, looking at him as if waiting for something. Finally he said, "They say a Blade can never rest if his sword doesn't hang in the hall. Friend, you have my word on this—he has been returned to the elements in proper fashion. I lit the pyre myself. He was not a volunteer."

Would they eat Herat instead? But it was welcome news. "Thank you."

"I brought you some water and food. Two days due west, then aim for the two peaks like breasts—that'll bring you to Koburtin. The tribes have mostly gone south at this time of year. You should be all right."

Disconcerted by the painful lump in his throat, Durendal said, "Thank you. Look . . . I wish I could say I'm sorry about Herat. I never met a swordsman to match him."

"Yes," Everman said sadly. "He was no coward. He didn't shout for help, and he was risking a lot more than . . . But he had his faults. I haven't congratulated you on beating him. Let's let it go at that, shall we?"

"Yes," Durendal said. "We'd better let it go at that."

"One other thing. I am authorized to offer you his place, if you want it. No tricks, I swear. You can join us, and welcome. Forever."

"No thank you."

Everman smiled. He blinked as if he had dust in his eyes. "I'm not surprised. I'm sorry, though. You don't know what you're turning down. Just tell me this: Is our brotherhood so much more evil than yours? You don't think I'm worth all the lives it takes to keep me alive, but is your precious king?"

The outrageous question took Durendal's breath away. "I risk my life voluntarily to—"

"So do our challengers."

"Oh, that is absurd! That's crazy! Blast you! We were friends at Ironhall. We were close as brothers. Now to see a man I trusted and admired and loved turned into . . ." Into what? There was a stranger behind that familiar face. Argument would not bring back the old Everman. "We did agree to let it go at that, didn't we? You'll make it home all right?"

The monk chuckled. "Oh, I'll be stiff and so on, but I'll make it. I brought you a gold bar, as a memento. Throw it away if you don't want it. You can ride a camel?"

"Not well, but I'll get by."

They drank from a water skin and bade each other farewell as friends who know they can never meet again. They mounted and rode off in opposite directions.

MONTPURSE

V

Home proved to be very far away. Everything conspired against him—caravans, weather, and finally war. A man alone was fragile. Many times he escaped robbery only through his ability to stay awake all night. Twice he felt the approach of fever and had to bury all his valuables in a secret place and hope he would live to dig them up again. He found half Eurania up in arms. Chivial was at daggers drawn with both Isilond and Baelmark, so he was forced to return through Gevily, and even then he was fortunate not to fall into the hands of Baelish pirates. He landed at Servilham on a blustery morning in Ninthmoon 362, more than five years after he left. Converting the very last of the King's money into a dapple mare, he set off to ride the length of the kingdom.

He found his homeland strangely changed. Ambrose was no longer the popular hero he had been. Taxes had risen sharply, trade was depressed by the war, harvests had been poor for three years in a row. Queen Sian had been beheaded for treason and replaced by Queen Haralda. Bizarre fashions now ruled the cities. Gentlemen sported ruffs, vast plumed hats, grossly puffed sleeves, slashed tabards, embroidered surcoats, fur-trimmed capes. Ladies had disappeared inside clouds of drapery, sleeves trailing to the ground, and little lost faces peering out from beneath elaborate turbans. As he neared the capital, Durendal learned that he must seek out his sovereign at the great new palace of Nocare. But reporting to the King could wait a couple of days; he had a mission more important than that.

He rode in over Starkmoor around noon, being spied first by a pair of horsemen who veered to intercept him. At first glance they knew him for a Blade, but they saluted with no sign of personal recognition.

"Candidate Bandit at your service, sir."

"Candidate Falcon, sir."

Judging their eager faces, flushed pink by the wind, he would have taken them for juniors, and yet they were both armed. They were so typical and he had been away so long that they seemed almost like twins to him. He noted that Falcon had an upturned nose and Bandit's heavy eyebrows met in the middle. He berated himself for using such trivia to distinguish men with as much right to be counted individuals as he had, but he had nothing else to go on in a first encounter, out here on the blustery heath.

He did not give his name, which must have been forgotten by now. They would assume he was making a joke in very poor taste. He said only, "I come to return a sword. I cannot stay."

They exchanged frowns, then Falcon wheeled his mount and galloped off to give warning, while Bandit escorted the visitor in. He had both the sense to realize that Durendal did not wish to converse and the poise to remain silent. When they rode through the gates, the great bell was tolling.

Durendal dismounted before the monumental main door and handed the reins to a groom he did not know. "I shall not be staying. See to her needs and bring her right back."

He had thought that time had blunted the heartache, but he felt it all anew as he extracted Fang from his pack and strode up the steps. He mourned again for Wolfbiter; for friendship; for absolute loyalty, quick wits, unfailing endurance; the great promise that had been wasted to so little purpose. He mourned his own guilt. Never would he accept another Blade from the King. He had sworn that oath a hundred times since Samarinda, and he swore it again there, in the shadow of the Hall. Monarchs might bear such burdens, but not simple men like him.

No task took precedence over a Return. All the school had assembled under the sky of swords: masters, knights, candidates, with anonymous servants huddled in the background, hushed and solemn. His tread tapped a slow knell on the stone as he entered, holding the sword before him. No whispers of excitement greeted his appearance, for he had been five years gone. One or two of the most senior candidates might have witnessed his last visit, but they would have been mere children then. He had won no cups since, felled no foes. Even the faces at the high table took time to light up with recognition, and some of those were a surprise to him. Many he had expected to see were absent. There was a new Grand Master, a man who had been retired from the Royal Guard just after Ambrose's succession and whose name was Sexton or Saxon or Sixtus or something like that. The candidates seemed like babies to him, the knights like mummies. This was his fourth arrival at Ironhall, and now he knew he wanted it to be his last. He was thirty! He owned an estate, after all, Peck-something in Dimpleshire. He would not need to join that row of impotent pensioners when his arm grew slow. He had served his King well for eleven years, longer than most Blades. If she was still free, he would marry Kate and retire to be a country gentleman.

The tables and benches had been cleared away. He paced along the lines of candidates to where Grand Master stood waiting for him below the broken Nightfall. Already the second Durendal wished he had not come at all. Had he waited, the King might have given him permission to reveal some of the story, although that was not likely. As it was, the details must remain secret, and Wolfbiter's heroism untold. Bitter the injustice! On the other hand, Ambrose might have forbidden even this small tribute.

"I bring Fang," he said, hearing his voice echo dismally in the hush, "sword of Sir Wolfbiter, companion in our order. He died in a far land, defending his ward, whom he saved then and had saved several times before. Cherish his sword and write his name in the Litany, for none better deserves to be remembered there.''

Grand Master waited for more. Then, frowning, he stepped forward to accept the blade. He said only the required minimum: ''It shall hang in its proper place forever.''

Durendal stepped back one pace and drew Harvest to salute the broken blade on the wall. Then he turned on his heel and walked out. He rode away over the moors in the eye-watering wind.

· 2 ·

''By the eight, you've aged!'' Commander Hoare boomed cheerily. ''I hope I don't look as bad as that. Good to see what's left of you, though!'' He enveloped Durendal in a bone-breaking hug.

His face had not changed very much, although he had finally discarded his much-derided pale beard and there were flecks of premature silver in his hair. The rest of him was resplendent in a redesigned Guard livery, which seemed totally impracticable but might be appropriate within the new palace's sprawling wonders of gilt and marble. True, many parts of it were still scaffolding and ugly brick; to see gracious gardens in the current swamp and abandoned farmland required a considerable amount of imagination—but the inhabitants were all grandiose as peacocks.

''You look much the same,'' Durendal retorted. ''Congratulations, Leader! Is it permissible to ask what happened to your predecessor?''

"The Chancellor, you mean? Wench? *Wench!* Bring ale for our guest! Sit down, man, sit down!"

The visitor sank into a swansdown-padded chair and gazed all around the sumptuous office of quilted silk walls and ankle-deep carpets. Back in his day, the headquarters of the Royal Guard would have been rejected as stabling by the royal hostlers, while this looked like a potentate's harem. Then he stared in even greater disbelief at his elaborately bedecked host, observing that his surcoat was embellished with complex heraldry of anvils and flames and swords, topped by a motto, *To Be With and Serve.*

"Can you fight in that ensemble?"

Hoare cleared his throat and stretched out his legs to admire his elaborate buskins. "Probably not, but when was the last time we had to fight?"

"Things have changed?"

"You could say that. The King no longer campaigns in person." The Commander glanced a warning as a buxom maidservant bustled in with tankards and a small keg.

"Chancellor?" Durendal said. "Montpurse is chancellor? Um, good for him! What happened to Lord Centham?"

Hoare busied himself tapping the barrel until the door had closed behind the maid. "Treason. He was to be put to the Question today, actually."

"How is His Majesty?"

"Ah! Well, very well. Truly the *greatest* monarch Chivial has ever seen." The remark was accompanied by an expansive gesture with both hands, and a raising of expressive eyebrows. "We have a new queen, you know."

"The former Lady Haralda, I understand."

"And a real beauty! A very sweet sixteen. Just five years older than Princess Malinda. Your health, Sir Durendal, and your happy return!"

They clinked tankards.

Durendal smacked his lips. "I missed this. You really ought to try fermented goats' milk. Nothing ever tastes bad again."

"No wonder you've aged! Tell me where you've been all these years."

"Not until I have reported to the King, I'm afraid. How is Montpurse enjoying his new duties?"

"Like a double dose of crotch rot. Lord Montpurse, of course. Companion of the White Star and so on." Hoare donned an expression of cross-eyed idiocy that said nothing and hinted at a great deal. His humor bore a cynical odor it had lacked in the old days.

Yes, things had changed. All the myriad questions frothing up in the newcomer's mind had best be postponed until he learned better how the land lay. Ambrose must be . . . forty-five? Yes, forty-five. He should not be losing his grip yet. And a wife of sixteen! He would still crave a male heir, of course.

"I must request an audience to report on my mission."

"I'll arrange that for you," Hoare said. "I do have some powers, and access to the Secretary's ear is one of them. An unpleasantly hairy ear, yet a very acute one. But it was the Secretary . . ." He fell silent, staring.

Puzzled by the look, Durendal said, "I trust you can find a corner for me to call my own?"

"Absolutely! Will a two-wench bed be adequate? You realize you're officially dead, don't you?"

Durendal had been about to quaff ale. He lowered his tankard. "News to me. How did that happen?"

"I do believe that it was Secretary Kromman himself who originated that report. The King issued—"

"Kromman? Ivyn Kromman, the inquisitor? He's alive?"

His host kept an intent gaze on Durendal while taking a long drink. "Very much alive. Very close to His Majesty. Useful fellow. Relieves the Chancellor of many of his burdens."

"Do keep talking." Durendal caught himself transferring his ale to his left hand, which was a danger signal in a swordsman.

Hoare had noticed. "He returned from some foreign mission about a year ago. He had picked up some very valuable intelligence in Isilond—on the way back from somewhere else, rumor has it—and that brought him to His Majesty's attention. About a month ago, he was appointed personal secretary." Pause. "He has taken up his duties with celerity and diligence."

"Tell me how I died. I've forgotten."

"No details were revealed."

"Would it be possible for me to have that audience before the Secretary learns that I am undead?"

"How long since you came in the gates?"

"About fifteen minutes."

"Too late, then."

Silence.

"You know Master Kromman?" Hoare asked quietly. "But of course, he arrested your— I mean the late lamented Marquis. You met him that morning?"

"I have met him since, too." To reveal more, even to Hoare, might be very unwise.

More silence. Granted that Kromman had witnessed the rejuvenation conjuration in the monastery, had he actually managed to steal a sample of that revolting feast and use it to save his own life?

No. From what Everman had said, even a single mouthful would have bespelled him, so he would have been forced to go back to Samarinda and join the brethren or else die the following dawn. But Kromman's cache of inquisitorial conjurements had included spiritually enhanced bandages and simples, so it was just possible that he had managed to heal himself. Just barely possible— wounded, without horse or water, stranded in the endless wastes of Altain. Even if he had possessed some means of calling his horse back to him, it could not have been a pleasant experience. He would be no more friendly now than he had been before.

What had he told the King?

"I believe that an audience may be more urgent than I first thought, brother."

The Commander pushed away his tankard half full. "Give me an hour. He's going to be inspecting the west wing. I'll borrow livery for you—you can't meet him looking like that. You want an escort in the meantime?"

"Flames and death, man! In the palace?"

Hoare shrugged. "No, of course not. I'm just jumping at shadows."

"There must be a lot of them around," Durendal said grimly.

He had an hour. He went straight to the White Sisters' quarters and asked to see Mother Superior. Several of the sniffers came and went while his heels were allowed to cool in the corridor outside the ornate door, and he noted that they, at least, had not changed their traditional habit for any of the newfangled fashions.

The door opened again. Mother Superior was a very tall, gaunt woman with a supercilious nose and awl-sharp eyes. Her hennin almost touched the lintel, which was a good ten feet up, and she brought with her an eye-watering fragrance of lavender. She had not been Mother Superior when he left, but he remembered her. Judging by her expression, he had the spiritual attributes of a warm dung heap.

He bowed. "I am Durendal of the Royal Guard, Mother. I have been away for some time on His Majesty's business. I have just returned."

Her gaze traversed from his face down to his travel-scuffed boots and back again. Her pursed lips said *pity!*

"I wish to see one of the sisters. We were friends. Sister Kate?"

The pursed lips had become a clenched jaw. "We have no sister by that name." She began to close the door.

He stamped a foot in the opening in a fencer's appel. "She was transferred to duties in Brimiarde about five years ago, just as I—"

"There is no Sister Kate in Brimiarde," Mother Superior announced firmly. "There is no Sister Kate in the order. If you do not instantly remove your boot, I shall lodge a complaint with the Privy Council—just see if I don't!" She slammed the door in his face.

Homecoming was not turning out as he had expected.

· 3 ·

The clink of masons' hammers and a powerful stench of paint were reminders that the west wing was still under construction. Hoare knew where he was heading, though, and led the way to a huge emptiness that must be destined to become a reception hall. It was lit by enormous windows along one side, while plasterers labored in a high spiderweb of scaffolding covering the opposite wall and tilers crawled antlike around the floor, creating swirls of color. He set out across it, aiming for a group of men standing at the far end.

"If you think this is big, you should see—"

"Halt!" A squad of four Blades blocked their path, and the foremost had his sword drawn.

Hoare roared, "Snake!"

"Beg pardon, Leader. Standing orders, sir." Snake was trying with a notable lack of success to conceal his amusement at this opportunity to challenge his superior. He had been a new boy when Durendal left and now wore an officer's sash, but neither maturity nor the voluminous new livery could make him look much less like his namesake than he had before. He was still as thin as a rapier. "The Sisters are questioning your compan—" His eyes widened. "Sir Durendal! You're back! You're alive!"

Durendal said, "Wait!" before Hoare could say anything he would have to retract. Two White Sisters were hovering in the background, both of them mature, competent-seeming women. One looked close to nausea and the other not far from it, and the cause could only be the contents of the heavy bag he bore in his left hand. "I was intending to present this package to His Majesty. It is a conjurement, yes, but I did not expect it to be still active."

The three junior Blades were still adjusting to the presence of the famous Sir Durendal, but Snake himself—and, more important, Hoare also—had progressed to the next step. Their faces had hardened into doubt and suspicion. A man returns from the dead, heads straight for the King, and triggers the sniffers' alarms. Who or what was he?

"You had better leave it here, brother," Hoare said warily.

"It is fairly valuable, and I suspect the Sisters would rather have it removed from their presence." He looked at them to make the remark a question.

"Whatever it is, it is vile!" one of the women snapped.

"You speak truer than you can know. Well, let us send it to a safe place." Durendal laid down the bag and fished in his pocket for the golden bones. He transferred them to the bag without—he hoped—any of the watchers seeing either them or the gold block itself. "Leader, would you have this taken to your office, please? *Without* anyone looking inside it? And give orders for it to be kept safe and confidential."

Hoare seemed reassured but not totally convinced. "Of course. Fairtrue, see to that. Take it to my office; stay and guard it until I get back."

The young man thus addressed was sandy haired and fair complexioned, with a face suggesting more affability than intelligence. Durendal had met him before, because he had been introduced to all the candidates in Ironhall on the night of Wolfbiter's binding, and now he recognized the other two Blades also. The beefy one had been Wolfbiter's Second, by the name of . . . Bull-something.

Bullwhip. His eyes were bright with hope. So were the others'. All three of them would have been friends and contemporaries.

He shook his head. "Just me. He died with great honor, though. I returned his sword to the Moor on my way here." He watched their hopes die and imagined their reactions if they heard that Wolfbiter's killer was now within the palace. But he did not want them to get to Kromman before he did. He would explain at the inquest. He handed over the bag to the one called Fairtrue. "Careful! It's heavy."

Too late. Fairtrue dropped it with a thud that shook the hall, fortunately missing his feet. He picked it up again with an embarrassed laugh. "Must be solid gold!"

"We don't need a speech, Sir Fairtrue," Hoare snapped. "What is required in the present instance is prompt obedience to orders!"

"Yes, Leader!" Pink faced, the youngster hurried away, canted sideways by the weight of his burden.

The men all looked to the sniffers, who exchanged worried frowns. They did not seem very reassured. *Flames!* Durendal felt in his pockets to make sure he had not overlooked any more of the gold bones. None.

"Have you been carrying that package for some time, sir?" asked the elder.

"Three years, sister."

"Ah. You vouch for him, Commander?"

"I vouch for him before any man in the Guard."

She was relieved. "Then we shall assume that it is only some residual odor . . . taint, I mean, a residual taint of the conjurement."

The taint was on his soul, too. As Durendal proceeded on his way, he noticed Hoare gesturing to Snake to follow and bring his men. The incident was troubling, a shadow on his loyalty when he faced a showdown with Kromman over which of them was lying. And the King was obviously busy with other matters. To force bad news on him at such a time would be utter folly.

"Perhaps we ought to leave this for now?"

Hoare cocked a disbelieving eyebrow. "Second thoughts? You? You're certain that Kromman lied to him?"

"Yes."

"Telling fibs to His Majesty is classed as treason, and there is nothing to which Ambrose the Great assigns greater priority than treason in all its multifarious manifestations. Just watch. Wait here, all of you."

The King was consulting a roll of drawings, standing within an entourage of about two dozen men ranging from splendidly attired nobles to artisans in dirty rags, and dominating them like a swan among cygnets. At first he scowled when Hoare appeared before him, but his reaction to the whispered explanation was instantaneous, suggesting a full-force gale hitting a scatter of dry leaves on a courtyard. A moment later there was no one within twenty feet of him except Durendal, bowing low.

As he straightened, the King said, "You are very welcome back, Sir Durendal. Your return gladdens our heart."

"Your Majesty is most gracious. It is always an honor and pleasure to come into Your Majesty's presence." It was, too.

Ambrose was certainly bigger than he had been, but his height and the skill of his tailors had turned obesity into mere overwhelming mass. A lesser man must have collapsed altogether under the magnificence of his attire— fur, brocade, cloth of gold; ruff, gems, gold. Only his face gave him away: the shrunken mouth, the mountain of butter encroaching on the famous amber eyes. There was white in his fringe of beard, and the rest of it had faded to a dull brown, yet he was still an unquestioned monarch. Durendal felt small before him.

"You escaped from captivity? We shall look forward to hearing of your exploits."

"I was never captive, sire."

The piggy eyes shrank to pinholes. "Then how exactly came you to be separated from Inquisitor Kromman?"

"I left him for dead in the desert, sire. I tried to kill him and am sorry to learn than I failed."

A royal foot tapped on the tiles. "You had some reason for this, I presume?"

"Because he killed my friend and Blade, Sir Wolfbiter, and very nearly killed me also."

The King looked slowly around the great empty hall. All the spectators backed away even farther. "We are waiting, Sir Durendal."

"My liege. We arrived at Samarinda . . ."

He told the story in full detail. The King gave him his complete attention—he had always been a good listener. For twenty or thirty minutes the nobles and master craftsmen stood impotently silent, Blades and White Sisters conferred in faint whispers, tilers and plasterers worked their hearts out in case the King should glance their way. When Durendal had finished, two red blobs of fury glowed on the royal cheekbones.

"I was informed that you and your Blade insisted on breaking into the castle despite contrary advice from Master Kromman. When you did not come out at the agreed time, he returned to the lodgings you shared. He waited two weeks and when you still failed to appear he gave you up for dead and left the city."

A man could not say, I know you appointed him Secretary only a month ago and to put him on trial for treason so soon will be a public admission that he deceived you, but I am sworn to defend you from all foes and that man is a liar and a killer.

All he could say was, "I am prepared to repeat my story before the inquisitors, sire."

The King thumped the roll of drawings against his thigh a few times. "Trusting of you. Secretary Kromman told me his story in the presence of Grand Inquisitor herself."

Death and fire! A trickle of sweat ran down Durendal's ribs. The King was warning him that the inquisitors defended their own. Mention of Mother Spider raised the stakes considerably. If the King accepted his Blade's story, he must at least dismiss and perhaps destroy a senior minister. Would he even dare to try? The Office of General Inquiry might not cooperate in decapitating itself. To be certain that he had the truth of this affair, he would have to put someone to the Question, and that was using sledgehammers for drumsticks. The best Durendal could hope for now was dismissal from court. It was what he wanted, wasn't it—retirement? Honorable retirement, though.

"I have the gold I mentioned, sire. Did Master Kromman describe the gold, and, if so, how did he explain his knowledge of it?"

The shrewd little eyes grew no warmer. "He said little about gold, but I am sure he can present other explanations of how you acquired it. I want to see this gold. Where is it?"

"In a bag in the Commander's office, sire. The sniffers took exception to it."

"Damn the sniffers. You may have brought a profit for . . ."

The King had turned to look for his Blades. Hoare was grinning, having just finished saying something humorous. The other three and the two White Sisters were all shaking with suppressed laughter, unaware of the royal glare suddenly fixed upon them. It felt like a month before one of them noticed.

Hoare came hurrying over. "My liege?"

"Go and bring me Sir Durendal's bag."

"Sire, the White Sisters were very . . . Um, yes. At once, Your Majesty!" The Commander backed away, bowing. His sovereign's fury seemed to follow him all the way to the door like tongues of fire.

"Your return is most timely, Sir Durendal," the King muttered.

Not sure what that implied, Durendal said, "For further evidence, I must have imprinted a substantial scar on Master Kromman's belly."

The King left off glowering after Hoare to glower at

Durendal instead. "He was wounded when brigands attacked the caravan on his way home."

Shit! "Sire, he has obviously kept his lies as close to the truth as possible. But he did follow us into the castle, he did not wait two weeks for us to emerge, he did close the trapdoor *and* the gate on us, he certainly possessed an invisibility cloak, which—"

"Those were his orders."

"Sire?"

"The cloaks are a state secret, to be denied at all times. They do not confer invisibility, only a sort of unimportance, and they are extremely difficult to use. If an assassin walked in here wearing one, you would probably see a page or another Blade, and you would pay no heed—but only if the man kept his head. If he let his own attention wander for an instant, the cloak would reveal him. Kromman could no more have loaned you his cloak than you would loan an unruly horse to a man who has never ridden. It would have been useless to you. And if he did follow you into the killers' den, then he was taking little less risk than you were."

The swamp grew deeper every minute.

"He did not wait two weeks! He fled right away. He lied to you."

"A man may reasonably conceal his own cowardice."

"He used the cloak against me, sire, which is hardly the act of an innocent. He might just argue that closing the trapdoor was a necessary precaution with dawn breaking, but never that locking the gate was." Was this now the extent of his complaint against the King's personal secretary?

Ambrose glared at him as if he were a cast-bronze idiot. "It was already light. He assumed that you were either dead or had found a hiding place within the castle. The next night he went back and unlocked the gate and waited until dawn. He will also claim he tried to run from you later because he did not know who was pursuing him. He has hairs growing out of his nose. Is there anything else about him you dislike?''

That thumping noise must be earth falling on his coffin lid. ''If that is what Your Majesty believes, then you had better put me to—''

''No!'' bellowed the King. The watchers all shivered and retreated a few more paces. ''I don't believe it,'' he continued in his former tones of quiet menace. ''Accept an inquisitor's word over a Blade's—what kind of dunce are you calling me? He tried to steal all the glory and leave you to die, but I can't prove it without putting one of you to the Question, so I won't. He is a bottom-feeding worm, but a prince must use the tools available to him, and very few are beyond reproach, as you are. I congratulate you on a superb accomplishment. You have lived up to your glorious reputation, Sir Durendal.''

Speechless, his Blade bowed.

The King said, ''Name your reward.''

Fire! He thought of that estate he had never seen. Release? No, not that. And he had sworn to obey his liege, not to pander to his feelings. ''Justice for Wolfbiter's death, sire.''

The King swelled, his fat fists clenched, his beard bristled. ''Sirrah, remember your place! Not even you can speak to me like that! Name another.''

''I want nothing else except to continue to serve Your Majesty as best I can.'' To Be With and Serve—that would be Harvest's answer if he could ask her the same question. It was the purpose for which he had been made.

Ambrose accepted the amendment with reluctance. ''Very well, I will grant you that. But you will remember that justice is mine, Sir Durendal. I will have no duels or blood feuds in my court.''

Oh?

The hall stilled like a mill pool after a trout has taken a fly. Courtiers and Blades fell silent; even the busy artisans paused in their clinking and shuffling, as everyone sensed the confrontation—the mysterious newcomer glaring rebelliously at his sovereign, the King's face growing steadily more inflamed while he waited for assent so dangerously withheld. Veins began to bulge at his temples. His foot tapped. The onlookers exchanged shocked glances, held their breaths.

Long seconds crept by as Durendal wrestled with his soul. His friend and defender had been foully betrayed; he had bungled the necessary retribution. How could he claim one speck of manhood if he did not seek out Kromman again at once and complete the job? What use would he be to himself or anyone else if he had to live with that crushing shame? It would destroy him.

But defiance now would destroy him even sooner, certainly before he could empty Kromman's blood on the floor. Even if he were merely banished instantly from court, he would be ruined: a Blade without a purpose. What else was he good for except guarding the King?

How could he serve any king who decreed such injustice?

But he could almost hear Wolfbiter warning him not to be impulsive, arguing with cold-blooded logic that this man was the only king he had, and a good one in spite of his faults. Ambrose had more pressing concerns than the death of one of his Blades. Blades were dispensable. They accepted their powers and privileges in full understanding of the price. A monarch with a kingdom to rule, responsible for millions of lives, could not shatter the smooth running of his government by deposing Grand Inquisitor and her minions over a petty personal squabble. Sometimes even the best of kings must dilute justice with policy. And so on.

Oh, Wolfbiter!

He bowed his head in misery. "As Your Majesty commands." *Wolfbiter, Wolfbiter!*

Ambrose continued to scowl. "We trust that any wishes we may convey in future will be granted more seemly acknowledgment, Sir Durendal?"

A last flicker of rebellion: "No command Your Majesty can ever give me will hurt more than that one."

And a final spark of royal anger . . . but then a grudging nod. "You have not lost your brash insolence. A little of that can be refreshing, but don't overdo it. And no one understands better than we do how readily a ward is inspired with countervailing loyalty to his Blade."

"Thank you, sire."

"Your return is timely," the King repeated. "Commander Hoare frequently displays an inappropriate attitude to his duties. You replace him now as commander of our Guard. And I won't have him as your deputy, either."

Speechless, Durendal knelt to kiss fingers like thick pink sausages.

· 4 ·

It was typical of Ambrose that he left Durendal the job of breaking the news to his predecessor, which he did as soon as they returned to the overembellished Guard headquarters. Hoare heard of his dismissal in his own bordello of an office.

He closed his eyes in rapture. "Oh, bless you! Bless you! Bless you!"

"You mean that?"

"I will kiss your feet if you promise not to tread on my tongue. Flames, I'll do it anyway!"

"Get up, you idiot!"

Truly, the former commander did not seem to be faking his delight. He hurled himself into a chair and bellowed, "Wench! Wench! A bottle of sack for a celebration!"

"I shall need your help," Durendal said unhappily.

"Anything you want, brother, but I know you—it won't take you long to pick up the reins." Hesitation. "Did he mention release for me?"

"Um, no. I can recommend it, of course. You don't want to crawl off and rot on Starkmoor, do you?"

Blades typically resisted release vehemently, but Hoare was always an exception to rules. He beamed. "I want to go off and rot at a place called Sheer, whose lord has a most gorgeous daughter of seventeen with the sort of breasts that inspire poets to write epics."

"You mean sonnets."

"Not in this instance."

"Is she crazy enough to want a lecherous, broken-down swordsman?"

"She is mad about me. So is her father, but I can fight him off. No, I mean he approves of me as a man, but he doesn't want his only child tied to court, that's all."

With wistful thoughts of Kate, Durendal congratulated him. Times were a-changing when the Guard's most celebrated rake settled into matrimony. He wondered how many more Blades had such ambitions.

"You won't mind," Hoare said, "will you, if I go and tell her now?"

As he ran out, he almost knocked over the wench bringing the bottle of sack. Durendal sent it back to the cellar and proceeded to explore Guard headquarters. The first door he opened revealed an assembly of seven bored Blades playing dice and drinking. All of them dated from after his time, except Felix, one of his old classmates, but they all leaped to their feet to embrace him and welcome him back to the world of the living.

Touched, he broke the news that he was their new commander.

"Ha!" Felix bellowed. "Now you'll see some changes, you slipshod tadpoles! Now you'll find your backbones stiffened."

"Quite possibly," Durendal said. "And you can start by carrying a message for me, brother. Kindly inform Mother

Superior that the commander of the Royal Guard needs to see her at once upon a matter of extreme urgency. Don't mention my name. I give you fifteen minutes.''

When the formidable and somewhat breathless lady was ushered into the ostentatious office, she recoiled in horror at the sight of the man behind the great desk. A wrinkling of her nose suggested that the taint of the Samarinda conjurement had not yet faded very much. She herself had brought the same penetrating odor of lavender.

''Do be seated, Mother,'' Durendal said without rising. ''His Majesty has just appointed me to succeed Commander Hoare. I am exceedingly concerned about the King's safety, a matter on which I have overriding authority, of course.'' He scowled at a handful of papers he had snatched at random from a drawer. ''These schedules!''

She perched stiff-backed and awkward on the edge of a chair designed for lounging. ''What schedules, Commander?''

He assumed a threatening glower. ''About an hour ago, Mother, I took a very obvious conjurement into His Majesty's presence. I was not challenged until I was less than twenty feet from our sovereign lord. That is clearly unacceptable.''

''But . . .''

''Yes?''

''Nothing. Do continue.''

''I intend to.'' He slapped the unoffending documents. ''I am going to double all the guards on the palace. That will apply to both Blades and White Sisters, of course.''

She gasped and clutched both hands to her monumental hat, as if it were about to fall off. ''Double? You mean His Majesty wishes to contract for additional assistance from our Order?''

''No, I regret that the budget will not allow hiring more staff. Advise your charges that they will be working double shifts from now on.''

The old witch glared at him. ''I do not believe this!''

Durendal was ashamed to discover that bullying could

be a pleasurable occupation in certain circumstances. "If I fail to have your complete cooperation, Mother, I shall lodge a complaint with the Privy Council—just see if I don't!"

She colored in fury. She chewed her lip for a moment. Just when he had concluded that she was going to call his bluff, she said, "I investigated your previous inquiry, Commander. There was a Sister Kate, as you said. She resigned from the White Sisters almost five years ago, which is why she had slipped my mind."

"Indeed?"

"Indeed."

They eyed each other appraisingly, like fencers after a first exchange. He dropped the papers on the floor and leaned back in the chair. "And where is she now?"

"Our last information is that she returned to her parents' home."

"Married?"

"I understand not."

"In that case—and only in that case—I wish you would find her for me. I shall be posting the new duty rosters in . . . let me see—three days?"

She stood up. "Make it four!"

After so many years, what was one more day? "Four it is." He rose and bowed across the desk to her. "I look forward to working with you, Mother, on all matters pertaining to the safety of His Majesty."

"It will be interesting," she said as she swept out.

• 5 •

After the King had been safely seen off to bed that night and guards posted, the Commander was treated to a private supper in the Chancellor's opulent suite, and that august personage rewarded him by returning his sword breaker. Montpurse had aged less than anyone, for his hair had always been ash blond and he had not lost it. He even retained his Blade trimness inside vestments as sumptuous and bulky as the King's. Despite his disclaimers, he did not seem to be finding the golden chain too onerous. His worst burden, he said, was the King's creation of the office of private secretary and the man he had chosen to be the first incumbent.

"Then why don't we drink to his swift but painful demise?"

"An excellent suggestion!" The Chancellor refilled the glasses. "Kromman is a hagfish. He attaches himself and sucks out the life. Tell me what he did in Samarinda."

Cautiously Durendal asked, "How much do you know already?"

Montpurse's eyes were still the color of skimmed milk and could still twinkle in candlelight. "More than the King suspects. He swallowed some tale of the philosophers' stone and threw away a few lives on it. But one of his strengths is that he's never afraid to try something new. That's rare in aristocrats, you know? I hear you lost a good Blade. Was there anything behind the legends?"

"Quite a lot. Everman would have been after your time. . . ."

Even to Montpurse, he told little. Just a few words seeping back to the younger Blades would give the King that blood feud he did not want.

As evening drifted toward morning the Chancellor became quite talkative, passing on valuable information about ministers and nobles and even some noteworthy commoners in Parliament, supplying Durendal with an expert's eye view of Chivian government. But then he returned to the subject of Master Secretary Kromman.

"He is definitely after my job. I'd give it to him gladly if I thought I could escape with my life." That was a gentle twisting of the truth, of course. It was obvious by now that Montpurse reveled in being chancellor. "And when he has stuck my head on a spike, I am sure he will go after yours."

"I'll drink to that as an order of battle. Er, not tonight, though. I seem to have reached my limit."

"Oh, I'll come first, no question. He's efficient, Master Hagfish. He can lie to you, but you can't lie to him. The King realized his mistake very quickly. He was going to remedy it back into the cesspool it came out of, but now you've changed all that."

"Me? You're saying that I saved Kromman's job?"

The Chancellor sighed and refilled his glass. "I fear so. Court intrigue is very like fencing in some ways: thrust, parry, feint, riposte. Where was I? Oh, yes. You convinced the King that Kromman is a liar, right? And had actually lied to him. So now the King has a noose he can drop around Kromman's neck any time he wants. That increases his value immensely. I'm truly surprised Ambrose would put an incorruptible like you in charge of the Guard. He likes to use people he can menace."

"You are calling me incorruptible? What are you guilty of—clandestine nose picking?"

"Many things. Letting His Majesty believe he could fence worth a spit, for example, until a braver man than I rubbed his nose in the truth."

Durendal hurriedly reached for the decanter. "Maybe I could manage one more glass."

Montpurse laughed. "Never forget, Leader, that the best player in the game is Ambrose himself."

"I don't like the game. I don't want to be part of it."

"You will. It grows on you."

By the following noon, Durendal had interviewed every member of the Guard. Far too many of them were of his own generation, those who remembered the Nythia campaign. He made tactful inquiries about romances, ambitions, outside interests. He discovered that Ambrose had not visited Ironhall in more than eight months and Grand Master's reports told of a dozen ready seniors cribbing their stalls.

When he had prepared his report, he set off to seek an audience. He caught the King after lunch, when he ought to be a good mood; but the way he bunched his eyebrows and rumbled, "Well, what is it?" was not promising. He made no move to take the scroll being offered him.

"Briefly, sire, half your Blades are rotting from old age; they contaminate the rest. I have here a list of fifty-seven who ought to be dubbed knight and released. You don't need so many guards." The royal mouth opened, but before the foam could start to fly, he continued: "And Ironhall is bursting at the seams. If you keep those boys waiting any longer you will ruin their edge." That was as close as he dared come to saying that his sovereign should move his fat carcass to Starkmoor and stop torturing all the anxious youngsters.

But the King took it that way. His face flamed red and his beady yellow eyes glinted like those of a wild boar. "Nobody talks to me like that! I will shorten you by a head, you upstart pigsticking serf!"

Durendal knelt. "My life is Your Majesty's, always, but I swore an oath to serve you and will not serve you in any way except the best I can. To withhold unwelcome truth is no true fealty." If he was remembering a certain night when an upstart recruit had given his liege a brutal lesson in fencing, it was a reasonable wager that the King was remembering it also.

The King glared.

After about two minutes, he said, "Arrange it. And get out of here before I throttle you!"

The Commander rose, bowed, and withdrew.

· 6 ·

On the third day, heading up a wide granite stairway, he saw an odiously familiar figure in black robes mincing down toward him. Kromman's face had returned to its former pallor, but it was thinner, and the dangling hair framing it was streaked with white. They halted to appraise each other. A couple of White Sisters came by, going down. They pulled faces and went on without a word.

This was the moment Durendal had been dreading, the encounter he had wanted to put off as long as possible. It was going to take all the self-control he possessed not to draw his sword and revenge the treachery that had slain his friend. Fortunately Kromman was unarmed.

When the Sisters were out of earshot, Durendal said, "So even the vultures rejected you?"

"I fail to understand that remark, Commander." The Secretary's voice had not lost its unpleasant hoarseness. "I do wonder on what terms you obtained your release from the brethren."

"Go and get a sword!"

Kromman smiled. "If you wish. We know that you are destined to betray your king and if I must die to stop you then I shall willingly lay down my life for His Majesty. Do you plan to call me out?"

"He has forbidden it."

"How unfortunate! Of course your exalted new office pays an additional fifty crowns a year, which you will not wish to jeopardize by defying him."

Fire and death! "Don't push me any further, Kromman."

"I will push all I want, Commander," the inquisitor whispered. "I will plot and scheme, and one day I will find your blind spot and drag you down. The next round will be mine."

"No, it will be mine, because I am already old for a Blade. One day quite soon I will be released from his service, freed of my binding and my pledge. That day you die. Enjoy life while you can, Ivyn."

This was a very narrow interpretation of what he had promised—a slippery, forked-tongued, inquisitor-type of hedging—but it was all he had, and he meant what he was saying. Kromman could see that he did, and a shadow of doubt showed in his face. Durendal strode on up the staircase.

He appointed Snake as his deputy, for he seemed the brightest of the youngsters and had shown resolution in drawing on Hoare when that was his duty. The King approved the promotion without comment.

On the third day, Commander Durendal walked in on the squirrel-like bureaucrats of the Ministry of Royal Forests and explained that he was taking over their offices but they could—if they wished—occupy the Guard's old space, which was four times the size, much more luxurious, and hidden away where no one would ever bother them again.

He put two desks in the front room and set his own name on one of them. Now anyone could find the Guard without delay, and usually get the commander in person. He sent the King a note.

On the fourth day, Snake arrived at the Guard office to

find his commander in conference with six fawning tailors. Blade Fairtrue, who had been unfortunate enough to be the first man to catch Durendal's eye when he needed a victim, was being employed as a mobile tailor's dummy. His stolid, boyish face was screwed up in misery as he pranced around to order, waving his sword.

"Cockroach!" said the Commander. "Swan. Rainbow. No, that neckline is going to throttle you. Take it off. Snake! Tell me what you think of these britches."

Alarmed, Snake pulled his superior aside and hissed in his ear. "The King himself designed our livery!"

"That explains it, then. Get your pants off and try on these."

Snake glanced out at the hallway where about two hundred people were parading back and forth. "Yes, sir. If you promise not to recommend me as your successor in your famous last words."

"I won't if you behave yourself." Durendal, too, eyed that open door, realizing that more than just modesty recommended a move to more private premises. If the King had designed the livery, then he must not be allowed to hear what was going on until the entire Guard had been outfitted and the old uniforms were safely burned. Spring it on him at a big banquet, maybe—one for the Diplomatic Corps or something. Then he would have to pretend that it was his own surprise. That was Kate standing in the doorway.

Words lodged in his throat. He just stared, and she just stared—no longer as young but every bit as desirable. Smaller even than he remembered, a little plumper. And her companion . . . No mistaking those rebellious dark eyes, the brows already thicker than most, the widow's peak. Numbers whirled through his head.

Finally he said, "He's tall for his age." Then, to the consternation of the observers and for the first time since he had been only about five himself, Commander Durendal burst into tears.

· 7 ·

His years as leader flew away like swallows, perhaps because twenty-four hours were never enough for all the living he needed to do in a day. There was Kate, above all, and a mutual love that never produced a single cross word. There was winning the trust of the hitherto fatherless Andy, who had named himself by mispronouncing the name they shared and was quite the most stubborn child ever spawned by a swordsman. He was also reckless to the point of insanity, a fault that his mother would not admit must spring from her bloodlines. Soon, too, there was Natrina, the loveliest baby Chivial had ever seen.

The Treaty of Fettle brought the Isilondian war to an end, at a price. Parliament screamed that it was a national humiliation, which it was, but Lord Chancellor Montpurse retorted that a Parliament that does not vote enough funds to wage a war properly cannot expect to approve of the results. The lopsided Baelish struggle continued, with raiders ravaging the coasts almost at will: burning, looting, raping, slaving without mercy. Chivial had no way to retaliate, for Baelmark itself was impregnable, a poor and sparsely populated archipelago ringed with reefs. Parliament reluctantly granted funds to build half a dozen fast ships. The Baels caught four of them in port being outfitted and burned them. There was little cheering now when Ambrose appeared before his people.

Durendal kept the Guard youthful, undermanned, and strung tight as a lute. He escorted the King on his progresses and royal visitations—except to Starkmoor. There he sent Snake. The first time a binding was scheduled, he arranged for Montpurse to mention in passing to the King that the founder's name might possibly receive a louder ovation than the King's. Ambrose took the hint and did not insist on the Commander accompanying him.

He won the King's Cup twice more and then retired from competitive fencing, but he pointed out that only members of the Royal Guard had ever won it and vowed fearful vengeance if that tradition were to be broken. It never was while he was in charge.

Amid the pomp and panoply, when orders glittered and trumpets sang, he was closer to the King than any man. He stood with drawn sword beside the throne when the King addressed Parliament, when the King received ambassadors, when the King judged major disputes between great landowners. He developed a deep respect for the wily fat man's ability to steer his realm the way he wanted it to go. One of his duties as chief Blade was to stand guard inside the door at meetings of the Privy Council, so he was soon aware of all major state secrets. He was amazed at the way the ministers submitted to the King's browbeating, even Montpurse sometimes. Could they not see that Ambrose would respect only those who chose their ground correctly and were then prepared to defend it to the death?

On the shadowed side of the road sat the hated Kromman, lurking in his webs, ever plotting against Montpurse, always ready to exploit a mistake but seemingly making none of his own. The battle was unequal, for a chancellor must act while the secretary was a mere shadow of the King himself and rarely offered a target. Nevertheless there were some victories, as when Grand Inquisitor dropped dead and Ambrose accepted Montpurse's candidate as her successor instead of Kromman's.

There were even triumphs, as when Queen Haralda gave birth to a healthy young prince. The exultant king decreed a month's national rejoicing and named the boy after himself. There were also tragedies. The Queen died a week later, and for half a year Montpurse ran the kingdom until the King came back to his senses.

That shattering sorrow reinforced Ambrose's virulent hatred of conjuration, whose seeds had been laid by the long-dead Countess Mornicade. No number of assurances from the White Sisters would persuade him that his wife had not been slain by some antagonistic conjurer. This obsession led in turn to the King's Great Matter and thus to the downfall of Chancellor Montpurse.

· 8 ·

The epochal meeting of the council at which the Great Matter was unveiled was held in Greymere on a dreary day in early winter, with sleet beating on the windows. Ambrose's overworked ankles could no longer support his bulk for hours at a time. A couple of years ago, Secretary Kromman had introduced a chair of state into the council chamber, and the King now used it as a matter of course. His ministers remained standing, although several of them were much older than he was and there were empty chairs all around the walls.

The Privy Council was a strange mixture of hereditary nobles with resounding titles and efficient commoners who did the actual work—the High Admiral, the Earl Marshal, the High Constable, the Second Assistant to the Master of Forests. They ranged in age from thirty to eighty and were all, with the possible exception of Montpurse, terrified of the King. Black-clad Kromman stood at a writing desk in the shadows, officially taking notes but in practice fixing every speaker with his unnerving, lie-detecting stare.

The meeting was going poorly. Negotiations for the

King's marriage to Princess Dierda of Gevily had been dragging on for months, growing ever more complex, until now the draft contract included clauses on lumber exports and fishing rights. Montpurse argued for a conciliatory response, the soft line. When no one else objected, the King did. Debate raged until he had his way, and the Chancellor was instructed to send a very hard response.

To the Blade observer by the door, it was quite clear that Ambrose had only opposed the original recommendation to see if Montpurse had done his homework and would defend his position. Once the King began to argue a case, though, he usually convinced himself; he quite often ended by imposing solutions he did not really want. Durendal wondered if Montpurse had foreseen this and therefore had begun by defending the wrong goal. It was possible.

The First Lord of the Exchequer presented a harrowing account of the national finances, ending with a plea that Parliament be called into session to vote more taxes. Chancellor Montpurse warned that there was much unrest in the country and a Parliament would certainly seek redress if given the chance. Redress meant concessions, and concessions were easier to start than finish. And so on. Ambrose had been growing more and more flushed. The chief Blade was laying bets with himself on how soon the thunder would start. He won and lost simultaneously.

"Flummery!" roared the King. "Parliament? I'll give those pettifogging stall keepers something to redress. Chancellor, why do you not impose our taxes uniformly? Why does a fifth of the kingdom benefit from our rule and justice, yet contribute not a copper mite to the upkeep of the realm? Is this fair? Is this justice?"

Montpurse's face was not visible to the watcher by the door, but his voice sounded calm. "I regret, sire, that I do not understand to what Your Majesty—"

"Master Secretary, read out that report you gave me."

Kromman lifted the uppermost sheet of paper from the pile on his desk and tilted it to the gloomy winter light.

"Your Majesty, my lords. A preliminary survey of lands held by elementaries and conjuring orders indicates that they constitute in aggregate approximately nineteen one-hundredths of the arable land and pasture of Chivial. As examples, the Priory of Goodham owns more than half of Dimpleshire and large tracts in neighboring counties, the House of Fidelity at Woskin controls one third of the wool trade of the eastern counties, the Sisters of Motherhood at—''

"Sisters of Lust!" the King bellowed. "They sell love potions. The House of Fidelity traffics in mindless sex slaves. Foul conjurations! If you want an enemy cursed or a virgin enthralled, you take your gold to these purveyors of evil. And yet they pay no taxes! Why not? Answer me that, Chancellor!"

Montpurse's voice was less calm now. "I have no idea, sire. The matter has never been put to me until now. As Secretary Kromman has obviously had time to investigate the—''

"Because it has always been done that way!" said the King triumphantly. "Because no one ever had the gumption to suggest otherwise. In my grandfather's day it didn't matter. The sickness was a matter of a pox here and a pox there. But year by year these cancers grow richer and acquire more land, until now they are a blight upon the whole face of Chivial. Put that to Parliament, My Lord Chancellor! If we levy taxes upon the orders, we can reduce the impost on everybody else and still raise the revenue. How do you like that idea?"

"It is a breathtaking concept, sire. But—''

"But nothing! Why didn't you suggest it to me? Why didn't any of you? Why do I have to rely upon a mere secretary to point out this injustice in our rule, mm?" The King leaned back in his chair and smirked. "You see, not one of you can think of an objection!"

Durendal resisted a strong desire to whistle. He felt a distinct chill up and down his backbone.

"Many of these orders do good work, sire," Montpurse

protested. "The houses of healing, for instance. Others enhance seed corn, end droughts, treat—"

"They can do all that and pay taxes too! I see no reason why they should wax ever richer while the crown goes penniless. Summon Parliament, Lord Chancellor, and prepare a bill to levy taxes on them."

Montpurse bowed and the rest of the council copied him like sheep.

As soon as the meeting was over, Durendal went back to his office and tore up a recommendation to release eight Blades from the Guard. He consulted the latest report from Ironhall and penned a letter to Grand Master. He wrote another requesting a meeting with the Grand Wizard of the Royal College of Conjurers. Finally he went to call on Mother Superior, who received him in her private withdrawing room, offering him dainty plates of sweet cakes and a glass of dry mead. They were fast friends now.

The writ to summon Parliament was issued the following week, but rumors of the Great Matter had escaped already. Durendal waited upon the King.

Kromman had long since ousted the Chamberlain from the anteroom and assumed his duties there. It was well known that persons not in the Secretary's favor might need another haircut before they gained admittance to His Majesty, but that restriction did not apply to the Commander of the Royal Guard. Only once had Kromman dared to challenge his right of immediate access and then Durendal had emptied an inkwell over him.

Falcon was senior Blade on duty, with Hawkney assisting. They sprang up as Durendal entered.

"Who's in there now?"

"His lordship the Warden of Ports, sir."

That was excellent news. The Warden was a notorious windbag, whom the King suffered only because he was an uncle of the late Queen Haralda. "Poor Screwsley! I can't let the poor boy suffer like that. I shall relieve him." Durendal headed for the council room.

Kromman's dead-fish eyes glittered angrily as he went
by the desk. "You can't interrupt—"

"Then stop me."

He opened the door, causing young Sir Screwsley to
jump like a spooked frog. His lordship the Warden was
in full drone, while the King brooded by the window,
staring out at frosty branches. He spun around with a glare.
What happened next must depend on the King's reaction.
Durendal could merely gesture Screwsley out and take his
place—a breach of etiquette but hardly high treason. His
gamble paid off, though.

"Commander!" the King boomed. "My Lord Warden,
you will have to excuse us. Sir Durendal brings urgent
business, which I do believe may take some time." Laying
a meaty arm on the surprised noble's shoulders, he propelled him to the exit. Then he banished Screwsley with
a dagger glance and shut the door himself, chortling.

That left Durendal.

"Lord Warden of Windmills," the king muttered. "*Do*
you have urgent business?" His jocularity turned to
suspicion.

"Vital, sire, if not quite urgent."

The suspicion increased. "Namely?"

"Majesty, you are about to declare war on most of the
conjurers in the kingdom."

"You are not supposed to know that!"

"Half the population knows it. My job now is to prepare
a defense against the inevitable retaliation."

The next few minutes were at least as stormy as he had
expected. On one hand, the King refused to believe that
anyone would dare attack him by conjuration. On the
other, he had a deep-seated dread of exactly that. He detested his Guard's attempts to mother him, although this
was its duty. He had no lack of courage, except that he
feared being thought a coward. If Parliament heard that
he had increased his personal guard, it might refuse to
pass the bill. And so on.

Eventually Durendal went down on his knees. "My

liege, I must humbly beg you to relieve me of my duties as com—"

"Blast you! Double blast you! No, I will not relieve you of your duties. Get on your feet. Why do I tolerate your stubborn impudence? There isn't one man in the realm who defies me the way you do. I ought to fire you!"

The glare stiffened and then slowly melted. The King guffawed. "That wasn't too logical was it?"

Tricky. "It was too subtle for me, sire."

The King boomed out another laugh and thumped his Blade on the shoulder. "I just hope I don't cut off your head one day before I change my mind. How can I get rid of you this time? What's the absolute minimum you will accept?"

"Sire, I have always kept the Guard below official strength. In normal times, this keeps them on their toes. I do think times may not be normal for the next little while. There are eight seniors ready at Ironhall."

"Eight? Last report I saw said three."

"Grand Master will approve eight, sire. Mother Superior can obtain another dozen White Sisters . . ."

"At what price, mm? Blasted women bleed the treasury dry." The little amber eyes peered suspiciously out of their caves of fat. "If I go to Ironhall and let you hire six more sniffers, will that shut you up?"

Durendal bowed. "For the moment at least, sire."

"Go!" As his Blade reached the door, Ambrose shouted, "I'm only humoring you because you got that warden windbag out of my hair, you understand?"

Impulse . . . "Sire, when is his next audience?"

"Out!" roared the King.

The King rode to Starkmoor four days later, and that time Durendal went with him. He had warned Grand Master in advance about the cheering problem, and the word had been passed down the ranks. His Majesty and the Commander entered the hall together, receiving a memorable ovation. Eight excited new Blades swelled the King's escort when he departed.

Durendal, meanwhile, had quietly investigated the next crop. He urged that they be brought on as fast as possible. He held a long meeting with the knights, laying out his concerns for royal safety in the days to come.

Parliament convened. Durendal stood beside the throne while the King read his speech to the assembled Lords and Commons. Things began to go wrong very soon after that.

The Lords were quite amenable to the Great Matter. As major landowners themselves, the peers disliked the way the elementaries were gobbling up the countryside, so if the King thought he could bring them to heel, they would willingly cheer from a safe distance.

The Commons had other ideas. Taxing the conjuring orders was low on their scale of priorities, even dangerous, not necessarily advisable. The elementaries were good for business. Everyone needed healing magic, perfectly respectable burghers changed the subject when there was mention of love charms or aphrodisiacs, and many an honorable member wore a good-luck amulet under his shift. The Commons were much more interested in curtailing monopolies, raising import duties, reducing export duties, and especially in ending the accursed Second Baelish War, which had been dragging on now for more than a decade. Nor had the Commons forgotten the Treaty of Fettle.

As the voices droned, day after day, a consensus emerged—the Commons decided they particularly disliked the King's first minister. The Chancellor's duties included bullying Parliament into carrying out the sovereign's wishes, but now the Commons began to bully the Chancellor. It was his fault that taxes were so high and the cost of building the palace of Nocare had drained the treasury. He was to blame for the monopolies and perhaps the bad harvests, too. He was certainly responsible for the Fettle humiliation and the Baelish monsters turning the coasts to desert.

No decision had been reached when Parliament recessed for the Long Night festivities. The King was furious. Durendal relaxed a little.

Montpurse promised action as soon as the holiday season was over, and he was as good as his word. With flagrant intimidation and wholesale bribery, he jostled the bill along. It passed second reading in the early days of Firstmoon. One more vote would bring it to the palace for the royal seal.

If anything was going to happen, it ought to happen before that.

· 9 ·

Durendal had gone to bed. He went to bed every night, on principle, to make love or just snuggle. Even after six years of marriage, it was almost always the former—a man had to uphold the legend—and he was frequently back at Kate's side again when she awoke, for much the same reasons. While she slept, he attended to less important matters, like business, fencing, reading, or carousing. Poised on one leg, he had just put one foot into his britches when she screamed. He regained his balance and ripped the curtains aside. She was sitting up, but he could not make out her face in the dark.

"Where?" he said.

"Everywhere!" She screamed again. "It's terrible! Stop it!"

He snatched up his sword and an enchanted lantern—one of a score that he had bullied out of the College—and dashed for the door. Any normal man who abandoned his wife and children like that would be a despicable poltroon, but a Blade had no option. Kate knew that. It was shock that had made her react as she had, never fear. She would cope.

He raced across the children's room, where a five-year-old girl and a ten-year-old boy were just waking in terror at the noise. He shouted, "Look after your mother and sister, Andy!" and was halfway across the salon. Those three rooms comprised his personal world when court was at Greymere, and they were much more luxurious than any other member of the Guard enjoyed. As he reached the corridor beyond, he realized that he was wearing next to nothing. Had the alarm come five seconds sooner, he would not have had even that.

By the wavering light of the lantern, he sprinted for the King's quarters. The palace was dark and silent, although he assumed that every White Sister would be reacting as loudly as Kate had—the building was just too huge and solid for him to hear them yet. He had a long corridor to traverse and two staircases to climb. Common sense might suggest that the Commander should be billeted close to the King. That was the case in most of the other palaces and had perhaps once been the case in Greymere; but the old building had been extended and modified a hundred times, until now it was a labyrinth and any such convenient arrangement had been lost. Moreover, Blades did not sleep, so common sense did not apply to them.

He was not greatly concerned, even yet. The royal suite could only be reached through a guardroom where three Blades were always on duty. For the last three months, that number had been increased to twelve as soon as the King retired. Nor was Ambrose aware that rooms just outside the royal suite held another dozen swordsmen and more kept vigil in the grounds below his windows. The entire Guard, now comprising eighty-seven men, was on high alert and should be able to rally within minutes. Seventy-two knights had been called back from retirement and smuggled into the palace. If the king learned of them before they were needed, he would roast Durendal whole.

The problem, of course, had been to know what form the assault might take. If it involved an attack on the building with the sort of thunderbolt power wielded by the Destroyer General and his Royal Office of Demolition, then swords would be useless. Defense against fire and air was the responsibility of the conjurers of the College. Durendal had alerted them, nagged them, and—he hoped—persuaded them to take all possible precautions. The Guard was concerned only with personal assault by people, probably crazed people roused to killer madness by enchantment, like the assassins who had cut down Goisbert II.

Or so he had thought.

He had just reached the bottom of the staircase when something hurtled out of the darkness into the light of his lantern, coming straight at him. He thrust out Harvest instinctively and skewered it through its chest.

It was only a dog.

There were scores of dogs around the palace, every palace. They varied from enormous deerhounds to the cute little bundles of fluff that the ladies cuddled when they had nothing better to cuddle. This one was about the size of a sheep, of no discernible breed. No, it was *not* only a dog. It had been coming on its hind legs, so he had struck it as he would strike a man, and it ran right up the sword at him. With a yell of horror, he let go of the hilt just before the monster sank its teeth in his hand. It fell to the floor, snarling and yelping while he jumped clear of the snapping fangs, wishing he was wearing boots, thick boots.

Now he could hear uproar in the distance, two floors above him. Spraying blood around Harvest's hilt, the dog hauled itself upright, then reared on its hind legs and came at him again. He beat at it with the lantern, and it went down again. He rammed the lantern into its jaws so he could snatch the hilt and drag Harvest free. In sudden gloom, the dog rallied and attacked again, this time going for his legs. Now he knew better than to stab—he slashed, splitting its skull through one eye and one ear.

262 · Dave Duncan

It rolled in the sea of blood it had already lost. But still it was not dead. Leaping backward from its attack, he slashed and hacked, blood sticky on his hand, the lantern light winking uncertainly. He cut off the monster's head. The body reared up, front paws clawing at him. He swung mightily, and cut it in two. The halves flailed helplessly, while the head was still snapping. It couldn't move, though, so he left it and went racing up the stairs.

In the distance, the great bell began to toll, the signal he had arranged. At the first landing, he could hear tumult along the corridor in both directions—men cursing, women screaming—but he had to keep going upward, heading for the King. The dog-thing had attacked him on sight, so while the attack might be aimed at the King, everyone was vulnerable.

Halfway up the second flight of stairs, he heard claws following him. Ignoring them, he reached the top and sprinted along the passage. Lights flickered and flashed ahead of him, showing men and monsters fighting. There were bodies on the ground—men with their throats torn out, fragments of dog still thrashing and snapping. But the men were winning and now more of them were emerging from the doorways.

"Silence!" he bellowed. "Blades stay with the King." That was inevitable, of course. "Knights, go and hunt down the rest. Clear the palace!"

Close on his heels came a pack of monsters, streaming out of the darkness with eyes glowing in the light of the lanterns. Sheepdogs, mastiffs, bulldogs, wolfhounds, terriers, cuddly lapdogs—so they had been. Now many were teetering on hind legs and most of them were man-sized or even bigger, with slavering nightmare jaws. But there were twenty or more men in the press of defenders, so he squirmed through them until he reached the first door. He rapped the agreed signal—three, two, one.

Locks clattered and the door opened a slit. Terrified eyes peered out at him, and then he was allowed in. The doorkeeper was Falcon, the one with the upturned nose he had first met years ago, while returning Wolfbiter's sword to Ironhall. Now Falcon was one of the officers, although more because of his sword skills than the quality of his judgment. He slammed the door again and locked it, but by then his leader was already running through the warren of the royal suite.

He passed four dead dogs in pieces and two dead men before he reached the bedchamber. The bed curtains were ripped and torn down, revealing a girl sitting there with covers up to her chin. She was so high on the heaped mattresses that he could see her over the heads of the men standing in a ring around the bed, and he registered her ashen face and wide-stretched eyes and bloodless lips. She looked as though she wanted to scream and could not find air.

At the foot of the bed stood the King in a purple robe, with his scanty hair all awry, steadying his hands on the hilt of an upright broadsword. His expression suggested that somebody was going to die to pay for this, probably several somebodies. All around him stood Blades and knights. There were four dismembered dogs on the floor, the pieces still thrashing. Big dogs. Huge dogs, they had been. And a whole lot of blood. The air was foul with the stench of blood and offal. The expensive rugs would be ruined.

Muffled tolling of the bell and distant screaming—but in the room, sudden silence.

"You should not appear before us improperly dressed, Commander." The King was more shaken than he wanted to show, but obviously in control of himself. Starting to enjoy himself, in fact, the fat bastard.

"Anyone hurt in here?"

"Nothing serious," said Dreadnought, who had succeeded Snake as deputy commander. He had blood all over his arms and in his sand-colored beard. There was a makeshift bandage on his left wrist. "We lost a couple out there, though."

"I saw them." Durendal made a fast count. Thirty or

so. If that wasn't enough, he couldn't imagine what would be. The King, thank all spirits, was not given to sleeping with dogs. His last queen had been, though—four or five at a time—but she was gone. Lucky!

He said, "They're not just coming here, sire. They seem to be attacking anyone. I think we can keep you secure, but I'm afraid we have casualties elsewhere."

To confirm his remark, a chorus of deep baying had almost drowned out the tolling of the bell. It sounded like a choir of thousands.

The King's dawning smile shriveled away. "Has anyone any idea of how many dogs there are in the palace?"

"Not as many as there were," Fairtrue growled.

"You must have them hunted down, Commander!"

"I've arranged for that, sire."

Before Durendal could comment further, the nearest window collapsed in a shower of glass and lead and wood. The thing that came in through the drapes was roughly dog shaped, but as big as a bull. It had six-inch canines and claws almost as long. As four men converged on it, another window crashed.

Durendal jumped for the King and manhandled him toward the corner of the room. Ambrose was big. He instinctively resisted, dropping the broadsword to fight off this assault, but Durendal had more muscle and a binding to aid him. He thrust his sovereign bodily into the garderobe, slamming the door.

The King tried to open it. Durendal threw all his weight against it. "Stay there until I tell you to come out!"

The first monster was a heap on the floor, methodically hacked to pieces. The second was now being given the same treatment, but not before it had crushed a man's head in its jaws. Who had that been? There were four windows in the room. He began organizing precautionary defense at the other two. If the hound things could climb three stories up the side of the palace, the outer walls were not going to keep them from invading the grounds. How many dogs were there in Grandon? What was the range of this conjuration? How huge were they going to become?

How many windows led into the royal suite? "Flint! See to the next room!"

Another monstrosity started to come in the first window. Fairtrue hacked off a taloned paw and it toppled back and vanished into the darkness with a long, discordant howl, cut off abruptly as it met the rose garden far below.

"Nice one," Durendal said. He ran over to look out. He caught a brief glimpse of the palace with innumerable windows flickering lights and what seemed to be scores of enormous ants scrambling upward. Then a huge set of slavering fangs opened in front of him. He jumped back and rammed Harvest into the jaws.

He heard more windows shattering and a door going down in the distance, suggesting that all the defenders in the corridor were dead or wounded. It was going to be a long night. He snapped orders, setting guards on each window, with backups to spell them off and clear away the debris so that the fighters had room. The King had emerged from the closet, but just far enough to reach the bed and catch hold of the girl, who had fainted. He dragged her to him and carried her into the garderobe. He came out again, scowling at Durendal.

"I'll stay here. If they get close, I'll even hide inside."

To his own astonishment, Durendal laughed. "If they get close, I'll join you!"

Several voices shouted at once, "Leave room for me!"

Bloody flesh was making the floor slippery. The stench of eviscerated dog was appalling. Monsters fought their way in through the windows almost on one another's tails, but the Blades had their measure now—hack at the muzzles to cut away the deadly jaws, chop off the legs. The flesh still writhed, but it could do no harm.

Men began screaming out in the dressing room. Flint and his helpers fought a determined rear action, retreating back into the bedchamber before the ghoulish attackers. Soon the doorway was almost blocked by corpses.

Durendal had begun to feel better, though. His initial impression had been wrong—the sheer weight of this attack showed that it must be directed at the King. There could not be enough dogs in all Chivial to put so many into every window in the palace. Unless they started tearing their way through the stonework he could hold this room. Blades protecting their ward would fight for days before they dropped dead, and he did not think the hounds' attack could match that defense. Everyone in the room now was soaked in blood. Young Ebony was sure to lose that crushed arm and was weeping on the bed, being tended by Sailor.

It was going to be butchery, but nothing worse than that. Just a very long night.

· 10 ·

Lunch in Durendal's quarters the next day was a boisterous celebration. Snake was there, and so were a score of old friends from the past—Felix who was Keeper of Brimiarde Castle; Quinn, now Master of Rapiers at Ironhall; Hoare who was father of four—his wife produced them in pairs—and many more. It was a school reunion. Parsewood, on his knees, was lecturing the solemn Andy on what a great man his father was. Scrimpnel jiggled Natrina on his lap, and the little minx was playing up atrociously. Kate, the only woman present, was being hailed as the heroine of the hour. Nonsense, she said, every White Sister in the palace had pealed like thunder; it hadn't been detecting the conjuration that was the problem, it had been doing something about it. She beamed proudly at her husband and nagged the footmen to distribute the wine faster.

From cellar to turrets, Greymere reeked of dog guts. Flesh was being carried out in barrows. Thoughts of the death toll lurked just below the gaiety, but the Blades had won the most dramatic victory in their entire history. Every success must have a price, and in warfare it was often the price that measured the victory—a dozen members of the order had died to write this epic in the annals.

Brock, who had ambitions to be master of rituals at Ironhall one day, was pontificating on how the thing could have been done in apparent defiance of the rule that spirituality could only be applied with an octogram. Enchanted dog food, he opined, with much more confidence than conviction. Audience response was moving from scathing to outright hostile when the Chancellor walked in. Everyone who had found a seat stood up; those already upright bowed.

"No, no, no!" Montpurse pulled off his chain of office and thrust it at Kate. "Hide that in the laundry bin!" He pecked her cheek. "I'm not here officially. I just want to be one of the gang again, like old times. Franklin, you young scoundrel, what's this I hear about you and the ambassador's daughter . . . ?" He began working his way through the overcrowded room, greeting everyone by name without hesitation. Kate hung the chain around her neck for safekeeping and headed for a mirror.

"How is the big man?" asked Hoare when his turn came.

"Preening," Montpurse said with a cautious smile. "Accepting congratulations from all the peers of the realm. Don't anyone mention garderobes for the next ten years."

"Congratulations to you also," Durendal said, fighting his way through with a glass of wine. "This ought to put paid to our mutual unfriend!"

"Why do you say that?"

"Well, taxing the orders was his idea, wasn't it?"

Montpurse sipped his wine. A ripple of silence flowed out from him until he was the focus of every eye. He had never been one of the gang—even at Ironhall he had always been a chief.

"Not so simple, I'm afraid," he said quietly. "Whom do you think Parliament will blame?"

The room erupted in protest. Durendal felt a touch and turned to see the worried face of Hawkney, one of the new juniors.

"The King wants you, Leader."

Montpurse smiled thinly at Durendal and said, "Good luck."

What did that mean?

The King was in his dressing room, which alone among the rooms in his suite had escaped assault in the night. Feet had tracked bloodstains across the rugs, but there were no other signs of damage, and the stench was bearable. He was busily complicating the efforts of his valet to undress him.

Royal toilets were frequently public occasions, but this one was as private as could be, with only old Scofflaw, the valet, and a single Blade by the door—Flint, who was discreet. His commander did not post gossips to such intimate attendance on the King.

Durendal bowed when the royal head appeared from inside an undershirt.

"I owe you my life again, Commander."

"My duty, sire. And my pleasure, too."

If the King had been preening earlier, he wasn't preening now. He scowled as he stepped out of his britches. "What's the latest toll?"

"Much the same—twenty dead, seventeen mutilated, a couple of dozen bitten less seriously. About half those were civilians, the rest swordsmen. Six of the dead were women, sire, which—"

"And where did all those swordsmen come from?"

"The Blades? Oh—you mean the knights?"

"You flaming well know I mean the knights!" Ambrose said with a sort of wry menace. He was amused, though. "Hurry up, man, I'm freezing to death." That was to Scofflaw.

"Well, from all over, sire. Starkmoor, a lot of them. From the length and breadth of Chivial. They were all very glad to have a chance to serve again. . . ."

"But it was you who thought to summon them and have them standing by. I was wrong; you were right." The King sighed. "Give me your sword."

Durendal felt a jolt of alarm. "Sire, if you are planning what I think you are, I must respectfully point out that the danger has not yet—"

The King held out his hand. "I have kept you bound too long, my friend. How old are you now?"

"Thirty-five, sire." Thirty-six in a few days. "But I'm still—"

"And how old is the next oldest Blade in my Guard?"

"Four or five years younger, I suppose." Nearer ten. Panic! A Blade released from his binding was a lost soul. "Sire, I beg you to remember that reading the inquisitors made. If I'm not bound then you can't trust—"

"Readings are camel drippings!" the King boomed cheerfully. He seemed quite unaware that he was wearing only his underwear and exposing a belly that would have filled a wheelbarrow. "Bound or unbound, I trust you before anyone in the realm. Now give me your sword and *kneel*!"

Many times Durendal had watched Blades whining and pleading when faced with this terrible moment. He had always promised himself that he would not be such a fool when his own end came. Nevertheless his shaking fingers took a shamefully long time to remove his ruff, open his doublet, unbutton his shirt, and expose his shoulders. He knelt before the king. The sword that had bound him touched his flesh—right, then left . . .

"Arise, Sir Durendal, knight in our Loyal and Ancient Order."

There was no peal of thunder, no sense of change, and yet now the burden must be gone. No longer need he worry night and day about defending his ward. Perhaps it would take a few days for that realization to sink in. What was he going to do with the rest of his life? He could leave court! Kate would dance on the ceiling. Aha! He could kill Kromman!

He should have known that something dramatic would happen right after he went back to Ironhall. It always did.

Smiling, the King held Harvest out to the side. Flint came forward to take it, carefully avoiding Durendal's eye.

"Baron Roland, as I recall?"

"I suppose so, sire." Strange—it still felt like a loss.

"Your— Blast you!" That remark was directed at old Scofflaw, who had seen an opportunity to leap forward and plunge a garment over the royal head. Ambrose reluctantly put his arms through the armholes. "Your recommendation for your successor, Lord Roland? Dreadnought?"

Durendal glanced toward the door, where Flint now stood again. The King frowned and gestured for the Blade to leave, which he did, taking Harvest with him. The door closed. That left Scofflaw, but he never spoke to anyone except perhaps the King. He was older than Ironhall, probably half-witted, a bent and desiccated husk of a man. Junior Blades and younger courtiers told terrible Scofflaw jokes. (What has four legs and steams? Scofflaw ironing the King's britches.) Scofflaw did not count.

"Bandit, sire." Dreadnought was twenty-eight, much too old.

"Bandit?" The King frowned. "Which one is he?" Once he had known every Blade in his guard personally. "Not that corset, you blockhead! It pinches. The old one."

"The one with the eyebrows, sire. He never enters the Cup contest, but he's the best man by far. They'll follow him into a furnace."

The King shrugged. "Send him up, then."

"I may tell him that you asked for him?"

A chuckle. "If you wish, my lord."

With half his buttons still undone, Durendal started to bow.

"Wait. I'm not finished." The King gasped in agony, but that was merely the corset being tightened. "Pull, fool, pull! You expect me to go out looking like a butter churn? Tighter!" He groaned. "Find Chancellor Montpurse for me."

Someone tipped another bathtub of icy water over Durendal. "Your Majesty?"

"And bring me his chain."

"*Sire!* But—"

"No buts. It's for his own good. If I don't do this, Parliament will impeach him."

Sick at heart, Durendal muttered, "As Your Majesty commands." The rank injustice of it burned like ice in his belly. All this uproar was Kromman's fault, not Montpurse's. He began to bow again.

"Wait," the King said again. "We'll settle this now. I have every confidence that you will be an excellent chancellor. It brings an automatic earldom at the next investiture."

"Me? *Me?* You're joking . . . er, Your Majesty. I'm a pigsticker, not a statesman, sire!" The floor rocked under his feet.

Trailing Scofflaw on the end of his corset strings, the King stumped over to tower above Durendal. "Would you recommend I appoint Kromman?"

Oh, bastard! Couldn't he at least have found a more honorable argument than that? "Sire, I am not capable. I am only a swordsman. But Kromman is a liar and a killer and a human slug. Your Majesty cannot possibly be serious about—"

"No, I am not. Now kneel and kiss my hand and then go and get that chain."

Bugger! Gross, fat, conniving bugger! Unbound or not, Durendal could not refuse his sovereign. He knelt as Baron

Roland to kiss the King's hand and rose as first minister of Chivial.

Happily wearing his sword again, he went down to the Guard Office, where he found Bandit listening with a tolerant smile to a dozen bragging juniors. This party was more sober than the riot going on in his own quarters, but no less exuberant.

"The King wants you."

"Me, Leader? Me? He doesn't know me from a long-eared owl. Why?" Bandit was little changed from the fresh-faced kid Durendal had met on the moors the day he returned Fang to Ironhall, but he was as solid as Grandon Bastion and personable to a fault. He would handle the King as deftly as he wielded a rapier.

"I have no idea. He specifically asked for you, though."

The thick line of eyebrow bent in a frown. "There's been a mistake! He must be confusing me with one of last night's heroes. I did hardly anything."

"Tell him so to his face."

Bandit straightened his doublet and hurried off. His excessively puzzled expression was a small ray of pleasure on a very gloomy day. Durendal glanced around the company and was satisfied that none of them had guessed.

"Again I tell you that I am proud of all you," he said, "and so is His Majesty. He sends his thanks and his congratulations."

He would have done if he had thought of it.

Nor did Durendal's face give away anything when he returned to the party that was rapidly turning his quarters into a rook's nest—not even to Kate, who could usually read his features through an oak door, and who at last sight had been wearing the gold chain he was seeking but was not wearing it now. He summoned her with a glance. Frowning, she came squirming through the merrymakers to reach him. He backed out to the corridor. At close quarters she sensed the absence of his binding and lit up with a smile like a fanfare of bugles.

They hugged.

"At last you're mine!" she said. "And I am Baroness Kate?"

"And Countess Kate after the next dubbing."

"Oh?"

"He made me chancellor."

Her smile wavered. She tried to hide her feelings behind coquetry, which she was never good at. "I shall need a whole new wardrobe!"

"If that's all it takes to compensate you, then I'm a far luckier man than I deserve." He kissed her, wondering what he had ever done to deserve such a woman. "Can you forgive me?"

Someone roared his name, the old name he had been so proud to bear.

Her smile was back—a little thinner, but very fond. "Forgive? I am bursting with pride. You wouldn't be the man I love if you'd refused him. Can I wear the chain sometimes?"

"Only in bed."

"That sounds a little bizarre."

"Wait and see—we'll both wear it."

Even his bedroom was packed with revelers, so he could not shed his Guard livery yet. He gave the party a few more minutes, then slipped away again and plodded off in search of his predecessor, whom he found alone in his office, setting heaps of papers in rows on the desk. For once—perhaps because he was stooped or because the room was dim—his flaxen hair made him seem old. He looked up with a smile and lifted the chain from his shoulders.

"You knew!" Durendal said with relief. "You might have given me a hint!"

The ex-chancellor shook his head. "I guessed, that's all."

"You put him up to this!"

"I swear I did not. We never discussed it. You are the obvious choice. There just isn't anyone else he would consider for a moment. Here.'' He set the chain around Durendal's neck. "Suits you. Congratulations.''

"Condolences are more in order.''

"Oh, you'll be a great chancellor, but I admit that there is a sense of relief.'' He sighed contentedly. "I've had seven years of it—he's drained me.'' He was showing no bitterness, no regret. He had always had grace. "I was terrified he'd appoint some birdbrain aristocrat. Oh, by the way, that chain is gilded copper, not gold. Make sure the receipt you give Chancery for it says so, just in case someone accuses you of embezzlement one day.''

"You're joking!''

Montpurse chuckled. "Some of our predecessors fell into even sleazier traps than that. Now, I've sorted these by urgency. Start at this end.'' He waved his successor to his own chair and took another. "Let's see. What isn't in here? What's too secret to be written down? Well, as one ex-Blade to another, let me warn you about Princess Malinda.''

Durendal wondered how soon he could resign. Would half an hour be too short a term? "You are telling me that the King's children are my concern now?''

"Everything is your concern now,'' Montpurse said cheerfully. "She's sixteen and has her daddy's temper only more so. The sooner you can get her judiciously married off, the better.''

Amen to that! Durendal had already had some clashes with Princess Malinda, but if Montpurse had not heard about those, then he need not be troubled with the information now. He was a free man.

"And there's the war,'' the free man said. "There's only one way to stop that, of course.''

Durendal realized that he knew very little about the Baelish War. The council never discussed it. "Which is?''

Montpurse gave him a long stare. "You don't know that story?'' He spoke more softly than before. "No hints, even?''

"I haven't a clue what you're talking about.''

"Ambrose started it. The whole bloody Baelmark disaster is all his fault. I'm astonished it hasn't leaked out by now." He smiled, a smile much like his old smiles. "Well, Lord Chancellor, in this case what you don't know won't hurt you. Keep as far away from that whole Fire Lands business as you can. Perhaps, but only perhaps, it will end when Ambrose is ready to make a groveling apology to King Radgar. He knows that, but I've never had the courage to suggest it. Good luck there."

"I am not qualified for this! You have tact and—"

"But you have courage, friend, which matters more. That's what he needs—someone to tell him the truth when he's wrong and save him from himself. You're the man." Montpurse leaned back with a smile. "Anything I can do to make the transition easier, of course, just ask. I'll be glad to help all I can. But there is one more thing I must warn you about."

Durendal fingered the accursed chain. "All right, tell me the worst."

The buttermilk eyes were guarded. "We've been friends a long time."

"Flames, yes! Ever since that night I gave you your sword and you came and thanked me—you realize how long ago that was? And when I was a green Blade, just come to court. . . . I disgraced myself and everyone else fencing with the King. You could have slaughtered me and you didn't. And what you did for me when the Marquis—What's wrong? *Why even mention it?*"

There was sorrow in Montpurse's smile—and amusement, of course, and appeal, perhaps. "Because Parliament will have my head."

"No!"

"Or the King will. Be quiet and listen. Princes are not easy to serve. They in turn serve their realms, and realms are without mercy. One of the first things you will have to do is—"

"I'll stuff this damned chain down his throat first!"

"No you won't. I did the same to Centham. Will you

button up your lip a minute? Ambrose has made a mistake, several mistakes, but kings can't make mistakes. They all have to be my fault. A chancellor's job is to bear brunts.''

''Kromman—''

''Kromman wins this round. He's too insignificant to blame.'' The ice-blue eyes seemed to darken for a moment. ''Never take your eyes off that one, friend! Remember that Ambrose loves to yoke the ox and the ass together and play them off against each other. But you can handle Kromman. Parliament is another matter.''

''I won't be a party—''

''You'll do what the King needs. I tell you that it is your duty, that I bear no malice, that I did the same thing myself. May chance preserve you when your day comes, brother!''

Durendal felt ill. ''Fire and death, man! If that's what's in the wind, then we've got to get you out of the country, and fast!''

Montpurse shook his head resignedly. ''No. I swore long ago to give my life for him, and this may be the way I have to do it. It will give him a fresh start, and you also. Parliament will simmer down once it has tasted blood. Now I'm going to go home and tell my family the good news. The bad news will come when it comes.'' He rose and offered a hand. His palm was dry, his grip firm, his gaze steady. ''You'll see they don't suffer too much, won't you?''

Many a fencing bout was decided by the first appel. Some instinct told Durendal that he would never meet the King's standards as first minister unless he began with a decisive move. He had everything to learn about fighting in this new arena, he had huge amounts of backlog to absorb, and suddenly the days were a third shorter than they had been—he must waste the nights in sleeping. Nevertheless, he had attended every meeting of the Privy Council for more than five years. He knew the King, he knew the issues, and he felt very confident when he presented himself for his first formal audience as chancellor.

He had to wait more than an hour for it to begin, because the river had frozen over. His Majesty was off roistering at a court skating party, complete with an orchestra and marquees set up on the ice. Ale was being mulled, chestnuts roasted, and whole oxen turned on spits. The former commander wondered how many of the Guard could attend their royal ward on skates, but that was one worry he had been spared, in return for the many hundreds he had acquired. Eventually darkness ended the joyous occasion, sending the King back to the palace and the council chamber.

Durendal was relieved to see that the Blade on duty by the door was Bandit himself—who had guessed that Durendal was responsible for his promotion and had almost forgiven him already. Bandit would not tattle if his predecessor made an unholy fool of himself in the next hour.

However, finding Kromman about to follow him into

the council room also, Durendal said, "Out!" and shut the door in the Secretary's face.

Ambrose was already slumped in his chair of state like a heap of meal sacks. He straightened, glowering, as Durendal bowed to him.

"What did that mean, Lord Chancellor?"

"With respect, Your Majesty, I crave the right to make my confidential reports to you alone."

"Or?"

"No 'or,' sire. I merely ask that I make my confidential reports to you alone." He met the resulting anger squarely. He *could* resign now, although it would hurt horribly.

The King drummed fingers on the arm of his chair. "We shall reserve judgment. For now, you may proceed. What are you doing about my marriage?"

Even having watched the fencing at innumerable council meetings, it still felt strange to be a player. The question was designed to throw him off balance, but Ambrose was not being deliberately unkind to his tyro chancellor. It was just his style. He treated everyone that way.

"Nothing, sire." The real question was whether the fat old man really wanted the fuss and bother of a fourth wife at all, but he probably did not know the answer himself. "Since no ships can sail for at least a month, I wish to make a humble suggestion that Your Majesty use the breathing space to consider appointing a new emissary— a fresh start to go with your new ministry."

The King grunted, which was usually a good sign. "Who?"

"Have you thought of the Lord Warden of Ports, sire?"

"Why?" There was sudden threat in both the question and its escorting glare. The King might consider the warden the greatest bore in Chivial, but the man was an aristocrat and a sort of relative; and no upstart gladiator was going to make fun of him.

"Sire, as a member of your family, he would carry weight with the Gevilian royal house. He is also an accomplished negotiator." And Ambrose would love to send him overseas, far from the royal ear.

"Talks like a pigeon, you mean." The King grunted again, meaning he wanted time to think about it. "You have to go before Parliament tomorrow. What are you planning?"

This was the day's business, why Durendal had come.

"I ask Your Majesty's permission to tender this brief bill for its approval." Durendal extracted a sheet of paper from his case and offered it. He had spent half the night with two attorneys on that one page: A Bill to Wreak Justice upon Those Responsible for the Late Outrages at His Royal Majesty's Palace of Greymere and Divers Other Persons Transgressing by Conjuration Against the King's Peace and Public Decency.

Ambrose would not admit that he needed glasses. He heaved himself out of his chair and stomped over to the window. He read the offending document at arms' length, then returned it with a shrug of contempt. He began to pace.

"Chicken drippings. Sparrow feathers. You can't identify the culprits, can you?"

"The inquisitors say that's a job for the Conjurers, sire, and the College says it is up to the Dark Chamber. They may be able to narrow it down to a dozen suspects between them, that is all. Even then, they're only going by—"

"Don't blather. If you mean no! then say no! Save the pig swill for Parliament. Talk all you want there—although never, ever, tell an actual lie, not even to some lowly, smelly fishmonger."

The King continued to pace, warming to his task. No one knew more about directing parliaments without letting them know they were being directed than Ambrose IV, who had been at it for nineteen years and was now starting to train the fourth chancellor of his reign. "The second thing to remember is that everything has its price. Parliament is a great beast that gives milk only when fed. If it wants redress, it must vote taxes. If we want revenue, we must make concessions.''

Durendal wondered what Bandit was making of this, his first insight into the innermost kitchen of the state.

The King turned at the window and stood with the cold winter light at his back. ''Tomorrow, they'll start with a lot of huffing and puffing about the Night of Dogs, with loyal addresses to me, demands for the culprits' heads— the sort of drivel you just showed me. Then they'll get down to business, and the first thing you will tell them is that you have had Montpurse arrested.''

So soon! Montpurse had warned him, but must it be his first act? ''Sire! But—''

''I have not finished, Chancellor.'' Give him his due, the King did not look as if he was enjoying this. ''I just told you, everything is done by trade. We need revenue. We give them Montpurse. If we don't, they'll pass an Act of Attainder against him. Then he'll be even worse off and we'll have gained nothing—understand? And you're the new boy. We must make you popular, the Champion of Parliament. If you can just hang on to that for the first couple of sessions, you may achieve something.''

''Sire, my loyalty—''

''Is to me. The better Parliament likes you, the better you can serve me. You've gone over the books, I hope?''

''I have had them explained to me.''

''That's what I meant. The Exchequer is bankrupt. We shall have to give enormous redress to win any additional revenue—your predecessor's head will be only the start.'' The King scowled and resumed pacing. ''Our Great Matter will be defeated now. They'll claim it puts the stability of the realm at risk. You have a hard campaign in front of you, sirrah! I hope I have chosen a fighter to lead my troops?''

So here it came, the lunge he was counting on. He might doom his career as chancellor with this one suggestion. Or he might win a glorious victory and even manage to save Montpurse. ''Your Majesty's counsel will be invaluable to me. I have so much to learn. . . . But may I presume to ask . . . to offer a proposition, which is probably out of the question because of some legal snag I don't appreciate, but which in Your Majesty's greater experience may—"

"You're blathering again." The King planted his fat fists on his even fatter hips and eyed his new pupil warily. "What would you do?"

"That bill I showed you—it would authorize you to close down any elementary which offends against public decency. If it is approved, I shall advise Your Majesty to prorogue Parliament." That would save Montpurse.

"What?" The King's jaw dropped onto a layer of chins. "Go on, man, go on!"

"Well, why just tax them if Parliament will let you shut them down? You could confiscate their lands entirely. Begging your pardon, sire, but who needs taxes?"

The King stumped over to his chair of state and lowered his bulk onto it. Durendal waited to be told that he was an ignorant blockhead with congenital insanity. If the solution was so simple, surely Kromman or Montpurse or the King would have seen it long ago? Ambrose was going to laugh him to scorn and in a few months—just long enough that he would not have to admit he had made an error of judgment—he would find himself a new chancellor, one who did not advocate absurdities.

Yes, the King did begin to laugh, but he laughed until his belly heaved and tears streamed down his roly-poly cheeks into his beard. When he managed to catch his breath, he wheezed, "And I accused you of not being a fighter! You're proposing outright war! Stamp them out!"

This sounded promising. "They started the war, sire. Of course, there will be considerable danger when they realize what we are up to." The Guard would have a thousand fits—Bandit already looked as if he had just been kicked in the duodenum.

But Durendal had guessed his king would not shrink from the prospect of danger and the supposition was correct. The royal fist thumped on the chair. "Blast them all!

If we have to call on the Destroyer General, we'll do it! How will you proceed? Who'll bell this cat?"

"The inquisitors will want to, of course, and so will the College. I'd prefer to set up an independent Court of Conjury. Investigate, convict, disband, expropriate, and move on to the next. Obviously, some of the orders are beneficial—license them and let them continue. I don't for a moment suppose you can reclaim the entire one fifth that Secretary Kromman mentioned, and you may glut the real estate market, but I doubt that your treasury will run dry for a year or two."

"By the eight, I was right to pick you! A pox on Parliament! This is sumptuous!" The King smacked his lips, but then his habitual suspicion returned. "Who's going to run this Court of Conjury?"

"Your Majesty will name the officers, of course, but what I suspect you will need most is a band of fighting men brave enough to storm these lairs of evil. It will be close to war, I am sure. And the obvious men to recruit, sire, are the knights of my order. As you saw on the Night of Dogs, sir, there are dozens of them still fit and strong, loyal to Your Majesty—some married, some not, some rusting away in Ironhall, many of them with no real purpose in life. They will leap at such a chance to serve you." That was the part of his plan that appealed to him most, and he would give all his teeth for the chance to lead the army. Alas, he knew he could not hope for that.

The King muttered, "Sumptuous!" a few times. "By fire, we'll do it!" He seemed about to heave himself out of the chair, then he paused. He smirked at Durendal with his fat little mouth. "I reward those who serve me well. What do you need?"

Montpurse safely out of the country? Kromman's head in a bottle? Ten more hours in the day? "I have given you only promises so far, sire. Should not rewards wait until I can show results?"

The piggy eyes seemed to shrink and withdraw, making Durendal think of two hot chestnuts on butter. He wondered uneasily what was brewing inside the sly, unpredictable mind behind them.

"Blast honest men!" the King muttered. "I could deed you a county and you'd stuff it in a drawer and forget it. There must be some way to make you fawn like the others!"

"Your Majesty's approval is ample recompense for what I have achieved so far." That sounded like bootlicking, and yet it was true. On his first bout in the political arena, he had impressed this devious, lifelong schemer, and that felt like winning the King's Cup.

"Ha! I know what's wrong with you. Thought you looked peculiar! You're running around half naked." Ambrose peered around him. "Guard? Oh, it's you, Commander, er, Bandit. Get me the Chancellor's sword!"

With an understandable blink of surprise, Bandit opened the door and called to one of the Blades in the anteroom, who were guarding Harvest as a minor part of their duties.

What?

The King heaved himself out of his chair. "Secretary!"

Kromman scuttled in like a giant, unwinking beetle. "Your Majesty?"

"Make out a warrant!" said the King. "A decree of . . . Oh, make up a name. Addressed to the Guard." He accepted the sword from Bandit. "Henceforth, at all times and places, Baron Roland may come armed into our presence."

Durendal, Bandit, and Kromman all said "What?" simultaneously.

Then Kromman bleated, "But the readings, sire . . ."

Bandit growled, "He's worth three of . . ."

Durendal protested, "Your Majesty, I am not . . ."

The King silenced them all with a glare and extended Harvest hilt first to Durendal. "No, you're not bound now. We reward you with our trust, my lord."

Speechless, Durendal hung his sword back in her proper place at his belt. Armed and unbound! It was an honor he could not have dreamed of—the only man in the kingdom so trusted. For once, the Secretary's face was an open book, and the fury written on it was worth a dukedom. The King was smirking, so probably the Chancellor was being fairly readable himself.

Moments like those taught a man a lot about loyalty.

· 12 ·

Even the King had underestimated the fury in Parliament. Merely throwing Montpurse in the Bastion did not sate his enemies—it just whetted their appetites. Suddenly the ex-chancellor was the greatest villain since Hargand the Terrible, and neither Lords nor Commons would debate anything except a Bill of Attainder, condemning him out of hand to the Question. Duly passed by both houses, it arrived at the palace one snowy evening to receive the King's signature and become law.

The new chancellor slept very little that night and doubted that his sovereign did either. To accuse Montpurse of treason was absolute insanity—incompetence perhaps, for all men made mistakes. Indiscretion in accepting gifts from inappropriate persons was possible, but he could have done nothing to deserve what the act demanded. Yet if the King refused consent, Parliament might cut off his revenues. The decision was his to make; his Chancellor must advise him. By morning Durendal had almost convinced himself that duty to King and country required throwing Montpurse to the weasels. After all, although the Question was very harrowing, it was not fatal and would certainly clear him of the charges.

Almost convinced himself.

That must have been the right decision, though, because

Montpurse agreed with it. Even then he served his King or his former friend. His signed confession arrived not long after dawn, leaving Durendal no choice. He took the bill into the King's bedroom to be ratified.

Later that day he rode to the Bastion, accompanied by a squad of Blades. He had adamantly rejected the King's offer to assign personal Blades to him—quoting a precedent set by Montpurse—but he could hardly refuse an escort. The lads enjoyed the unnecessary outing with their former leader.

In less than a month, Montpurse had aged ten years. His scalp showed through his hair, his face was dragged down in pouches, his arms were thin. Much more surprising was an apparent serenity quite improbable in a man confined to a dark and malodorous cell with chains on his ankles and only a prison shirt and britches between his skin and the cold.

"You have absolutely nothing to fear," Durendal said. "You will throw their charges back in their faces."

Montpurse smiled sadly. "Everyone has secrets, my lord. When will it be done?"

"I'm hoping I can hold them off until the King prorogues Parliament."

"No, no! Get it over with, please. As soon as possible."

"As you wish. I'll see to it."

Knowing the man, Durendal had anticipated that request and had already given the necessary orders. He did not need to countermand them, as he would have done had Montpurse wanted a delay. He sat with the prisoner and talked about the good old days, although to him all past days must seem good now. And when the inquisitors came, Montpurse was taken by surprise.

He drew one sharp breath and then said, "You are efficient, my lord! Thank you for this."

In a case of high treason, a member of the Privy Council must attend when the suspect was put to the Question. Durendal would not delegate that terrible duty, but if it was not the worst experience of his life, he could never

286 · Dave Duncan

decide what else was. It went on forever. The elementary
in the Bastion was just another stinking dungeon, so small
that he must lean against a slimy wall with his toes almost
on the lines of the octogram. Montpurse sat bound to a
chair in the center, his face mercifully concealed by the
near darkness. Halfway through the ritual, Durendal realized with fury that one of the chanting conjurers was
Kromman, but by then the spirits were gathering and he
dared not interrupt.

The conjuration invoked water and fire, but mostly air,
until the silences seemed to whistle with hurricane winds.
Montpurse whimpered a few times and writhed against his
bonds. At the end, he sat with his head slumped forward.

"Have you injured him, you fools?"

"He has merely fainted, my lord," Grand Inquisitor
said calmly. "Quite normal. Do you wish us to throw a
bucket of water over him?"

"Of course not, you idiot! Put him to bed and call
a healer."

"I hardly think that is necessary, Chancellor."

Interpreting the regulations as liberally as he dared and
telling himself that he was merely being considerate of
his patiently waiting escort and Montpurse's own feelings,
Durendal left and returned to the palace.

Having to waste time on sleep was a nuisance. Being
deprived of it was a torment. Two days later, he went to
the King feeling as if his head had been marinated overnight in vinegar. He dropped an inch-thick statement on
Ambrose's lap.

"Drivel!" he said. "Claptrap! Picayune maundering!
There is nothing in here to convict a fox of stealing chick-
ens. He accepted gifts—but they never influenced his decisions. He spoke harshly of you behind your back—what
sort of a man would he have been if he had not? I have
said much worse myself. He delayed carrying out orders
in the hope you would change your mind—which you did,
several times. He let you beat him at fencing. When did

flattery become a capital offense? Sire, this man is innocent! You can never have had a truer or more faithful
servant."

The King scowled at him with his piggy little eyes.
"Go and talk with him!"

"What?"

"Go and talk with the prisoner! That is a command,
Chancellor!"

So Durendal rode back to the Bastion.

He found Montpurse in the same dark, stinking cell as
before, frantically trying to write in the near darkness—
on the floor under the narrow shaft that admitted what
little air and light there was, because he had no table.
Heaps of paper surrounded him.

"Lord Roland!" He scrambled up eagerly, rattling his
shackles. "I am so glad you have come!" He sounded
close to tears.

"I have read your statements and—"

"But there is more, much more! So many things I
wanted to include and they would not let me! Oh, my
friend, I welcome this chance to tell you how I betrayed
you. I was jealous. I hated you for your skill with a sword!
When you defeated me in the King's Cup I wanted to
come after you with a real blade. When you fenced with
the King on your first night at court, exposing us all as
toadies and lickspitters, I said such awful, dreadful things
to you! I detested you for my own shame, the disgrace I
had brought upon myself and the whole Guard. The first
time we ever spoke, on the night of my binding, I came
and thanked you, but not because I was in any way grateful to you. No, only to make me feel gracious and lordly.
I was a detestable person in those days. Do you know I
played with myself, back there at Ironhall? Oh, I know
every boy does, but that doesn't excuse all the lecherous
images and unclean thoughts . . . Wait, I have it all in
writing here."

He began to scrabble among his papers. He would not,
could not, stop confessing to every imaginable sin or fault

he had ever committed or even contemplated, no matter how trivial. In minutes Durendal was pounding on the door and yelling for the guards to let him out. The change, he was informed, was permanent.

He went back to the palace. In silence he took the death warrant to the King, and in silence the King signed it.

Kate

VI

·　1　·

The coach crawled interminably through the snowy night, following the lackey who walked ahead with a lantern to keep it out of ditches. Shivering even with two of the three rugs wrapped around his old bones, Lord Roland was tempted to reach for the third also, because his young companion did not seem to need it. Pride would not let him.

He was brooding again. He must say something.

"You know, it's almost exactly twenty years to the day since the King made me his chancellor—Firstmoon, 368. About the time you were born, I suppose?"

"Roughly." Quarrel's face was invisible. His tone implied that it was shameful to be so young, so another topic was required.

"Not very far to go now. Ivywalls is nearer Nocare than Greymere, of course."

"It's a beautiful place. I look forward to seeing it in spring."

Would the malevolent new chancellor allow either of them to see spring? Worry about that tomorrow. "When the King suppressed the elementaries, it was my share of the loot."

"My lord!" Quarrel sounded almost comically shocked. He would have been only a child during the suppressions.

"I speak crudely but not inexactly. It was never used as an elementary itself, or my wife couldn't go near it even now, but it was a fairly typical case. The land had belonged to the Curry family since the previous dynasty. . . . The house is much more recent. In his last

291

illness, old Lord Curry called in healers from the Priory of Demenly. While they were supposedly enchanting him back to health, they enchanted him to leave his entire estate to the priory. His wife and children were thrown out in the fields.''

"Spirits! What? That's outrageous!''

"Oh, we uncovered much worse things than that—children turned into sex toys, men and women enslaved or deliberately addicted so that they would die or suffer horrible pain unless they paid for fresh conjurations every day. Some of the ways the orders used to fight back were equally vile. It wasn't called the Monster War for nothing. Had you been my Blade in those days, Sir Quarrel, you would have had your work cut out for you. The assassins usually tried for the King or Princess Malinda, but they honored me a few times.''

The Night of Dogs had been only the start. Fortunately, Ambrose IV had never been a coward. The more they attacked him, the more determined he became. No chancellor ever had better backing.

"I'd like to hear some of those stories, my lord.''

"Ah, old man's rambling! Ancient history. The point is that we won. The King brought conjuration under the rule of law, and a lot of other countries envy us now. He did very well out of it, of course. He sold off the lands, usually; but sometimes he made gifts of them, and Ivywalls was one of those. He gave it to me like a huntsman throwing the entrails to his dog.''

"My lord! No! You weren't his dog. You were his army.''

"Not I, lad, nor the Guard, either. It was the Old Blades we called back who were his army, and Lord Snake was his general. I was just the spider in the attic, plotting where we would strike next. In time we ran out of enemies and life became much less exciting.''

After a moment, Quarrel coughed politely. "It wasn't exciting this evening?''

"Indeed it was!'' Durendal said, abashed. "Please don't

think I am not grateful. You may have set an Ironhall record—saving your ward only three days after your binding.''

''I didn't even draw!''

''You did exactly what was required, neither more nor less. Few Blades ever draw in anger. No, I am very grateful when I think where I would be now without you.''

Emboldened, Quarrel said diffidently, ''Then . . . I know a Blade should never question, but it does seem . . . I mean I don't see . . .''

The poor kid wanted to know why he was going to have to die.

''You're wondering why the King assigned a Blade to me last week and today sent Kromman to charge me with treason?''

''It puzzles me, my lord, if you don't mind my—''

''I don't mind at all. It puzzles me, too. Being unpredictable is an attribute of princes, I suppose. His Majesty certainly did not mention assigning me a Blade the last time I saw him.'' To leave the story there would be a snub. ''I went to visit him just before Long Night. You know he's at Falconsrest.''

''I've been told of it, my lord. There's a house on a crag and some other buildings below it in the valley.'' Quarrel was demonstrating that Ironhall's political lessons were up to date. ''Only the King and his intimates stay at the lodge.''

Only idiots went there at all in midwinter, but Ambrose had shut himself up at Falconsrest a month ago. Was that the action of a completely rational man?

''He did not mention Blades. To be honest, he was not at all pleased with me. Bestowing honors on me was very far from his mind. He was rather curt, I'd say.''

He was also dying, but no one said that.

· 2 ·

As Sir Bowman came twitching and shambling across the scenic spread of the Chancellor's office, Durendal rose to greet him. He honored any fellow Blade that way, and the deputy commander was always amusing company. He was a gangly, sandy-haired man, who gave an impression of extreme clumsiness, as if all his limbs were moving in different directions; but this was pure illusion, as he had proved by twice winning the King's Cup. He usually seemed ready to burst into tears, yet he had a sense of humor to rival Hoare's—whom no one remembered anymore, of course.

"Pray be seated, brother."

"How may I assist, my lord?" Bowman flopped into the chair as if he had tipped himself out of a sack. He peered morosely across the desk at the Chancellor.

"A couple of things. First, I'm trying to locate a place called Wizenbury. No one seems to know where it is. But you have Guards from all over, so if you wouldn't mind asking around the—"

"Appleshire," Bowman said gloomily. "I was born near there." Blades never discussed their past, but he had still a trace of the west in his voice.

"Ah, thank you." The Chancellor had found the sheriff he needed for Appleshire, and he suspected that Bowman knew perfectly well why he had asked that absurd question. "The second thing is a little harder. I must go and visit the King. Do you think you could find a couple of patient souls who might bear the tedium of walking their horses beside my palfrey?"

Bowman uttered a moan of ironic disbelief. "Suicidal daredevils who might just be able to keep up with you, you mean? I think I have some crazies who may accept the challenge. The entire Guard," he added with an abrupt descent into ever deeper melancholy.

Five days before Long Night, the palace of Greymere ought by rights to be bespangled with decorations and throbbing with jollity. This year it was a drab barn of boredom, and the longest faces were the Blades'.

"You miss His Majesty. We all do."

"Mice don't play when the cat's away, my lord. They die of irrelevancy. I wish Dragon would let us rotate the men, but he's stopped doing even that. Useless wear and tear on the horses, he said. He doesn't think of the rust on the men."

"Would you consider a suggestion?"

"Very happily, my lord—from you."

"Your livery's frowzy and old-fashioned. I can say so, because I designed it myself, but that was years ago. Something more modern would make them feel better, liven them up."

Bowman gave him an especially lugubrious look. "You think His Majesty would approve it? He doesn't even like to change his socks these days."

"No, I don't suppose he would, but . . . Never mind."

"Yes. Well, my lord, I will very gladly provide you with an escort. When?"

"An hour before dawn. We'll be back for the festivities."

The Blade sighed. "I doubt if you'll miss much if you aren't. Nothing more?" He began to lurch upright.

"Not for me. Anything I can do for you?"

Bowman sagged back again quickly, as if he had been hoping for such a question. His voice dropped to a confidential murmur. "Well . . . it isn't really any of my business, my lord, nor of yours either, and I know you'll pardon my presumption saying so, but I know that Grand Master has seniors stacked up to the roof. I just thought, if you get a chance to sort of drop a word to the King, maybe? We could use some young blood in the Guard; but even if he doesn't want to go there himself just now, he might assign them to others, perhaps?''

Durendal shrugged. It certainly was not his business, because he was government and the Order was in the King's personal prerogative. Ambrose was very touchy about that distinction. ''I'll see what I can do. You don't have to tell me that he doesn't answer his mail.''

At first light, Durendal rode out of the gates on Destrier, in the company of three boys. They would be furious if they knew he thought of them as that, but their ages combined would not exceed his by much. Their names were Foray, Lewmoss, and Terror, and they were all glad of a chance to seem useful. He noted that they were well mounted and all had good seats, which meant that Bowman had sent his best horsemen—probably with strict orders to prevent any repetition of the embarrassing incident that had marred the Chancellor's last journey to Falconsrest, when a certain geriatric Chancellor had shown certain young Blades his heels. Well, he would see how he and Destrier felt on the way back.

A miserable wind moaned under a dreary sky, once in a while throwing snowflakes just to warn that it had plenty in hand. Falconsrest was an all-day ride from Grandon, but they could stay overnight at Stairtown if the weather turned worse. Going two by two, his guards took turns riding at his side, courteously wheedling tales of the past from him, flattering him by asking about the Monster War or even the Nythia campaign—none of which ancient history could possibly be of any interest to them.

They were all hoping that Commander Dragon would let them stay on at Falconsrest, relieving three of the dozen or so men he kept there. Durendal found this ambition amusing, because there was absolutely nothing in those wild hills that should attract spirited young men in the middle of winter. It was their binding talking. They pined at being kept away from their ward. When Foray even had the audacity to ask why the King had shut himself up in such a burrow over Long Night, Lord Roland sternly suggested he ask the King himself. The answer, alas, was that he hated people watching him die.

He questioned them about recent news from Ironhall. They would not realize that it was none of his business; as a knight of the Order, he was expected to be interested. They confirmed what Bowman had said about a surfeit of seniors waiting for assignment.

Between chats, he pondered the unfamiliar future that lay beyond the King's death. For the first time, he would be free to do what he wanted. Travel, probably, because Kate wanted to travel. He had friends and correspondents all over Eurania now, and standing invitations to visit. He would be a private citizen, but a famous one, welcome in a dozen great cities. Thanks to Ambrose, he was rich. It would seem very strange.

He led the way into the valley as the winter afternoon faded out in despair. The group of thatched buildings cowering under the snow-covered hills was commonly known as the village, although it consisted entirely of overflow accommodation. The lodge on the rock that loomed almost directly above it was the palace proper, but it had only four rooms. There was something bizarre about the court of Chivial sheltering in sheds.

While he shed his cloak and stamped snow off his boots, he was greeted by Commander Dragon, who was a beefy, thickset man by Blade standards, with a luxurious black beard and a swarthy complexion that made him seem older than his twenty-eight years. In complete contrast to his deputy, Dragon had no sense of humor at all. He was a plodder who would never question an order or think for himself, which was precisely why the King liked him.

"Much the same, my lord," he said before Durendal could ask the inevitable first question. "I'll send someone to tell him you're here. A posset to warm you now?"

"Add some hot bran mash for my horse and I will be in your debt till the sun burns out. Although I think that may have happened already."

"It will be back," Dragon assured him solemnly.

Shack or not, the barn-sized room was bright and hot. Some amateur musicians were screeching out dance music. Strips of colored muslin added a seasonal gaiety above the long tables at which people were guzzling great slabs of pork, while the rest of the hog sputtered and sparked on a spit. Durendal's insides rumbled imploringly for attention.

Sternly telling them to wait their turn, he sent for the royal physicians and conjurers. They would not commit themselves on their patient's condition, perhaps deterred by the law that declared imagining the King's death to be high treason. They certainly offered no hope. He looked around the ring of haggard, tight-shut faces and resisted the temptation to try a royal bellow on them.

"I trust you will give me as much warning as you can of any change you foresee in His Majesty's condition?"

They nodded in noncommittal silence. He went off to eat. Just when he was about to start on a high-piled platter, a Blade with snow on his eyebrows appeared to inform him that the King would receive him at once. On his way out he had to pass Foray, Terror, and Lewmoss, all chewing vigorously with grease running into their beards. He hoped they choked on their stupid grins.

As he was donning his damp cloak at the door, Dragon appeared again, glancing around furtively.

"My lord?"

"Leader?"

"If you get the chance to drop a word to His Majesty . . . I know he listens to you, my lord."

"Sometimes he does. What can I do for you?"

"The Guard, my lord." The Commander was whispering, which was very unlike him. "I've got twenty men I want to release, you see. They're all well past due. I've mentioned this, but . . . well, he won't even discuss it with me. It would be a nice Long Night present for them, I thought.''

Durendal sighed. ''Yes, it would. I'll see what I can do.''

Obviously Ambrose was neglecting his precious Blades, and that was a very bad sign. Was he incapable of making decisions or merely clinging to the past, the old familiar faces?

Huddled against the snow, the Chancellor rode a dogged little mountain pony up the steep track to the lodge. Where the village had been festive, the lodge was dreary as a tomb, although it was crammed full of men. To cross the guardroom he had to pick his way along a narrow path through a clutter of bedding and baggage, passing half a dozen Blades playing a morose game of dice by the light of a single candle. The stairs took him up to another dormitory, which was little brighter and so congested with men that it was hard to believe they would all find room to lie down later. They seemed to be grouped into three snarly arguments. He wondered who they all were: cooks, hostlers, valets, doctors, nurses, secretaries? He had seen no women, but he had not looked into the kitchen, which probably also served as a communal bathhouse and another bedroom. People swarmed on a king like bees on a queen—there might well be tailors, musicians, falconers, vintners, or even architects and poet laureates in attendance at Falconsrest. Every one of them would fight for the right to live in the squalor of the lodge rather than the relative comfort of the village, just to prove that he was of the indispensable elite. This is what happened when monarchs tried to escape.

At least the King's bedroom was not stuffed like a fish barrel. It held a few chests and a great four poster, whose faded purple draperies rippled in drafts that rattled the shutters and baffled the best efforts of a roaring fire. The other rooms had reeked of bodies and overworked garderobes, but here those stinks were overwhelmed by the rancid stench of the suppurating ulcer that was killing

Ambrose IV. He sprawled back on heaped pillows, a face of melted tallow above an enormous heap of furs. Were those just shadows under his eyes or mildew?

He had outlived four wives and his son; he had never seen his grandsons. After a reign of thirty-nine years, his realm had shrunk to this windy kennel, and every gasping breath was a noisy effort. Durendal knelt to him.

His voice rasped disturbingly. "Get up, fool! Can't see you down there. Sorry . . . drag you all this way . . . such weather."

"It is a pleasure to get some exercise, Your Majesty. They tell me that your health is improving."

"Told you . . . all I needed was a rest!" The King glared defiantly. He was still not yet admitting anything.

With extreme annoyance, Durendal noted the odious Kromman standing inside the closed door, almost invisible in his midnight robes. He was stooped now, a sinister cadaverous scarecrow, but the fish eyes still held their sharklike menace.

"What's this I hear," the King wheezed, "about you steeplechasing, beating my Guard?" The question showed, and was intended to show, that he had other sources of information—Dragon in this case, of course, but Kromman ran an efficient spy network quite apart from the Office of General Inquiry. There were undoubtedly others. Wily old Ambrose had not loosed his grip on his kingdom yet.

"Sire, if you must give me a horse like Destrier, you cannot expect me to haul fish with him." He could still flinch under the royal glare. "On the way back last time I did suggest a small race. My escort agreed, and I won by a nose—purely because I had the best mount. It was foolish and unkind to the horses." Luckily Kate had not heard of the incident.

The King gasped a sort of cough that was probably meant to be a laugh. "Two fell off, you won . . . three lengths. Won't hurt brats . . . know best man still best." His tone changed to annoyance. "Why're you here, bothering me, interrupting vacation?"

Durendal turned to look at Kromman.

"Oh, let him be," the King snarled. "Only eavesdrop in the crapper. Can't keep secrets, this place."

Why torture a dying man with a personal squabble? "As Your Majesty wishes." Durendal reached in his pack and brought out his folder of papers. "I need your instructions about a few matters, sire. The Nythian rebels are the most urgent, as they are due to be hanged in three days. A royal pardon at Long Night is—"

"Hang 'em."

"Two of them are only boys, sire, thirteen and—"

"Hang 'em!"

Very rarely in his twenty years as chancellor, Durendal had gone so far as to kneel and offer Ambrose the golden chain. There were some places even loyalty could not go and hanging children ought to be one of them; but his resolution failed when he looked at the dying despot. Even if the King had no pity for those rebel brats, Durendal felt pity for him and could not desert his liege lord now.

"Yes, sire. Next item. The Exchequer requests approval of this warrant."

He held out the paper, but Kromman moved in like a stalking cat to take it. He placed it on a writing board and extended it to the King, offering a quill. Ambrose signed without looking, a wandering scrawl. The Secretary removed the board and withdrew to the shadows. How much influence had the former inquisitor gained over the invalid? At least the privy signet was still on the royal finger.

After that, the King listened to the problems in silence broken only by his labored breathing. Each time he waited for the Chancellor's recommendation, then nodded. Kromman obtained his signature and took it away to seal.

With rising distress, Durendal pressed on. At first they had been teacher and pupil, then a team—a quarrelsome but effective team—for almost twenty years. Now he made the decisions and the King approved them. Chivial was ruled by an aging chancellor, which was not good enough. He wanted to retire and enjoy a little of the private life he had never known, but he could not abandon his post now. It was hard not to curse or weep.

At the end, he bowed. "There is nothing else of great moment, sire. The rest can wait until your return. Er, Parliament? It is summoned to convene in three weeks, sire. Do you wish to postpone—"

The King barked, "No!" and was convulsed by coughing. When he recovered, he just glared.

"Then your speech, sire . . . ?"

"Send me . . . draft, what you need."

He would never be well enough to journey back to Grandon and address Parliament, but obviously that was not to be said.

Alas, the good old days! In his first ten years as chancellor, Durendal had spoiled Ambrose, letting him rule as an autocrat. Squandering the wealth of the elementaries with mad abandon, he had needed no taxes and brooked no interference with his own will. When he had at last been forced to summon Parliament again, he had run into ten years' backlog of complaint. It hadn't ended yet. Each Parliament seemed worse than its predecessor.

"That's everything, then, sire." One last paper. "Oh . . . It is not urgent, but you still need a new sheriff for Appleshire. I was wondering if you would consent to appoint Sir Bowman. He would—"

"Who?"

"The deputy commander."

The King recognized his slip and reacted with anger. "You keep your meddling fingers off my Guard, you hear?"

"Of course, sire, I was merely—"

"None of your business! I'll see to, all that when . . . get back."

"No, sire. I realize."

The invalid made a feeble effort to heave himself higher on the pillows and then sank back with a groan. "Did . . . daughter reply . . . your letters?"

"No, sire."

"Did . . . tell her I'm sick?"

That question could kill a man coming and going. No would mean that Durendal had not done enough to convince the Princess. Yes would contradict the King's official policy. Any hint of dying was treasonous. "I did mention that your health was causing some concern, sire."

"Just want see them. Did . . . tell her so? One at a time, if won't trust me."

Durendal sighed. "I have sent every message and messenger I can think of. I have even dispatched an artist, with a plea that he may be allowed to sketch the princes. I haven't heard from him yet, but you must make allowances for the weather at this time of year, sire. No ships are crossing. Why not let Secretary Kromman try writing to her and see if he has any more luck?" He had nothing to lose by making this suggestion, because it was certain Kromman would have tried already, with or without permission. Princess Malinda's feelings toward Lord Chancellor Roland need not be mentioned.

A tremor of the old anger shook the King's moribund mass. "Take hostages. Seize Baelish ambassador, merchants . . ."

"You don't mean that."

"Cockscomb!" Color showed now on the pale butter cheeks. "Upstart peasant! Think you can run kingdom, when . . . can't even manage one stiff-neck slut? Willful biddy!"

That was hardly fair when they were discussing his daughter, who was also the wife of a foreign ruler. There was much more to the Princess problem than her personal spite. Parliament had always detested the idea of a barbarian Bael succeeding to the throne of Chivial, even if the marriage treaty did stipulate that Malinda would reign in her own right and her husband would be no more than consort. Parliament had grave doubts that a notorious pirate chief like King Radgar would pay much attention to that legal nicety. Worse, Parliament was going to be grievously concerned, meaning mutinous, if the King was too ill to address it in person while his heir was far away on those barren rocks. There would be talk of a regency, moves to tamper with the succession, delegations sent hither and thither. Time was running out for the part-time ruler—but Ambrose was shrewd enough to know all that.

"I have done my best, sire. I am sure that your grandsons will turn up to visit you in the spring, when the sailing improves."

The King turned his head away. *What spring?*

"My business is complete, my liege. I humbly beg leave to withdraw."

Ambrose did not look around, but after a moment he muttered, "Have safe . . . ride home."

Durendal lifted the pudgy hand to his lips. It was as cold as the winter hills beyond the shutters. "I won't go above a canter. You know I never do."

There was no reply.

Kromman held the door open for the Chancellor. Their eyes met as Durendal went by, and he saw a gleam of triumph that twitched his old fighting dander. Was that odious intestinal worm gloating because the King was about to die and then Lord Roland would no longer be chancellor? Very likely! He probably considered himself so indispensable that the new Queen would have to retain him in her service. Good luck to her! And to him—they deserved each other.

Of course the King's death would also free Durendal from his pledge of good conduct. He still owed vengeance to Wolfbiter, but over the years his anger had faded to sad resignation, a private fantasy to amuse himself when the Secretary was being particularly obnoxious. Justice belonged to the King, and by failing to act against Kromman, the King had effectively pardoned him. Durendal had sworn his oath as a young and footloose bachelor, a vagabond newly returned from wild lands where blood feuds were common as fleas. Now he was a husband, a father and grandfather, and a respected elder statesman with rich estates, not a man who would throw away his life and destroy his family's happiness to so little real purpose. Must he admit that he was just too old? That he no longer had the juice in him to be an executioner? No, the slug just wasn't worth the scandal now.

· 3 ·

Three days after Long Night, the courier's bag that carried routine business back and forth between the King at Falconsrest and the scriveners of the Privy Purse at Greymere produced a warrant assigning a Blade to Lord Roland—a standard form bearing the King's signet and signature, with the recipient's name inserted in the King's hand. It was promptly sent along the hall to Durendal, who puzzled over it for an hour, wondering not only why the King had sent it but also why it had not come to him directly. A companion bag had brought him other documents.

It might be a simple error. Ambrose's illness had not dulled his wits so far, but if he had decided to clear the backlog of seniors at Ironhall by distributing them to ministers and courtiers, as he sometimes did, then perhaps he had inadvertently written the wrong name. An inquiry to Privy Purse brought the response that it had been the only assignment received.

Other routine papers the King had dealt with showed no signs of mental confusion. Eventually Durendal took the riddle home to show Kate, and they argued over it into the night. The most plausible explanation they could devise was that the King was at last preparing to die and knew that his chancellor's reign would end as soon as the new Queen could lay her hands on a pen and a stick of sealing wax. Durendal had inevitably made enemies in serving his sovereign; how could he refuse such a farewell gift? Eventually Kate persuaded him he must accept.

The next morning she left to visit their daughter and he set off for Ironhall. He did not call at the palace to obtain an escort—partly because it would have taken him out of his way and partly because he had still not definitely decided to go through with the binding. If he changed his mind, he would not want the Guard to know about the warrant. He went alone, confident that his swordsmanship was still capable of dealing with any reasonable peril.

Besides, Deputy Commander Bowman was still being difficult about what had happened to Lord Roland's last escort.

At noon, when Durendal reached the moors, he was almost ready to turn back, but some deep stubbornness drove him on. After all, he could visit Ironhall without ever mentioning the warrant. By the time he reached the doors, night was falling and he knew that he was going to go ahead with the binding. Whatever the King's motives, he was still the King, and a lifetime of obedience was not to be set aside now. It did seem a shabby trick to play on some eager youngster, though.

The current Grand Master was Parsewood, whom he had known only briefly before starting his trip to Samarinda, but who had distinguished himself in the Old Blades during the Monster War. Having never married, he had settled down at Ironhall to end his days in teaching; the Order had elected him its chief three years ago. He was depressingly grizzled and had lost most of his teeth, but he greeted the Chancellor with enthusiasm and a very welcome mug of hot mulled ale to drive away the winter chill. He must be curious to know why Lord Roland was being assigned a Blade now, after twenty years as chancellor, but he did not ask. They settled on either side of the fireplace in his private chamber.

"Prime? Name of Quarrel. Rapier man." He shrugged.

"Nothing exceptional, nothing to worry about. He'll never take the Cup, but a good, sound lad. Very charming. He shines there. Will break a few hearts, I'm sure, but that's the legend, yes?" Grand Master sighed nostalgically.

If there was nothing exceptional about Candidate Quarrel, then he could not hold the key to the King's strange decision. "Can he ride?"

"Like a centaur."

That did not sound as if the King was just trying to put an end to steeplechasing, which had been one of Durendal's wilder theories.

"He doesn't compare with Foray, Terror, or Lewmoss, of course," Grand Master said in an odd tone. "Superb equestrians, all of them."

"What are you implying?"

"Story is that you wrecked half the Guard. I heard three broken legs, one collarbone, and a severe concussion. Assorted ribs."

"An unfortunate accident! The hedge hid the ditch completely, but that black of mine has feet like a cat. I shouted back to warn them, but I was too late. That's all. I was extremely lucky."

Grand Master leered and took a drink.

Annoyed that such embarrassing tales were going around, Durendal said stuffily, "I'm told you have a surfeit of seniors just now."

"Officially twelve. More, really. It could have been worse, but we cut back enrollment about five years ago, when the King's health began to, er, cause concern. Lately we've picked up again. Why are you smirking?"

"That was not a smirk, Grand Master. Chancellors never smirk. That was quasiregal approval you detected. I was just thinking how well His Majesty is served—hundreds or thousands of people all quietly doing their best to promote his interests."

"His? The Crown's. When they think we're not listening, the seniors refer to themselves as the Queen's men."

"This is not a frown," Durendal said, "it's a quasiregal caution against imagining the King's death."

"Well, he is over seventy," Grand Master protested, adding, "brother," as a precaution. "How is his health, hmm?"

"Not as good as he would like, frankly. His leg bothers him a bit. Still sharp as a den of foxes, though."

"We'll all be the Queen's men one day, I expect. The bindings translate, because we swore allegiance to him and his heirs. You will give the seniors a few pointers with the foils tomorrow, won't you?"

"Me?" Durendal laughed. "Grand Master, my wind is hopeless these days! I'm slower than a spring thaw."

"But your technique, man! Ten minutes watching your wrist will do 'em more good than a month's practice."

Oh, flattery! "If you insist. But not for very long, especially on an empty stomach."

"Knew I could count on you." Grand Master chuckled. "They have their own name for you, you know? They call you 'Paragon.'"

Paragon? Horrors! Didn't they realize what politics did to a man? *Paragon* was obscene! Durendal opened his mouth to call the whole thing off, but Grand Master was already on his feet.

"Ready to meet your Blade now?"

Suppressing his doubts, Durendal consented. They went to the chilly little flea room, and in a few minutes the Brat opened the door for Prime and Second. It was all horribly reminiscent of that first sight of Wolfbiter, half a lifetime ago.

Within Blade limits, Quarrel was tall, much taller than Wolfbiter, but equally dark, lithe like a rapier himself. Second was a stocky, broad-shouldered redhead, probably a slasher—Candidate Hereward. Babes, both of them. Had they even been born the last time Durendal came to Ironhall?

The ritual words were spoken. The boys turned, and Candidate Quarrel had his first sight of the old man who would claim his absolute allegiance—shock, horror, and dismay. Durendal knew that he had made a mistake, but it was too late to back out. The poor kid was stuck with him now.

The embarrassing moment passed as soon as the antiquated visitor was named, when Prime made a very fast recovery, feigning wild enthusiasm. "Incredible honor . . . never dreamed . . . admired here in Ironhall beyond any other . . ." He was wasted as a swordsman. He should have gone on the stage.

· 4 ·

The following night, Quarrel was bound. On the third night after that, Kromman came to Greymere with the king's writ. . . .

"Her ladyship returned this afternoon, my lord." Caplin lifted the cloak from Durendal's shoulders. Candlelight from the chandelier glistened on the steward's shiny scalp and the bunched cheeks of his smile. "An uneventful journey, she said. She is in the library. May I take that for you, Sir Quarrel?"

"No worry." Quarrel tossed his cloak over a chair, Ironhall fashion.

It would not be tolerated there for long in Caplin's demesne. His standards were much narrower than his person, which almost rivaled the King's in width and depth, if not in height. A jewel, was Caplin—about twenty million carats. He had shed his smile as he noted the absence of the gold chain. "Her ladyship has already dined, my lord. You did say you would be remaining at the palace tonight."

"A welcome change of plan. Have Pardon attend to the horses and see that the coachman and the lackeys are suitably boarded—can't send them back tonight. Tell Churpen I want to clean up and change, please. Then I will second Sir Quarrel at one of those celebrated banquets you call snacks. I think he can last another half hour before he dies of starvation."

His Blade flashed a winsome grin. "I estimate just short of forty-two minutes, my lord."

"Come and meet my good lady."

Durendal led the way through to the library, his favorite room, scented by leather bindings and wood smoke. A pine fire crackled merrily on the slate hearth and rows of books smiled down from tall shelves.

He braced himself to break the tidings and did not have to. She missed the chain instantly and hurried to him, her eyes hunting out all the implications before he could even open his mouth. Her hair had never lost its golden shine and was well served by the current fad for small bonnets. On the other hand, her figure was too delicate for the tight bodices worn with the newfangled farthingale, which favored the voluptuous. Tonight she was rustling voluminous skirts of a fiery red that would have shocked her five years ago, but such was fashion. Inside the shifting styles the basic woman never changed—although tonight she did look a little fatigued by her journey.

He did not try to tell her what had happened, just hugged her in silence. Then he murmured, "Natrina and the children are well?"

"Yes." Kate loosened her embrace just enough to look him in the face. "Was this your idea or his?"

"His."

"And who replaces you?"

"Kromman."

"That wretch?"

He released her with a quick frown of warning. "Dearest, let me present my honored guardian, Sir Quarrel. Lady Kate."

She rewarded the Blade's bow with a bob and a flawless smile. "I have already heard of Sir Quarrel! I came home to find all the female staff staggering around and bumping into things because their eyes were full of stars. Now I see why. You are very welcome indeed, Sir Quarrel. I am sure the service around here will improve dramatically."

Whatever the boy might have been up to with the maids during the last two nights, he could not possibly have any more experience of women than that; yet he took the teasing with an easy smile, like a seasoned gallant. "And I see that their extraordinary tales of their mistress's beauty were not exaggerated at all."

Kate's laugh was still pure birdsong. "What an outrageous untruth! Sir Blade, you should be ashamed of yourself. But I thank you for it." She rose on tiptoes to kiss his cheek. "Now tell me about your binding. My husband's arm has not lost its skill, I hope?"

"He skewered me like the expert he has always been, my lady—all over before I even knew it. It is a tremendous honor to be bound to the greatest swordsman of the century."

"And an even greater one to be married to him, I assure you! Now show me your sword."

Beaming, he drew and went down on one knee to proffer it as if he were pledging it to her. Kate took it. She found the point of balance, then held it correctly in a rapier grip, one finger over the quillon.

"You are a point man, Sir Quarrel!"

"Few are as versatile as his lordship, ma'am."

"She is wonderfully light. What is she called?"

"Reason, my lady."

Durendal had not thought to ask that and Quarrel was glowing like a candle flame because Kate had. She had stolen his heart as she could steal any man's. His lordship could almost feel jealous—not because he doubted her love, but because he knew he could not charm a woman as she was enchanting this boy.

"A valiant name for a noble sword," she said, returning it. "May Reason win all your arguments, Sir Quarrel!"

"We'll go and change, dear. I asked Caplin to prepare a snack for us."

Kate concurred at once. As he turned to the door, he caught her eye and saw she was not smiling anymore. She understood the problems.

Quarrel, only three days bound, was still in what Montpurse had called the bathroom phase. (Why did he keep thinking of Montpurse tonight?) To spare him unnecessary anguish, Durendal left the door open while he bathed. While Churpen dressed him, he stood where his Blade could see him from the tub, and then waited for him to dress in turn—wondering with amusement whether Quarrel would run after him naked if he tried to leave. Together they returned to the library, where a modest feast for six was laid out on a portable table. Kate sat by the fire working at her spinning wheel under the candlelight. She was never idle.

"I must drink to my release and retirement," Durendal announced. "You will have a glass, Kate? No? Sir Quarrel?"

"Just one, my lord. As you warned me, that seems to be my limit."

"Tell me what happened," Kate said without looking up. It was unlike her to be impatient.

"Kromman brought a warrant from the King. I took off my chain, throttled him with it, and came home."

"I wish I could believe you." She rose and came over to him. "The warrant was genuine, of course?"

He stared up at her in blank astonishment. "Absolutely no question. Signed and sealed."

"Seals can be stolen. The signature?"

"The King's. I have seen it a million times. Very firm."

She removed the knife from his fingers. She lifted his hand to lay it against her cheek. She kissed it. Then she spun around and went back to her place by the fire. What on earth?

"Kate?"

She started the wheel turning again. "You have a serious problem, husband dear. You will have to leave the country, of course."

He glanced at his companion. Quarrel was chewing lustily but missing nothing.

"Cannot this wait until we have finished our meal, dearest?"

"I'm not sure it can, if Kromman is involved. You may gamble your own life—you always have. But a few days ago you accepted a Blade. You must not throw him away so lightly."

Quarrel said, "My purpose is only to serve, my lady. I am of no other consequence."

"Rot. If the King's men come to arrest my husband, what will you do?"

"Kate!"

"Die, I suppose," Quarrel said quietly.

"Exactly. Has he explained to you why he accepted a Blade from the King now, after twenty years of managing without one?"

The boy's dark eyes looked from one to the other of them appraisingly, and for a terrible moment he was Wolfbiter—Wolfbiter almost thirty years dead, Wolfbiter who would be over fifty now had he lived.

"No, my lady. Just that it was His Majesty's decision."

Durendal refilled his glass angrily. Why was Kate in such an overwhelming rush? He had entirely lost his appetite, but he must allow Quarrel to satisfy his. He could feel quite nostalgic watching the way the boy put away food, although there wasn't a pennyworth of fat on him.

"Rubbish!" Kate said. She would not be diverted when she was in this mood. "He has refused the offer many times before. Is that not so, my dear?"

"Once or twice."

"So five days ago the King honors you by assigning

you a Blade and today he fires you. I think you owe your companion an explanation."

"I wish I had one." Durendal swirled the red wine in his goblet, studying the play of light through the crystal. He forced himself to look up and meet Quarrel's questioning stare, painfully reminiscent of another boy's, long ago. . . . "The King is dying."

He watched color drain from the peach-bloom cheeks. No, Quarrel was not Wolfbiter. He never would be. But he was a brave and dedicated young man, decent and likable and in deadly peril through no fault of his own— only because a useless old man had accepted him as a gift out of stupid sentimentality. Quarrel took life less seriously than Wolfbiter ever had or ever would have, but that did not mean he was any less worthy. He would do his duty as stubbornly. If necessary, he would die as bravely, perhaps even more bravely, for he would regret the need more.

"Soon?" the boy asked.

"Soon. He's over seventy. He's been grossly overweight for most of his life. Sometimes he can hardly breathe now. He has an oozing ulcer on his leg, can't walk. A month or two, no longer."

Quarrel began to eat again. Life must go on. "Surely healers can be found for a king, my lord?"

"They have done all they can. Time and death yield little to conjuring. He would have died five years ago without the healers."

"Princess Malinda?"

"To the best of my knowledge, she is in good health." If Durendal was not to eat more, he may as well talk. "You are surprised that I am not sure? Well, the Princess is no friend of mine, Sir Quarrel." He twirled his wineglass. "Nor of her father's. King Ambrose has his virtues, but being a fond parent was never one of them. She was as self-willed as he is and she never forgave the callous way he discarded her mother. I earned her dislike when I was still Commander."

"You don't need to tell that story, Durendal," Kate said flatly.

"I think I do." Hearing a few of the sleazy things a chancellor did in the course of twenty years' service might cool Quarrel's incandescent hero worship. "When Malinda reached adolescence—I was still Commander—her father suggested deeding her some Blades of her own. I looked into the historical precedents and argued strongly against it. It seemed that letting an unmarried damsel bind a twenty-year-old swordsman was not merely asking for trouble but virtually insisting on it. I do not believe she was promiscuous by nature, but she was young and she was surrounded at all times by dashing young guardsmen."

Quarrel smirked knowingly with his mouth full.

"There are two ways of losing your head over a woman, Sir Quarrel, and we are discussing the permanent way."

Quarrel sobered instantly, mumbling an apology.

"I chose her escorts carefully and made sure every man jack of them knew about certain obscure methods of committing treason. The Princess fell head over heels for two or three of them—in succession, I mean, not simultaneously. They reported to me when the fire got too hot for them, and I transferred them to other duties."

Neither the King nor Montpurse had known what was happening, but Malinda had accused Sir Durendal of spying on her, harassing her, and meddling in her private life. Her enmity had begun then.

"Just after I was made chancellor, Dark Chamber agents caught the Princess and her current passion in compromising circumstances—meaning together in a dark corner. There was very nearly a major scandal. It was only to prevent one that the King refrained from throwing Commander Bandit and several other people in the Bastion—and me, too, when he found out that this was not her first flirtation. Kromman thought I was done for at that point. So did I."

"It was the stupid little honey's own fault!" Kate

snapped. "Why she should have blamed you for it, I can't imagine."

Durendal shrugged. "She thought I'd set her up. She'd have done better to blame the inquisitors. And don't be too hard on her. Ambrose had her examined by a panel of doctors and midwives to make sure she was still a virgin, and no sixteen-year-old would appreciate that humiliation. He decided to marry her off as fast as possible, especially because he was about to marry Princess Dierda of Gevily, who was a month younger than she was. He wanted no court jesters asking which was which. Then the queen of Baelmark died and he saw a way to end the war; kill two birds with one stone." Better to offer his daughter than a humiliating apology . . .

"What did she think of the idea?" Quarrel asked thoughtfully.

"Princesses marry whom they are told to marry. Most of them do, anyway—I really thought Malinda would have to be driven aboard the ship at sword point, but no. She is her father's daughter and she kept her dignity. She was convinced that the match had been my idea, though."

Quarrel tensed. "Does she still think so, my lord?"

"I'm sure she does. In fact, I argued against it as strongly as I dared. The King told me to mind my own business. Parliament might have stopped him, but he didn't need to call Parliament then, because Lord Snake was suppressing elementaries all over the place and gold was pouring in. He already had a son to succeed him. He was convinced he could father a dozen others on Dierda—he was not yet fifty. Besides, no king of the Fire Lands has ever died of old age. He expected Malinda to come slinking home to him as a widow very shortly.

"He was wrong on all counts. King Radgar still rules in Baelmark. Dierda proved barren. His son died that same year. Malinda has never written him a note and will not receive his ambassadors. He learned about the birth of his grandsons from public reports. If she cannot forgive her father, her feelings toward me had best be left unspoken."

Obviously the Ironhall classes on the court had included little of this, for Quarrel's eyes were wide. He was still eating, though.

"Perhaps he keeps her chained in a tower," Kate remarked.

"The Dark Chamber spies say not. She seems healthy and happy and popular. Baelmark is not nearly as primitive as most Chivians believe, and Ambrose knew that. We assume that when he dies she will come home to claim the crown, but this may be wishful thinking. Her oldest son is almost eighteen, so she may send him in her stead. The only thing certain is that she will not tolerate me as her chancellor for an instant. I knew my term of office was drawing to a close even before Hagfish came to call today."

"Hagfish, my lord?"

"Chancellor Kromman. He was nicknamed that by . . . an old friend of mine." Montpurse again! Durendal's conscience hadn't died after all. Today it had taken on a new lease of life. Fertilized by fear, no doubt.

The conversation veered to lesser matters then, because Caplin returned, alerted by some stewards' telepathy to the need to refill Sir Quarrel's plate. The life-and-death question was whether Kromman and Malinda were already in cahoots. Was today's sudden dismissal the start of the Princess's revenge?

When the meal was over, Durendal settled into his favorite seat by the fireplace and watched Kate spin. Quarrel pulled up a chair between them. It would feel strange having the lad hanging around all the time, almost as if Andy had never gone. But Andy was thirty now, wrestling trade winds in the Pepper Islands. And this quiet home life was not going to last very long anyway.

"Durendal, my love," Kate said, without looking up from her busily whirring wheel, "you described the Princess's career in great detail for Sir Quarrel, but you did not explain why it involves him."

"Ah! Forgive me! Well, a few days ago, the King sent

that warrant assigning a Blade to me, with no explanation. I was puzzled. Angry, in a way. I eventually decided he was offering me a sort of farewell present. There are very few rewards he has not bestowed on me. I have declined many more, for excessive honors attract enemies. We have fought and argued bitterly for twenty years, but I always served his interests as best I could. Even when he was most enraged at me, he knew that. Rank and lands and wealth—everything he had to give, he gave me. One exception was a Blade.''

Quarrel nodded, frowning slightly. At his age, Wolfbiter had been led off by his ward to the ends of the world, but he had to sit here and listen to social gossip and talk of grandchildren. Durendal could not forget the dismay that had flashed across the boy's face when he turned to greet his future ward. He had found an ancient, broken-down politician, destined for the scrap heap very soon. Although he had hidden that reaction instantly and skillfully—and ever since had shown no sign of resentment whatsoever—it must still rankle. Antiquated Lord Roland could not be as bad as the Marquis of Nutting, but he was hardly a cause to dedicate a life to. What could a fresh-minted Blade care about colic and teething troubles?

''It seemed that he was warning me not to count on his protection much longer. If he was admitting that, then he must have accepted the gravity of his condition at last. I decided to accept, mostly for his sake. I could have refused, because he is too sick to fight me now, but I could not bear to. I hope you will understand and forgive me.''

''There is nothing to forgive that I know of, my lord!''

''Flames, I do not need a Blade, lad! When I look at you I see a thoroughbred harnessed to a broken-down tinker's wagon.''

''I see one of the great men of the age, my lord, and my heart swells with pride that I may serve you.''

No comment was possible except, ''Thank you.'' How could one so young be such a polished liar? It was disconcerting.

Quarrel's eyes gleamed. "And with respect, my lord, I think you do need a Blade. The King thinks so. Aren't you in danger? Isn't that what her ladyship meant? Wasn't Hagfish threatening you in your office this afternoon?"

"You can't fight the government all alone, Sir Quarrel, and Kromman is the government now."

"Flee the country!" Quarrel said triumphantly. "It is no shame, my lord. You have done nothing wrong."

A jaunt to Samarinda, perhaps? It was close to midnight, so Everman must be almost as old as Durendal, heading fast into his morning senility. But at dawn he would be restored to youth—like Quarrel: supple, vigorous, beautiful.

Of course, Quarrel knew nothing of Samarinda. Travel to him meant exotic adventure, endlessly receding horizons. To Durendal it implied purposeless exile, waiting to die in some queer little foreign town, with no company but strangers and Kromman's assassins lurking in doorways. Flee the country he had served so long?

He seemed to have arrived back where he had started. Could that be exactly what the King had had in mind? But . . .

Kate said, "You have not explained to me why, after all these years, the King should suddenly promote Kromman to chancellor."

"Because I don't know why. I can only suppose that the man's whining finally wore him down. They are shut up there together in Falconsrest—have been for weeks. Or it may be that he thinks a new chancellor will have better luck making the Princess see reason."

She snatched up a skein of wool and hurled it at him. "Durendal, you are being excessively stupid!"

"My love?"

Quarrel's surprise flashed to high amusement and then polite inattention.

Kate's cheeks were flushed, which they had not been a moment ago, so it was not the fire's doing. "There is far more to this than you admit or even see. When Kromman brought that warrant, did you touch it?''

"Of course. I opened it and read it.''

"Have you handled anything else unusual today?''

What in the world was troubling her? "Dearest, you talk in riddles.''

Kate hugged herself as if she felt chilled. "Your hands smell of enchantment,'' she said.

· 5 ·

About a hundred possibilities flashed through Durendal's mind and were discarded. "What sort of enchantment?''

"I don't know, but I certainly do not like it! I have met it before somewhere. Sir Quarrel, my husband was not entirely truthful with you, but then I have not been entirely truthful with him. A week ago, when the warrant for your assignment appeared, he brought it home to show me. In twenty-five years he has never once discussed state business with me, because he is bound to secrecy by his privy councillor's oath, but this was a personal matter.'' Kate was obviously annoyed that she had to make such excuses; she must have a very good reason for doing so. She had *never* behaved like this before!

Quarrel nodded eagerly. Perhaps he thought the Roland household was always this exciting. "Of course.''

"He did not decide to accept the Blade the King offered. I decided. I talked him into it.''

"I am very glad you did, my lady.'' Nobly said! Quite convincing.

"There was enchantment on that warrant, too.''

The men said, "What!'' simultaneously.

Kate clenched her lips angrily for a moment. "I should have told you, dear, but it was very faint, so I was not quite sure of it. I am now, because it was the same enchantment I detected on your hands when you came home tonight. Whatever it is, it is no conjuration that ought to be around the court."

"Some new healing?" Durendal suggested, but the glare he received dismissed his question as an insult to her intelligence.

Quarrel's mind was more nimble or less hidebound. "Are you saying that these documents are fakes, my lady, or that the King himself has been enchanted? Is he the source of the conjuration?"

"I am saying that there is something seriously wrong, and now Kromman has had my husband evicted from court." Kate never galloped off on wild byways of imagination like this.

He must believe her. "Could Kromman be the source of the enchantment?"

She shrugged. "If he is, he should not be allowed near the King. What are the White Sisters doing?"

"The King is at Falconsrest."

Kate put a hand to her mouth in shock. "So he is!"

Quarrel glanced from one to the other anxiously.

Kate explained. "The lodge had been used as an elementary. What they did there I shudder to think, but it absolutely reeks of conjuration. The octogram is still there. I can't go near it, even yet. No White Sister can."

Candles were starting to gutter, and the library grew dim. Durendal threw another log on the fire.

"I don't recall seeing any White Sisters at Falconsrest, but I probably did and just didn't register them. There must be some!"

"In the village, not the lodge," Kate said, frowning.

"But if enough enchantment is leaking out for you to detect it here, then they would have to be aware of it, surely?"

She nodded reluctantly. "That sounds logical. I wish I

could remember where I met it before. It is horribly familiar. One of the suppressed orders, I suppose. You took me to a few of them.''

"Can you go back to Falconsrest, my lord?" Quarrel asked quietly.

"I'm technically under house arrest." Kromman would use any such move as an excuse to have Durendal thrown in the Bastion—not that Kromman needed any more excuses. He tried to envision what might happen if he did go. Would Kromman be there or at Greymere? How would Commander Dragon react? Even if Ambrose was informed that his former chancellor had arrived—which was by no means certain—would he not just assume that Lord Roland had come crawling on his knees to ask for his job back? "The King would not receive me."

"Where is Mother Superior?" Kate asked. "At Greymere or Oakendown?"

"I have no idea."

"You can't go to the palace, so I must go to Oakendown. I'm the one who's blowing trumpets, after all. If she isn't there I'll dump the problem on the Prioress."

He smiled at her admiringly. Even the short carriage ride today had fatigued her, yet now she was blithely talking of the much longer journey to the White Sisters' headquarters, and in midwinter, too. "A letter would suffice, dearest. We can send Pardon with it." Quarrel would be better, but Quarrel could not leave his side.

"The King was quite normal when you saw him, my lord?"

"Not unless you call dying normal. But if something happened—and I'm not convinced yet that anything has happened—then it must have been about Long Night itself, after my visit to Falconsrest and before he issued the warrant for your binding." The handwriting on that had been surprisingly firm and legible, he recalled. Was that significant?

"Well," Kate said, "we must sleep on it." She rose, the men jumping up also. "We can sleep more soundly knowing we have a Blade to defend us from burglars.'' She took up a candle and lit it at another.

Quarrel chuckled gleefully. ''When you have the second Durendal beside you, ma'am? He would slaughter the whole gang of them before I could draw Reason from her scabbard. It is well known that that's why the King never bothered to waste a Blade on his lordship.''

''He did have a Blade once. Didn't you know?''

''Well, yes. He died overseas somewhere, didn't he? I haven't heard any details.''

That innocently smiling young scoundrel had been trying to worm the story out of his ward since they left Ironhall. Kate did not know that. What she did know was that Durendal had written a detailed account of the Samarinda adventure to be placed in the Ironhall archives after his death. She was the only person who had ever read it.

''Up there,'' she said, ''that black volume. You can reach—''

Durendal snapped, ''No! I forbid it!'' He was still bitter that Wolfbiter had not received the honor he deserved, but to spell out for his present Blade how he had failed his first one would be an intolerable humiliation. He turned to snuff out the candles.

Like the deadly bolt he was named for, Quarrel flashed across the room and caught Kate as she fell, scooping her up in his arms and stamping on the candle she had dropped before Durendal had taken a step. He strode over to the couch and set her down.

''Just a faint, I think, my lord. A healer . . . but she can't, can she? Perhaps a cold compress? Summon her maid to loosen her, er, bodice, my lord?''

''Ring the bell.'' Durendal knelt at his wife's side, alarmed and furious at his own dismal performance and even more furious that he was worrying about that just now. All his life he had been *fast* and proud of it.

''No, I'm fine!'' Kate said. ''Don't, please, Sir Quarrel. Just a slight dizzy spell.'' She made a brave attempt at a smile and reached down to adjust the rumpled gown over her farthingale.

"Wine!" Durendal said, jumping up. Quarrel beat him to the decanter.

"A cushion for my head, dearest? Thank you." She was still pale, but she laughed and squeezed her husband's hand. "My, it is nice to have men dancing attendance on me like this. Relax, dear! I'm not having a baby."

Quarrel almost spilled the wine he was offering her. In a moment, though, Lady Kate was sitting up, composed and insistent that she was recovered.

Durendal sat on the couch beside her. "I've never known you to do that before."

"Neither have I! And you won't again." She pressed her lips together for a moment, thinking. "I got up too quickly. And the shock, I suppose. I remembered."

"Remembered what?"

"Where I met that enchantment before. Give me your hand again." She held it to her cheek. "Yes. It comes from Samarinda."

Durendal's mind shied away from the implications. His flesh crawled. Not that horror again, surely? Here in Chivial? "That's what you sniffed? How could you possibly know?"

She set her chin as she did when she was not to be moved. "Because when you came back, you stank of it for weeks. If I hadn't loved you so much and wanted you so much, I couldn't have borne to be near you. It faded eventually, but I remember it."

"It was the gold. The gold bones."

"I don't care what it was." Kate shuddered. "Ghastly! But whatever contaminated you then is back on you now, and I smelled it on the King's warrant, too."

• 6 •

It was Quarrel who fitted the last piece in the puzzle, but that came in the morning.

Not for many years had Durendal found trouble sleeping, but too much had happened too quickly that day. As he lay wide-eyed in the darkness, listening to Kate's soft breathing, he remembered the book and knew that Quarrel would be tempted to pry. The youngster had been officially given the dressing room outside the bedchamber as his own, but a Blade had no use for a bed. He might be anywhere in the house by now.

Which would be worse—having him learn all about Wolfbiter's death or letting him know that his ward was too nervous to sleep? Could Durendal possibly get to the book first without being detected? He slid gently from beneath the sheets, found his dressing gown, and tiptoed barefoot to the door. Sneaking around in the dark when there was a freshly bound Blade in the house was not exactly prudent, but it was worth a try. He eased the door open. In the darkness beyond, a girl was whispering, "Oh yes, yes, yes . . ."

Sighing, the master of the house closed the door again. Blades did have a use for beds.

He felt gritty-eyed and dejected when he came down to breakfast. The winter day was as gray as his mood, with casements rattling and rain beating on the panes. Quarrel glowed like a summer noon, working his way through a heaped plate of ribs and a tankard of spruce beer. He rose and bowed and beamed simultaneously. Kate smiled a wary welcome.

Evaluating her husband's expression in the light of long experience, she tactfully informed Caplin that they would serve themselves from the sideboard. As the steward went out, Durendal was very tempted to call him back, just so his wife could not talk business, which was what she obviously had in mind. They had never quite agreed on suitable topics for breakfast conversation. He poured himself a beaker of cider.

"I read your book, my lord," Quarrel announced cheerfully.

Durendal roared. "You what?"

The boy did not flinch an eyelash. "I read your book about Samarinda."

"I expressly forbade you to do any such thing!"

"Yes, my lord. I heard you." He shrugged.

"Dearest," Kate said gently, "you look just like the King."

"The King? I look absolutely nothing like the King! What do you mean?"

"I mean you are glaring at Sir Quarrel merely because he has been attending to his duties with exemplary diligence."

With even greater diligence, Durendal took himself off the boil. Perhaps there was some justice here; he was being given a dose of the medicine he had prescribed for Ambrose often enough. He glanced at his wife's amusement, then at his Blade's polite stubbornness. The boy must have had a busy night. "I apologize. Of course the book is now relevant to your responsibilities, and you did right to read it. What did you conclude?"

Quarrel eyed him warily for a moment. "That I have even higher standards to live up to than I feared. I—I wept, my lord."

That was absolutely the most effective thing the damned kid could have said. Was he really an incredible actor, or could he possibly be genuine? Durendal grunted.

Kate made a noise that sounded suspiciously like a smothered snigger. "Would you care for some ribs, Your Maj— my lord?"

"No thank you! And stop making jokes about me and the King. Did you gain any valuable insights into our problem, Sir Quarrel?"

"Just that that enchantment is the most evil thing I ever heard of. Immortality supported by endless murders!" He stole a quick look at Kate, as if hoping for support; but she had risen and gone to the sideboard to clatter the silver covers. "You know His Majesty better than anyone, my lord. If Kromman offered him that conjuration, would he have accepted?"

Durandal almost yelled, "Why do you think I couldn't sleep all night?" He said quietly, "Not the king I have served all my life." The silence festered for a moment— was he being dishonest? "But when a man sees that last door opening before him, the one that has nothing on the other side . . . when his life's work is threatened—Blood and steel, lad! I don't know! And he may not have had any choice. You must have read what Everman told me, how they addicted him to the monstrous feast with one mouthful. He was not the Everman I knew at Ironhall— he looked just like him, but his mind was twisted out of shape somehow. If Kromman prepared the conjurement and then gave it to the King . . . But how would Kromman have known the ritual? Can we reasonably suppose that he sent another expedition back to Samarinda to steal it? He's only the King's secretary."

"Face facts, dear." Kate thumped a heaped plate down in front of him and resumed her seat. "He has had a quarter of a century to arrange it. He is very close to the inquisitors still, and if anyone can steal a secret, they can. Perhaps the King himself—"

"No! I will not believe that of Ambrose! And I'm not hungry."

"You need to keep your strength up. His health began

to fail about five years ago. That's just time for someone
to make a round trip to Samarinda.''

"Rubbish! If anyone had organized such an expedition
for him, I'd have heard of it." He glared at her. If it had
happened, it must be Kromman's fault, not Ambrose's!

"Pardon me," Quarrel said. "You met Hereward—he
was my Second, ma'am. His grandfather was an inquisitor.
He told me once how the old man used to tell him stories.
He didn't read them—he remembered them. He could repeat any book he had ever read, word for word. Inquisitors
are given a memory-enhancement conjurement.''

When the cold, sick feeling had waned a little, Durendal
said, "I apologize."

"Nothing to apologize for, my lord."

"There is much. I should have seen that years ago. If
Kromman followed me into the monastery in his invisibility cloak and witnessed the ritual, he could have remembered it . . ." *Blood and fire!* Was that why Kromman
had tried to kill both him and Wolfbiter—so that he would
be the only one with the dread secret? Had the King
known Kromman knew the ritual, all these years? Or even
suspected? Could that be why he had put up with the
odious slug for so long?

"What are you going to do about it," Kate asked, ever
practical, "in all this rain?"

That was the question. He considered his options. Run
away, go abroad? Not now. Tell someone? Who? Who
would not just assume that he was spreading such impossible lies about his successor in the hope of getting his job
back? If he had no one but himself to consider, he would
go and find Kromman and kill him, as he should have
done years ago. But Chivial was not Altain. Killers were
hanged, so Kate would be a murderer's widow; and if
Quarrel guessed what he was planning, he would try to
beat his ward to it.

"If Kromman's doing what we suspect, he has to murder someone every day. How can he possibly get away
with that? Who would help him?''

"The Guard, of course," Quarrel said angrily. "If a ward needs a body to save his life, his Blade will provide a body." His face paled, and he laid down the rib he had been waving. "Or volunteer?"

"Oh, no," Kate muttered. "No, no, no!"

The King *eating* his way through his Guard?

"They couldn't possibly get away with it," Durendal said, trying to convince himself as much as his listeners. "People don't vanish in Chivial without being missed. If the King is doing that, then he can only meet outsiders once a day, when he's at about the right age . . ." A little after sunset, when he had received Durandal himself? No, the stink of his leg had been genuine. It had happened later—if it had happened at all.

If the answers were anywhere, they must be at Falconsrest.

Quarrel knew that, too. "You're under house arrest, my lord. Kromman has a spy in your household."

"I expect he— You *know* this?"

"The housemaid Nel, my lord." Actor or not, he couldn't quite hide his delight at being so efficient a bodyguard.

"And who told you it was Nel?"

"Er . . . Marie, my lord. And Gwen."

"Both? Separately?"

"Oh, yes, my lord, of course! I mean . . ." He was blushing at last.

Kate slammed a hand on the table. "I shall have a word with Mistress Nel!"

"She more or less admits it, my lady," Quarrel muttered, even redder.

"What? Are you debauching my entire staff, Sir Quarrel? Because—"

"Don't nag the man," Durendal said, "just because he has been attending to his duties with exemplary diligence." And incredible stamina.

Quarrel grinned sheepishly.

"Men!" Kate glared just like the King did. That was

not very fair, because her husband had warned her exactly what would happen if they brought a Blade into the house. She had even agreed that they would have to take financial responsibility for any unwanted results. "Very well! I shall drive to Oakendown and lay the problem before the Sisters."

Quarrel said, "But . . ." and looked at his ward.

"No need for you to go, dearest." Durendal realized he had cleaned his plate and tried not to show how annoying that was.

"I see it as my duty. I shall take Nel with me for company, and I may stay there a few days to recover from the journey. What you men get up to while I'm gone, I shall probably be happier not knowing; and what I don't know, inquisitors can't get out of me."

Incredible woman!

"Sir Quarrel, would you wait outside for a moment, please?"

His Blade frowned, then rose obediently and headed for the door—checking the windows on the way to make sure they were securely locked. The heavy oak door thumped shut behind him.

Kate waited defensively for her husband to speak. She looked tired already, although it was only morning; her thinness was more than just an illusion of the current fashions. He had been working fourteen hours a day during the King's illness, but he should have noticed. Even more galling was the obvious fact that the servants knew what he had missed.

"When Quarrel went to your aid last night, my dear, he made a remark about healers. I didn't pick up on it then, but now I know what he almost said. He knows you cannot tolerate healing."

"Many White Sisters can't."

"But not all. How does he know you're one of them? Obviously he has been gossiping with the maids. Joking aside, part of his duty is to understand my household. But why should they have told him that about you?"

Kate's chin came up stubbornly. "Bah! Pillow talk. I expect they were discussing childbirth."

"I am quite certain Quarrel was not discussing childbirth."

"You must ask him—he is a man of many talents. Meanwhile, my dear, we both have duties to attend to. When the present crisis has been resolved, I trust we shall have leisure to discuss our future together."

"Oakendown is—"

"I am quite capable of journeying to Oakendown, Durendal. I want that future of ours to be as long as possible, you understand? So you will please deal with Master Kromman—finally and expeditiously!" She rose, defiance in every inch of her. "I do not expect you to sit here warming your hands at the fire while I am gone."

He caught her in his arms before she reached the door. "Won't you tell me?"

"Later. Your problem is much more urgent than mine."

"Then take care, my dearest!"

She laid her head against his shoulder. "And you, my love. Come back safely. I don't want to be alone."

· 7 ·

The answer lay at Falconsrest, so there he must go, although he could not guess what he would do there.

If a watch had been set on Ivywalls, the drenching rain would be worse than a thick fog for the watchers, and it had removed the snow that would have held tracks. Leading the way on foot through the orchard and the coppice, Durendal was virtually certain that he was departing undetected. On impulse, he asked Quarrel if he thought he could handle Destrier and received the inevitable answer. Annoyingly, the big black seemed equally enthusiastic about the new arrangement—fickle brute!—and the two of them were beautiful together, moving like a single dream animal. That left Durendal on Gadfly, who had no great turn of speed or agility but would thump along all day without complaint. A long, miserable ride it would be.

As the first cold trickle penetrated his collar, he mused that the previous day he had been effective ruler of all Chivial, and today he became a felon just by leaving his house. For a lifetime he had served his King with all his heart, but now he was contemplating murder and treason. Kromman . . . if he had Kromman within reach, would he kill the new chancellor? Perhaps. He had owed Wolfbiter a death for too long. Only thoughts of the inevitable consequences to Kate and Quarrel made him doubt his own resolve now.

He stayed clear of the main Grandon road, lest he be recognized by some passing royal courier—incredibly unlikely but a risk that need not be taken. He had decided to avoid Stairtown for the same reason, going south to Great Elbow, which was slightly closer to Falconsrest anyway.

The weather made conversation on the road difficult. It was only during a most-welcome break for a meal in a wayside inn that he told Quarrel what he had decided.

"We need a base, even if it's only for one night, and an old friend of mine runs a tavern just outside Great Elbow. He calls himself Master Byless Twain, but he's really Sir Byless. He was my Second, so he's another broken-down old ruin like me. Don't smirk at your ward like that; it's disrespectful. He may be able to help us and certainly won't stand in our way. I warn you now—he's more than a little odd. He's usually friendly enough with me, but he has no love for the Royal Guard or even the Order."

Quarrel waited for an explanation, but it did not come.

"It's a couple of years since I saw him. . . . He has a

very pretty daughter. Let your conscience be your guide, of course, but in my hunting days I regarded other Blades' daughters as off limits. They're not so easily impressed by the legend, anyway."

"I understand, my lord. If I gave offense at your house—"

"No, I expected it. I did exactly the same at your age. The legend's a side effect of the binding conjuration."

Furthermore, being a Blade was a job that deserved its compensations. Of Lord Bluefield's four Blades, one had died resisting his arrest. The other three had been waylaid successfully by Montpurse, but only Byless had survived the reversion conjuration, and even he had not brought all his wits back with him. Quarrel would be happier not knowing the story, for Bluefield had been only the first of King Ambrose's chancellors to fall from favor.

Another reason to use Byless's tavern as their headquarters was that the King's Blades shunned it. They disapproved of its name, The Broken Sword.

Never having called there in winter, Durendal was dismayed to see how bleak and depressing it was, a thatched hovel cowering by the road under dark and dripping trees. He was even more dismayed to realize how many years must have passed since his last visit, for the woman in the doorway could only be the formerly pretty daughter. She had lost most of her teeth while gaining a great deal of weight and at least three children, two of whom clung to her like burls. She was suckling the smallest and might be going to have a fourth in the foreseeable future. Both her face and her hair needed washing.

She looked at Durendal without recognition. "I can give you a meal and a bed, sir, if you won't mind looking after your own horses. The men have gone out. There's only me and the brats here."

He agreed they would stable their own horses. As they went to do so, Quarrel remarked acidly that his conscience was in complete control so far.

Despite her unprepossessing appearance, their hostess produced a passable meal between cuffing and scolding children, and the ale was tolerable. Having served her guests, she dropped platters for herself and her oldest at the far end of the long table and she set her remaining teeth to work at a gallop.

Durendal talked horses with Quarrel until the meal was done and then explained that they would be making an early start in the morning but might return to spend another night. He slid a gold coin along the planks to her. He asked for directions to Stairtown, thereby confirming his impressions of the local roads and the way to Falconsrest without actually mentioning its name. Finally he asked, "And where is Master Twain on this wretched day?"

"Went with Tom, sir. My man."

"Where to?"

She wiped her platter with the last of her bread. "Hunting for Ned, sir, over at Great Elbow. Disappeared. They're all out looking for him. He's simple, you see. Must have wandered off."

Ward and Blade exchanged horrified glances.

• 8 •

Durendal slept. Quarrel wakened him when the second candle was two thirds gone. He wrapped himself in his cloak and trudged out into the night, shivering and still half asleep, to find that his efficient Blade had already saddled the horses and brought them to the door. Although the rain had stopped, the night was dark as a cellar. That should be an advantage when they reached Falconsrest, because skulking around any place guarded by Blades was a very dangerous occupation; but it made their chances of ever arriving there much slimmer. As it was, the horses could go no faster than a walk.

They were on their way before he realized that he was astride Gadfly again. Quarrel had held a stirrup for him without a word and he had accepted without looking. A very neat maneuver! He would not be petty enough to make an issue of the matter now, but if Junior thought that Destrier was to be his mount from now on, he was grievously mistaken.

"Just reconnaissance?" Quarrel asked as they rode into the wind.

"I hope so. If they're doing what we fear they're doing, then it must be done in the lodge itself. It has two rooms up and two down, separated by chimneys, garderobes, and a stair. An elementary has to be on the ground, of course, and there used to be an octogram laid out in the room they now use as a kitchen. It's probably still there. The outside door's in the other, the guardroom. Ideally, I'd like to creep up to the kitchen shutters at dawn and listen. If I hear chanting, we'll be certain. If I don't, we'll know we're wrong."

"You better let me do that, my lord. No point in both of us going."

Blast that binding!

Receiving no reply, Quarrel muttered, "Must we do this at all? That simpleton's disappearance seems like pretty strong evidence to me. If we asked around Stairtown and learned of any other people gone missing, then we would know, wouldn't we?"

"You're right, I suppose, but I . . . Curse it, this is the King we're accusing! We're saying he's turned his Guard into a wolf pack. I just can't be as logical as you, I suppose."

"It must be another side effect of the binding," Quarrel said indignantly. "I never used to be logical or cautious or anything like that!"

"Nothing wrong with logic, and you're only cautious where I'm concerned. You'll be rash to madness with your own life."

"I certainly hope so."

"Not necessarily. A good Blade uses his head. There's a time to lunge and a time to recover, a time to thrust and a time to parry. When Wolfbiter and I were trying to escape from the monastery, I didn't stop to argue that I was the better swordsman and ought to bring up the rear. I let him do his duty and ran like a rabbit. It's where you get to that matters, not how."

Having delivered himself of that profound homily, Lord Roland promptly got lost. When the clouds turned brighter before the slow winter dawn, he managed to find a road that he thought was the one he wanted. He had to leave the trail before it reached the outer gate, for there would be a guard there. Then he had to find a way through the patchy woods that cloaked the hills, navigating by instinct and hoping to come out somewhere near the lodge. He got lost again. Curse Byless for not being available as a guide!

The sun was glinting between the clouds and the horizon when he reined in at the edge of the trees above the little cup-shaped valley. Below him, the lodge stood on a spur that protruded like a ship's prow from the steep hillside—a small stone house and a wooden shed for horses. The royal standard still flew from the flagpole. Down on the flats, the village slept on, showing no signs of life.

He said, "Too late. If they did it, they've done it already."

"We can wait and see if they bring out a body . . . remains of a body."

"I'm not sure what they'll do with it. The bones are too valuable to throw away."

Growing steadily more chilled by the wind, they waited to see what might happen. Soon a carriage and two outriders emerged from the village and crept slowly up the steep trail to the lodge. A man came out to wait for it, then scrambled inside. It turned and went back down, then headed off along the road to the outside world.

"I would almost swear that was Kromman," Durendal said. "Wearing black?"

"He moved like a young man, my lord. I've only seen the Secretary once."

Was the new Chancellor commuting to Grandon every day? If he was now a Samarinda immortal, then he would seem roughly his proper age by the time he arrived at Greymere. He might be able to spend two or three hours on business there and depart before he became too old to manage the journey. Would it be possible to ambush him on his return?

Down in the village, people were stirring, tending livestock, heading to the mess for breakfast. Then half a dozen men came out of the lodge and went into the stable shed.

"My lord, we should leave. They may have spotted us."

"I think I agree with that cautious remark," Durendal said, turning Gadfly's head.

Infuriatingly, clouds hid the sun so effectively that he managed to get lost again, or at least became uncertain how far from the palace they were. When they emerged from the trees onto the road, he said, "I'm not sure we're outside the gate."

"Nor I, sir."

"Let's take it gently, in case we have to make a sudden detour."

They rode at a slow trot along the narrow trail, which wound through woods, roughly following a noisy, rain-swollen stream. Quarrel studied the ground with youthfully sharp eyes.

"Horses have come along here since the carriage did, my lord. There are hoofprints on top of the wheel marks."

"Relief for the guard on the gate?"

"Possibly. Or those six may have gotten ahead of us. You suppose they've gone hunting another victim?"

"Don't even talk about it! It makes me ill!"

In a few moments the road emerged from the dense

wood to cross an old clearing, now overgrown with thick thorns and scrub, impenetrable to man or horse. The trail was barely wide enough for two abreast.

"I think I know this spot," Durendal said. "We're outside. Another couple of miles and we'll be into farmland near Stairtown."

They rode across the clearing, back into pine woods, around a corner, and came almost face-to-face with six mounted men, lined up in two rows of three.

Dragon bellowed, "Halt in the King's name!" and spurred his horse forward. The others came close behind.

"Ride!" Quarrel yelled, wheeling Destrier.

Durendal copied. A second later he decided that they had made the wrong decision and should have tried to bull their way through, but by then they were into a chase and it was too late. They were heading back to Falconsrest. Through the clearing again, then pine woods . . . Hooves thundered, mud sprayed. Quarrel was struggling to hold the black in so that Gadfly could keep up. Durendal glanced behind and saw that four of the pursuers were gaining, two lagging behind.

"Turn at the next corner!" he yelled. "We'll double back."

But the next corner was too late. Straight ahead was the guardhouse. Three more Blades had heard the approaching hooves and were mounting—on the near side of the gate. Nine Blades were not good odds. The trees rushed past, the gate raced toward him.

"Over it!" he shouted. He thumped his heels against Gadfly's ribs with little effect, while Destrier shot forward like an arrow. The guards were drawing their swords, their mounts shying away from the great stallion charging them. Quarrel had drawn Reason, but there were two horses converging on him and he had a gate ahead. Confused voices shouted, "Spirits, it's Paragon!" "Take them alive." "I know that horse." "Stop them!" Quarrel parried one man's sword, trying to dodge a stroke from the other and gather his horse for the jump all at the same time. Destrier flashed a bite at one of the horses, then the beat of his hooves ended as he took to the air. *Oh, beautiful!*

Again Dragon bellowed, "Take them alive!"

Ignore the swords, then. Close on Destrier's tail, Durendal gathered his reins, sat down tight, dug in his heels, and whispered, "Do it, Gadfly!" He knew she couldn't, though. Even he could not put her over that gate.

She tried her best. She might even have succeeded, had not one of the guard's mounts cannoned into her as she took off. She clipped the top rail and pitched. He saw trees whirled against the clouds and filthy black mud coming up and nothing more.

· 9 ·

The chant was familiar. So was the scent of fresh-cut greenery. Yes, this was a conjuration for healing wounds, the one the Guard used and Ironhall used. And—*Uh!*—the surge of spirits was painfully intense. The last time he'd felt it this strong was when he'd broken his leg fooling around on the armory roof with Byless and Felix.

There must have been an accident. He was lying on a straw pallet in the center of the octogram. He was the one being enchanted . . . might explain why he hurt, although not why hurt in so many places . . . couldn't have been fighting . . . unless chopped to pieces. Not falling off roofs again, surely? He peered up blearily at a dim plank ceiling and a whole army of men, swaying like trees above him, far too many. Bare stone walls, chimney, underside of a wooden stair. Things were coming and going.

The conjuration ended. Two round, pink, identical faces

peered closely into his eyes. Fingers pried. A voice complained fussily.

"Well, that's the best we can do for him here. I think he'll be all right in a day or so. How many fingers am I holding up, my lord?"

Eight fingers waved in front of Durendal's eyes. The question did not feel as if it had been directed at him, so he did not interrupt the conversation.

"Can you speak?" asked the two faces.

Stupid question.

The faces went away. The sixteen or so men all looked down from an enormous height. He ought not to lie here or he'd get stepped on. Too much effort not to.

"Let him rest for an hour or two," the petulant voice said. "Then we may try again. I really do not understand what has gone wrong with this octogram. The balance of elements is very wrong, very strange. It was all right last week, I know it was." It grew confidential. "It is perhaps just as well that His Majesty has chosen to discontinue the treatments here. I do think you should bring in a conjurer to attempt a realignment. Now, you said there was another patient?"

"A sword wound, Doctor. He's lost a lot of blood."

Durendal felt strong hands lift his pallet and bear it away. His annoyance at this impiety turned to interest as he noted corn mills, chopping blocks, water butts—two of everything. Shelves, bins. Two door lintels, even. Another room, just as cold. Being set down again . . .

"I don't think he's faking," said a new voice, "but don't take your eyes off him for a second. Just remember who he is. Even half dead, he's still a match for any of you lubberly lot."

Someone draped another blanket over him. Chair legs scraped on flagstones. Soon the chanting began again, farther away.

The mists cleared, swirled again, cleared again. He was in the guardroom of the lodge at Falconsrest—lying on the floor, not as close to the fireplace as he would like and about as far as possible from the outside door. There were four Blades with him, two sitting, two standing— guarding him, of course. He wasn't going to be making any breaks for a while yet, though. Left wrist hurt. Face hurt—mouth and left eye. Ribs aching. Could have been much worse; the old man not too fragile yet. Vision still blurry, so better to keep eyes shut, listen to the sounds of conjuration drifting in from the kitchen. Quarrel being repaired, too? Two heads better than one. Time to think of escape when they were both mobile. Have to do it before breakfast time tomorrow.

He could drift off to sleep if he tried . . .

"Well, he's young," said the prissy voice. The doctor had come into the guardroom. The chanting was over. "He'll make up most of the blood loss within a couple of hours. Plenty to drink, plenty of red meat, and he'll be a tiger again in a week. Now, I'll just take a quick look at His Majesty and—"

"His Majesty does not wish to be disturbed." That was Bowman's voice. Where was Commander Dragon? When had Bowman left Greymere?

The doctor made a sound of distress, although a hushed and subdued one, because the King's room was directly overhead. "But, Sir Bowman, it's over a week since he accepted any medical assistance or advice at all! The dressing on his leg—"

"You saw him last night, Doctor."

"Only, er, socially. I admit that his appearance was extremely encouraging, but—"

"And the way he threw you all out of the room was almost like old times, wasn't it? Well, he plans to go down and sup at the village tonight. I expect you can thrust all the medicine and conjuration you want on him then."

"Thrust?"

"Manner of speaking. Thank you for your help, Doctor. Now Sir Torquil will see you safely—"

"Ah, I shall just have another look at Lord Roland first."

Fuzzy or not so fuzzy, Durendal knew he could not fake coma to a doctor. He opened his eyes and smiled. "Much better, thank you. Is it permissible for me to sit up now?"

"My, what a quick recovery!" muttered one of the watchers.

"He always was quick," said another, equally sarcastic.

The doctor beamed and knelt down to investigate pulse rate and pupil size and other phenomena. "Do as much as you feel able, but don't force it. You had a very nasty tumble, my lord. You remember?"

"I fell off a horse?"

"You did indeed. How many fingers?"

"I assume three, although I can see about four and a half."

The plump man chuckled politely at the lordly wit. "Vision still a bit blurred? Rest today, and we'll see how we are feeling tomorrow."

One or both of them might be feeling very dead tomorrow. Obviously the doctor—his face was familiar but his name was still at large—was not in on the plot. His life might be hanging by a fine thread at this very moment, depending on what instructions had been given to Sir Torquil.

As if he had read those thoughts exactly, Bowman spoke from somewhere overhead. "Lord Roland will confirm for you, Doctor, that his presence here at Falconsrest just now is a confidential matter."

"Yes, indeed," Durendal said. "His Majesty is most anxious that it not be known. Could cause a great deal of trouble at this juncture."

"Certainly could," Bowman agreed.

The medic scrambled to his feet while spewing out protestations that of course he understood perfectly and had never doubted what the Commander had told him and as a court physician he had always observed the strictest discretion—blah, blah, blah. He was hustled away by Sir

Torquil. The room brightened and then dimmed as the door opened and closed. A gust of cold air swirled smoke and flames in the fireplace.

The ensuing silence felt ominous. Boards creaked upstairs, and logs crackled on the hearth. The wind rattled a window somewhere.

"Flaming idiot, that one," Bowman said.

Sparing his left arm, Durendal heaved himself up to a sitting position. The room lurched sickeningly and then steadied. He saw tables, chairs, a couple of chests, but all the bedding that had cluttered the guardroom on his previous visits had disappeared, other than the pallet he was sitting on. Inevitably everyone except the conspirators would have been banished from the lodge. The King and the Blades would be living here now, probably Kromman, not likely anyone else.

He peered disbelievingly around the circle of faces— six young men staring back at him as if they wanted his funeral to be the next item on the agenda. Fire! These were Blades! These were Ironhall boys, like him, brothers. Never before had he seen the King's defenders from the outside, as it were, and the revelation was chilling. As enemies, these youngsters were terrifying. For the first time since childhood he was without a sword, and he had fallen into a den of lion cubs.

Bowman was in charge. When and why had he been brought from Greymere? His presence was unwelcome news, because he was a lot more subtle than Dragon. Any swordsman who moved as if he had spastic palsy and cracked jokes with the solemnity of a professional mourner was certainly paradoxical and probably capable of being deliberately devious. Durendal had always rated Bowman far ahead of the Commander. Bowman was saying nothing, waiting for him to speak first.

If his head would stop spinning, he might try a bluff . . . think up some reason why he had come to Falconsrest, ask after His Majesty's health. . . . It wouldn't work; they would merely wait for the inquisitor to return. So let them say something. He waited.

Before anyone said anything, the door from the kitchen was flung open and a young man came hurtling into the room as if he had been thrown out of a tavern by a squad of bouncers. His doublet and britches were blackened by dried blood from his chest to his knees. He tripped over a chair and for a moment seemed to hang there, arms out flung, chalky face twisted in terror, then he sprawled on the floor with a scream of agony. He curled himself up in a whimpering knot. He was the second casualty, the second patient to be enchanted. But he was not Quarrel.

Two more Blades followed him in. "Where do you want this scum, sir?" asked one of them, closing the door. Inexplicably, all the burning anger in the room, which a moment earlier had been directed at Durendal, was now aimed at the boy on the floor.

He wailed into his knees, "Why didn't you let me die!"

"Because you'll keep better this way till the Fat Man's ready for you!" said the other, preparing a kick at his back.

Before he could deliver, Bowman snapped, "That'll do, Spinnaker!"

"Just tenderizing the meat, sir!"

"I said that'll do! Get upstairs, Lyon. And you," he told Durendal. "You'll be safer up there."

Safer for whom?

One question was now answered—Ambrose was not in the lodge, or no one would be talking about the Fat Man.

Another remained: Where was Quarrel?

Durendal made a performance of struggling to his knees, then to his feet, although this required no great dramatic ability. The young Sir Lyon took even longer and could not manage to straighten at all, keeping his arms wrapped around his belly. He was obviously still in terrible pain. The onlookers made no effort to help either of them. Side by side, they hobbled toward the stair.

That cloak draped over that chair . . .

That was Quarrel's cloak. Durendal had helped him choose it and had spooned out an absurd number of gold crowns to pay for it, because Quarrel had displayed both a grandiose taste in clothes and very exalted ideas of what the Lord Chancellor's Blade ought to wear. He had, admittedly, looked exceedingly good in it all. But now that costly, sable-trimmed cloak was a mud-splattered, blood-soaked discarded ruin, so the urgent question was answered. It should have been obvious that no one could treat a Blade's ward as Durendal was being treated unless the Blade was finally, definitely, permanently . . . dead.

· 10 ·

Like the guardroom, the dormitory had been tidied since Durendal had last seen it. Although a Blade rarely slept, he shared other men's need for a place of his own—to store his kit, to be alone, to take a woman. Only the King could be alone in the lodge at Falconsrest, but each Blade had a token bedroll, sixteen of them laid out in neat military rows, filling the room. Sir Lyon hobbled over to one that must be his, as far from the fireplace as any. He lay down painfully and turned his face to the wall.

Durendal crouched close to the smoking embers on the hearth, looking up expectantly at Bowman, who had followed them upstairs and now stood awkwardly slumped against the door frame, deceptively boyish despite his fringe of sandy beard and habitually morose expression.

"What's for breakfast tomorrow?" asked the uninvited visitor.

Bowman's gaze wandered briefly in the direction of

Lyon and then back again. "Whoever was on that horse of yours—Martin's gone to bring him in."

"You mean he escaped?"

The Deputy Commander cocked a tawny eyebrow. "We heard you bound a Blade a few days ago."

Who must therefore have been his lone companion. "Name of Quarrel. Good kid."

"Well, then."

Well, then he's dead. Escaping wasn't something Blades ever tried to do. "How?"

Bowman's shoulders twitched in an uncoordinated shrug.

"Flames, man!" Durendal shouted. "What happened?"

"Torquil got him as he jumped. The horse ran away with him. He must have bled to death right after—he was leaving a trail a foot wide. Don't worry, we'll find him."

What they would do with him did not need to be asked. The Guard's overriding concern now must be to find a fresh body every morning. Durendal fought a tide of nausea. *Oh, Quarrel!*

"Where's Kromman?"

"Grandon."

"And the King?"

"Gone for a gallop. He likes the exercise. And there's a shepherd's daughter up in the hills who struck gold a few days ago."

Durendal gazed into the fire for a moment, trying to think. Nothing much happened, except he decided that a decent man like Bowman must be under enormous strain. He jabbed at that weak spot. "How do you feel about all this?"

The only answer he received was a mawkish, pitying smile. How Bowman felt didn't matter. He was ruled by his binding to save the King's life, and now the King was in deadly peril every day at dawn. His Blades had no choice except the one Lyon had tried and botched.

Durendal gestured inquiringly in the direction of the smothered sobs.

"That was your doing, I reckon, my lord."

"Mine!?"

"When he saw who we'd brought down. That was the last straw. He fell on his sword—he just wasn't man enough to do a proper job of it."

Death and fire! "And was he the first to do that?"

Bowman shook his head reluctantly.

"Volunteer breakfasts? Fire and blood! If more of you were man enough to do it, then this evil wouldn't prosper."

Bowman colored and straightened up. "That's easier for some of us to say than others, your lordship. You're special. Suppose the King gives you a choice? Which end of the spoon will you choose?"

For a moment, that simple question left Durendal speechless. He had not considered so appalling a possibility. He licked his lips. "I believe that immortality on such terms is utterly evil, Sir Bowman. If I am given a free choice, I hope I will have the courage to refuse it. If I am forced into accepting, I hope I will have the courage to kill myself at the first opportunity, so that I do not go on extending the evil. But a good friend of mine was trapped into accepting and was not the same person after, so I do not know if I shall be able to do that."

"I think you have the courage, my lord."

"Thank you."

Bowman chuckled hoarsely, but his gray eyes gleamed like steel. "Don't thank me, my lord—it's my job to identify the King's enemies. I know where you stand. You stay in this room, Lord Roland, and behave yourself. No talking, no trying to escape. Understand? I'll tie you up and gag you if I have to."

"I understand perfectly. Just one more question?"

"What?"

"Do the Blades on the menu qualify for the Litany of Heroes?"

The Deputy Commander bared his teeth angrily and

went slouching back down the stair. As he disappeared, he began shouting names.

Durendal rose and limped across the room to the prostrate boy. He eased down on one knee. "Sir Lyon?"

The kid looked up. His eyes were red, his lips almost blue.

Durendal squeezed his shoulder. "You've got more courage and honor than the rest of them put together, lad. Don't worry, we'll find a way to stop this."

The boy whispered, "Sir . . . my lord . . . they don't trust you!"

"Never mind me," Durendal said. "I can look after myself. Don't give up yet!" and headed back to the fireplace. He had never congratulated a would-be suicide before.

Moments later, Spinnaker and two more men came in to guard the captives. The stair was the only way out, and there were more men down in the guardroom. When Durendal tried to talk, he was again threatened with being bound and gagged.

By Bowman's estimate, he would not be eaten for at least two days—Quarrel first, then Lyon, then Lord Roland. He would prefer that fate to being forced into the conspiracy and made to eat part of his own Blade. Whether Kromman would agree with either of these programs remained to be seen.

It was odd that they were taking so long to find Quarrel's body. There could be no doubt that he was dead, after all. He would have crawled back into the fight on his belly trailing his guts if he weren't. Gone to organize a rescue? No hope of that. Even if a Blade could act like that, the lodge was guarded by the world's best swordsmen. They could hold it for weeks against any force except the Royal Office of Demolition, and that would be no rescue. The rest of the Guard, back at Grandon, knew nothing of what was going on, would not believe it anyway, and was equally bound to the King.

Durendal stretched out on the nearest bedroll to wait

upon events, but however hard he sought to make plans for his own extremely precarious future, his mind kept wandering back to Quarrel, that fresh-minted Blade, that meteor who had flashed through his life and vanished before he could know it. Had he been like that boy once—sharp and sparkling diamondlike, not counting costs or weighing alternatives? He could not remember.

So much promise wasted.

He was hard on his Blades. Wolfbiter had lasted two years, and Quarrel only five days.

QUARREL

VII

Quarrel parried a slash from the Blade on his right, half dodged and half tried to fend off a cut from his left. He felt a searing pain in his shoulder, but before he took time to worry about that, he put Destrier at the gate and was flying. *Wonder horse!* Again a voice yelled, "Take them alive!"

Destrier came down with perfect grace, and then it was reaction time. Spooked by the scuffle and smell of his rider's blood, he laid back his ears and fled off along the track as if all the spirits of fire were after him.

Quarrel must put Reason back in her scabbard before he dropped her. He must do something about the bleeding, or he'd never get back into the fight. He must turn the horse, or the fight would be over before he did get back to it. He looked behind him just in time to see Gadfly tumble and Paragon thrown free. By the eight, that was disaster! Even Paragon couldn't jump up from a fall like that and fight off nine Blades. Oh, turn, blast you! But Destrier hurtled along the track, heedless of reins and heels.

First he must stop bleeding. He needed his right hand for the reins. His left hand wasn't moving properly. Spirits, but his shoulder did hurt now! He let Destrier have his head for a moment while he grabbed the left side of his cloak and tried to pull it tight to staunch the bleeding, but then a swerve by his horse almost threw him. His cloak caught on something, tore its pin, and was gone. Let it go. Forget the blood—he was going to die anyway. He had to get back in the fight and die there. No Blade ever ran away. Not one single Blade had ever run away, not in almost four hundred years.

A wagon loomed up unexpectedly, blocking the trail, its two ponderous cart horses looking almost as astonished as the driver. Destrier slid to a halt and reared, bucked a few times and spun on two feet like a cat. He took off again. Somehow Quarrel stayed on, although by all odds he shouldn't have, and every impact jolted fire from his wound. Now they were going back to the fight. Except there wouldn't be a fight. Paragon would have been stunned by the fall at the very least, if he hadn't broken his neck. Dragon had shouted to take them both alive, but a Blade must never let his ward be taken alive while he lived himself.

He had failed horribly. Only five days ago he had been bound to Paragon himself—the second Durendal, Earl Roland, Lord Chancellor, the greatest swordsman of the century, perhaps the greatest ever, Ironhall's most celebrated son since the first Durendal. Not since he had been the Brat had he ever dreamed of an honor like that—Paragon's Blade! He still had a very clear mental picture of all those green, green jealous faces at his binding, from Hereward all the way down to the sopranos, just drooling at the thought of being bound to Durendal himself. After only five days he had let his ward be killed or captured. Back into the fight! He must die. There could be no life with such shame, not an hour, not an unnecessary minute.

There was his cloak in the road, staining the mud red. Then five horseman ahead, coming after him. He tried to reach for his sword, and Destrier took the chance to leave the track altogether. Angry shouts faded in the background as the big black pelted across a meadow at full gallop, dodging willows, dodging boulders. The pursuers shouted and followed.

Quarrel doubled up with his head alongside the horse's sweaty neck to avoid having it knocked off by branches. He tried not to scream. He yelled instead. "Turn 'round! Turn 'round! That's twice you've done this to me, you carrion brute! I've got to fight. I've got to die with Reason in my hand.''

Destrier raised his ears for the first time since the gate, appraising the river ahead: steep banks, foaming white water, sharp rocks.

''You can't!'' Quarrel screamed, then gathered up the reins and sat into the saddle and did everything he could to help as the black took wing.

They made it with about an inch to spare, but it felt as if they landed on his shoulder and the world swam in blackness.

Loss of blood was making him feebleminded, perhaps. He howled at his horse to turn back, but Destrier refused. The Guard had balked at that impossible leap and even at trying to ford the torrent, which meant that Sir Quarrel, companion in the Loyal and Ancient Order, etc., had escaped when he was never supposed to escape. He would be the first Blade in four hundred years to run away and leave his ward to die. Just dying of loss of blood in the woods would still be a disgrace, if he couldn't do it nearer his ward. But it would be better than nothing.

The dog-food horse had found a game trail to race along.

If only he were certain that Durendal was dead! Then he could dismount, unsaddle Destrier, and happily bleed to death himself. But Dragon had been shouting to take the fugitives alive. Human sacrifice—they wanted Paragon so the King could eat him. First Blade ever to run away, first Blade to let his ward get eaten. If they did take him alive, they might not kill him until they were ready to do the conjuration—dawn tomorrow.

Rescue?

He'd tried to die. If he hadn't been wounded he could have controlled this worthless hack, and then he would have died as he was supposed to. It wasn't his fault that he was alive! But since he was, wouldn't it be a sensible idea to try and organize a rescue, just in case his ward was still alive?

Who?

Having lost most of his terror, Destrier was growing rather tired of all this exertion. He slowed to a trot, which jarred hot knives into Quarrel's shoulder. He kicked the brute back into a canter.

Who? Who would help a disgraced, wounded, runaway, cowardly Blade against the King and his Guard?

The Queen's men, of course.

Mad! Crazy! Absurd! They were half the kingdom away. Delirium.

He would never reach them. His horse had worn itself out already. He was still bleeding and covered with blood, so he'd certainly be challenged and stopped by somebody. He would die and drop off before he got close. Even if he made it, he couldn't possibly convince them and bring them back before sunrise tomorrow. They wouldn't believe him. The masters and knights wouldn't let them do anything about it if they did. They couldn't possibly achieve anything against the Royal Guard.

The fires they couldn't! A dozen of the best swordsmen in the world?

A time to thrust and a time to parry, Paragon had said.

He patted his horse's lathered neck.

"Home, Destrier," he whispered. "Take me home."

· 2 ·

It seemed to Durendal that he had achieved a sort of immortality already, for that morning went on forever. His guardians would neither speak in his presence nor let him speak. It was a commentary on their tortured state of mind that they did not even fall to playing dice, the Blades' traditional pastime of last resort. He heard men being relieved and sent off down to the village to eat. He heard a meal arriving for the King, because the royal household could not know that the dying man had gone off to gallop a horse over the hills.

He was startled to discover that there was another reborn in the lodge. A pale-faced man, young and stringy in servant's livery that seemed too short for him, came scurrying out of the King's bedchamber, shot a frightened, wide-eyed gaze at the prisoner, and disappeared rapidly down the stairs. It took Durendal several minutes to realize that it had been Scofflaw, the King's eternally ancient valet, who wasn't ancient anymore. The pump down in the kitchen squeaked for a while, then he came trudging back up with a metal bucket in either hand. Without looking at Durendal at all, he placed them on the dormitory fire to warm, filled two more, and took those into the bedchamber. Later he went down to fetch firewood also, but he was no more talkative in his youth than he had been in his old age, and rather more obviously short of wits.

It was past noon when sounds of horses outside, then new voices down in the guardroom, caused his guards to break into smiles of obvious relief. The King had returned safely.

Memory: Before he was Durendal, on his second night in Ironhall, when he had been very new as the nameless Brat, very lonely, and very frightened by this strange new life—things had turned suddenly even worse. He had been informed that he must participate in a conjuration, not merely with the exalted Grand Master, but also with Prime Candidate Montpurse, whom the rest of the school almost worshiped already, and Crown Prince Ambrose, who had come to bind Prime to his personal guard. He'd been almost thirty, just three years before his father died—a domineering young giant, fiery and handsome, with brilliant amber eyes, with hair and beard of fine-spun red gold. He had filled all Ironhall with his personality, rousing the candidates to wild enthusiasm for the glory that would come when he ascended the throne. He had not noticed the Brat, and the Brat had been so afraid of forgetting his lines that he had barely noticed the Crown Prince.

Heavy tread came up the stairs. First to enter was Dragon, hairy and suspicious, a black bear of a man. He looked the prisoner over and then stood back beside Spinnaker and the others, his hand on his sword hilt.

Durendal stood up, having already decided on his strategy. Whatever the ethics, Ambrose was still his liege lord. Outright defiance would be profitless, while unquestioning deference would not deceive anyone who knew him as well as the King did. Between those two extremes, he must be respectful to the monarch and opposed to his actions. Nothing new in that.

In rolled Ambrose, restored to the prime of manhood, virile and intimidating. There was even something of that long-ago demigod about him once again, but the conjuration had not removed his fat, so the big man was a grotesque parody of what he should have been. Nor had he yet had time to acquire a suitable wardrobe. Even allowing for the predictable horse sweat and grass stains and general dishevelment, he was an untidy mess, with clothes bulging in the wrong places and loose in others. He stopped and stared at Durendal, fat hands on widespread hips. What he saw seemed to amuse him.

Durendal bowed.

"By the eight, you look old!" The fat man laughed, but his laugh was heartachingly familiar as the King's laugh, which no one had heard for almost two years. It took all the sting out of the remark. He had his charm back.

"Your Majesty looks much better."

The tiny boar's eyes seemed to stab through his guard and scan his innermost thoughts. "And you are pleased to see this, Lord Roland?"

"I rejoice to find you in good health, sire."

"But the medicine disturbs you? Long live the King!"

His little mouth puckered in a smile. "Say it, my lord. Say the words."

It had not taken him long to demolish Durendal's defenses and drive him back to that one place beyond which he could not retreat. The King is dead, long live the Queen? But that would be suicide. The Blades were already glaring dangerously. Bowman had come to join them.

Durendal said nothing, waiting for the thunderbolts.

But the King was in excellent humor, chuckling as if he had expected that reaction. "Come on in. We need to talk." He began to move, and the Blades surged forward in a mass. "Not you!"

Dragon hesitated. Bowman growled, "Leader!" warningly.

"This one's dangerous, sire!" the Commander said.

"Dangerous? That old man? Here!" The King pulled out his dagger and tossed it hilt-first to the Commander, who caught it with a catlike flash of his hand. "There! No weapons. Do you think I can't handle him now?"

He was a head taller than Durendal, twice his weight, thirty years younger. Chortling, he marched into the bedroom with his former chancellor slinking at his heels like an aging hound. Durendal closed the door, although he was certain that Bowman would eavesdrop through the chinks in the garderobe wall.

"Took you long enough to get here!" The King hauled off his coat, brushing away Scofflaw's fussy attempts to help him.

"Was that why you sent me that assignment warrant, sire? To bring me running?"

Off came the sweaty shirt, buttons flying. "I thought it might. You always got loud and impudent when I tried to give you a Blade. But this time you accepted. Well, that kept you out of the Bastion, didn't it? You should have heard Master Kromman! Blast you, Scofflaw, can't you even heat a bath properly?"

The King proceeded to sit down in a copper basin much

too small for his blubbery mass. Water cascaded over the brim and drained away between the floorboards.

"You didn't keep him long, sirrah! Flaming waste of one of my Blades. Give me the soap, man! I suppose you think he belongs in the Litany, when he died fighting his king? They haven't found his body yet. Well, he can still serve me when they do!" The piggy eyes glanced at Durendal, appraising his reaction to this abomination.

"Sire, how long have you known that Kromman knew the ritual?" That was a gamble on the King's good humor, for monarchs should never be questioned.

Today he was too pleased with himself to take offense. "I guessed right away. Surprised you didn't. Memory enhancement's standard for inquisitors." Ambrose lathered and splashed for a moment. "Immortality didn't interest me much in those days, of course. He brought up the subject . . . oh, about ten years ago, I suppose. Parliament being stingy voting taxes. Could have used the gold."

"That would certainly have saved me from listening to a lot of boring speeches."

A throaty chuckle. "Ah, but you wouldn't have liked the price! I wouldn't pay the price. Kromman's price was always your head—old man." The youthful king made an effort to bring one fat pink foot inside the basin with him and gave up. "Here, you wash 'em!" Throwing the soapy flannel at Scoffflaw, he leaned back, sending more torrents into the guardroom. "I wouldn't buy. Hope you appreciate that, my lord. Ten years! But Kromman trapped me in the end. I was dying last time you were here, yes?"

"Yes."

"Yes. He couldn't bear to think of the country falling apart. That mad daughter of mine has no following except Baelish barbarians and Chivial would never stand for them. Don't know why I listened to you when you talked me into sending her off to live with those savages on their seagull-infested rocks. There was going to be civil war after me. Kromman could see that. He wouldn't let the country suffer."

Ambrose heaved his bulk out of the basin with a display of youthful agility, swamping the floor again and also Scofflaw, who had not been expecting the move. The valet rushed for towels.

"Master Kromman has always been loyal to Your Majesty," Durendal admitted, lacking any way to deal with the King's readjustment of facts.

"Yes, he has. He told the Blades how they could save my life, right here at Falconsrest. It was fortunate that we had an octogram here, already seasoned, and none of those snoopy sniffers in the house." The King peered at his audience to see if he was being believed.

"And who was the first victim?"

Ambrose leered with a full set of shiny white teeth. "A murderer. A highwayman who robbed and slaughtered travelers. He was hanged at Stairtown right after Long Night. The Commander and his men rode over and cut him down. Does this trouble your conscience, Lord Roland?"

Durendal shook his head—it didn't if it was true. But what about Ned, the simpleton? Why were Blades going mad and killing themselves? "I suppose they made Kromman try it first?"

"Oh, of course! When they saw what it did for him, they slipped a taste of it to me. I knew what had happened right away. Not that shirt, you idiot!"

So Kromman really was one of the reborn! He had seemed more sprightly than usual on the night he came to collect the chancellor's chain. Durendal had noticed but assumed that it was just because he was having fun.

The rest was all lies. None of it could have happened unless the court had come to Falconsrest, which had certainly been Ambrose's decision. Dragon was a stolid plodder—loyal as any Blade, but bereft of imagination. He would never have obeyed any order from Kromman until he had cleared it with the King. On his lonely deathbed, Ambrose IV had sold his soul and agreed to pay his secretary's price. Now he was lying about it.

"So what happens now, Your Majesty? You have a new chancellor."

"Not those hose, blockhead! Yes, I do." The King winked. "But not for long, mm? At the moment, Master Kromman is in Grandon, suppressing the White Sisters. Once we've disposed of them, we can move court back to Greymere without creating ripples. We don't need him anymore, do we? The Blades know the ritual. The only possible source of trouble is Parliament, and Parliament won't ever tolerate Kromman. You, they will. Even the Commons trust you."

So it was double-cross time. Durendal knew he ought to be pleased and wondered why he felt so ill.

"I'm afraid I still don't understand why you sent me that warrant, sire."

The King just grunted, but his piggy eyes flashed warning. He was afraid of the listeners. And that was why he had not simply written Durendal a letter—because he had been prevented. By accepting the rejuvenation ritual, he had put himself in Kromman's power. When the Blades had seen the monster their ward had become, they had feared that the people would find out and rise up to tear him limb from limb. Kromman would have played on those fears, and the King had found himself a prisoner of his own guard at Falconsrest. It was obvious.

How had the wily old fox managed to dispatch even the warrant? Because those warrants were standard forms and every Blade knew what they looked like. So the royal rogue must have filled it out and handed it very innocently to one of the juniors, perhaps even young Sir Lyon, who would not think to question an assignment when there were so many seniors waiting at Ironhall. "Forgot this— just drop it in the mailbag, will you?" So it had slipped by Kromman and the Guard. Very simple and very cunning!

It had not quite worked. Instead of hammering horseshoes all the way out to Falconsrest to demand an explanation, Durendal had accepted the warrant at face value. But now he was here anyway. The only difference was a dead boy, stiffening somewhere out there in the bushes.

"The other jerkin!" the King snapped. "An immortal monarch and an immortal chancellor. Yes, you also, my lord. People don't like upset and uncertainty. I've been king, and a good king, for as long as almost anyone remembers." He considered Durendal carefully. "Don't worry about it. One mouthful will change your mind. I will see that you swallow that mouthful—whether you want to or not." He guffawed. "Tomorrow we may try a little fencing, Sir Durendal! What do you say to that, mm?"

· 3 ·

A wounded man, covered with blood, riding across Chivial on a bleak winter's day should have been stopped by now, or even robbed of his horse and thrown into a ditch to die. He should have fallen off a thousand times, for the world came and went behind black clouds. He kept waking to find Destrier had languished into a weary walk, so he would kick him into a canter again. Oh, his stiffening shoulder hurt! He wasn't even sure of the way, but Destrier seemed to know it. Faster, faster!

He was roused by a whinny, then an answer and dogs barking. Stupid horse was pacing into a barnyard. The idiot, carrion brute had scented a mare or just wanted company. Quarrel tried to sit up and take charge, but the black fog swirled closer and drums beat in his head. Thatched buildings seemed familiar—Destrier had headed back to the only warm stall he knew within reach, the last place he'd been given oats, The Broken Sword.

"No! No! No!" Quarrel kicked and tugged on the reins

to turn him. Losing his balance, he slid neatly off the stallion's back and fell into the waiting arms of the innkeeper himself, Master Twain.

He was seated by a fire, wrapped like a parcel in blankets, drinking something very hot with soup and brandy in it, and being told to finish his story. His arm had been trussed in an old enchanted bandage that had belonged to the Guard once, very long ago, but ought to have some power remaining, Sir Byless said. Sir Byless kept shouting at the pregnant woman, who shouted back, and the younger man, who was twice his size, and the children, who were wailing in terror.

"Father, you're crazy!" the younger man said. "He's bled dry; he's in terrible pain. He's in shock and doesn't know what he's talking about. Put him to bed and get a healer here right away and he may just possibly have a chance. Let him back on that horse and he won't go a mile. You're going to kill him!"

Sir Byless threw a platter at him—which he dodged—and yelled at him to get the mounts ready and yelled at his daughter to warm those clothes before the lad put them on and yelled at the brats to shut up. He kicked a dog out of the way, making it yowl to frighten the children even more. The boy was a Blade, he screamed, tough as steel. More soup, wool socks. Keep talking, lad.

Could this twitching, slobbering old wreck really have been a Blade once upon a time? Durendal's own Second? Paragon had said so, and Byless himself had confirmed it—do anything for Lord Roland, he said, and bugger the rest of them. He had tufts of white hair sticking out everywhere. His eyes rolled and he slobbered and he was never still, never quiet. Keep talking, lad! His clothes were a rummage of mismatched patches, far from clean, far short of his bony wrists and ankles.

Quarrel swallowed, burning his throat. His head seemed to be spinning faster and faster; it must fall off soon. He was so weak he kept weeping. "Did I tell you they're going to eat him?"

"Aye, that you did. Doesn't surprise me. Nothing would surprise me about that gang of brutes. Or that fat criminal who runs them. Bring the lad more soup, I say! Makes up the blood he lost. Let me get those boots off." He hurled the empty brandy bottle at the younger man, who dodged it as if he had had much practice. "Thomas Peeson, you will do as you're told or you will get your hulking carcass out of my house and take all your ugly spawn with you! Now saddle up the gelding for me and Sir Quarrel's black and be quick about it. We leave in three minutes or I take the horsewhip to you."

· 4 ·

Bowman spent the afternoon down in the village—talking, listening, and frequently confirming that, yes, His Majesty's health was much improved, and yes, he did intend to come down there that evening and eat a meal in court. Yesterday's summoning of the doctors and their subsequent dismissal before they had a chance to examine their patient had been a master stroke, a brilliant preparation for the grand reappearance. Rumors of the miraculous recovery would have spread as far as Grandon already. Tomorrow there would be bells ringing. Kromman had orchestrated it all.

Still, this evening's visit would need very careful supervision. First, the King must be restrained from making his entry too early, while he was still visibly too young. Secondly, he would have to be hustled away before he became too obviously old. Kromman had suggested keeping him in as small a room as possible and circulating the audience through, but Ambrose never took kindly to being managed. Tonight he would be his own worst danger—he would glory in all the praise and attention and want to stay on till dawn. People would certainly notice when his hair and teeth began falling out.

Toward sunset, the deputy commander returned to the lodge and went in search of Dragon. Doubtless the Commander would be a solid performer at massacre and mayhem. He was a stickler for detail and never argued with the King, but when it came to subtlety he couldn't draw his sword without gelding himself. That was why Secretary Kromman had brought Bowman out from Grandon to take charge here. He had not believed a word of the story until the following sunrise, when he had seen three fading geriatrics transformed into kids again. The King, Kromman, and the valet—just three so far, but if the King had rewarded a mere sock washer with eternal youth, then he would certainly confer it on a faithful bodyguard when the need arose.

Dragon was in the dormitory, staring morosely into the fire. Half a dozen other Blades sprawled around the room, not talking, not playing dice, just brooding. It was not good enough. They were all bound by oath and conjuration to preserve their ward. They had always known, every one of them, that this might involve killing. Why should they suffer from scruples now?

Paragon lay stretched out near the fire, apparently asleep—which in itself was a chilling demonstration that old age had not blunted his nerve yet, for he must be aware of his peril. His wits were still sharp enough. He was Danger Number One at the moment.

Bowman caught Dragon's eye and beckoned with a nod of his head. Frowning, the Commander rose and followed. Bowman clattered down the stairs to the guardroom, but that was under the King's chamber. All the walls and ceilings had more gaps than picket fences—there was nowhere safe to talk in the lodge. He went outside in the twilight and then around the corner, out of the wind.

"What by the eight is eating you?" Dragon demanded grumpily.

"They didn't find the kid's body, did they?"

"No."

"So who do we serve up tomorrow?"

The Commander tugged at his beard. "Lyon, I suppose. Poxy little coward. It's what he wanted."

"What does the Fat Man say?"

Dragon winced and glanced at the nearest window, which was safely closed. "He says Kromman."

Bowman had expected that. "Why?"

"Says he's getting too big for his britches. Says Paragon's the better man and he can't keep both of them any longer or they'll tear the place down between them. At each other's throats, he says. He needs Paragon to handle Parliament, he thinks."

"He's a fool."

Dragon did not argue. He pulled his cloak tighter around him and stared at the moon sailing through the silver clouds. Lights were twinkling in the village, where the great feast for His Majesty was being prepared.

Bowman said, "Durendal doesn't approve of the new arrangement."

"I'm not sure I do."

"But you got no choice. Nor I. He does."

"He won't when we feed him the meat. King says that'll change his mind."

"But will it? King has a blind spot when it comes to Paragon. Maybe you do, too?"

Dragon turned quickly, showing anger. "What are you implying?"

"Would you die for a cause?"

"Die for my ward if I have to."

"Yes, but for a cause? A moral principle? Never mind. I don't care if you would or not. I don't know if I would. But I think Durendal would. Even if he discovers he's twenty again and can go on becoming twenty again every sunrise for a thousand years—he'll give all that up if he has to, won't he? If he thinks it's wrong? Why do the kids all call him Paragon?''

"Same reason I do, I suppose." Dragon did not understand rhetorical questions.

"So let's play it safe. Who do we serve up tomorrow?"

After a long pause, the Commander said, "Paragon."

"I'll see to it." Bowman turned to go.

Dragon shouted, "Not yet! Wait and make sure Kromman gets back safely."

"Right," said Bowman. "Good idea." The Secretary would want to watch, anyway.

· 5 ·

Marie began having hysterics again, and Cook slapped her face again. Quarrel had been carried in by Master Caplin and Pardon the hostler, and was now lying on a couch by candlelight with Cook holding a mug of something to his lips. It tasted like scorched milk. Mad Sir Byless had collapsed in a chair near the fireplace, all wet rags and tufts of white hair and slobber.

"We've sent for a healer, Sir Quarrel," the fat steward said. "Pardon's gone to fetch a healer."

Panic deadened the awful pain of weariness for a moment. "No! Tell him, need horses. Paragon in danger." He saw the blank looks, fought for strength to explain again. "Told you—Durendal. His lordship. Got to rescue him. Need the book. Just came for the book. Go on." He drank again, greedily. The doublet Sir Byless had given him was so stiff with blood that it crackled with his every move.

"Stop Pardon!" Caplin said, sending Gwen running. "Go where, Sir Quarrel?"

"Ironhall. Take them the book. Rescue Paragon." He grabbed the steward's soft arm and squeezed. "He'll die! Got to rescue him!"

"He's out of his mind!" Cook protested. "And that other one . . ." She scowled at the prostrate Sir Byless. "Go on? Tonight? Blathers! They're neither of them fit to go another step."

"I'm sure Sir Quarrel will," Caplin said. "He's a Blade, has no choice. We don't have a coach, lad. I can borrow one, but it may take time."

"No time. Need horse."

"It'll kill him!" Marie screamed.

Caplin told her to be silent and bring the first-aid box. "Pardon, saddle two horses. Is your friend going on with you, Sir Quarrel?"

Byless lifted his head and rolled his eyes in every direction. "Course I'm going with him!" he screeched hoarsely. "Just a tick weary. Got any brandy? I'm sure my old friend Durendal keeps some good brandy handy!"

"Sir Byless," Quarrel explained, although he thought he must have done so already. "Was Par—his lordship's Second at Ironhall."

Caplin seemed to conjure a bottle of brandy out of the air. He handed it to the visitor without even suggesting a glass. Byless tipped it to his mouth.

"We have a conjurement for wounds, Sir Quarrel, but you've lost a great deal of blood. Never seen anyone so white. Cook, some hot broth, please—quickly! What book? Gwen, bandages, clean clothes."

They lifted him back into a saddle—Twosocks, this time, not Destrier. Sir Byless managed to mount Patches with some help from Pardon. Quarrel took the reins in his good hand and led the way out of the yard.

· 6 ·

As Dragon and Bowman headed back inside, Durendal quietly closed the window. He had heard few of the actual words, but the mood had been obvious—and so had the intended victim. He was in more danger from the Guard now than he was from either the King or Kromman. He went back to the hearth. None of the Blades showed any interest in his actions as long as he stayed away from the stair and the King's bedroom. Dragon returned, looking windswept and chilled.

About ten minutes later, Scofflaw appeared and approached Durendal in a crabwise shuffle, wearing an expression of extreme alarm. He had lost his youth, and wisps of loose hair on his shoulders suggested that he was rapidly going bald under his hat. Also, his stoop and wrinkles were starting to return. He opened and closed his mouth a few times.

"The King wants me?"

Eager nod. The valet turned and shuffled off again, while still contriving to watch Durendal and make sure he was coming. The faithful half-wit had given his king lifelong devotion, so now his life had been extended indefinitely. A new order of chivalry—the Cannibal Companions.

Durendal followed. Most of his aches and scrapes had gone now, banished by the healing; but he felt badly off balance, missing the weight of the sword he had borne for thirty-seven years. He went into the King's room and closed the door behind him. Scofflaw was already down on his rug in the corner like a spaniel.

All afternoon, Ambrose had been rummaging through papers that Kromman had brought from Greymere the previous day, probably just to keep him occupied. Every hour or so, the King had sent for his previous chancellor to question something. Now he was standing in the brightness below a chandelier of a score of candles, reading a sheet of parchment. He had aged uncannily since morning—hair and beard gray, breath wheezing. His ulcer had not reappeared, though.

He shot his visitor a suspicious sidelong glance. "You were keeping things from me!"

"Nothing important, sire."

"Ha! How about this? Gaylea wants to marry this ward of his. He's thirty years older than she is, or I'm a chicken. But you've been sitting on his petition for two months—and he's a duke! You still bearing a grudge against him because of that King's Cup thing?"

"I won, remember?"

"He can deliver a lot of votes in Parliament."

"That's why I was sitting on his petition. You always told me that want was stronger than gratitude."

Ambrose grunted. "So I did." He threw that document down on the littered bed and took up another to query. The audience continued. His wits were as sharp as ever. It was almost like old times.

Finally he abandoned the papers and began pacing back and forth. "Your attitude displeases me. I've been a good king so far."

"A very fine one, sire."

"And that crazy daughter of mine knows nothing! She's been shut away for twenty years on those islands, breeding barbarians. She's not capable of running a civilized kingdom. Everything will go to pieces." He waited for an answer. Not getting one, he turned his full royal scowl on his former chancellor. "Well? You deny it?"

"She may make mistakes at first. So did you. Isn't she entitled to her turn, just as you were?"

The King's face darkened. "Not now we have a better

alternative. Now a good king can continue to be a good king forever. What troubles you? You think I'm planning to hunt down innocent people and slaughter my loyal subjects? Nonsense! Felons, convicts—that's the answer! Kromman estimates that more than two thousand men are hanged in Chivial every year. What you will do, my lord, is explain to Parliament that we have a new conjuration to turn their bones into gold. The corpses will henceforth belong to the crown. Simple, yes? You won't need to mention rejuvenation yet. That can leak out gradually. I think the Commons will be pleased to hear that their beloved prince is about to abolish taxation altogether, don't you?"

"I expect they'll be happy for a year or two." Durendal thought of that cellar in Samarinda. "After that your gold will be as common as sewage and worth less."

"Bah! Details! The country will benefit. If it's that pretty wife of yours who's worrying you, then we can include her. What other persnickety complaints have you got?"

"Two, sire. First, mortal men won't take kindly to being ruled by an immortal. I don't think the country will stand for it."

"The country can eat dirt. What's the second?"

"Change, sire. Variety. New blood. Anything can go on too long. People go stale, even kings. Even kings who eat human flesh."

"Spirits! I could have your head for that!"

"Then take it. I would sooner die than watch Chivial wither under a permanent tyranny." Durendal could imagine what the listeners in the garderobe would make of that remark.

The King dropped his voice to a needling whisper. "Well I shan't give you that pleasure! At dawn you will be reborn too and then we'll see how you feel about life and death. You've been a good chancellor, I admit—best I ever had—and you can damned well go on being a good chancellor till the sun cools. Get out of here!"

Durendal went back out to the dormitory. The King thought rejuvenation would change his mind and restore his loyalty. He hoped it wouldn't. He did not think Kromman and the Guard would give either of them the chance to find out.

· 7 ·

The last many hours were a blank. He had been riding in a daze, letting Byless find the road, letting Twosocks follow Patches. Poor brutes were staggering, but they had come to Ironhall now. The lights were out. Of course. It was after midnight.

Quarrel roused himself. He was freezing, ice to the core. "That window. Throw rocks." He was too weak to sit straight in the saddle. He was one agony from top to toe and the world was going up and down, up and down. Twosocks had come to a stop, head down in exhaustion.

"Think I don't know the seniors' nursery?" Byless mumbled.

He fell flat on the ground when he dismounted, and he needed four attempts to hit a casement. Glass shattered. A moment later a face appeared—Bloodhand's unfortunately, but then Hereward was there beside him.

"Quarrel," Quarrel said. "Need the Queen's men. Rescue Paragon."

Somehow they carried him into the dormitory without waking any of the masters, the servants, the knights, or even the juniors; and they laid him on a bed. They reluctantly let Byless accompany him, goggling at the idea that this filthy, staggering scarecrow had been Second to Paragon, as if Paragon hadn't needed a Second like any other Blade. Byless flopped down on the nearest bed and was asleep at once.

A dozen of them gathered around in the candlelight, most of them half naked, rubbing their eyes and stretching. Someone fetched a few fuzzies who ought to be seniors but were being held back. Quarrel flogged his brain awake to explain as much as he must: the King locked away in Falconsrest, Samarinda, the book, Paragon's secret mission before they were born—which everyone had heard of but knew nothing about—Wolfbiter likewise . . . terrible conjuration, eating human flesh, evil Kromman, the King changed into a monster, dispossess the Queen, rescue Paragon. His voice would die away in a croak, and they'd give him another drink and he would go on. A couple of them read rapidly through the book.

"He's raving," Crystal said.

"He didn't cut his shoulder himself," said Hereward, red brows clenched down in a frown.

Another voice. "Paragon's book confirms what he's saying."

"Paragon must have needed a Blade for something, after all these years." That was Crystal, who was Second now.

"He's an old man," Willow suggested.

"He beat you at rapiers, didn't he?"

Passington next. "If we try anything like this, they'll fart the lot of us."

"Queen's men," Quarrel whispered. "Won't ever be a Queen."

"You left your ward in a fight?" That was Bloodhand, who was a dog's backside.

He explained again about Destrier bolting and him being wounded and Paragon thrown and Dragon wanting him alive. And eating human flesh.

"Got go," he said, heaving himself upright. The room spun and would not steady. "You come or not, I got be there a' dawn." He had been dreaming—they weren't companions like him, just kids. They hadn't had the sword through the heart, the final forging. But they were all he had or could have had, because they weren't bound to the King and all other Blades were.

"I'll come with you," Hereward announced, "for Paragon. Anyone else wants to come, stay close. The rest go back to the wall there."

One or two began to move away. Then they shuffled closer again. All of them. The Queen's men. Quarrel wept with impatience while they dragged on clothes and slung on their swords and planned how they would break into the stables. Falconsrest was hours and hours away and the night was flying.

◆ 8 ◆

The King's coach arrived an hour or so before midnight to transport him down to the village. Most of the Blades went with him, but three remained behind to guard Lord Roland and the despised Lyon. Durendal slept, making up for two sleepless nights. The weather turned stormy, rattling the casements and blowing smoke from the fireplace.

The King's return seemed to fill the whole lodge with noisy men, laughing and joking. Obviously the public appearance had been a great success.

Dragon and Bowman helped the aging monarch up the stairs. His bulk was as great as ever, yet softer and flabbier now. His head was bald, his white beard wispy, and he had trouble walking, even while leaning on the Commander's shoulder. At a guess, he was the equivalent of about eighty. He paused to catch his breath at the top of the stairs, rasping like a water mill.

"Chancellor Kromman back yet?"

"No, Your Majesty." Bowman shouted, as if the King were now hard of hearing.

"He's late! Send some men out to look for him."

"It's a nasty night, sire. I expect that's slowed him."

The antiquated monarch mumbled toothlessly. "What time is it?"

"About three hours until dawn, sire."

"Get the octogram ready. I need some sleep first, but remember to wake me in plenty of time."

"So's we can carry you down as usual?" muttered a resentful voice in the shadows, but the King did not hear. He lurched into his chamber, leaning on the doorjamb as he went through. Dragon followed, closing the door.

"What does he look like by dawn?" Durendal inquired of the dim room.

"Like a dead pig," someone said.

In a while the Commander came out of the other room, having presumably tucked His Majesty into bed. He disappeared downstairs. Half a dozen men remained, sitting around the dormitory, exchanging comments on the night's events. They were vastly more cheerful than they had been all day, confident that the deception had been successful and might continue to be so in future. Gradually they fell silent, waiting for dawn and the daily conjuration. Young Sir Lyon cowered alone in a corner, ignored and terrified. The pump squeaked in the kitchen below as men attended to their toilet.

Durendal wandered over to the fire and stacked more logs on it. The watchers watched, but none objected. He had slept on his problem and found an answer—not a very satisfying one, but one that his conscience would accept.

Even now, he could not kill the King outright. After a lifetime of service, that was an impossible thought. But he could block another rejuvenation—he was certain he could bring himself to do that much, and he knew how to achieve it. He might be choosing a particularly horrible death for himself, but he was going to die anyway, as soon as Kromman returned.

The conjuration was evil. True, the use of convicted felons was more acceptable than the Samarinda swordsman lottery. A hanged man had no use for his corpse, and the rotting bodies that dangled from gibbets all over Chivial were disgusting eyesores. True, Ambrose was a fine ruler and might continue to rule well for many years—unless immortality changed him. It had changed Everman. Equally true, his daughter was an unknown quantity. Durendal bore no especial love for Princess Malinda, nor any great personal loyalty either.

So why did he feel he must play traitor now and destroy his king? Who was he to oppose this grand scheme? Was he wrong to think it wrong? No, for he had one advantage no one else had—he had seen the evil in full flower in Samarinda. He wished he could discuss it with Kate and benefit from her practical common sense, but he was sure she would agree with him. Kate could not even tolerate healing, so it was not surprising that the rejuvenation conjurement repelled her so strongly. In a strangely perverted sense, that was another advantage he had. He could not be tempted by rebirth when she could not share it.

No, the answer lay in something Grand Master had said to him when he went back to Ironhall: "We'll all be the Queen's men one day, I expect. The bindings translate, because we swore allegiance to him and his heirs."

Several times in his life, Durendal had sworn to be true to Ambrose IV, his heirs and successors. That Ambrose was dead. The person who inhabited his body was someone else, an imposter who looked like Ambrose, talked like Ambrose, and wore the crown that ought now to descend to the Princess and eventually one of her sons. This was slippery huckster talk, not the sort of creed a former Blade should follow, but his conscience needed a crutch.

The fire was starting to crackle and blaze brighter. Then a thumping of hooves and a rattling . . .

"The spider's back," a Blade muttered.

Durendal rose. All eyes turned on him, but the prisoner walked away from the stair and the royal bedchamber, over to a window. He peered out. The carriage he had seen depart that morning squeaked to a stop below him, its two lamps casting a bleary light through blowing snow—the ground was coated white already. A couple of Blades emerged from the lodge to greet it. They opened its door and pulled down the steps.

Kromman would be as old as the King, now. He would probably have to be carried in. No. Surprisingly, the black-clad figure was coming out by himself, teetering unsteadily and not using his left arm. He kept his head down, hardly showing his milk-white face between his collar and his hat. He reached the ground, staggered, and recovered, pushing away an offer of help. A man in Guard livery appeared behind him.

The two outriders had dismounted. Three footmen leaped down from the back of the coach, the driver and another from the bench. The King's men shouted and reached for their swords, and the newcomers jumped them, bearing them to the ground. More passengers sprang out of the coach, others were emerging on the far side and running around. Several raced for the door of the lodge.

Whatever was going on, that was not Kromman who had arrived, and obviously it was time for Durendal to make his move. He took three swift strides to the fireplace and grabbed up the tongs. He lifted a glowing log and hurled it across the room to land in a cascade of sparks. Then another. Blades leaped up with howls of fury and shock. Another, another . . . A sword came flashing toward him and he parried it with the tongs: *Clang!*

"Stop him!"

"Never mind him—help me here!" shouted another.

"Fire!" roared another.

Bedding was bursting into flames all over the room, spewing smoke and a reek of burning feathers. Men dived on the blazes, trying to smother them with blankets, but Torquil and Martin drew and lunged at Durendal. He parried them both, tongs in one hand and poker in the other, standing at bay with the fireplace at his back. *Clang! Clang!* This was going to be it—once he might have had a chance against two, but not these days. Not unarmed. *Clang!* How many strokes could he survive?

"Leave me, you fools!" he shouted at them. "Save the King!"

His assailants were too intent on vengeance to listen. *Clang!*—close one. Then Lyon smothered Martin from behind with a blanket over his head, dragging him down to the floor. Startled, Torquil let his attention waver; Durendal cracked the poker down on his sword hand and heard bones break. Torquil screamed.

"Thanks, lad!" Durendal raised his voice. "Everyone save the King!"

Coughing, spluttering, frantic Blades were trying to stuff burning quilts and mattresses out through the windows. The wind blew flames back in their faces. But Bowman had hurled open the door to the King's room and disappeared inside. Others followed.

Durendal stumbled, choking, to the stair. Lyon dived ahead of him, making his escape. They went down the precipice in a slithering rush and ended on the guardroom floor. Half a dozen more Blades were trying to fight their way out through the invaders, but there was room for only two at a time in the doorway. Whoever the newcomers were, they had efficiently caught the Royal Guard with their pants down—literally so in a couple of cases—and bottled them up in the lodge.

"Fire!" Durendal scrambled painfully to his feet. He wanted only to make the octogram unusable, not burn anyone to death. "The lodge is on fire! Save the King!"

The Blades spun around and ran past him, up the stairs, all except the pair battling in the entrance.

"Put up your swords!" he roared. "In the King's name, put up your swords, all of you! Stand aside and let me deal with them."

The defenders stepped back, and he took their place,

peering through the whirling snowflakes at a dozen unknown and inexplicable swordsmen.

Their leader shouted, "Come out with your hands up!"

Durendal dropped the tongs and raised his hands. "No more fighting! We must let them rescue the King. Put up your swords, I say!"

"It's Paragon!" a voice cried.

Overhead, part of the roof collapsed, blasting flames skyward and making the scene bright as noontime. Coughing, he emerged into the storm. He wiped his streaming eyes and then stared with stunned disbelief at the stocky boy clutching the scimitar. He had lost his hat, and his red hair shone like gold in the light from the blaze.

"Hereward!"

"Lord Roland!"

He looked around at all the other youthful, nervily grinning faces, and knew he was seeing the seniors from Ironhall. *Fire and death! What were they doing here, battling the Royal Guard?*

"We came to rescue you, my lord," Hereward said. "Looks like we arrived just in time." He laughed. "Stand clear of the door there."

Durendal obeyed and impudent hands thumped his shoulder as he went by. Two bodies lay in the snow—dead or unconscious? More of the roof collapsed. The horses panicked at the flames and smoke, taking the coach off with a rush into the night. A moment later it overturned on the hill in a rending crash and screams of terror from the team.

"My lord!" croaked a voice. The counterfeit Kromman lurched forward, a flutter of black garments and a white face, one arm in a sling. *By the eight, it was Quarrel!* He fell into his ward's arms and buckled.

Durendal hugged him, taking his weight, although he seemed to weigh nothing at all. "You're alive!" Blasted stupid thing to say! And was it even true? How could any man look like that white skull and live? "You're hurt!"

"Been hurt a long time," Quarrel whispered. "You all right?"

"I'm fine. But what happened?"

"Went for help. Got the Queen's men." He tried to smile.

Durendal lowered him to the ground and knelt there, supporting his shoulders. "Ironhall? You rode there and back?" That was not humanly possible, and yet a dozen boyish faces were grinning proudly down at him from man height all around. Even with the benefit of surprise, who else could have given the Guard a fight? They seemed to be waiting for his orders.

"Let the Guard out. Disarm them, though."

"We're doing that, my lord," Hereward said.

Choking and blinded men were staggering from the lodge, being expertly overpowered and stripped of swords and daggers before they could recover enough to object. The stone shell was an inferno, white fire showing through every window, half the roof gone. Harvest was in there somewhere.

A cheer greeted a band of Blades struggling out of the lodge with a bulky package that was presumably the King. That seemed to be the end of it. Anyone left inside would be dead now, for the floor beams were collapsing. The shed, too, was ablaze, but someone had released the horses.

"My lord?" Quarrel whispered. "Did I do right?" The snow was clinging to his eyebrows and hair.

"Yes, yes! You're a champion! You saved the day! You made idiots of the Guard. Magnificent! You go on the Litany of Heroes tomorrow."

"Got something for you . . ." Quarrel groped at his soiled robe.

"It can wait," Durendal said, still cradling his Blade's head.

Evidently it couldn't, so he reached where the powerless hand fumbled, and in the pocket found a loose collection of cold . . . ? Cold links! He hauled out the lord chancellor's chain of office, glittering like a fiery snake.

"Your gold chain," Quarrel mumbled. "Yours."

Not ever again, but that did not matter. "Thank you. I'll keep it safe." Durendal looked to one lanky youth and groped mentally for his name. "Willow, we must get a healer for him. Run down to the village and . . ." But a healer could do very little without a conjuration, and the octogram was under the blaze. He shuddered as he realized that his terrible act had probably killed Quarrel. "No, we'll have to take him to Stairtown."

The Queen's men exchanged worried glances.

Hereward said, "And the King, my lord? The companions want their swords back."

"No! No! Don't return them yet." The emergency was far from over. There might still be time for the Guard to rush the King to another octogram, although shouts from the trail meant a hundred witnesses were on their way. He could not imagine what sort of confusion was about to result, what sort of charges and countercharges would fly. More necks than his would be laid on the block over this night's events, but the fewer the better.

"Look, Prime, I think you should all disappear now. Take the Guards' swords with you, but go. You did what you set out to do—you and your army. I'm proud of you all. And I'm especially proud of . . . Quarrel? Quarrel!"

Willow knelt in the snow and felt for a pulse. He did not find one. "I'm not surprised, my lord. It was only his binding that kept him going. I think the rest of him died hours ago."

No, it was not a surprise, but it hurt. Oh, how it hurt! In cold dismay, Durendal laid the body flat. He closed the empty eyes and folded the hands over the chest. There were too many things to do now to spare time for mourning. Far too many things. He had already believed Quarrel dead, so why did it hurt so much more the second time? If only he could have had a son like . . .

An animal scream howled through the night and was

instantly joined by others. He lurched to his feet as the Blades began to rampage.

The hero of the hour was Candidate Crystal, who had been left with Bloodhand to guard the confiscated swords. When he saw the inanimate baggage that was the King being hustled out, he had the wit to gather up the weapons and hurl them through a window into the burning lodge.

Compared to some former massacres, such as the Blade Riot after the death of Goisbert IV, the resulting battle was a brief and minor affair. Less than a dozen of the Royal Guard were still active, and they were all unarmed. Even so, the fifteen Ironhall seniors on hand were boys against madmen, reluctant to use steel on unarmed opponents. Three of them went down before Hereward and Durendal rallied the rest and convinced them that this was a life-and-death matter.

Lord Roland was the obvious target, of course. The berserkers swarmed at him like starving weasels, intent on tearing him to pieces, and he could do nothing except hide behind his youthful defenders. Eventually he gained a sword from one of the wounded, but by that time most of the Blades had been disabled and had collapsed into pathetic, weeping impotence. The last one to fall was Bowman, stabbed through the thigh. The brief horror was over. The Queen's men had prevented catastrophe. For that, at least, they could claim credit at their trial.

Feeling drained and deathly weary, Durendal went over to look at the King in the fading firelight. The courtiers had all fled into the night, but now they started creeping back like ants to a picnic, and most of them came to where he stood, to gaze like him in silent disbelief at the remains of the man who had ruled Chivial for so long. He seemed peaceful and very old, although probably not so impossibly old that anyone would suspect enchantment. The body bore no signs of burns or injuries, so either the smoke had killed him or his heart had given out as he was being rescued. Perhaps Ambrose, who had never feared anything, had died of fright. There were to be no last farewells, no harsh words of recrimination. The King is dead. I did this, Durendal thought. I killed my king. Whatever happened now, life would never be the same.

Snow was drifting around the corpse already. The storm was rapidly becoming a blizzard. Why was nobody taking charge? He had no authority. He just wanted to go away and weep, but someone must restore order. He recognized the fussy healer who had treated him in the lodge.

"You! Gather a work party and take His Majesty's body down to the village."

The little man jumped as if he had been asleep. "Oh, of course, my lord. Here! You . . . and you . . ."

Feeling that all his bones had been turned to lead, Durendal plodded back to the swordsmen. The Queen's men were busy helping the Blades, wrapping on makeshift bandages, offering what comfort they could.

There was someone missing.

"Willow? Where is the Chancellor Kromman—does anyone know?"

"Oh!" said Willow, looking all around. "He was in the carriage, my lord. Quarrel recognized it and we stopped it. His guards got hurt, but they'll live. We left them at a farmhouse and brought him—tied up, my lord."

The coach was a heap of wreckage, so Kromman was very likely dead already. He would have to wait.

A kingless court was a headless animal. Still everyone else was waiting for leadership. Durendal drew a deep breath and bellowed over the hubbub. "The King is dead! Long live the Queen!"

The Ironhall candidates shouted approval. "Long live Queen Malinda!" Courtiers took up the cry.

Dragon was sitting in the snow, recovering from a blow to the head. His face was sooty and bloodied, his doublet scorched; he had lost much of his great beard, but sanity was back in his eyes again.

"Are you ready for duty, Leader?"

He nodded grimly. "But I don't take orders from you."

"I'm not trying to give orders, only advice. It may be weeks before the Queen can get here. There is no Parliament, for it dies with the sovereign and a new one must be summoned. There is no chancellor, for even if Kromman is still alive, he cannot live past dawn. I was officially dismissed, and your duty now is probably to see me locked up in the Bastion. Just at the moment, Leader, you are the government of Chivial."

The Queen's men reacted with snarls of disapproval. Hereward raised his scimitar, looking almost furious enough to use it. A youthful voice shouted, "Paragon!"

"Put that damned scythe away before you hurt somebody!" Durendal bellowed. "Thank you! Commander Dragon is in charge. All I can do is advise."

Courtiers were crowding in, eager to meddle and participate in historical events. Soon there might be far too many leaders. But Dragon wiped a sleeve over his forehead and clambered to his feet with some help from Hereward.

"I'd appreciate your advice, my lord. We must arrange for the body to be conveyed back to Grandon."

He was still confused. Dragon was not the man for this. Durendal explained patiently, "No, Commander. Normally the first priority would be to escort the King's heir to Greymere so that she could prevent a massacre when the rest of the Blades hear the news. As that isn't possible, I suggest you head for Grandon with as many men as you can spare and disarm them one at a time. When old King Everard died they did that. Catch each man in turn in a net and have a dozen others around him shouting, 'Long live the Queen!' until he comes out of shock and joins in."

Dragon scowled. "It's my privilege to take the King's signet to Her Majesty and inform her of her accession!"

What better way for a courtier to gain advancement from a new monarch? The messenger who delivered such tidings could expect an earldom at the very least. But give Dragon the benefit of the doubt—his binding must be burning like a rash, driving him to find his new ward.

"You going to walk to the Fire Lands?" Bowman

limped forward out of the flying snow, leaning heavily on Spinnaker's shoulder. "No ships sail in Firstmoon." Here was competence, even if he was misinformed on that last point.

"Yes, it is your right," Durendal told Dragon. "And Baels can sail in any weather. There's one of their ships standing by in Lomouth for just this purpose. The captain's name is Ealdabeard. The harbor master will direct you to him."

"Oh?" Bowman asked with quiet menace. "And how do you know all this, Lord Roland?"

"Because I arranged it with the Baelish ambassador months ago, of course. We knew something like this might happen. Ealdabeard will get you to Baelmark if anyone can, Leader. In fact, if you leave right now you may just be able to catch the tide."

Fortunately Dragon did not ask how Durendal could possibly know how long the ride would take him in this weather or when the tides ran in Lomouth. He merely said, "Take charge here, Deputy," and disappeared into the snowstorm.

Durendal turned hopefully to Bowman.

"Got advice for me, too, have you?" the Blade inquired sarcastically.

"If you want it."

"Let's hear it."

"First, seal this valley behind you so nobody gets out for at least three days. The snow will help. When you get to Grandon, find the Lord Chamberlain or the Earl Marshall. The King's will is in Chancery, in the top drawer of the crown chest." Neither Ambrose nor Kromman should have seen any reason to meddle with it in the last few days. "It provides for a council of regency until the new queen can arrive to take the oath. Here—" He held out the gilded chain that Quarrel had died for. "Give them this."

Bowman took it as if he were afraid it might bite him. It certainly did its wearers little good in the long run. Apparently he was going to do as Durendal had suggested.

"Meanwhile," Durendal said, "half your men are disabled. I suggest you put these admirable youngsters under your orders for the time being."

The Deputy Commander glowered at the self-styled Queen's men. They grinned cockily back at him.

"Even if they have written an epic chapter in the annals of Ironhall," Durendal added, "they are probably in no hurry to go home and face Grand Master."

Cockiness became apprehension, and grins worried glances.

"Good idea," Bowman said. "You're all conscripted. You can start by giving us your swords."

It was over. Now a man could break out in a sweat and shiver. Durendal wandered off into the darkness to be alone.

The trouble had barely begun. And there were still loose ends. What of young Lyon, who had been only the first man to save his life this night? Where had he run off to? Where was poor Scofflaw? Had anyone rescued him? Even if he had escaped the fire, he would die when the sun came up. The rippling circles of tragedy would continue to spread. But none of that was his concern now.

Kromman. What about Kromman?

· 9 ·

The carriage was a heap of twisted wreckage lying on its side. Three horses had escaped or been rescued, but the fourth had been put out of its agony by someone who had apparently not thought to look inside or had not done so carefully. When Durendal clambered up and peered down through the shattered door, his lantern at first showed only a jumble of fallen benches. Then he identified two bare legs protruding underneath, tied together at the ankles. Climbing down without putting his weight on the debris was no easy task in the uncertain glow of the lantern. Balancing awkwardly, he began to lift away the remains and throw them out through the roof.

Soon Kromman's glassy eyes stared back at him. The face was a skull, plastered with dried blood and wisps of white hair. It might have been dead for years. "So you won!" it said.

Durendal almost dropped the bench he was holding. "I don't feel as if I won. I'll cut those ropes and get you out of here." He cleared away the last of the wreckage.

"But there is no octogram, is there?" The familiar croak had shrunk to a sound like rats gnawing rafters. "The lodge was burning."

"No, no octogram. The King is dead."

"The reading was correct, then. I knew you would kill him one day."

"I think you killed him." Durendal drew his borrowed sword. "You gave him that filthy conjuration. The man I met today was not the king I served all my life."

"Hairsplitting. You seek to justify your treason."

"Perhaps." He cut the ropes binding the spindly ankles, horrified at how cold the flesh was to his touch.

"You are wasting your time," Kromman whispered. "How long till sunrise?"

"About an hour."

"Hardly worth the effort, then, is it? My back is broken. I am in very little pain."

Durendal moved the lantern closer. Kromman's clothes were caked with blood. It was incredible that this frail and brittle old man had not died an hour ago, even if only from the cold.

Baffled, Durendal said, "I have to go and get help. You take a lot of killing, Inquisitor, but I daren't try to move you."

The bloodstained mouth twisted in a grimace. "If my pride allowed me, I would ask you to use that sword. Would it give you a lot of pleasure to kill me now?"

Durendal sighed wearily. "None at all. I grew too old for vengeance. You had nothing to fear from me."

"Only the death of my king."

He was abhorrent and contemptible, but he was dying. He could be pitied for that. There was certainly nothing to gloat about.

"I grant you that some of your motives were honorable."

"My, is that the best you can do? Well, if we are making up, then I ask you, out of common kindness, to put me out of my misery. I beg you. I implore you, Sir Durendal. You would do as much for a dog." The corpse eyes gleamed with mockery. Even now he was playing his spiteful games.

"You want me to feel guilty, whether I agree or not, don't you? Well, I don't feel guilty about you, Kromman. I don't hate you, I just despise you, because all you ever wanted was power over other people—and when you had it, you used it only to hurt. I don't think you were ever really human. You certainly aren't human now. I'll go and fetch some help."

There was no reply. Leaving the lantern, Durendal climbed out of the wreckage and trudged back up to the lodge. He sent a healer and two stretcher bearers, but the old man was dead when they got there.

When the sun came up, turning the blizzard white instead of black, Durendal was standing in a makeshift morgue in the village. The King lay in improvised state in another room. This one held the rest of the night's grisly toll: Scofflaw, Kromman, four Blades, three Ironhall candidates, one footman who had been caught in the rampage—and Quarrel.

They gazed in silence upon the hero.

"He died saving his ward," Durendal said. "Take his

sword, Prime. Her name is Reason. See she is put in her proper place and honored forever.''

"That's your job, my lord."

"I have other commitments."

He was a regicide. He would be taken back to Grandon to pay the penalty for high treason. In himself he was unimportant, but he feared that the entire seniors' class of Ironhall might die with him, and that would be a tragedy.

• 10 •

The Lord Chamberlain was Durendal's son-in-law. The High Admiral was his neighbor at Ivywalls. Three other members of the Regency Council were former Blades, and two more had been his protégés in Chancery. The Council's first act was to summon him to Greymere and order him to resume running the government. He moved back into his old rooms as if nothing had happened. The country remained peaceful, mourning Ambrose with more nostalgia than love, plus no small apprehension for what might follow him. His body was brought to Grandon to lie in state and was then returned to the elements with all due pomp and respect.

The Baelish ship had sailed from Lomouth while the storm still raged, much to the astonishment of local mariners. Commander Dragon's introduction to ocean travel must have been a memorable experience, but would a middle-aged woman venture the return voyage at that season, or would she send a regent? Or would she, Durendal wondered in private, ignore the summons and throw Chivial into chaos and civil war?

Three weeks to the day after Kromman had brought him

his dismissal, a meeting of the Council was interrupted by news that a flotilla of Baelish ships had been sighted on the Gran. According to its minutes, the Council then voted to adjourn. In fact its members stampeded out the door and up the stairs to the south gallery, which commanded a good view of the river. The Baels had wasted no time. No one had expected a reply for at least another ten days, but there they were—sleek, beautiful, and sinister in the winter sunshine; three long vessels being rowed against both wind and tide into the heart of the capital. Although Durendal could make out no details at that distance, the Admiral asserted that they were indeed dragon ships. The absence of dragon prows or red war sails, he said, was a sign that they came in peace. The largest of them was flying an elaborate banner that might be a royal standard.

Lord Roland retired to his quarters and settled down to read a book. It was less than two hours before a squad of men-at-arms arrived at his door with a warrant for his arrest. It must have been almost the first document issued in the new reign, but somehow he did not feel especially flattered.

Lord Thernford, Warden of Grandon Bastion, had once been Sir Felix and before that a close friend at Ironhall. He greeted his new guest warmly and installed him in a comfortable suite of rooms—bright, airy, and large enough for Lord Roland to bring his wife to stay with him if he wished, and keep two or three servants as well. The following morning fresh orders arrived and a shamefaced Felix escorted him down to the dungeons. He was locked up in the very same cell Montpurse had occupied, many long years ago. It was clammy and cold and dim, and also infinitely boring, for he was allowed no visitors and no news, but at least he was not shackled as Montpurse had been. Queen Malinda was not quite so malicious as the late Inquisitor Kromman.

Nine or ten days later, he was taken up to a bright room and interrogated by Grand Inquisitor and one of his men.

Why only two of them? And why did the interrogation last a mere hour or so? He must assume that they had already decided to put him to the Question and were trimming the preliminaries to a legal minimum.

Another two weeks went by. If the new Queen chose to exert the full letter of the laws concerning treason, not only would he be put to a very shameful death, but Kate and the children would suffer with him. His grandchildren would be left penniless orphans. Malinda had nursed her hatred of Lord Roland for many years, but now she could enjoy as much revenge as she wanted. There was nothing she could not do to him and his.

One afternoon, with no prior warning, two warders brought a bucket of warmish water and a bundle of fresh clothes. Clean and respectably dressed, the prisoner was taken back up to the world of light and fresh air. He had to wait a long hour in unnerving silence before he was led in to see the visitor, but he knew that he would not have been treated like this if he were to be put to the Question. That might come later, of course.

He knelt to await her pleasure, blinking at the winter sunshine pouring through the window behind her. She had always been a tall woman, heavy boned and powerful. In bearing three children, she had lost any trace of youthful charm, but at least she had the sense to dress in sober, matronly style. The diamond coronet that was her only adornment added dignity to a face both cold and arrogant. She looked convincing enough.

"We have read your statement. You plead guilty to murdering our royal father."

"I did kill him, Your Majesty, with great sorrow." His intention had only been to deprive Ambrose of another rejuvenation, but that was picayune hairsplitting. The intent and the results condemned him.

"Why?"

"Because I believed that the monarch I had served all my days was already dead. When he embraced that terrible conjuration, he became something not human.'' More hair-splitting, legal rubbish.

There were only two other people present, both standing behind the Queen, both wearing the livery of the Guard. One was Commander Dragon, glowering darkly, but the other was young Hereward, and he was smiling. With that realization, hope twisted in Durendal's heart like a dagger.

"So we owe our throne to your regicide?" the Queen asked.

Almost anything he might say in reply to that damnable question could kill him. "I did my duty as I saw it, Your Majesty, which is what I have always done. Your noble father was my liege lord but also my friend, inasmuch as a master and servant may share friendship. I shall honor his memory for whatever time is left to me, forgiving him that one final error."

"You rank yourself competent to judge your sovereign's errors?"

"Ma'am, he had access to that conjuration for twenty years and chose not to touch it. He was tricked into it during his final illness, when he was in a very distressed state of mind. If I judged him, then I judged him as my friend, not as my lord. If I have done nothing else, I believe I have preserved his memory from shame."

The Queen pursed her lips.

He persisted. "I know this sounds foolish, ma'am, but I am sure in my own mind that the man I served so proudly and so long—the father you knew, ma'am . . . I think he would have approved."

Silence. Then the Queen nodded almost imperceptibly. "My father died in a fire of unknown origin. A conjuration has been prepared that will prevent you from ever saying otherwise. Will you submit to that?"

"Gladly, ma'am!"

"Then we shall include your name in the general pardon."

Fighting back tears, he bowed his head. "I am indeed

grateful for Your Majesty's mercy.'' He would see Kate again!

Malinda had not done, though. "I have found little cause to like you over the years, Lord Roland.''

"If I ever caused Your Majesty distress, it was with deep regret, and only because I believed that I was doing my duty.''

"It is only because I know that and respect you for it that your head is going to remain on your shoulders, my lord. And I am not ungrateful. Sir Hereward, when the prisoner has submitted to the conjuration we mentioned, you may give him back his sword, but not before. Take him away.''

Durendal rose, bowed, and backed, and bowed again. . . . Hereward came forward solemnly, but grinned again as soon as the Queen could not see his face. At her back, Dragon was smiling, too.

Harvest, Hereward explained later, had been located in the ashes and refurbished at Ironhall. The new cat's-eye was less bright than its predecessor and the armorers had some doubts about the quality of the blade, but they assumed that Lord Roland would not be putting it to any strenuous use in future. Lord Roland agreed with that prediction and kissed her.

No longer welcome at court, he lived quietly at Ivywalls with Kate until she died in the summer of the following year. Thereafter the mansion seemed an absurd extravagance for one bored old man of almost sixty. He yearned for the company of his peers and something useful to do. When Andy came back from sea the next time and announced that he was through with voyaging to far quarters of the globe, his father happily gave him the house and estate outright. He belted on his sword, mounted Destrier, and rode off to the west.

· Epilogue ·

"That was very good," Grand Master said. "I did not expect you to catch those last two."

"Kids' stuff!" The boy sneered.

"You think agility is of no importance to a swordsman?"

"Um. Suppose tis."

"You are exceptionally agile. I think you would do very well, but the choice is entirely yours, not mine or your grandmother's. Yours. If you wish to enlist, I accept you. If you do not, then I shall tell your grandmother that I refused you. I warn you that you will be embarking on a whole new . . ."

As he went through the set speech, he watched the play of emotions on the pinched and sullen face: fear, contempt, a distrusted dawning of hope and excitement. The spindly limbs showed no signs of rickets, so a few good meals would do wonders for them, and a little pride would heal the wounded soul. What boys of fourteen needed were fences to climb over. If the gates were left open, they assumed nobody cared. They could never understand that, though, and if this young terror walked out of here today, he would be hanged within a year.

"Have you any questions?"

"What about the other stuff?"

"It doesn't matter. It's forgotten. Your name is forgotten. What people think of your new name will depend entirely on what you do in future."

"Who chooses my new name?"

"You do."

"I want to be Durendal!"

"Oh, do you?" Grand Master chuckled. "I'm afraid you can't have that one yet. He's still alive."

"He is? But Grandmother says—"

"He's very old, but still quite healthy. Master of Archives will help you choose another. There have been many fine heroes whose name you can take. Pick a good one and try to live up to it."

"Durendal was the best!"

"Some say so. Now, what is your decision?"

The boy looked down at his bare feet. Grand Master held his breath. In five years he could turn this young rogue into a first-rate swordsman. If he didn't have five years left, others would finish the work.

"You really want me? After what she told you 'bout me?"

"I do."

"All right. I'll try. I'll try real hard."

"Good. I'm pleased. You are accepted. Brat, go and tell the woman waiting outside that she may go now."

We hope you've enjoyed this Eos book. As part of our mission to give readers the best science fiction and fantasy being written today, the following pages contain a glimpse into the fascinating worlds of a select group of Eos authors.

In the following pages experience cutting-edge sf from Eric S. Nylund, Maureen F. McHugh, and Susan R. Matthews, and experience wondrous fantasy realms of Martha Wells, Andre Norton, Dave Duncan, and Raymond E. Feist.

SIGNAL TO NOISE

Eric S. Nylund

Jack watched his office walls sputter malfunctioning mathematical symbols and release a flock of passenger pigeons; his nose was tickled with the odor of eucalyptus. Inside, the air rippled with synthetic pleasure and the taste of vanilla.

"I need to get in there," he told the government agent who blocked the doorway.

"No admittance," the agent said, "until we've completed our investigation on the break-in."

Puzzles, illegalities, and dilemmas stuck to Jack—from which he then, usually, extracted himself. That gave him the dual reputation of a troubleshooter and a troublemaker. But the only thing he was dead sure about today was the "troublemaking and sticking" part of that assessment.

The agent stepped in front of Jack, obscuring what the others were doing in there. National Security Office agents: goons with big guns bulging under their bullet-proof suits. And no arguing with them.

Today's trouble was the stuff you saw coming, but couldn't do a thing about. Like standing in front of a tidal wave.

Jack hoped his office *had* been broken into, that this wasn't an NSO fishing trip. There were secrets in the bubble circuitry of his office that had to stay hidden. Things that could make his troubles multiply.

"I'll wait until you're done then."

The agent glanced at his notepad and a face materialized: Jack's with his sandy hair pulled into a ponytail and his hazel eyes bloodshot. You have an immediate interview with Mr. DeMitri. Bell Communications Center, sublevel three."

Jack's stomach curdled. "Interview" was a polite word that meant they'd use invasive probes and mnemonic shadows to pry open his mind. Jack had worked with DeMitri and the NSO before. He knew all their nasty tricks.

"Thanks," Jack lied, turned from the illusions in his office, and walked down the hallway.

From the fourth floor of the mathematics building, he took the arched bridge path that linked to the island's outer seawall. Not the most direct route, but he needed time to figure a way out of this jam.

Cold night air and salt spray whipped around him. Electromagnetic pollution filtered through the hardware in his skull: a hundred conversations on the cell networks, and a patchwork of thermal images from the West-AgCo satellite overhead.

Past the surf and across the San Joaquin Sea, the horizon glowed with fluorescent light. Jack regretted that he'd stepped on other people to get where he was. Maybe that's why trouble always came looking for him. Because he had it coming. Or because he was soft enough to let little things get to him. Like guilt.

Not that there was any other way to escape the mainland. Everyone there competed for lousy jobs and stabbed each other in the back, sometimes literally, to get ahead. He had clawed his way out with an education—then cheated his way into Santa Sierra's Académe of Pure and Applied Sciences.

But it wasn't perfect here, either. There were cutthroat maneuvers for grants, and Jack had bent the law working both for corporations *and* the government. All of which had helped his financial position, but hadn't improved his conscience.

He had to get tenure so he could relax and pursue his

own projects. There had to be more to life than chasing money and grabbing power.

Now those dreams were on hold.

His office had been ransacked, and the NSO had got too curious, too fast, for his liking. Had they been keeping an eye on him all along?

He took the stairs off the seawall and descended into a red-tiled courtyard.

In the center of the square stood Coit Tower. The structure was sixty meters of fluted concrete that had been hoisted off the ocean floor. It had survived the San Francisco quake in the early twenty-first century, then lay underwater for fifty years—yet was still in one piece.

Jack hoped he was as tough.

The whitewashed turret was lit from beneath with halogen light, harsh and brilliant against the night sky. Undeniably real.

Jack preferred the illusions of his office; sometimes reality was too much for him to stomach.

No way out of this interview sprang to mind, and he had stalled as long as he could. The crystal-and-steel geodesic dome of the Bell Communications Center was across the courtyard. Jack marched into the building, took the elevator to sublevel three, and entered the concert amphitheater.

On the stage between gathered velvet curtains, the NSO had set up their bubble.

Normal bubbles simulated reality. Inside, a web of inductive signals and asynchronous quantum imagers tapped the operator's neuralware. It allowed access to a world of data, it teased hunches from your subconscious, and solidified your guesses into theories. They made you think faster. Maybe think better.

But this wasn't a normal bubble. And it was never meant to help Jack think. It was designed for tricks.

THε DεATH OF THε
nεCROMANCεR

Martha Wells

She was in the old wing of the house now. The long hall became a bridge over cold silent rooms thirty feet down and the heavy stone walls were covered by tapestry or thin veneers of exotic wood instead of lathe and plaster. There were banners and weapons from long-ago wars, still stained with rust and blood, and ancient family portraits dark with the accumulation of years of smoke and dust. Other halls branched off, some leading to even older sections of the house, others to odd little cul-de-sacs lit by windows with an unexpected view of the street or the surrounding buildings. Music and voices from the ballroom grew further and further away, as if she was at the bottom of a great cavern, hearing echoes from the living surface.

She chose the third staircase she passed, knowing the servants would still be busy toward the front of the house. She caught up her skirts—black gauze with dull gold striped over black satin and ideal for melding into shadows—and quietly ascended. She gained the third floor without trouble but going up to the fourth passed a footman on his way down. He stepped to the wall to let her have the railing, his head bowed in respect and an effort not to see who she was, ghosting about Mondollot House and obviously on her way to an indiscreet meeting. He would remember her later, but there was no help for it.

The hall at the landing was high and narrower than the others, barely ten feet across. There were more twists and turns to find her way through, stairways that only went up half a floor, and dead ends, but she had committed a map of the house to memory in preparation for this and so far it seemed accurate.

Madeline found the door she wanted and carefully tested the handle. It was unlocked. She frowned. One of Nicholas Valiarde's rules was that if one was handed good fortune one should first stop to ask the price, because there usually was a price. She eased the door open, saw the room beyond lit only by reflected moonlight from undraped windows. With a cautious glance up and down the corridor, she pushed it open enough to see the whole room. Book-filled cases, chimney piece of carved marble with a caryatid-supported mantle, tapestry-back chairs, pier glasses, and old sideboard heavy with family plate. A deal table supporting a metal strongbox. *Now we'll see,* she thought. She took a candle from the holder on the nearest table, lit it from the gas sconce in the hall, then slipped inside and closed the door behind her.

The undraped windows worried her. This side of the house faced Ducal Court Street and anyone below could see the room was occupied. Madeline hoped none of the Duchess's more alert servants stepped outside for a pipe or a breath of air and happened to look up. She went to the table and upended her reticule next to the solid square shape of the strongbox. Selecting the items she needed out of the litter of scent vials, jewelry she had decided not to wear, and a faded string of Aderassi luck-beads, she set aside snippers of chicory and thistle, a toadstone, and a paper screw containing salt.

Their sorcerer-advisor had said that the ward that protected Mondollot House from intrusion was an old and powerful one. Destroying it would take much effort and be a waste of a good spell. Circumventing it temporarily would be easier and far less likely to attract notice, since wards were invisible to anyone except a sorcerer using gascoign powder in his eyes or the new Aether-Glasses invented by the Parscian wizard Negretti. The toadstone itself held the necessary spell, dormant and harmless, and in its current state invisible to the familiar who guarded the main doors. The salt sprinkled on it would act as a catalyst and the special properties of the herbs would fuel it. Once all were placed in the influence of the ward's key object, the ward would withdraw to the very top of the house. When the potency of the salt wore off, it would simply slip back into place, probably before their night's work had been discovered. Madeline took her lock picks out of their silken case and turned to the strongbox.

There was no lock. She felt the scratches on the hasp and knew there had been a lock here recently, a heavy one, but it was nowhere to be seen. *Damn. I have a not-so-good feeling about this.* She lifted the flat metal lid.

Inside should be the object that tied the incorporeal ward to the corporeal bulk of Mondollot House. Careful spying and a few bribes had led them to expect not a stone as was more common, but a ceramic object, perhaps a ball, of great delicacy and age.

On a velvet cushion in the bottom of the strongbox were the crushed remnants of something once delicate and beautiful as well as powerful, nothing left now but fine white powder and fragments of cerulean blue. Madeline gave vent to an unladylike curse and slammed the lid down. *Some bastard's been here before us.*

SCENT OF MAGIC

Andre Norton

That scent which made Willadene's flesh prickle was strong. But for a moment she had to blink to adjust her sight to the very dim light within the shop. The lamp which always burned all night at the other end of the room was the only glimmer here now, except for the sliver of daylight stretching out from the half-open door.

Willadene's sandaled foot nearly nudged a huddled shape on the floor—Halwice? Her hands flew to her lips, but she did not utter that scream which filled her throat. Why, she could not tell, but that it was necessary to be quiet now was like an order laid upon her.

Her eyes were drawn beyond that huddled body to a chair which did not belong in the shop at all but had been pulled from the inner room. In that sat the Herbmistress, unmoving and silent. Dead—?

Willadene's hands were shaking, but somehow she pulled herself around that other body on the floor toward where one of the strong lamps, used when one was mixing powders, sat. Luckily the strike light was also there, and after two attempts she managed to set spark to the wick.

With the lamp still in hands which quivered, the girl swung around to face that silent presence in the chair. Eyes stared back at her, demanding eyes. No, Halwice lived but something held her in thrall and helpless. There were herbs which could do that in forbidden mixture, but Halwice never dealt with such.

Those eyes— Willadene somehow found a voice which was only a whisper.

"What—?" she began.

The eyes were urgent as if sight could write a message on the very air between them. They moved—from the girl to the half-open door and then back with an urgency Willadene knew she must answer. But how— Did Halwice want her to summon help?

"Can you"—she was reaching now for the only solution she could think of—"answer? Close your eyes once—"

Instantly the lids dropped and then rose again. Willadene drew a deep breath, almost of relief. By so much, then, she knew they could still communicate.

"Do I go for Doctor Raymonda?" He was the nearest of the medical practitioners who depended upon Halwice for their drugs.

The eyelids snapped down, arose, and fell again.

"No?" Willadene tried to hold the lamps steady. She had near forgotten the body on the floor.

She stared so intensely as if she could force the answer she needed out of the Herbmistress. Now she noted that the other's gaze had swept beyond her and was on the floor. Once more the silent woman blinked twice with almost the authority of an order. Willadene made a guess.

"Close the door?" That quick, single affirmative blink was her answer. She carefully edged about the body to do just that. Halwice did not want help from outside—but what evil had happened here? And was the silent form on the floor responsible for the Herbmistress's present plight?

With the door shut some instinct made the girl also, one-handedly as she held the lamp high, slide the bolt bar across it, turning again to find Halwice's gaze fierce and intent on her. The Herbmistress blinked. Yes, she had been right—Halwice wanted no one else here.

Then that gaze turned floorward, as far as nature would let the eyes move, to fasten on the body. Willadene carefully set the lamp down beside the inert stranger and then knelt.

It was a man lying facedown. His clothing was traveler's leather and wool as if he were just in from some traders' caravan. Halwice dealt often with traders, spices, and strange roots; even crushed clays of one sort or another arrived regularly here. But what had happened—?

Willadene's years of shifting iron pots and pans and dealing with Jacoba's oversize aids to cooking had made her stronger than her small, thin body looked. She was able to roll the stranger over.

Under his hand his flesh was cool, and she could see no wound or hurt. It was as if he had been struck down instantly by one of those weird powers which were a part of stories told to children.

ThE GILDED ChAIN
A Tale of the King's Blades

Dave Duncan

Durendal closed the heavy door silently and went to stand beside Prime, carefully not looking at the other chair.

"You sent for us, Grand Master?" Harvest's voice warbled slightly, although he was rigid as a pike, staring straight at the bookshelves.

"I did, Prime. His Majesty has need of a Blade. Are you ready to serve?"

Harvest spoke at last, almost inaudibly. "I am ready, Grand Master."

Soon Durendal would be saying those words. And who would be sitting in the second chair?

Who was there now? He had not looked. The edge of his eye hinted it was seeing a youngish man, too young to be the King himself.

"My lord," Grand Master said, "I have the honor to present Prime Candidate Harvest, who will serve you as your Blade."

As the two young men turned to him, the anonymous noble drawled, "The other one looks much more impressive. Do I have a choice?"

"You do not!" barked Grand Master, color pouring into his craggy face. "The King himself takes whoever is Prime."

"Oh, so sorry! Didn't mean to twist your dewlaps, Grand Master." He smiled vacuously. He was a weedy, soft-faced man in his early twenties, a courtier to the core,

resplendent in crimson and vermilion silks trimmed with
fur and gold chain. If the white cloak was truly ermine,
it must be worth a fortune. His fairish beard came to
a needle point and his mustache was a work of art. A
fop. Who?

"Prime, this is the Marquis of Nutting, your future
ward."

"Ward?" The Marquis sniggered. "You make me
sound like a debutante, Grand Master. *Ward* indeed!"

Harvest bowed, his face ashen as he contemplated a
lifetime guarding . . . whom? Not the King himself, not
his heir, not a prince of the blood, not an ambassador
traveling in exotic lands, not an important landowner out
on the marches, not a senior minister, nor even—at
worst—the head of one of the great conjuring orders. Here
was no ward worth dying for, just a court dandy, a parasite. Trash.

Seniors spent more time studying politics than anything
else except fencing. Wasn't the Marquis of Nutting the
brother of the Countess Mornicade, the King's latest mistress? If so, then six months ago he had been the Honorable Tab Nillway, a younger son of a penniless baronet,
and his only claim to importance was that he had been
expelled from the same womb as one of the greatest beauties of the age. No report reaching Ironhall had ever hinted
that he might have talent or ability.

"I am deeply honored to be assigned to your lordship,"
Harvest said hoarsely, but the spirits did not strike him
dead for perjury.

Grand Master's displeasure was now explained. One of
his precious charges was being thrown away to no purpose. Nutting was not important enough to have enemies,
even at court. No man of honor would lower his standards
enough to call out an upstart pimp—certainly not one who
had a Blade prepared to die for him. But Grand Master
had no choice. The King's will was paramount.

"We shall hold the binding tomorrow midnight,

Prime,'' the old man snapped. ''Make the arrangements, Second.''

''Yes, Grand Master.''

''Tomorrow?'' protested the Marquis querulously. ''There's a ball at court tomorrow. Can't we just run through the rigmarole quickly now and be done with it?''

Grand Master's face was already dangerously inflamed, and that remark made the veins swell even more. ''Not unless you wish to kill a man, my lord. You have to learn your part in the ritual. Both you and Prime must be purified by ritual and fasting.''

Nutting curled his lip. ''Fasting? How barbaric!''

''Binding is a major conjuration. You will be in some danger yourself.''

If the plan was to frighten the court parasite into withdrawing, it failed miserably. He merely muttered, ''Oh, I'm sure you exaggerate.''

Grand Master gave the two candidates a curt nod of dismissal. They bowed in unison and left.

KRONDOR
The Betrayal

Raymond E. Feist

The fire crackled.

Owyn Belefote sat alone in the night before the flames, wallowing in his personal misery. The youngest son of the Baron of Timons, he was a long way from home and wishing he was even farther away. His youthful features were set in a portrait of dejection.

The night was cold and the food scant, especially after having just left the abundance of his aunt's home in Yabon City. He had been hosted by relatives ignorant of his falling-out with his father, people who had reacquainted him over a week's visit with what he had forgotten about his home life: the companionship of brothers and sisters, the warmth of a night spent before the fire, conversation with his mother, and even the arguments with his father.

"Father," Owyn muttered. It had been less than two years since the young man had defied his father and made his way to Stardock, the island of magicians located in the southern reaches of the Kingdom. His father had forbidden him his choice, to study magic, demanding Owyn should at least become a cleric of one of the more socially acceptable orders of priests. After all, they did magic as well, his father had insisted.

Owyn sighed and gathered his cloak around him. He had been so certain he would someday return home to visit his family, revealing himself as a great magician, perhaps a confidant of the legendary Pug, who had created the Academy at Stardock. Instead he found himself ill suited for the study required. He also had no love for the burgeoning politics of the place, with factions of students rallying around this teacher or that, attempting to turn the study of magic into another religion. He now knew he was, at best, a mediocre magician and would never amount to more, and no matter how much he wished to study magic, he lacked sufficient talent.

After slightly more than one year of study, Owyn had left Stardock, conceding to himself that he had made a mistake. Admitting such to his father would prove a far more daunting task—which was why he had decided to visit family in the distant province of Yabon before mustering the courage to return to the East and confront his sire.

A rustle in the bushes caused Owyn to clutch a heavy wooden staff and jump to his feet. He had little skill with weapons, having neglected that portion of his education as a child, but had developed enough skill with his quarterstaff to defend himself.

"Who's there?" he demanded.

From out of the gloom came a voice, saying, "Hello, the camp. We're coming in."

Owyn relaxed slightly, as bandits would be unlikely to warn him they were coming. Also, he was obviously not worth attacking, as he looked little more than a ragged beggar these days. Still, it never hurt to be wary.

Two figures appeared out of the gloom, one roughly Owyn's height, the other a head taller. Both were covered in heavy cloaks, the smaller of the two limping obviously.

The limping man looked over his shoulder, as if being followed, then asked, "Who are you?"

Owyn said, "Me? Who are you?"

The smaller man pulled back his hood, and said, "Locklear, I'm a squire to Prince Arutha."

Owyn nodded, "Sir, I'm Owyn, son of Baron Belefote."

"From Timons, yes, I know who your father is," said

Locklear, squatting before the fire, opening his hands to warm them. He glanced up at Owyn. "You're a long way from home, aren't you?"

"I was visiting my aunt in Yabon," said the blond youth. "I'm now on my way home."

"Long journey," said the muffled figure.

"I'll work my way down to Krondor, then see if I can travel with a caravan or someone else to Salador. From there I'll catch a boat to Timons."

"Well, we could do worse than stick together until we reach LaMut," said Locklear, sitting down heavily on the ground. His cloak fell open, and Owyn saw blood on the young man's clothing.

"You're hurt," he said.

"Just a bit," admitted Locklear.

"What happened?"

"We were jumped a few miles north of here," said Locklear.

Owyn started rummaging through his travel bag. "I have something in here for wounds," he said. "Strip off your tunic."

Locklear removed his cloak and tunic, while Owyn took bandages and powder from his bag. "My aunt insisted I take this just in case. I thought it an old lady's foolishness, but apparently it wasn't."

Locklear endured the boy's ministrations as he washed the wound, obviously a sword cut to the ribs, and winced when the powder was sprinkled upon it. Then as he bandaged the squire's ribs, Owyn said, "Your friend doesn't talk much, does he?"

"I am not his friend," answered Gorath. He held out his manacles for inspection. "I am his prisoner."

MISSION CHILD

Maureen F. McHugh

"Listen," Aslak said, touching my arm.

I didn't hear it at first, then I did. It was a skimmer.

It was far away. Skimmers didn't land at night. They didn't even come at night. It had come to my message, I guessed.

Aslak got up and we ran out to the edge of the field behind the schoolhouse. Dogs started barking.

Finally we saw lights from the skimmer, strange green and red stars. They moved against the sky as if they had been shaken loose.

The lights came toward us for a long time. They got bigger and brighter, more than any star. It seemed as if they stopped, but the lights kept getting brighter. I finally decided that they were coming straight toward us.

Then we could see the skimmer in its own lights.

I shouted, and Aslak shouted, too, but the skimmer didn't seem to hear us. But then it turned and slowly curved around, the sound of it going farther away and then just hanging in the air. It got to where it had been before and came back. This time it came even lower and it dropped red lights. One. Two. Three.

Then a third time it came around and I wondered what it would do now. But this time it landed, the sound of it so loud that I could feel as well as hear it. It was a different skimmer than the one we always saw. It was bigger, with a belly like it was pregnant. It was white and

414

red. It settled easily on the snow. Its engines, pointed down, melted snow underneath them.

And then it sat. Lights blinked. The red lights on the ground flickered. The dogs barked.

The door opened and a man called out to watch something but I didn't understand. My English is pretty good, one of the best in school, but I couldn't understand him.

Finally a man jumped down, and then two more men and two women.

I couldn't understand what anyone was saying in English. They asked me questions, but I just kept shaking my head. I was tired and now, finally, I wanted to cry.

"You called us. Did you call us?" one man said over and over until I understood.

I nodded.

"How?"

"Wanji give me . . . in my head . . ." I had no idea how to explain. I pointed to my ear. "Ayudesh is, is bad."

"Ask if he will die," Aslak said.

"Um, the teacher," I said, "um, it is bad?"

The woman nodded. She said something, but I didn't understand. "Smoke," she said. "Do you understand? Smoke?"

"Smoke," I said. "Yes." To Aslak I said, "He had a lot of smoke in him."

Aslak shook his head.

The men went to the skimmer and came back with a litter. They put it next to Ayudesh and lifted him on, but then they stood up and nearly fell, trying to carry him. They tried to walk, but I couldn't stand watching, so I took the handles from the man by Ayudesh's feet, and Aslak, nodding, took the ones at the head. We carried Ayudesh to the skimmer.

We walked right up to the door of the skimmer, and I could look in. It was big inside. Hollow. It was dark in the back. I had thought it would be all lights inside and I was disappointed. There were things hanging on the walls, but mostly it was empty. One of the offworld men jumped up into the skimmer, and then he was not clumsy at all. He pulled the teacher and the litter into the back of the skimmer.

One of the men brought us something hot and bitter and sweet to drink. The drink was in blue plastic cups, the same color as the jackets that they all wore except for one man whose jacket was red with blue writing. Pretty things. I made myself drink mine. Anything this black and bitter must have been medicine. Aslak just held his.

"Where is everyone else?" the red-jacket man asked slowly.

"Dead," I said.

"Everyone?" he said.

"Yes," I said.

AVALANCHE SOLDIER

Susan R. Matthews

It lacked several minutes yet before actual sunbreak, early as the sun rose in the summer. Salli eased her shoulder into a braced position against the papery bark of the highpalm tree that sheltered her and tapped the focus on the field glasses that she wore, frowning down in concentration at the small Wayfarer's camp below. They would have to come out of the dormitory to reach the washhouse, and they'd have to do it soon. Morning prayers was one of the things that heterodox and orthodox—Wayfarer and Pilgrims—had in common, and no faithful child of Revelation would think of opening his mouth to praise the Awakening with the taint of sleep still upon him.

The door to the long low sleeping house swung open. Salli tensed. *Come on, Meeka,* she whispered to herself, her breath so still it didn't so much as stir the layered mat of fallen palm fronds on which she lay. *I know you're in there. Come out. I have things I want to say to you.*

The camp below was an artifact from olden days, two hundred years old by the thatching of the steeply sloped roofs with their overhanging eaves. Not a Pilgrim camp by any means. No, this was a Shadene camp built by the interlopers that had occupied the holy land in the years after the Pilgrims had fled—centuries ago. A leftover, an anachronism, part of the heritage of Shadene and its long history of welcoming Pilgrims from all over the world to the Revelation Mountains, where the Awakening had begun. Where heterodoxy flourished, and had stolen

417

Meeka away from her. And before the Awakened One she had a thing or two to tell him about that—just as soon as she could find him by himself, and get him away from these people . . .

Older people first. Three men and two women, heading off in different directions. The men's wash house was little more than an open shed, though there wasn't anything for her to see from her vantage point halfway up the slope to the hillcrest. The women's wash house was more fully enclosed. That was where the hotsprings would be, then.

Where was Meeka?

The sun would clear the east ridge within moments, and yet no man of Meeka's size or shape had left the sleeping house. In fact the younger people were hurrying out to wash, now, and there were no adults whatever between old folks and the young, so what was going on here?

Then even as Salli realized that she knew the answer, she heard the little friction of fabric moving against fabric behind her. Felt rather than heard the footfall in the heavy mat of fallen palm fronds that cushioned her prone body like a feather-bed. Well, of course there weren't any of the camp's men there below. They were out here already, on the hillside.

Looking for her.

"Good morning Pilgrim, and it's a beautiful morning. Even if it is only a Dream."

She heard the voice behind her: careful and wary. But a little amused. Yes, they had her, no question about it. She could have kicked the cushioning greenfall into a flurry in frustration. But she was at the disadvantage; she had to be circumspect.

"How much more beautiful the Day we Wake." And what did she have to worry about, really? Nothing. These were Wayfarers, true, or if they weren't she was very much mistaken. But there were rules of civility. She had meant to get Meeka by himself, without betraying her presence; but she had every right to come here on the errand that had brought her. "Say, I imagine you're wondering what this is all about."

STEPHEN R. LAWHEAD

THE CELTIC CRUSADES

A story rich in history and imagination,
here is the magnificent saga of a
Scottish noble family and its divine quest
during the age of the Great Crusades

THE IRON LANCE
BOOK I

0-06-105109-8 • $7.99 US • $10.99 Can

THE BLACK ROOD
BOOK II

0-06-105110-1 • $7.50 US • $9.99 Can

THE MYSTIC ROSE
BOOK III

0-380-82018-8 • $7.99 US • $10.99 Can